THE NAMING

THE FIRST BOOK OF PELLINOR

Alison Croggon

CANDLEWICK PRESS

Copyright © 2002 by Alison Croggon
Map drawn by N. Puttapipat

First U.S. paperback edition in this format 2017

First published as *The Gift* by Penguin Books Australia, 2002

The Library of Congress has cataloged the hardcover edition as follows:

Croggon, Alison.
The Naming / by Alison Croggon. — 1st U.S. ed.
p. cm. — (The first book of Pellinor)
Summary: A manuscript from the lost civilization of Edil-Amarandh chronicles the experiences of sixteen-year-old Maerad, an orphan gifted in the magic power of the Bards, as she escapes from slavery and begins to learn how to use her Gift to stave off the evil Darkness that threatens to consume her world.
ISBN 978-0-7636-2639-6 (hardcover)
[1. Supernatural—Fiction. 2. Magic—Fiction. 3. Identity—Fiction. 4. Orphans—Fiction. 5. Fantasy.]   I. Title.
PZ7.C8765Gi 2005
[Fic]—dc22   2004045165

ISBN 978-0-7636-3162-8 (paperback)
ISBN 978-0-7636-9443-2 (reformatted paperback)

17 18 19 20 21 22 BVG 10 9 8 7 6 5 4 3 2 1

Printed in Berryville, VA, U.S.A.

This book was typeset in Palatino.

Candlewick Press
99 Dover Street
Somerville, Massachusetts 02144

visit us at www.candlewick.com

FOR JOSH

One is the singer, hidden from sunlight
Two is the seeker, fleeing from shadows
Three is the journey, taken in danger
Four are the riddles, answered in treesong:
Earth, fire, water, air
Spells you OUT!

Traditional Annaren nursery rhyme
Annaren Scrolls, Library of Busk

A NOTE ON THE TEXT

I T is with considerable nostalgia that I write this introduction for
a new edition of *The Naming*, the first volume in the series now
widely known as the Books of Pellinor. My translation of the
Naraudh Lar-Chanë (*The Riddle of the Treesong*), which comprises the
four volumes *The Naming*, *The Riddle*, *The Crow*, and *The Singing*, was
first published over ten years ago, but to think back to its blithe beginnings is like remembering another lifetime. So much has changed
since I idly thought, some time in 1999, that a translation aimed at
the general reader might be a good idea.

I suspected that perhaps this classic epic of Edil-Amarandh,
knowledge of which was confined to a tiny community of scholar-
ship, might appeal to those who would love it for its virtues as a
story as much as for the vivid illumination it throws over the varied
societies and cultures of a long-lost civilization. As so many readers
have let me know since, my hope has been rewarded beyond my
highest expectations. To these readers I owe my gratitude and my
thanks: their enthusiasm for these stories sustained my labor through
many rocky moments when it seemed that I would never find the
words to match the glories of the original. The worker knows best
where her labors are deficient; it's perhaps more difficult for her to
see its achievements. It was the responses of readers that took me
out of the anxious prison of my ego and reminded me that, however
inadequate my translation might seem to me, it still communicates
something of the epic resonance and beauty of the *Naraudh Lar-Chanë*
in the Annaren language. It was these responses that encouraged
me to translate another, shorter Annaren classic, *Illarenen na Noroch*

(*The Fading of the Light*), which tells of events a half century before those chronicled in the *Naraudh Lar-Chanë* and which is now published as *The Bone Queen*.

For those new to the marvels of Edil-Amarandh, I recommend Clark Jackson's popular short history, *The Bards*, a lucid introduction to the Annaren Scripts documenting their discovery by a shepherd in a cave in the Atlas Mountains of central Morocco in 1991. Unlike some other, grievously inaccurate, popular publications, *The Bards* gives an excellent portrayal of the society of the Bards without any need to add the spice of sensationalism. Claudia J. Armstrong's *Uncategorical Knowledge: The Three Arts of the Starpeople* and Christiane Armongath's indispensable *L'Histoire de l'Arbre-chant d'Annar* remain the standard references, but it is impossible not to mention Jonah Jones's magisterial three-volume *Elements of Mind: Thought, World, and Act,* a landmark study of Bardic ethics that shows their application to the problems we face in the twenty-first century.

Even given the enormous growth in Edil-Amarandh studies, very few readers will have the chance to compare my efforts with the blazing achievement of the original text. It is here that I most feel my inadequacies: much is inevitably obscured and lost. It is often said of translation that the beautiful ones are not faithful and the faithful ones are not beautiful. As some of my sterner colleagues have averred, I have sometimes favored beauty over accuracy. In my defense, I suggest only that, in this text in particular, qualities of feeling seemed to me to hold their own profound necessities and truths, and I was unwilling to sacrifice these virtues in cases where a closer pedantry might eclipse them.

Subsequent discoveries have thrown new light on areas that were still obscure when I was creating the Pellinor series. However, I have decided not to amend the texts: where it seems pertinent, I will note relevant items of interest in the introductions.

The Naming consists of the first two of the eight books that make up the *Naraudh Lar-Chanë*. As a courtesy to the reader I have included notes on the pronunciation of Annaren names and some general appendices on the society and history of Edil-Amarandh. However, I hope that the tale stands without these notes and that the reader who seeks primarily the pleasures of a compelling adventure will be satisfied by the narrative alone.

There are many people to whom I owe thanks, and I can mention only a few here. Nicholas, Veryan, Jan, Richard, and Celeste Croggon read the manuscript at an early stage, and their generous responses encouraged me greatly. Thanks are also due to Dan Spielman for his enthusiastic advocacy of the project, and to Sophie Levy of Corpus Christi College, Cambridge, for illuminating some of the more obscure aspects of Bardic social life during many fascinating conversations. I am grateful also to Alphonse Calorge, of the Department of Comparative Literature, Université Paris IV—Sorbonne, for invaluable advice on some nuances of translation, and to David Bircumshaw for suggestions on the prosody of the poems, which was often very difficult to render in English. Lastly, but by no means least, I would like to thank my husband, Daniel Keene, for his unfailing support, his acute comments on some tricky questions of Annaren syntax, and also for proofreading the manuscript, and my editors, Chris Kloet and Suzanne Wilson, for their excellent and painstaking counsel on all aspects of this book. Any remaining faults and mistakes are, naturally, solely my own.

Alison Croggon
Melbourne, Australia, 2016

A NOTE ON PRONUNCIATION

MOST Annaren proper nouns derive from the Speech, and generally share its pronunciation. In words of three or more syllables, the stress is usually laid on the second syllable: in words of two syllables (such as *lembel, invisible*) stress is always on the first. There are some exceptions in proper names; the names *Pellinor* and *Annar*, for example, are pronounced with the stress on the first syllable.

Spellings are mainly phonetic.

a — as in *flat; ar* rhymes with *bar*.

ae — a long *i* sound, as in *ice. Maerad* is pronounced *MY-rad*.

aë — two syllables pronounced separately, to sound *eye-ee. Maninaë* is pronounced *man-IN-eye-ee*.

ai — rhymes with *hay. Innail* rhymes with *nail*.

au — *ow. Raur* rhymes with *sour*.

e — as in *get*. Always pronounced at the end of a word: for example, *remane*, to walk, has three syllables. Sometimes this is indicated with *ë*, which also indicates that the stress of the word lies on the *e* (for example, *ilë, we*, is sometimes pronounced almost to lose the *i* sound).

ea—the two vowel sounds are pronounced separately, to make the sound *ay-uh. Inasfrea, to walk,* thus sounds: *in-ASS-fray-uh.*

eu—*oi* sound, as in *boy.*

i—as in *hit.*

ia—two vowels pronounced separately, as in the name *Ian.*

y—*uh* sound, as in *much.*

c—always a hard *c,* as in *crust,* not *ice.*

ch—soft, as in the German *ach* or *loch,* not as in *church.*

dh—a consonantal sound halfway between a hard *d* and a hard *th,* as in *the,* not *thought.* There is no equivalent in English; it is best approximated by a hard *th. Medhyl* can be said METH'l.

s—always soft, as in *soft,* not as in *noise.*

Note: *Dén Raven* does not derive from the Speech, but from the southern tongues. It is pronounced *don RAH-ven.*

Contents

NORLOCH

APPENDICES

GILMAN'S COT

Speak to me, fair maid!
Speak and do not go!
What sorrows have your eyes inlaid
   With such black woe?

My dam is buried deep
Dark are my father's halls
And carrion fowl and wolves now keep
   Their ruined walls.

From *The Lay of Andomian and Beruldh*

I

ESCAPE

FOR almost as long as she could remember, Maerad had been imprisoned behind walls. She was a slave in Gilman's Cot, and hers was the barest of existences: an endless cycle of drudgery and exhaustion and dull fear.

Gilman's Cot was a small mountain hamlet beyond the borders of the wide lands of the Inner Kingdom of Annar. It nestled at the nape of a bleak valley on the eastern side of the mountains of Annova, where the range split briefly and ran out, like two claws, from near the northern end. Its virtue, as far as the Thane Gilman was concerned, was its isolation; here he could be tyrant of his domain, with nothing to check him.

It was a well-defended fortress, though no one came to attack. At the cot's back was the stone cliff of the Outwall, the precipice cutting sheer some thousand feet from the Landrost, the highest peak in that part of the range. Around the cot were walls of roughly dressed stone, rising to a height of thirty feet from a base twenty feet wide. They tapered to four feet at the top, enough room for two men to walk abreast. At the front were stout wooden gates, which eight men or a wagon could enter with ease. The gates were barred at night and most days, except for hunts and when the hillmen came in their big wagons to trade goods, salted meat, cheeses, and dried apples for swords and arrows and buckets and nails.

About a hundred and fifty souls lived there: the Thane Gilman and his wife, who had been beaten to a shadow after bearing him twelve children, of which five still lived, and his henchmen and their women and bastards. The rest were slaves like Maerad, captured in raids in Gilman's youth, or bargained for at the gate, or simply born there. They lived in dormitories, long huts under the shadows of the walls.

The buildings were ancient, older even than Gilman guessed, the walls raised in forgotten times by grim northern men to keep out wolves, and worse. Under Gilman, the walls were mostly used to keep people in. The small enclosed meadows were tilled and harvested by slave labor, his tables and cloths and cheeses and sour drinks were all made by slaves, and Gilman wanted none running away. His many guards served to reinforce his tyranny, and, not inconsequentially, gratified his own opinion of his authority. Like many who ruled far vaster territories, Gilman was not above the pettiness of vanity.

If anyone did escape, there was nowhere to run to; their most likely fate was to be hunted down by untamed beasts in the forests that stretched below the mountains. And even to this isolated cot came rumors of stirrings in the outside world: whispers of unnamed shadows that haunted the forest deeps, or of forgotten evils that now woke and walked in the day-lit world. Grim though Gilman's Cot was, these vague stories of horror worked as well as any wall, gainsaying any attempt to leave.

Maerad was still too young to have given up hope of escape, although as she approached adulthood and began better to understand her own limitations, she understood it to be a childish dream. Freedom was a fantasy she gnawed obsessively in her few moments of leisure, like an old bone with just a trace of meat, and like all illusions, it left her hungrier than before, only more keenly aware of how her soul starved within her, its wings wasting with the despair of disuse.

*　*　*

The Springturn began like every other day of Maerad's life, with the iron clang of the dawn bell wrenching her from sleep. It dumped her on the rim of consciousness, sore and heavy and blind, and her dreams sank into the darkness of her mind, as if they had never been.

Yawning, she staggered out of the slaves' quarters to the courtyard well, her skin wincing at the icy air. She hunched her cloak around her shoulders and, scarcely glancing at the dim shapes of the buildings around her, pumped some water and splashed it over her head. Gasping, she shook the water off her heavy hair, and her breath plumed in white swirls out of her nostrils and through her chattering teeth. Her limbs still felt like lead, her face was numb as a brick, but at least she was awake.

She was drying herself with her cloak when she heard a heavy step behind her. Maerad turned, quick as a wild dog, her hackles bristling—but it was only Lothar, the huge, doltish man in charge of the buttery.

"Late night?" asked Lothar, sniggering.

Maerad turned contemptuously back to the well.

"You could hear the lords until cockcrow," he said. "And who took you last night?"

"Shut your muddy mouth, pea-brain," she said curtly. "Or I'll put the evil eye on you." She turned to face him, glaring, and began to raise her arms. Lothar went pale and crossed his hands before his eyes. "Ward! Ward!" he cried. "I meant no harm, Maerad."

"Then keep your mouth from evil gossip," she hissed. "Get! Go!"

Lothar scuttled off, and Maerad permitted herself a grim smile before she savored a precious minute to herself. The cot was only just stirring; it was before cockcrow, and there were still a few moments before the summons bell. Most of the slaves huddled greedily into their little patches of sleep-warmth, reluctant to leave until the very last second.

Maerad leaned back and breathed in hard, gazing up at the distant stars, tiny points of frosty fire high over the mountains. She searched as she always did for the dawn star, Ilion, burning brightly over the eastern horizon, and sniffed a new freshness in the early air. It's the beginning of spring, she thought. Despite her tiredness, her spirits lifted. Then she looked down at her callused hands and sighed. But not for me; I'm already withering. What will become of me?

She stared at the miserable dwellings around her with a dull hatred. Apart from the Thane's quarters and the Great Hall, which were better maintained than most, the cot consisted of dirt-floored stone hovels, roofed with rotting wooden shingles. Many were crumbling under their age and had been badly patched with clay and straw poultices, giving them an odd, diseased appearance. They stank of rotting middens and human filth. From inside the dormitory Maerad could hear the high, thin cry of a sick child, and someone else shouting angrily, and then the dry sob of a woman. What will become of me? she asked herself again, uselessly, and then the clang of the summons bell broke into her thoughts and she shook herself and tramped to the common room for her meager breakfast of thin gray porridge, and to be assigned her tasks for the day.

That morning Maerad was sent to the milchyard, Lothar's section. She grimaced at her bad luck. She would have to deal with him all day after she had slighted him, and today she was especially tired. Last night had been one of the Thane Gilman's riots, a special gathering to mark the first spring hunt, and his men had come back hungry, wild-haired, spattered with blood, quarrelsome, shouting for beer and voka and roast meats and music. For Gilman it was one of the high points of the year, and the work of all the slaves was doubled for the day. Maerad had worked an extra shift in the kitchen, turning and basting the deer carcasses on the iron spits. Then, because she was the only musician in the cot, she had sat in the Great Hall all night playing the ballads she found so tedious: tales of the slaughter of deer and the valor of men and dogs — and later, drinking songs, and the bawdies, which Maerad hated most of all.

The Great Hall was a grand name for what was really a large barn, roughly crossbeamed, with a blackened hole in the roof to let out the smoke from the great fire that always burned in the middle of the floor. Maerad sat in a corner with her lyre, blank-faced to hide her contempt, while twenty men seated at a long, roughly hewn wooden table set against the wall tore meat from bones with their bare hands and drank themselves insensible on the voka, a harsh, eye-stinging spirit distilled from turnips and rutabagas. They hadn't bothered to wash, and their acrid smell and the wood smoke made her eyes water. No one tried to paw her, to her infinite relief, but even so, the hot red eyes of the men made her feel filthy. As the night wore on, the hall grew hotter and stuffier, and Maerad felt dizzy with the reek and her tiredness. She played badly, something that seldom happened even under such circumstances, but nobody noticed.

The riot finished shortly before dawn, when the last drunken thug crashed facedown on the long table and snored among the rest, who lay dribbling on their hands or fallen in their own vomit. Then at last, trembling with weariness, Maerad picked up her lyre and left the hall, stumbling between sleeping dogs, tossed bones and filth, spilled voka, and snoring bodies to the sweet air outside. She stank, but she was so exhausted, she had simply made her way to the women's slave quarters and slipped onto her meager straw pallet for a bare hour of sleep.

* * *

In the cowbyre she leaned her forehead into the warm flanks of a dark-eyed cow, who stood patiently chewing cud as she kneaded its full udder. The milk splashed rhythmically into the pail. Maerad was on the brink of sleep when suddenly the cow almost kicked her and then tried to rear. Maerad started awake, rescuing the pail—spilled milk would mean a beating—and tried to calm the animal. Normally a word would do, but the creature kept snorting and stamping, pulling the chains that held her hind leg and head as if she were distressed or frightened.

The hair on the back of Maerad's neck prickled. She had a strange, taut feeling, as if there were about to be a storm and the air was crackling with imminent lightning. She looked around the byre.

A man stood there, not ten feet away, a man she had never seen before. For a moment, shock stopped her breath. The man was tall, and his stern face was shadowed by a dark, roughly woven woolen hood. She stood up and reached for a rushlight, uncertain whether to shout for help.

"Who are you?" she said sharply.

The man was silent.

She began to feel afraid. "Who are you?" she asked again. Was it a wer out of the mountains? A ghost? "Avaunt, black spirit!"

"Nay," he said at last. "Nay, I am no black spirit. No wer in a man's skin. No. Forgive me. I am tired, and I am wounded. I am not quite—myself."

He smiled, but it was more like a wince, and as the rushlight fell past his hood and illuminated his features, Maerad saw that he was gray with exhaustion. His face was arresting: it seemed neither young nor old, the countenance of a man of perhaps thirty-five years, but somehow with the authority of age. He was high-cheekboned, with a firm mouth and large, deep-set eyes. He held her gaze. "And who are you, young witch-maiden? It takes sharp eyes to see the likes of me, although perhaps my art fails me. Name yourself."

"Who are you to ask me?" said Maerad pugnaciously. It occurred to her, with a pang of surprise, that she didn't feel afraid—although, she thought in that split second, she ought to be.

The man looked hard at her, searching her face. He staggered slightly and corrected himself, and then smiled again, as if in apology.

"I am Cadvan, of the School of Lirigon," he said. "Now, mistress, how do they name you?"

"Maerad," she said, almost whispering. She felt suddenly at a complete loss, confused by his politeness.

"Maerad of the Mountains?" the stranger said with a wry smile.

"Of . . . of Gilman's fastness," she said. And then with a rush: "I'm a slave here. . . ."

"A slave?"

Steps sounded outside and Lothar's bulk darkened the door. "Where's that milk? What are you doing there; have you lost your wits? Are you looking for the whip? If the butter doesn't turn, we'll know who to blame."

He was not pleased with her, after her rebuff that morning. But again Maerad caught her breath in shock. Although the stranger stood plain in his sight, Lothar seemed to look right through him.

"I'm—I'm sorry," she stammered. "The cattle are restless. . . ."

She sat on her stool and leaned forward to the cow again, who now stood patiently. Lothar watched her while she milked. She willed him to go away. After a short time, she heard his steps leaving and she relaxed a little. She kept milking, because she needed time to gather her thoughts. The stranger still stood there, watching her.

"Maerad," said the stranger quietly. "I wish you no harm. I am tired, and I need to sleep. That's why I'm here." He passed his hand over his brow, and then leaned against the wall of the byre.

"He didn't see you," she said, still milking steadily to cover her amazement.

"No, it is a small thing . . ." he said, almost abstractedly. "A mere glimmerspell. What is interesting is that you saw me." He stared at her again, with that searching, disturbing gaze. Maerad felt suddenly shy before him, as if she were naked, and turned her face aside. She felt his eyes upon her, and then a kind of release as he looked away. Involuntarily she shook herself. She heard him shift and sit down.

"I wish I were not so tired," he said at last, and then asked, "You were not always a slave?"

"My mother wasn't a slave," Maerad answered, speaking reluctantly, as if against her will. "Gilman bought her and kept her here, when I was very little. I think he wanted to ransom her, but none came to ransom." She paused, and added flatly, "And then she died." She coiled around to face him, with a flash of anger. "What business is it of yours?" she demanded. "Who are you to ask me?"

The stranger seemed unperturbed, meeting her gaze calmly.

"What was your mother's name?"

"Milana. Milana of Pellinor, Singer of the Gift, Daughter of the First Circle. My father . . ." She stopped milking, and her hands flew to her mouth in astonishment. "Oh!"

"Oh, indeed," said Cadvan.

"I mean, my mother was called Milana, that's all I remember. . . ." Maerad trailed off in confusion. "She, she died when I was seven years old. . . . I don't know anything about . . . about the rest. Did you make me say that?"

"Make? No, I can't *make* you say anything. I asked, and the doors of your mind flew open. There is more in that treasury than most people realize. The School of Pellinor," he said, as if to himself. "That was sacked, oh, years ago. It was thought all were killed." He fell silent, and Maerad, shaken, continued milking. What was this man talking about? Was he mazing her, as wild spirits were said to do, bewildering her senses before snaring her? But he did not seem evil.

"By what right do you come in here and say . . . and say such things? I could call the Thane's men. . . ." She stuttered to a halt. Somehow she knew she wouldn't call the guards.

The stranger put his face in his hands and didn't answer her. Maerad glanced at him angrily. She finished milking the cow and turned her loose, bringing in the next one. Cadvan was still sitting, unmoving, in the same position.

"You can't stay here, if you are of Pellinor," he said at last.

Maerad looked across at the stranger with a sudden wild hope. Did he mean that he knew some way to free her? But no one could escape from the cot. . . .

He looked up at her. "Could you—perhaps—spare some milk?"

Wordlessly she offered him the milk pail. After a long drink, he wiped his mouth and smiled. "A blessing on you, and on your house," he said. Maerad nodded impatiently, brushing off the courtesy. "Will you have to come to the byre again?" he asked. "Today, I mean."

She examined his face suspiciously. "Yes, I am sectioned here today," she said at last. "I'll be milking again in the evening. Why?"

"Good." He stretched and yawned. "I'll sleep now. We'll talk later—yes, when I am less tired."

He cast himself down on the hay and was asleep almost instantly. Maerad looked down at him, considering whether to kick him awake and make him answer her questions, or to call the guards after all. But for reasons she couldn't trace, she did neither. Instead, she finished the milking and left him there.

She was beaten for the missing milk.

That day Maerad was so absent-minded, she was lucky to escape a second beating. At her tasks in the milchyard—churning butter or setting the milk in bowls for soured drinks—she scarcely saw what she was doing. At first she didn't know what she felt about the man in the byre. Her mind, practiced at the evasions necessary for survival, skipped over the thought of him; he was, in a way, unthinkable. But every now and then an image of his dark face rose unbidden in her mind, and with it an unsettling feeling she couldn't name: a skin-prickling premonition, not exactly unpleasant, but not quite comfortable either. If she had been a child used to name-day celebrations, she might have likened it to the feeling of anticipating a present, but she knew no such celebrations. At the same time, the blank, impassive mask under which she survived seemed to have disappeared, leaving her exposed and a little frightened. It was as if the stranger had opened a door, long shut in her mind, and a cold fresh wind blew in, waking her from a stupor. Who am I? she wondered, and the question hurt.

She was used to her own strangeness. It had often been a protection as much as a curse. Because of her blue eyes and black hair, the fair-haired Northerners called her a witch, and she had played the part from an early age, making a virtue of what set her apart. And Maerad did possess the power of cursing: if she glared at someone, they might trip over and fall for no reason, or a beaker might fall from a shelf and break on their head, and once she had blinded a man for three days. She was also especially good with animals, another sign of witchcraft; those she tended grew fat and yielded twice the milk of the others. Most of the slaves feared and avoided her, and Gilman's men . . . well, the Thane's men had also learned to leave her alone.

Gilman was deeply superstitious and, like all bullies, a devout coward. He believed that if Maerad were murdered, her ghost would drive him to a grisly death: madden him until he ran out into the wolfhunt, perhaps, or skewer him slowly with invisible knives of fire. So Maerad escaped the worst details, which caused comment and petty malice among many of her fellow slaves. Recently this resentment had flared into open violence: a month ago six women had attacked her and tried to drown her in the duck pond. They had almost succeeded, but Gilman had rushed out of the hall, red-faced with panic, and hauled her out of the water. Though Maerad was cuffed for the trouble she had caused, the slaves who tormented her were whipped and given no food for three days. Saved by Gilman! She grinned without humor at the irony. It had stopped the persecution, for the moment—but now no one spoke to her at all, apart from idiots like Lothar.

If it hadn't been for her music, she might have killed herself, or let the demons in her head taunt her into madness. Or she might have just turned into stone and become like the rest of them, brutalized of all feeling. Her lyre was her one possession, the only thing she still had of her mother. It was small, fitting into the crook of her arms like a baby, a bare wooden instrument with no decoration except some indecipherable carvings, but its tone was pure and true. One of her earliest memories was of her mother playing it, plucking the strings and singing to Maerad; she guessed she must have been very young, because her mother had not been sad.

Maerad could play like a true minstrel; her ear was accurate, and she only had to hear a tune once to repeat it. Mirlad, Gilman's Bard, discovered her talent after her mother died. She was only seven years old then, and he somehow persuaded Gilman to relieve Maerad from morning duties so he could teach her. Mirlad, gruff, taciturn, sometimes cruelly harsh, had been her teacher until she turned thirteen: then Gilman demanded her labor in the fields again. Maerad remembered her misery at that decision, and Mirlad's odd response. "I've taught you everything I know about music," he had said, shrugging indifferently. "Anything else would be a waste here. You can play in the evenings, anyway."

Her musicianship compounded her isolation, but it was another reason Gilman tolerated her: Mirlad had died some two years before, although perhaps only Maerad mourned his passing, and she was now the only person in the cot with the skill to play at the riots. She played for herself, privately, whenever she could, and those snatched moments were the only consolation of her degraded life.

Milana. My mother. How long since I thought of you? You braided my hair each night, even if your hands shook with tiredness, and you played me pretty tunes when I felt sad or when someone beat me, and kissed me, just there, on my forehead. . . . Maerad's mind flinched from the memory of her mother's death, how she had sickened, wasted by fever and pain and grief. She had died, that was all, and after that Maerad was alone.

For as long as she could remember, Maerad had dreamed of escaping Gilman's Cot. But year after year passed and brought only the knowledge that escape was impossible. Hope had ebbed little by little, until, though Maerad did not know it, she wore the same sad beauty that she remembered of her mother. Now, this *Cadvan*—she said the name to herself, privately— had appeared out of nowhere, as if walls and guards and dogs did not exist.

As the day wore on, she turned over the morning's conversation with an increasing impatience. Sometimes she convinced herself that she had dreamed the stranger, that he was an illusion of her exhaustion, a shadowy projection of the longing that burned within. She had thought hope was dead inside her, but now she realized that it merely slumbered, like ash-gray embers that held yet a glowing heart, which the merest breath might fan into flame.

The hours dragged, but at last it was evening. Just before she went to the byre, prompted by a sudden impulse, Maerad slipped back to her quarters and took her lyre from where she kept it, wrapped in sacking under her pallet.

Cadvan was still there, lying on his back in the byre, his hands folded behind his head, apparently studying the ceiling. He was not so gray-faced now, although there were still dark circles under his eyes. He smiled at Maerad when she entered, but when he saw the fresh welts on her legs from the beating earlier that day, his smile faded. She looked back at him expressionlessly, waiting for him to speak. He sighed and stood up.

"Well, Maerad, I've had a little time to think," he said. "This is a foul, noisome place; the animals are better treated than the people here. That is unjust enough." He paused. "Do you wish to leave?"

Maerad almost laughed. The cot was guarded day and night, and the guards were vigilant. Some slaves had tried to escape, but all her life Maerad had heard of none who succeeded, although she had seen many savage beatings and a man torn to pieces by Gilman's hounds. It was enough to gainsay the attempt.

"Leave this place?"

"Seriously, Maerad."

"I've dreamed of nothing else these long years," she said. "It's impossible. Why do you think I'm still here?"

"Nothing is impossible." Cadvan paused and looked down

at the ground. "You could leave with me. But I am in a little dilemma as to what to do; it would be most unwise to take you with me. I am flying from danger into danger, and I do not have my full strength."

Maerad's heart dropped with disappointment. She hadn't realized, despite her frank scepticism, the resilience of her hope. But Cadvan continued.

"Neither could I leave you here, if you are indeed Milana's daughter, and you indeed wish to leave. Perhaps I could come back when I was stronger; but I have duties I can't abandon, and I would not be free of them for months. And my heart tells me . . ." He fell silent again, looking at the ground, as if he were weighing a difficult decision.

"I must leave now. If you want to come with me, you may. Leaving will be a simple matter. Other things will not be so simple, but we will have to take them as they come."

Maerad was suddenly breathless and could make no reply.

"Yes?" the stranger said. "Or no?"

"Why are you asking me this?" she said. "It's impossible! Are you tricking me?"

Cadvan merely looked at her without answering. She stared back at him stubbornly, refusing to lower her eyes.

"There come few times in a person's life where there is a clear choice," said Cadvan at last. "The difference between one person and another is how they meet that choice." There was a short silence, and then he gestured impatiently. "I have no time. I have made my offer. You can stay or leave as you wish. I am asking what you want. If you don't know, it is no concern of mine." He brushed some straw from his cloak and turned to leave the byre.

A feeling akin to panic surged through Maerad. For a second she felt as if she were drowning again: only this time there would be no hand to haul her out onto the bank.

"Wait!" she called out. "Wait."

Cadvan turned again to face her.

"I'll come," she said.

Cadvan looked at her bundled lyre. "Is there anything you must fetch?" Maerad shook her head. "Well, that is good. We'll go now, then."

"Now? What about the cows?" And indeed, they were lowing, asking her to relieve them of their burden of milk.

"Someone else will milk them tonight," said Cadvan. "I do not think Gilman will let his beasts suffer; they are too valuable. Now, quickly. Come here."

Maerad approached him warily, and he made her stand square in front of him. He put his hands on her shoulders and spoke. The words sent a thrill through Maerad; it was like plunging into cold, fresh water from a spring welling from the morning of the world.

"*Larnea il oseanna, lembel Maerad inasfrea!*" He dropped his hands. "'Turn the eyes of men from Maerad so she may walk unseen,' is roughly what I have said," he explained. "Now no man could see you, though you stood a span from his nose. The virtue will not work on objects, if you drop them. So keep your bundle close! Now, we must scale the walls."

He picked up a pack Maerad had not noticed and walked toward the low door. As he did so, Maerad was assailed by panic once again. Somehow she already felt her decision was irrevocable, yet she didn't know what it was she had decided: why trust this man? She knew nothing of him. But her doubts were overwhelmed by a fierce longing, as if all her desires for freedom, crushed by hopelessness for so many years, came back in a single urgent wave. It can't be worse than here, she thought, because here I'm certain to die, and out there — who knows? She took a deep breath and followed Cadvan out of the byre.

"We must hurry," he said. "No speaking. I cannot make us unheard as well."

They left the byre and made for the south wall. Maerad found it hard not to flinch in the open squares, where the Thane's men stood lounging against the walls, toying with their weapons; it was difficult to believe in her invisibility when she felt so visible.

Their way led them straight past the Great Hall. The chained dogs looked up and sniffed in greeting as they passed, but the men looked through them.

She kept close behind Cadvan, tiptoeing despite herself, until they came to the least-guarded section of the outer walls. The wall itself was not hard to climb; Maerad had often considered the logistics. Impossible, however, under the vigilance of the guards, whose sight covered every inch of the wall and who knew their lives were forfeit if anyone left. Cadvan set his foot on the wall, and Maerad helplessly showed him her sacking-wrapped lyre, which she could not sling on her back. He stopped thoughtfully, took it, and stowed it in his bag. Then they started again. When they reached the top, Cadvan paused, looking each way for the guards who patrolled the way. Choosing his time carefully, he took Maerad by the arm and pushed her across the narrow path, and then together they went down the other side.

As they did, Maerad heard the bell ring—once, twice, thrice—before it began a long, urgent peal. It was the signal for an escape. She started, feeling horribly exposed. Lothar must have discovered her absence already, but it was very quick—no doubt he wanted revenge for her slight this morning, and she would be whipped for sparking an alarm. A commotion rose in the cot. She half scrambled, half fell down the wall, beating Cadvan to the ground.

"Now *you* make the pace!" he said, laughing. "I thought I'd never get you out of there!"

"They'll send the dogs after us!" whispered Maerad, panting with fear. "There's no escaping Gilman's hounds. They'll track a stag for a week and they can tear a grown man to pieces in a minute!"

"Dogs are easy to deal with," said Cadvan. "Don't be afraid, Maerad. If dogs are the worst we have to face, we will be fortunate. But now we must move on. See the end of this valley? I want to be well clear of this before the night is over. Our doom tonight is, I am afraid, a long walk. Then we'll rest."

Maerad looked down the valley where she had been imprisoned most of her short life. The ground swept away before her, a constant, steady decline of boulders and mountain rubble covered with sparse scrub and the odd tree bent against the harsh winds that swept down from the mountains, the Osidh Annova, eastern border of the Inner Kingdom. A rudimentary track wandered down the center of the valley, strewn here and there with stones from some landslide.

She suddenly felt very small and frightened. She looked at the man who stood at her elbow, and swallowed. His face was dark and closed; the great dogs that figured in her nightmares, with their yelping bays and their long, loping gait, were but small trouble to him. No doubt he knew far worse. He now seemed remote, charged with some hidden power she only sensed. She didn't want to seem foolish before such a man. She squared her shoulders and took a deep breath.

"We'll walk, then," she said, turning her face toward the broken path.

At her back, behind the cot, reared the Landrost, its tip stained red by the setting sun, its massive bulk throwing all the valley into shadow.

II

THE LANDROST

THEY had not gone half a mile when Maerad heard the long halloo of the hunting horn and the bay of Gilman's hounds. Her heart constricted. Before long the gates of the cot flung open and three of the Thane's men emerged, shouting, roughly horsed, and the hounds poured after them, loping in the low light. Noses down, they cast around for a scent, the bloodlust already a fire in their eyes. Maerad fought a rising fear and unconsciously shrank toward Cadvan. He glanced at her swiftly.

"Maerad, they cannot harm us," he said. "The men cannot see us."

She nodded and trudged on, trying to contain herself. Suddenly another bay went up—the hounds had found their scent and were running. The horsemen followed, spurring on their mounts. Cadvan was still walking steadily.

"But the *hounds* can see us," whispered Maerad. "The hounds can see us, and . . ."

"They won't harm us," said Cadvan. "They're savage beasts, but innocent. They serve no dark purpose. Have faith."

The hounds were nearing them swiftly. As they drew close, Cadvan stopped and wheeled around. He raised his arms, and to Maerad it seemed that suddenly a light was gathered about him, or within him, although she could see no source.

"*Lemmach!*" he said.

The leading hound stopped dead in its tracks, so the dog behind it tumbled over its feet. The pack wheeled around and stopped.

"*Lemmach ni ardrost!*"

The lead dog came up to Cadvan and whiffled around his knees. Cadvan stroked its nose. "*Ni ardrost,*" he said again, gently, and the dogs each sniffed him and then, as if they had just gone for a drink at a pond, trotted casually back to the riders.

Maerad stood stock still, her face a cipher. "What did you do?"

"I told them to stop and asked them to go home," said Cadvan. "And being friendly beasts, they obligingly did so. They'll not hunt us now, no matter what their masters do. They obey older laws."

At her back, Maerad could hear the riders cursing the dogs, and their yelps as they whipped them. She realized she was trembling. A massive exhaustion swept over her, and she stumbled. Cadvan caught her elbow in quick concern.

"I'm sorry to drive you, Maerad, but we cannot rest here tonight," he said. "Gilman's hounds are no danger to us, but other things are. This is an unwholesome place. And already it grows dark."

Maerad shrugged off Cadvan's hand. Other things? she thought. What other things? All the recent rumors of wers and other creatures of the night crowded uncomfortably in her mind.

"I'm all right," she said sullenly.

"It is safest if we keep moving," said Cadvan.

The night had a cold edge, but this early it was still mild and clear. They walked for some time in silence, and as Maerad began to get her second wind, they started talking. Maerad asked Cadvan what he was doing in Gilman's Cot, but he evaded the answer, instead asking about her life there, and whether she had earlier memories, from Pellinor. She could tell him little on that point.

"Fragments," she said. "A man—I think it was my father—a handsome man, tall, with long, black hair, laughing. A chair with beautiful carvings with a strange-colored light falling on it from a high window. A few scraps of music. I thought that I dreamed it."

"It's no dream. The Schools are places of high learning and much beauty," said Cadvan sadly, as if he spoke of something loved that was vanishing. "The Lore is upheld, and the Light shines over all who dwell there. But now their power wanes, and darkness reaches into Annar."

"What are the Schools?" asked Maerad, feeling ignorant and coarse. "Is that where you learned those spells?"

He glanced at her, and to her confusion he laughed. "Maerad, it is so strange to me that one of the Gift should know nothing at all of the Schools."

"The Gift?" said Maerad. She looked down the valley; a long way before her, she could see the stars glimmering between the spurs where it ended, opening out onto the wide world, of which she knew nothing. She suddenly felt more alone than she ever had in her life; and she was so tired, more tired than she had ever been. A ball of grief rose in her throat, and she couldn't speak.

"Please forgive me, Maerad," Cadvan said. "I do not mean to tease your ignorance. Perhaps more tutored, you would now be dead, and your lack of knowledge has protected you from the sight of those who would otherwise have done you harm." He smiled at her, and Maerad, not quite understanding him, smiled wanly back. "Perhaps I should turn Loresinger for a while?" he said. "Tonight we could have an introductory lesson. It will pass the time."

"All right, then," said Maerad, glancing across at the shadowy man beside her. "Tell me about the Gift."

They had a long way to go, but they were making good time, despite boulders and loose stones that constantly threatened to turn an ankle. The last traces of daylight were retreating from the mountains, and it was the dark interval before moonrise. Her legs felt heavy and sore with tiredness, but talking took her mind off her discomfort.

"Where to begin?" said Cadvan. "What is the Gift? How to answer that, when nobody really knows?" He paused, as if gathering his thoughts. "Well, those of the Gift are like to the Loresingers of Afinil. All Bards are of the Gift, and it means they have certain powers and abilities. The most important is the Speech." He paused. "Bards do not learn the Speech, but are born with it already living within them. In the mouths of those with the Gift, the Speech holds an innate power; it is the source of our Knowing and much of our might. Those with the Gift also live for three spans of a normal life: I am already an old man by normal reckonings, although you would not think so, perhaps."

"An old man?" said Maerad, looking dubiously at Cadvan. He did not look old to her; she had already guessed his age to be about thirty-five years. She wondered briefly if he was making it up, but then she thought of how he had made her invisible.

"Not old in the measure of Bards," said Cadvan, smiling, "but old enough. A long life is a double-edged privilege, believe me. But there are other signs; Bards know other Bards, which is how I knew you. This morning I thought for a second my powers had wholly failed me, when you challenged me." He clutched his breast. "My heart stopped! But then I saw your eyes. . . ."

Maerad glanced at him, again uncertain of what he meant, or whether she should laugh. She noticed that as he spoke

Cadvan was constantly alert, but in ways she didn't recognize. He never looked around or behind him, but seemed to be innerly attuned to something she couldn't hear, as if inside him flowed a music that, at times, demanded intense attention. It felt a bit odd, as if he were only half there.

"There is much you should know about Bards and the Light," said Cadvan. "To have the Gift, and to be ignorant of what it means, can be a terrible thing." He began to speak in an oddly formal tone, almost a chant, which at first nearly made her smile. She had a swift unbidden vision of a stone hall with high windows, and of many people seated in a circle, their heads bowed in concentration. The vision vanished, and she looked around her at the empty night and the gloomy shadows of the mountainside; but Cadvan's voice continued steadily in the darkness.

"Know then, Maerad, that in Annar and the Seven Kingdoms the Bards are charged with the keeping of the Light. The centers of Knowing are the Schools, but it was not always so. Many lives of men ago, the center of the Lore was Afinil, Citadel of Song, built when the first Loresingers came to Annar. Some say a terrible cold drove them from their home, and others that they sailed here on great ships from a foundered land, and still others say they simply appeared here among other humans; whatever the truth, our origin is lost in legend. However they came, Bards appeared in Annar, bringing with them the remnants of an ancient Knowing from the very dawn of the world: the Gift of the Speech, and Reading and Making and Tending, the skills and knowledge known as the Arts of the Light. And here was built the great city of Afinil, which was the center of the Knowing in the ancient days.

"Many songs tell of its unmatched beauty, of the unwalled towers that rose like lilies beside the mere, beside the pure face of blessed water. And within this citadel dwelt the Loresingers, all those who loved and tended the beauty of the world. The Speech was on all tongues, and all met with understanding."

Cadvan's voice shifted subtly into a chant. Maerad's heart quickened; she couldn't remember the last time she had heard a new song. Even in her surprised pleasure, the musician in her noted coldly that Cadvan possessed a very good baritone.

> *"Dashed into darkness, deeper than heartgrief,*
> *All voices mourn thee, high and humble,*
> *Treespeech and beastspeech, manspeech and bard,*
> *All voices mourn thee, fruit of the dawn,*
> *Flower of ice enchanting the sunlight,*
> *Shadow of moonbeam woven from marble,*
> *Throat of the morning where all voices mingled.*
> *In Afinil, O Afinil!*
> *Thy dreams are lost, thy music still,*
> *The briars creep where thy towers were*
> *And the stars are dark in the shadowmere.*

"So it is remembered in song as an ache, a memory of something lovely, now lost forever. The story of its loss is an evil one. But you must know it, if you are to understand the Bards. For the gifts of the Light, alas, were its own undoing."

Maerad stumbled again and this time fell, scrambling up immediately. Cadvan stopped. "Are you all right?" he said.

"Yes," she snapped, embarrassed, pressing her hands together where she had grazed them on the rock.

Cadvan looked at her sharply. "You haven't rested, and after a heavy day's work, no doubt," he said. "We must press on; but perhaps we can stop for a little while now, to go all the faster afterward." He sat down on the ground, just where he was, and gratefully Maerad sat down next to him. Her legs were shaking. Cadvan opened his pack and drew out a bottle. "This helps weariness," he said. He drank some, then offered it to Maerad. It tasted like water, but with a faint hint of herbs. A fiery tingling rushed through her body, and some of her exhaustion immediately lifted. In the sudden quiet, the valley felt oppressively silent, and when Cadvan began to speak again, Maerad almost jumped.

"Afinil, as I said, fell in part because of its generosity. In the south there arose a king who feared to die like ordinary men and sought instead endless life, freed from the doom of the world's circle. He envied the powers of the Light and desired them for his own. Masking his intent, he approached the gentle Bards of Afinil and asked for tutelage, and harboring no suspicion in their hearts, gladly they gave it to him. He was an apt pupil and in time became more powerful in the ways of Speech, more subtle in the Lore, more skilled in the arts of Making and Unmaking, than any before him. When he was satisfied he had learned enough, he returned to his own land in the south, the kingdom of Dén Raven.

"The intention of the knowledge of Light is to make fair, to make grow, to keep the sacred Balance. But this king bent this knowledge to his own purpose. His first wrong was to cast off his Name."

"How can you cast off your name?" asked Maerad, fascinated and puzzled. "What did they call him, then?"

Cadvan laughed. "He still has a usename, this sorcerer, though it is seldom said. He is usually called the Nameless. Every Bard has a secret Name," he continued. "You do not know my Name. You do not even yet know yours. A Bard's Name is given at enstatement, when you come into your powers: it is, if you like, your true Name in the Speech. It says who you are. To cast it off is to reject yourself."

"But that's impossible!" Maerad objected. "How can you not be who you are?"

"Alas, it's not impossible at all," replied Cadvan. "The king rejected his Name, because then he could also reject death. But with the gift of death, he cast away also the knowledge of those who die, and found his heart was empty, a pain sharper than any that he had known. For he was not of the immortals, and had not the right to deathlessness. He looked out on the world, and his eye was dark. He sought then the dominion of all on the earth and the destruction of all that rebuked him with its beauty, and he challenged the Law of the Balance, and overthrew it. And then, with massed armies and Black Sorcerers — those corrupt Bards that we call Hulls — he marched on the lovely citadel of Afinil, and cast down its fair towers and darkened the mere, so the moon no longer bathed there and the stars fled its lifeless face. Then began the Great Silence, when the Song was no longer heard in the wide lands of Annar.

"That was not the total of his evil, but it was among the most grievous. Many things then were lost to the world, beyond restoration."

Maerad listened in silence, overwhelmed with wonder, not only at the tale, but at the sweet tautness the names began to awaken within her: *Afinil, Loresinger, the Light.* They recalled much of the scent and sound of her mother, her voice as she plucked the lyre, the dark fall of her hair as she kissed her, and other memories that she could not trace. She sighed also, and looked around them. They were now more than halfway down the valley, and the stars were massed above them, bright around a moon waxing to the full. She picked out the Five Gemmed Daughters, swinging high over them in their ceaseless dance. Ilion was now sunk beneath the horizon.

Cadvan stood up. "We should move on," he said. Maerad scrambled to her feet, and they began again the slow trudge down the valley. Maerad felt her exhaustion beginning to return, but she forced herself on, and Cadvan returned to his lesson.

"The story of the downfall of the Nameless One is long and hard and desperate, and many parts of that tale never returned from darkness," he continued. "Suffice it to say that he was at last defeated. After his fall, the Bards made the Schools, which keep and teach the Knowing of the Light throughout Annar and the Seven Kingdoms. The center of all high knowledge is now Norloch, a fair place of gardens and high halls and learning. But in one way it differs from Afinil: for Norloch is walled and provision is made for a great garrison, and the innocence that was the downfall of Afinil will not be its weakness again. And this perhaps is the greatest loss caused by the Nameless, although some argue it is not so, and that in its greatness Norloch surpasses even the ancient citadel."

"Have you been there?" asked Maerad, when he said no more.

"Yes," said Cadvan. "Many times. For I am no longer part of any School, and travel between them as I must. The Light once more is under attack. And Bards now are sent on dangerous and secret ways to spy out the tracks of the Dark, rather than singing the leaves of spring in the old ways and bringing increase."

"Was that why you were near Gilman's Cot?" asked Maerad.

A shadow of pain passed over Cadvan's face. "It is a little close to speak of that," he said. He was silent then for a long time.

In the quiet Maerad again felt the oppressiveness of their surroundings. It was now some three hours since sunset, and the moonlight illuminated the sheer edges of the mountains with a white dew, casting the ravines into impenetrable shadow. In the distance she thought she heard faint howls and shrieks. She thought also that Cadvan's face held traces of some great strain, although his voice had betrayed nothing.

Maerad remembered his exhaustion only that morning, and that he had said he was wounded. She saw no sign of a wound.

At last she ventured another question. "Do you think that I might be a Bard?"

"Didn't you hear anything I told you?" said Cadvan shortly. Maerad cast him a glance of dislike. Her feet were beginning to throb with pain, and she marched on in silence, wondering if they would ever leave this cursed valley. Cadvan halted then and gasped, and Maerad saw that sweat stood out on his forehead.

"Maerad," he said. "I must ask your patience. I contest the will of the spirit of this place, which would not have us leave here. It bears down on me, and it gets worse the farther we go."

After a short time he walked on again, but more slowly, as if he were pushing through deep water. Maerad saw with anxiety they still had a long way to go before they passed out of the valley. She could feel nothing herself, apart from an increasing sense of dread. She didn't dare to speak. It was difficult walking, as now they picked their way through broken boulders and piles of scree slipped from the sides of the mountain, and at times the track almost vanished altogether. Her boots were ragged, and her feet felt bruised and sore. And, for the first time that night, the cold began to trouble her. It seemed to creep into the marrow of her bones, forming crystals in her joints that made it hard to move. She gradually descended into a dull nightmare of exhaustion, and finally was concentrating only on putting one foot in front of the other. The mouth of the valley drew closer and closer, but as they neared it, so the cold increased and Cadvan's steps became slower.

At last he stopped altogether. Now sweat ran in runnels down his face, and the edges of his mouth trembled. "Maerad," he said. "I must rest, just briefly." He collapsed slowly to the ground.

Instinctively Maerad reached out and clasped his hand.

All at once she felt it: a cold, cruel will that crushed her mind like a vice. She dropped his hand as if the touch scorched her.

"What *is* it?" she whispered.

Cadvan looked at her in amazement.

"You can feel it?" he said.

"Something," she said, wincing. "Something horrible . . ."

"Take my hand again," he said. Maerad looked at him fearfully and flinched away. When she had touched Cadvan, it was as if her mind had been invaded by a malignant consciousness, implacable and terrifying.

Cadvan let out his breath in a gasp, and then braced himself to breathe again, like a man in pain. He held out his hand toward her, speaking steadily. "Maerad, at this moment I keep the entire mountain from toppling on our heads. Perhaps you can help me. Take my hand!"

Reluctantly Maerad reached out and clasped it again. His fingers were cold as ice. The feeling came back, worse this time. Cadvan clutched her hard, as if he were drowning.

"Hold it back," he said. "Command it to retreat."

Maerad felt bewildered. What did he mean?

Hold it back!

The command seemed not to be said out loud, but inside her head. It was Cadvan's voice. In the midst of the baleful darkness that disordered her mind, his voice seemed to be a light, a small white flame. . . . She turned toward it, fighting down her terror. She focused her thoughts. *Go away!* she cried. She didn't know if she said it out loud. *Begone!*

At once the crushing sense of malevolence lightened. Cadvan let out an enormous sigh.

"By the Light, Maerad, that is some Gift you have. Now perhaps we will be able to leave." Slowly, holding her hand so tightly she could feel the bones crunching, he stood up.

They crept on steadily, bent over as if they carried heavy burdens. Maerad found it difficult to concentrate both on walking and on shielding her mind. Once she twisted her ankle on a rock and almost fell, crying out, but Cadvan kept fast her hand and she limped on. The end of the valley came closer with excruciating slowness.

At last, as the mountains began to turn silver gray and then rose pink with the approaching dawn, they reached the end of the valley. As they passed the last of its outrunning hills, Maerad felt the will snap shut behind her, like a gate, and suddenly her body walked freely again. She laughed with relief.

"We're out!" she cried, turning to Cadvan with an open smile for the first time.

Cadvan glanced at her somberly. "But still we must walk! Even in its shadows, the Landrost has power."

As if to emphasize his words, a deep rumble echoed from behind them and a great slide of rocks and boulders slipped off the side of the mountain and fell in dust to the ground. Maerad turned and looked into the valley for the last time. Strange, she thought; she felt no emotion at all, neither gladness nor regret. Nothing.

Then she turned away.

Before them she saw the turfed knees of the mountains descending to a great forest, obscured by mists that even now were drawing up to the sky. The sun was rising over the green hills, and its pale light fell on her face.

III

THE SCRYING

MAERAD limped on, her legs heavy, aching for sleep. An hour after sunrise, when the mouth of the valley had vanished in the larger range, but before they had reached the edges of the forest, Cadvan stopped beside a small grove of white-barked trees. Maerad saw they were ancient, with wide, scarred trunks, and grew in a circle close together.

"The birch is a tree of high virtue," Cadvan said. "Even here, we can sleep in peace. This is a dingle planted of old by the northern Bards. It is called Irihel, Icehome, and traveling Bards would stay here. It is well placed for us!"

They passed between the closely planted trunks, and Maerad saw that within them the grass was short and close-leafed, making a soft, fragrant ground that dipped down like a bowl. The branches met and interwove over their heads, the new leaves filtering the light green-gold. Cadvan sat down, throwing his pack to the ground, and stretched out his legs.

"We are not permitted to make fire here," he said. "More's the pity. My bones are frozen."

Maerad cautiously sat down with him. Her rough life in the cot had taught her to be wary of men; it had taken all her guile, and all her summonings of witchfears, to ward off Gilman's thugs. She had seen what they did to others weaker than they were. She was acutely aware that she was alone in a wild place, wholly in the power of this Cadvan; but he wasn't like any man she had met before, not even Mirlad, Gilman's dour and taciturn singer.

Cadvan eyed her with empathy. "There is a rivulet nearby, if you would like to wash," he said. "I'll show you, and leave you there briefly. You will be within call, should you need me. If you are unable to call, shout my name in your head. I will hear you."

Maerad nodded, and he led her to a small stream that flowed, fresh and cold, from the mountains. Behind high bushes of gorse and bramble, a small bank of smooth grass shelved up from a pool, almost as if it had been made for bathing. Cadvan left her, and Maerad washed for the first time since the day before, gasping at the cold water. She soaked her swollen ankle. The sprain was not too bad: it would be better in a day or so.

Then she returned to the dingle, where Cadvan had taken a blanket and her lyre, still wrapped in sacking, from his pack. He had also spread some food: dried fruits and meats, and a tough-looking biscuit. "Eat," he said. "I'll be back in a minute."

Maerad picked up her lyre, shaking off the sacking, and cradled it, but she was too tired even to pluck the strings. By the time Cadvan returned, ten minutes later, she was already sound asleep with the blanket wrapped around her, the lyre tucked in the crook of her arm like a baby, the food untouched. He smiled wryly and ate some of the biscuit. Then he wrapped his cloak around him and slept.

Maerad was awoken by hunger pangs. The sun was already low in the sky. Cadvan was sitting with his back to her and turned when she stirred. He was eating and offered her some supper. They ate in silence. That simple food, seasoned only by hunger, burst on Maerad's tongue like freedom, and she felt as if her entire body were glowing with the taste of sunlight, of wind blowing in wide spaces and trees reaching their burdened arms to boundless skies.

When they finished eating, Cadvan brushed the crumbs off his cloak with almost fastidious care. "Now, Maerad," he said, not looking at her. "We must think of our plans. I must travel many hundreds of miles, through dangerous country, and quickly. And now I have a passenger, and no extra food. And I notice you brought not a blanket, nor any food, nor even spare clothes—only a harp, like a true Bard. What shall we do?"

Maerad looked at him, schooling her face to betray nothing.

"How should I know?" she said. "You asked me to come with you." But a sudden fear plucked her. What, indeed, was she to do? She knew nothing and no one. As far as she knew, her family was all dead. She had no home. And she could be nothing but a liability to this man, who had freed her from slavery though clearly in danger himself. Would he abandon her?

As if he read her thoughts, Cadvan said quickly, "Of course, I wouldn't leave you here. But we must have some thought of where to go. My way bends to Norloch, where I must report to the Circle. I can either take you to a closer School, where you may rest and heal and be taught, or take you with me to Norloch."

"I don't mean to be in the way," said Maerad.

"Maerad, Bards learn that little that concerns them is the consequence of mere chance. Our meeting seems to me of more weight than that. Those of the Gift are rare enough: to find you in a cowbyre, in such circumstances, is too strange. And I doubt I would have made it out of that valley without your help. That much is clear to me. It is also, to my mind, astonishing to find such power as yours, wholly untutored. I would not have believed it if I had not experienced it. There's much I should tell you, much you should know. A Gift of this kind is a double-edged blade, and its possession can damage you if used wrongly. You are a puzzle."

He smiled at her, but Maerad sat gloweringly and would not smile back. There was a short silence.

"May I look at your lyre?" he asked. "It caught my eye. . . ."

Maerad picked up her instrument, unconsciously stroking it, and passed it to him. He took it and examined it closely, his interest quickening, his long slender fingers testing its weight and balance. He drew his hand across the strings in a gentle chord. The notes rang out sweetly and hung in the air. Cadvan whistled softly.

"This lyre," he said. "Was it your mother's?"

Maerad nodded. Cadvan sat thoughtfully, turning it over in his hands, running his fingers over the carved script.

"Have you ever had to tune it?" he said. "I suppose you have never replaced the strings?"

"No," said Maerad. "Should I have? I didn't know. . . . Mirlad never said . . ."

Cadvan laughed, startling her. "Oh, Maerad," he said, when he regained his breath. "Should you have strung it?" He laughed again, softly, wonder palpable in his voice. "This is a thing precious beyond the ransom of kings. What would Gilman have done, had he known such a treasure lay hidden in his small cot? It is worth ten times, no, a thousand thousand times, the worth of everything in it. Such lyres have not been made for many a long age, not since the days of Afinil. It was carved by a great craftsman. I don't know this script at all, and I know many that are long fallen into disuse; no doubt it tells the name of who made it. Instruments like these are known as Dhyllic ware, and a great potency is woven into their making. The virtue on its strings is one now long lost. I have read of these instruments, but I have never seen one. It was thought they were all lost. What a riddle you are!" He looked at her, still smiling.

Maerad had no idea how to answer him. She was staggered.

Her humble lyre, a thing out of legend? But, suddenly serious, Cadvan reached out and patted her hand.

"We shall have to be friends, if we are to travel together," he said. "And we must trust each other. Don't mind my teasing. Nevertheless, we must decide what to do."

Maerad looked uneasily down at her hands and said nothing. She didn't know what to say to this man: did he mean her ill? How could she tell?

"In any case, we won't leave here tonight," continued Cadvan. "I am still weary, truth be told. And I need to think. Here we are safe, for the time being. Rest will harm neither of us. And there is a long road ahead, whatever we decide."

He opened his pack and drew out a lyre. "Of less noble lineage than yours, but noble enough to keep it company," he said. "And still true, and my first love." He struck some chords, tuning it, and then plucked a cascade of notes that pierced Maerad's heart. It was a song she knew well, the beginning of the tragic lay of Andomian and Beruldh, which Mirlad had taught her many years before. Cadvan began to sing the part of Andomian in a clear, beautiful voice:

"Speak to me, fair maid!
Speak and do not go!
What sorrows have your eyes inlaid
With such black woe?"

He paused, plucking the melody, and Maerad realized he was waiting for her to respond. She was still holding her lyre, and began to play the antiphon, singing the answering verse. She hadn't played a duet since Mirlad died. They continued to sing the alternate verses of the ancient lay, Cadvan's baritone and Maerad's contralto filling the grove with music. Maerad had the odd feeling that the trees were listening, bending inward the better to hear them.

> *"My dam is buried deep*
> *Dark are my father's halls*
> *And carrion fowl and wolves now keep*
> *Their ruined walls."*

> *"Stay and heal your hurt*
> *Lay down that brow of stone*
> *From this day forth my hidden heart*
> *Will be your own."*

> *"The curse of Karak binds me*
> *My brothers are his thralls*
> *And I must turn all joy and flee*
> *To his foul halls . . ."*

Maerad stopped, suddenly faltering. Cadvan ceased his play, and after the rippling chords of music there was a deep silence. "And so Andomian and Beruldh met, and wended their way to the dungeons of the Nameless, and there died, beyond hope or help of the Light," he said. "But none of the legends speak of his regret." He struck a sudden harsh, impatient chord. "You're right, Maerad. This is no song for such a place, unhoused, in the dark, where wers howl in the distance. You play well: you've had some good teaching, clearly, although with some odd variants. I see you know more than you choose to show. I should have expected that. We'll talk of this later."

He put away his lyre and spoke no more for some time, and now his brow was dark and troubled. Maerad sat disconsolate, wondering if she had been impertinent or coarse. This man was

beyond her ken: he seemed to regard her with tolerant irony, and
then, without warning, his mood would change and he would
become distant and withdrawn. He was nothing like the men in
Gilman's Cot, who were moved only by coarse, violent impulses,
nor like Mirlad, who had been brusque, but whose gruffness
concealed a deep kindness. An instinct had told her Mirlad was
deeply unhappy, and so she excused his disillusion and his odd
moods. He had never spoken to her of the history of Annar, or
the Lore, or the Speech, although he had taught her many songs,
saying dismissively that they passed the time. Thinking back,
she supposed he saw as little hope as she did of her escape, and
so sought to protect her from dreaming, as perhaps he did, of
another life. A life where Bards and Song were held in honor, and
were not merely the entertainment at crude feastings.

And he had died there. She felt a new compassion wash
over her for the degradation of Mirlad's life, and his lonely
death.

Cadvan, though, was quite different, and much less easy to
feel out. He seemed more mercurial; his face was mobile, and
his thoughts flowed over it like the sun rippling over water. Yet
paradoxically he seemed more hidden, full of secrets beyond
even those he hinted at. Perhaps, she thought, all real Bards are
like this, at once more present and more remote. At least he had
gotten her out of the cot—but she couldn't think of what she
should do now, unless she followed Cadvan. He said himself
this was dangerous country, and she had no knowledge of any
dangers, save those of being beaten, and fighting off the
Thane's men. She would be as vulnerable as a baby rabbit.

Maerad leaned back against one of the birches and gazed up
through its branches, which twined black against the deep blue
of evening. A few early stars shone through, white jewels
snared in an intricate net. I cannot understand this pattern,
she thought tiredly. But the stars, at least, remain the same.

At last Cadvan said curtly that she should get some rest, and so she curled into the blanket. It didn't take long for her to sleep, despite the disorder of her thoughts.

Maerad woke with a start. For a moment she forgot where she was and wondered why there had been no bell; then a shaft of light striking through the branches shone in her eyes, and as she blinked, the events of the past two days came back with a rush. She sat up, rubbing her eyes, and saw that Cadvan was already up and had laid out breakfast. He had been to the stream, and his dark hair fell wet across his forehead.

"Good morning," he said, bowing. "The mistress of the house must forgive our fare, which, alas, is the same as last night. But wholesome, for all its monotony. Does my lady wish to wash first, or after she breaks her fast?"

Maerad laughed. "Later, I think. It's a better breakfast than I'm used to!"

They ate in a companionable silence. Then Cadvan packed up. Maerad wrapped her lyre in its sacking, and Cadvan stowed it.

"We must leave here today," he said. "I have decided to vary my course somewhat, and go to a place I know about sixty miles hence. At a good pace, and all being well, we will make it in about a week. We need supplies, and you need some clothes. Bards are not welcome everywhere these days, and we will have to disguise ourselves. But I think they will not turn away travelers in need."

Then he paused, as if he were uncertain. "Now, I wish to ask of you a favor. Maerad, you are a sore puzzle to me, and such is the importance of my errand. . . . I want to ask if I can scry you."

"Scry me?" said Maerad. "What does that mean?"

"It's hard to explain, if you don't know," he said. "But I must tell you, that if you refuse, I will respect your decision and will attempt to place no weight on it. Scrying is a hard thing, and no Bard performs it lightly. It means that I wish to look into you and see what you are."

"Oh," said Maerad. She still had no idea what he was talking about. Doubtfully, she asked, "Does it hurt?"

"Well. Yes, it does, in a way. It's a little like my asking if you would take all your clothes off and stand in front of me while I pore over you with a seeing glass."

Maerad stared at him, nonplussed. Cadvan's eyes were frank and open, and there seemed to be no guile in his request. Still, she felt misgivings stir within her. "It sounds like you want to magic me," she said suspiciously. "Don't you trust me? Is that it?"

He sighed. "It's not a spell, not as such. At least, I would do nothing *to* you, apart from look."

Maerad still said nothing.

"I don't like to ask," Cadvan said. "I brought you out of that place in good faith, and I would not ask if all that were at risk were myself."

"What if I don't agree?" she asked.

"Then I won't do it," said Cadvan. "And we shall continue with our journey." His face was suddenly inscrutable, and he bent to pick up his pack.

"What do you have to do?"

Cadvan paused.

"I look into your eyes. I see into your mind. That's all."

"That's *all*?" Maerad considered for a short time. It seemed important to Cadvan. And she didn't believe he would hurt her; he had had plenty of opportunity already, if that was what he wished to do. "All right, then," she said, shrugging. "If it makes you feel better. What do you have to do?"

"Are you sure?"

"Do you want to do it, or not?" she said.

Cadvan dropped his pack again. "Then stand square in front of me, like you did in the byre. And place your hands on my shoulders."

She did so, and he put his hands on her shoulders. They stood face-to-face, and Cadvan looked into her eyes. Maerad had a sudden desire to giggle.

"Don't laugh, Maerad," said Cadvan softly. "Empty your mind."

He spoke words in the Speech, very rapidly so Maerad couldn't catch them. It seemed to Maerad that the light around them darkened, and that all she could see were Cadvan's eyes. They were a very dark blue and burned with an inner fire that seemed at first cold, but then, she realized, was hot at the center, hot enough to burn. And what was that sadness in them? A deep sadness, a wound . . . a face much loved, she could almost see it . . . and something else, a darkness, like a scar. . . . But then suddenly she was overwhelmed with memories of her own life: memories she had forgotten, or pressed into the back of her mind. They came in a flood, in no particular order, almost as if her whole life were occurring in a single second; but some stood out.

Memory after memory of Gilman's Cot, numbing exhaustion and boredom and pain, the humiliations of the riots and beatings, playing with Mirlad when she was a child, and listening to his dour teaching . . . Her mother, and an old woman, blue-eyed, holding her, and a garden full of sweet-scented flowers . . . Singing and music and laughter in a great hall filled with men and women and children in fine clothes and lit with great branches of candles . . . Her mother clutching her in terror and sickness and grief, lurching in a wagon . . . A small table, piled high with fruit . . . Her mother holding a small baby, her brother Cai, who was chortling and reaching for a red flower . . . Her mother's despair and her mother dying. Her mother yellowed and wasted on a pallet, her lips cracked and ulcerated, her voice a whisper, brushing back her hair and saying, "Maerad, be strong. Be strong. . . ." And the death rattle . . . Crows wheeling in a dark sky, and men shouting, and terrible screams, a man she knew was her father felled with a blow from a mace, falling among many bodies, and a high tower burning in the night and a shout as the roof caved in, sending forth a leap of flame . . .

An intolerable anguish possessed Maerad, beyond even the grief she had felt at her mother's death; it was as if all the pain she had ever experienced gathered into a white-hot node in the center of her mind. It grew and grew, a distressing coruscation of her whole being, until she could no longer bear it. Beyond her conscious will, she screamed *No!* and burst into a storm of scalding tears.

She was aware of nothing else for some time. After a while, she realized she was on the ground, weeping on Cadvan's shoulder, and he was stroking her hair. Her sobs subsided at last and she sat back, thrusting Cadvan away and rubbing the back of her hand over her eyes.

Cadvan looked pale and distressed. "Maerad, I am truly sorry," he said. "I am very, very sorry."

She wasn't sure if he was sorry for the scrying, or for what the scrying had revealed. She felt limp, and the beginnings of a slight headache pulsed behind her brow. She hid her face in her hands.

"It *did* hurt," she said in a muffled voice.

"I shouldn't have asked," Cadvan said, after a silence. "For all your power, you are not much more than a child, and even the great find scrying a hard thing. I was in such doubt, whether you were a spirit of the Dark, sent to trick me."

"*Me* trick *you*?" Maerad looked up in surprise. Cadvan grinned at her crookedly.

"You have the consolation that I have paid for my doubt.

The cry you sent out threw me over to those trees. I was lucky my neck wasn't broken!"

"I did that?" She stared at him, her mouth open in astonishment.

"Indeed you did. But it wasn't your fault." He grimaced, rubbing his head, and Maerad saw there was a mark on his forehead. "You need to learn how to control your power."

"You'll have a bump there," she said.

"Yes, I will."

"Is it all right, then?"

"What?"

"I mean, it's all right?"

"Oh, yes." Cadvan answered her almost distractedly. "There is no Darkness in you, if that's what you mean; I know that, even though I couldn't finish the scrying. If there were, I would have found different walls and different kinds of refusals." He looked at her oddly—almost, she thought, shyly. "It's a strange business, scrying. I haven't done it very often. But I can tell you, Maerad, that I have not scried one with so much anguish as you. I shan't do it again in a hurry, and you almost scried me instead!" He shook his head, and they both sat unspeaking for some time. Maerad's headache ebbed away. She felt dazed and emptied; but there was also a strange sense of relief, as if she had been lanced of a large abscess.

Abruptly Cadvan stood up and brushed himself off. He seemed possessed by a new decisiveness, as if the doubts that had troubled him earlier had now been resolved. "We must leave here," he said. "The sun is already high, and we have a long way to go."

Maerad squinted up at him. "Where are we going?"

"I think I must take you to Norloch. But that is a long way from here. First we must find food, and maybe some horses."

He stood in the middle of the dingle and bowed to the trees, signaling to Maerad to do the same. She scrambled to her feet. "We must thank the trees for their hospitality," he said. "They have been good to us." Then he picked up his pack and walked out of the dingle.

Maerad lingered briefly before they left the shelter of the birches, for a last glimpse of the early sunlight shafting through the spring leaves. She thought the grove was the most beautiful place she had ever seen. The light scattered itself in silver and gold glints over the ground, and the intricate shadows of the branches danced with the gleams over the soft grasses, which rippled gently in the spring breeze. *Thank you*, she said silently, and bowed, feeling the ceremony strangely appropriate: the birches seemed more alive than most trees. For a moment she almost felt they were about to speak back to her, and they seemed to rustle a little sadly, as if they were friends waving farewell.

IV

BATTLE WITH THE WERS

W HY is it so quiet?" Maerad asked. "Is it always like this around here?"

"No, it's not. I don't like it," Cadvan said. "There are birds, very high up. I can't see what they are. Perhaps they watch us. It's like the quiet before a storm, but there will be no storm tonight. Tomorrow, perhaps. No, it's something else."

"Can you guess what it might be?"

"Yes. But I might be wrong. What I guess is that the Landrost has sent his messengers out, and that the hunt is on. I have only seen crows today; all other birds are in hiding."

"The hunt?" said Maerad. She realized Cadvan was correct about the crows; she had seen no other birds all day.

They were steering southeast, with the mountains on their right and the forest on their left. The sky was clear and cold, a high pale blue, and all through the morning the sun scarcely warmed them. All around them the earth was alive with the pale green of early spring; snowdrops and jonquils pushed through the tangled herbs and grasses, and marjoram and wild mint released sharp fragrances as they bruised beneath their feet. Low thorny trees and scruffy clumps of pines grew in the lees of the hills, bent by the winds, surrounded by tangles of gorse and bramble. Everywhere crept a pale blue flower shaped like a star, which Cadvan said was called *aëlorgalen*. "Dawnflower, in the Speech," Cadvan explained. "It only grows this far north." Maerad tried repeating the name, but found that her tongue stumbled over it, and afterward she couldn't remember it at all.

It was a beautiful countryside, but Maerad thought it curiously lonely. Their footsteps sounded loudly in the emptiness; they seemed to be the only things moving as far as the eye could see. There was no sign of habitation anywhere, although strange grass-covered ridges and mounds, which seemed too regular to be natural, constantly threatened to trip them up; perhaps they were remains of buildings long vanished. And she saw few animals—only some rabbits running in the distance, but that was all.

"I thought the Landrost was just a mountain," she said, looking back at its high, snow-tipped peak. "You talk as if it were a man. . . . And what's the hunt?"

"The Landrost is a power, yes, a person. . . . The mountain is merely his dwelling. But he is not a man, and never was."

"Like the Nameless One?" said Maerad.

"Not so powerful as him, although the Nameless was once a man. The Landrost is but one of his slaves. I will not speak his name here, although I know it." Cadvan paused, and Maerad noticed again the exhaustion on his face: it was, she saw, a deep exhaustion born of long struggle and pain. "He captured me, and held me in his fastness, deep in the mountain. I saw things there that he would rather I did not know, because in his pride he thought to make me tremble before I died. But I escaped, and his vengefulness is deadly, and we are not beyond his reach, not yet. I only just held him back in the valley, with your help; he would have brought the mountain down on us, else. His power wanes the farther we go, but here we are still too close.

"He does not easily countenance escape from his claws. I think he sends out the wers, and that is why it is quiet. Their shadows track us, although they can do nothing while the sun

still shines. Only in the dark can they take their forms. It will
be a bad night."

He was silent for some time. His words seemed to magnify
the stillness around them, and Maerad again looked around her
uneasily. The landscape seemed peaceful and unthreatening,
but some more subtle sense told her otherwise. Her skin began
to creep with an indefinable dread.

"Maerad," said Cadvan at last. "I think I should have left
you, rather than draw you into my own danger. I didn't think
enough, when I stumbled across you in that cot. I was too
astonished, and too weary. And now it is too late to turn back."

"No," said Maerad warmly. She thought of the suffocating
despair of Gilman's Cot. At least here, now, she could breathe
freely. "No, you were right to ask me to leave. I would rather
die than stay there."

"Well, you might die," said Cadvan.

"At least I won't die a slave," Maerad answered. Proud
words, she thought, but she meant them.

Cadvan pushed the pace and they walked in silence, wrapped
in their own thoughts.

Maerad still couldn't quite believe she had escaped the cot.
Every now and then she caught herself thinking idly that she
should be performing some task—weeding the fields or churning butter or spinning the rough wool that made all their
clothes—and then she would catch herself, with a tiny shock:
perhaps she would never have to do any of those things again.
Even with the increasing sense of watchfulness, a feeling that
the very stones were spying on them, the present moment overwhelmed her. She couldn't imagine anything more amazing
than the mere fact of her freedom. Where she was going, or
why, were questions she couldn't even contemplate. And this
Cadvan—who was he? Why did she have this strange feeling

she could trust him? She knew nothing about him. She had never trusted a man before, save Mirlad, and even that trust had taken years to establish. Why start now?

They stopped for the midday meal beside one of the many streamlets that ran down from the mountains. Maerad's ankle was beginning to swell, and she eased it out from the boot and held it in her hands, massaging the muscles.

"It hurts?" asked Cadvan. "Let me see." He took her foot in his hands and gently turned it. "It's a little swollen. Nothing very bad. Now, breathe in." He pressed his hand hard over her ankle and Maerad gasped with pain; then she gasped again, because the swelling and pain had vanished.

"It's gone!" she said. "Are you a healer as well?"

"All Bards are healers," said Cadvan softly, still holding her foot. "You should have shown me before." He smiled at her, and Maerad felt suddenly uneasy and withdrew her foot abruptly, wriggling her toes in relief.

"What's happening?" she asked. "I mean, there's so much I don't understand. Maybe I could help?" She looked up at him from under her tangled hair. "You said you were wounded, but I can't see any wounds on you. Did you heal yourself too?"

Cadvan stood up and squinted at the sun. "We should move on," he said. "I'll tell you things in time, Maerad. I was sent here on a secret task, and I am not at liberty to tell you everything. But yes, I was wounded, and no, I couldn't heal myself. It's not a wound you can see. I am weaker than I should be, here without protection in the wild."

"But you can trust me," said Maerad, beginning to feel angry. "And if you're in danger, then so am I, if I am traveling with you. So you owe it to me."

"I owe you nothing, Maerad." Cadvan's voice was even, but Maerad saw the flash in his eyes.

"You wouldn't have got out of the valley without me," she said. "You said so yourself."

"Peace!" said Cadvan, and his face closed against her. "Maerad, you are a child. Don't bother me with all these questions, at least not now. We have a long way to go."

Maerad was suddenly furious. "And who are you?" She didn't care that she was shouting, although her voice echoed loudly in the empty land around them. "You turn up out of nowhere in rags and then expect me to believe you're some kind of grand person from the west, with your talk of Bards and magic? You could just be a tinker full of tricks, for all I know. And then you tell me I'm just a child, go sit in the corner and be quiet. Shut up, Maerad—you'll find out later! I'm not a child. I'm sixteen summers old!"

"There are more important things than the vanity of a young girl," Cadvan said coldly. Maerad realized she was standing before him, her fists clenched, trembling with anger. She flushed.

"I'm *not* a child," she said again, but with less conviction. All at once she felt very childish. Cadvan looked weary, but his eyes were hard. He turned and began to walk away. Maerad paused awhile and then followed him, afraid of being left behind in this eerie silence. He was walking very fast, and she had to run to catch up. When she did, she didn't draw even with him, but walked just behind. Her temper had ebbed as suddenly as it had appeared, but she didn't want to apologize.

They walked in stubborn silence for more than two hours. The sun was warm on their backs now, and Maerad was tiring. Cadvan kept the pace fast, and she was by no means used to this punishing trekking, no matter how trained she was for hard labor. She was too proud to ask him to slow down, and gritted her teeth. She was beginning to hate his straight, unbending back, always before her, always unforgiving. There were still hours to go before sunset, when presumably they would stop, although it was quite possible that Cadvan would insist they keep going through the night. She had just swapped one tyrant for another. . . . When they got to this place they were going, Norloch or whatever it was called, maybe she could find her own way through the world; but for the moment she was stuck with him. Sweat trickled down her face. She was thirsty, and Cadvan had the waterbag.

"We're making good pace," said Cadvan, turning at last. Maerad scowled at him, and he looked surprised. "Are you still angry? Put anger aside, child. It's no use."

"I'm not a child, I said," said Maerad sullenly. "Stop treating me like an idiot."

"If you are not a child, don't behave like one," Cadvan snapped. He turned to move off, then stopped, sighing, and turned back to her, holding out his hand. "Maerad, this is ridiculous. I'm sorry. I'm used to traveling alone. If I have been less than courteous to you, forgive me. I'm tired, and we have a long way to go unhoused. And this place worries me; I don't want to be out in the open tonight. Let's stop this bickering, yes?"

He held out his hand, and slowly Maerad took it and nodded, swallowing. She felt ungracious, hot, and sulky under Cadvan's grave gaze.

"I need your help," he said. "Maerad, be sure there are things that I will tell you, when it is the right time, and that I don't tell you now because I can't bear to, not because I think little of you. And there are other things I can't tell you, because I may not."

"As you like," said Maerad. Suddenly she didn't care. Let him have his secrets.

He gestured southward. "I want to get to a place I know

before nightfall," he said. "It's not a protection, like the Irihel, but it will be safer than the open. It's still a league or more hence, and the afternoon is half gone. That's why I hurry."

"Can I have a drink of water, please, before we start again?" asked Maerad.

He pulled the waterbag out of his pack and handed it to her, drinking some himself. Then they began their trekking again.

Cadvan led them closer to the mountains, and toward nightfall began to steer toward what looked like a spike or a standing stone set high on a small, oddly rounded hill. As they neared it, Maerad saw it was a ruin, bare even of moss, with empty slits for windows. It was getting late; the sun already threw the long shadows of the mountains over them, and Maerad could feel the chill of early dew. The land was now completely silent, and it frightened her; she felt as if the unseen hunt were drawing in, crouching, preparing for attack. She thought she would like it better if she could see what tracked them. This invisible stalking was unnerving.

As they walked up the hill, slipping a little on the smooth turf, she asked what the ruin was.

"It used to be a guardhouse," answered Cadvan. "Nothing else stands here but this. We did well to make it by now."

"What did it guard?" asked Maerad.

"A great city," Cadvan said. "Its name is now long forgotten. Before the Silence this was a rich and populous country. The Nameless razed even the memory of this place. He took all its palaces and gardens down stone by stone, save this tower. Perhaps it had a use for him."

They passed under a thick granite lintel into the roofless ruin. It had been a small tower, about fourteen feet square, and once a stair had led to a lookout high above. For the most part the walls, made of huge stones cunningly fitted together without cement of any kind, still stood high—although the roof had collapsed and the stairs and floors had long rotted, leaving the marks of fireplaces high on the walls where rooms once had been. There was only one doorway, and the slit windows were set high up in the walls. Cadvan threw down his pack.

"We have but little time, and we must use it well, if we are to survive the night," he said. "Fire is our hope. We need wood, quickly, before it grows dark."

They left the tower and went wood-gathering. Around the base of the hill grew some thorn trees, and two had been uprooted in a winter storm. "Dry, perfect firewood," Cadvan said. "I think there will be enough here." Maerad had opened her mouth to ask how they were to chop firewood with their bare hands when Cadvan drew a sword from beneath his cloak. "Forgive me, Arnost, for putting you to such usage!" he said, and began to hack the deadwood as easily as if he were cutting bread.

"I didn't know you had a sword," said Maerad. "I never saw it before!" Suddenly she felt almost lighthearted, as if they were preparing a bonfire for a party.

"There is much you don't know about me," Cadvan said. "Pray that you get the chance to find it out! Now hurry!"

Catching Cadvan's urgency, Maerad dragged bundles of branches up the hill, and soon, after he had split the trees, he helped her. It was difficult work, as she kept slipping on the turf. Before long they had a high pile of firewood inside the old guardhouse. Cadvan eyed it critically. "It will do," he said. "It will have to. It is almost dark. Gather some more branches while there's time. I have something else to do."

He drew a small, curiously shaped dagger and began to score a deep line around the base of the hill, and as she lugged more firewood to the guardhouse, Maerad could hear him chanting words in the Speech in a low, rhythmical monotone.

When he had circled the whole hill, he stood still and lifted his arms up to the sky. Again he seemed to be illuminated by a strange light, and for a second Maerad saw a ring of white flame leap around the tower; but then she blinked, and it was gone, and she thought it must have been a trick of the vanishing light.

She went inside the guardhouse. The pile of wood was high, and the sun was just now slipping over the horizon. Inside, it was almost completely dark.

Cadvan joined her and immediately knelt down and made a small pile of kindling by the door. Then, stretching out his hand with his two forefingers stiffened, he said: *"Noroch!"* A tiny white flame lit on the kindling and spread, and he tended it, building the fire swiftly until Maerad was forced to stand by the opposite wall because of the heat.

"It's a bit like saying, 'Here we are,'" she said. "Don't you think?"

"And you think they don't know we're here?"

"What happens when it's dark?"

"In the dark the wers hold their power," said Cadvan. "They will fear this fire. They cannot break the stone. I don't believe they will break the barrier I have made. We have, I think, enough wood to last until morning. Now, Maerad, I know this is not a good time to ask you, but can you fight with a knife?"

Maerad did, in fact, own a dagger she had stolen from one of the Thane's men and kept secretly in her belt next to her skin. "I can try," she said. "I've never really fought with one." She showed Cadvan the dagger and he examined it swiftly.

"It's of rough make, but serviceable, and your size," he said. "If you are attacked, go for the eyes, if you can, and remember to hold it firm in your fist, like this, so it will drive in. I'll have to give you lessons in swordcraft when we are in a less tight spot."

Maerad felt her stomach tighten. "What will attack us?" she asked. What use was a knife against shadows?

"I don't know yet," said Cadvan. "But remember, although they are of the Dark, they can be killed. Their worst weapon is fear. Hold back the fear with everything you have. And only fight if you are attacked. Otherwise, leave any fighting to me."

He drew his sword, and the faint ringing sound echoed off the stone around them. The fire snapped and cracked, throwing strange shadows over the ancient walls, leaping up into the abyss above them. Maerad could see no sky through the roof, only an impenetrable darkness. Cadvan stretched, and then reached for his pack. "But for now, I am ravenous!" he said. He tossed Maerad a biscuit and some nuts and fruit, and they ate, their backs to the walls, their feet stretched out to the fire, their faces glowing in the heat. Maerad could hear the silence of the empty land around them, stretching for miles beyond the friendly popping of the firewood. It bore down on her, like a weight. And then, the sound she feared: a long, drawn-out howl. She almost dropped her biscuit with fright, but Cadvan appeared unmoved.

"The sun has set," he said.

"Wolfwers?" she whispered.

"Yes, for the meantime. The hunt is starting. They will take a little time to work out what to do about the barrier. It's white fire. The Dark cannot pass it without breaking its power, and that will not be easy. You should get some sleep."

The howl came again, and then was answered.

"Sleep? Now?"

"Why not? I will watch." Cadvan turned and grinned at her. "Be assured I won't let you miss any fireworks. Remember: fear is their worst weapon."

Maerad obediently lay down and closed her eyes. She tried to act as if she were not afraid; she tried to relax, but it was diffi-cult, out in the wild, on a broken stone floor, with wers sent by some black magician howling for her blood. . . . She ached all over with weariness after the hard walk that day, and the fire was so warm. But her body sang with tension, and would not let her sleep. After a while she stopped trying and sat up, drawing closer to Cadvan, who nodded but said nothing.

The Bard sat very still beside her, carefully feeding the fire. His face relaxed; he might have been asleep, apart from the watchfulness of his eyes. His sword lay drawn by his feet.

The wers were circling the hill. Maerad and Cadvan could hear their feet padding around and around, trying to find a way past the barrier. Maerad listened hard and counted maybe twenty. Every now and then one would stop and howl, a long ululation that froze the blood, a sound of utter desolation born out of long years of horror and emptiness. The cries hit Maerad in the pit of her stomach. They seemed to her the very sound of unlife, of creatures neither dead nor alive, but caught in a tormenting void between, condemned to envy and hate everything that took joy in existence. She shuddered with nausea. Cadvan continued to feed the fire, apparently unmoved. Then they heard the wers bunch together, and Cadvan reached for his sword. "They're going to rush the barrier," he whispered.

Maerad's pulse was hammering in her ears; she clutched her dagger until her knuckles were white. She listened to the heavy thunder of the wers' paws, and their breath, and the collisions as they hurled themselves forward; but the barrier held, and they were repulsed, howling. Cadvan relaxed and sat back.

"First game to us," he said to Maerad. She saw the flash of his grin through the leaping shadows.

The wers' assault on the barrier lasted for more than an hour; they threw themselves again and again at the enchantment, or tried to break it with their claws and teeth. Cadvan and Maerad sat in silence the entire time. Cadvan's barrier held well; they were not strong enough to break it, and he wanted them to tire themselves in useless assault. He hoped that they would hurl themselves against it all night. Then they stopped their rushing, and he heard one wer, the leader, he guessed, begin to howl; but it was a different howl this time, a thin, almost human wail, with words in it. It started low and quiet, but as time went by, it grew louder and more insistent.

"The wer leader is making a counterspell," Cadvan said. "We're unlucky. It's rare for a wer to know sorceries."

Maerad met his eyes, fear clutching her afresh. "What does that mean?"

"Either my spell is good, or it is not. There is nothing we can do except wait to see if it holds."

Cadvan picked up his sword and waited, tense. Maerad felt the power outside build. It gathered at the weakest part of the barrier, the join; like an evil black blade it tried to force itself into Cadvan's mind. He fought back, his jaw set, the sweat starting on his forehead, and Maerad watched him with mounting anxiety. The voice built to a crescendo, an unbearable pitch of sound, and then suddenly came a noiseless explosion, a burst of black light, and Cadvan rocked back against the wall with a grimace of pain. But the barrier still held. The wers could not enter.

Then came a sound Maerad disliked even more: silence. The wers were regrouping.

Cadvan put down his sword and rummaged through his pack. "Drink something," he said. He passed her the bottle that contained the herbed drink. "Now we must be vigilant."

"What for?"

"Anything. Anything at all. Sit with your back to the fire. Try to remember that this tower is roofless. The only way they can get in now is from above. The fire will daunt them, but not enough."

Maerad grasped her dagger in her hand and sat next to Cadvan, straining to listen. She could hear nothing but the blood in her ears. Dread rose in her heart until she almost wished something would happen, anything, anything to break this horrible suspense. She stole a look at Cadvan. He looked almost serene, his face relaxed, his eyes watchful. She took a deep breath.

They sat in this silence for what seemed like hours. Every now and then Maerad moved to ease the aches in her body, but Cadvan never stirred.

"Maybe they've gone away," she said at last. "We've heard nothing for ages and ages."

"Ssshhh," Cadvan hissed. "The only thing we can be sure of is that they haven't gone away. *Listen*."

"But there's nothing to hear."

"They will wait. They want our wills to weaken in fear. They feed on our fear. It's their life, their bread. Starve them! Send your mind out into the night. Use the Gift you have. Send it out into the night. Then you will hear."

Maerad wondered what he meant. Perhaps she should . . . Experimentally she gathered up her mind and imagined it past the walls of the guardhouse. At once she felt cold, although she still had her back to the fire. It was as if she had stepped outside, although she could see nothing but the opposite wall. But she heard the slow flapping of wings, wings of creatures that she could not imagine, wings without feathers, taloned and heavy, and heard hisses, as of cold breaths drawn in and out of cold, leathery bellows.

"Wings," she whispered. "But giant wings. It's not bats, or it's bats as big as wolves."

"Yes. They are close. The barrier will not hold them. I cannot make it high enough."

"But I can't see anything, Cadvan, I can't see *anything*." Maerad turned to him, her eyes wide. "They're so big, I can hear how big they are. What are we . . ."

"Silence!" Cadvan turned with the fury of a snake. "I can't be patting your hand like that of a terrified child. If we are to get through this night with our hides in one piece, you must remember who you are. You are one of the Gift. Grow up, or we will die here."

Maerad swallowed. Cadvan was preoccupied again, taking no notice of her, listening and watching, his sword in readiness. She took a deep breath and pushed back the terror that had started to take hold of her mind, winding its way through her muscles, insidious and cold, like a poison mist. Her heart was pounding, but she forced herself to relax. She held her pitiful dagger in her hand. It seemed so small. She wished she had a sword and knew how to use it. Perhaps then she might feel more like a warrior. She sent out her mind again, not knowing what else to do, and heard the winged creatures, farther away now, higher up. They were flying to the top of the barrier. What was the barrier made of? She didn't know, but they were going to fly over it and down on top of them. She knew that now. Instinctively she stood up, and saw that Cadvan was also standing, staring above them, up the walls where the fire flickered into shadow and then blackness. She moved closer to the fire. Cadvan threw another few logs on, building it up so the flames leaped high. It was unbearably hot. She looked above her, straining her eyes, her nerves stretched to breaking point.

At last she heard something, but so slight she hardly knew if it was the wind. Cadvan's breath hissed through his teeth. Then, so fast she almost didn't see it, a huge shape came plummeting down on them from above. It veered briefly into the fire and shrieked, flapping back. Cadvan leaped forward and hewed its neck with his sword, jumping back as it crashed down, spouting black gouts of blood.

Maerad saw with surprise that it wasn't as big as she had

thought: the body was about the size of a goat. But she had no
time to look at it, for now the air was full of claws and wings
and hissing. One came straight for her; she saw its eyes burning red in the fire. Her dagger was useless, and with a sudden
inspiration she dropped it and dragged a burning branch from
the fire. She thrust it at the creature, which wheeled away and
crashed into the wall. It fell to the ground, its neck broken.

Immediately another came for her, landing on the ground
and rearing up to slash her with its claws. She swung the
branch around, and her shoulder jarred as she hit it hard. The
creature hissed with fury as the flames licked it, and its long
neck snaked toward her. Maerad hit it again, and the branch
broke. She leaped sideways, grasping another branch, and the
wer struck her a glancing blow to the head with its claws. She
didn't feel any pain; her fear was suddenly overcome by a
surge of anger. She held the brand in both hands and swung it
randomly; the room was so small it was impossible not to hit
something. She was aware of Cadvan to her right, slashing and
hewing, beset by three of them, and then another three, while
others hovered overhead. Maerad kept lashing out, remembering to go for the eyes, and the creatures swung away from the
flame, concentrating their attack on Cadvan.

Then one of them landed before her, and to her dismay she
saw its outlines blur and soften. At first she thought it a trick of
her eyes, but then to her disbelief it began to transform into a
man, startlingly white in the darkness. She cried out and thrust
a brand in his face. He fell back, but then came for her, his wings
melting into his back, his face blank and murderous, a black
broadsword in his clawed hand. Maerad ducked the swing of
his sword and with all her strength brought the burning branch
back as hard as she could against his body. The flames burst into
life and licked up his neck, setting his hair on fire. He screamed
horribly and fell writhing to the ground, trying to beat out the

flames, but they stuck to him like a deadly glue, spreading until he was wholly alight, a screaming torch.

Maerad watched in horror, almost forgetting her danger for a second, but another creature landed and rose on its hind feet and her horror burst again into rage. This time she swiped it with the brand before it could begin to transform. It fell stunned to the ground, which was now slimed and smoking with blood. She stepped forward to bash it again when Cadvan reached past her and slashed off its head. And suddenly the room was still.

They stood together, panting. Maerad sent out her mind to hear if any more wings were coming, but she heard only the night. The room was piled with dead creatures. She gasped, feeling suddenly sick.

Cadvan put more wood on the fire, and then started dragging the corpses out of the door. Maerad stood back, swaying with nausea. The stench of death was overpowering, and she was beginning to tremble. She realized that the branch she was holding was about to burn her hand. She dropped it back on the fire and then, fighting down her desire to vomit, helped Cadvan clear the room of the creatures, casting them out of the doorway and down the hill, although she couldn't bring herself to touch the one who had burned, the one who was still half a man. At last the room was empty, although it stank of burning flesh and hair and blood. Neither Cadvan nor Maerad felt like sitting down.

"What were they?" she asked at last.

"Wormfilth," said Cadvan. "Wers can take whatever shape they desire. But they are all evil shapes, mockeries." He looked at her, smiling grimly. "You did well, although you nearly got me once. A doughty fighter, but somewhat undisciplined."

Maerad tried to smile back. "Do you think there are more?"

"I don't know. I don't think so. I counted nineteen, and I

heard about twenty. Maybe one didn't chance the fire. And it's not long till dawn now."

They moved outside and sat down by the doorway, still watchful but too exhausted to speak. Cadvan did not relinquish his vigilance, and Maerad, despite her weariness, watched with him. They heard nothing else that night, and at last the eastern horizon began to lighten and the sun, with unbearable slowness, lifted its rim over the edge of the earth, sending level rays over the forest before them. Maerad thought she had never been so glad to see a new day. She turned to Cadvan and almost laughed. They were not a prepossessing sight: both were smeared and spattered with the foul blood of the wers, and their faces were black with ash.

"Well," said Cadvan heavily. "We made it."

V

THROUGH THE MOUNTAINS

THEY did not stop to wash or rest, nor even to eat. Maerad averted her eyes from the pile of corpses at the bottom of the hill. "We should burn them," said Cadvan. "But we haven't time. Our only chance is to keep moving."

Maerad had never felt so tired. The only thing stronger than her exhaustion was her desire to get as far away as possible from that deathly place. They walked steadily on, and she tried to ignore her aching head, smarting from the wound the wer had dealt her, and to concentrate just on keeping moving. She had no idea of a destination. She was beginning to think that Cadvan was made of wire; he betrayed little sign of weariness, while for Maerad walking was becoming a torment without end. Slowly, painfully, they approached a spur of the mountain range and rounded it. As they did, it was as if the land came back to life again. Birds were singing their morning challenges in the low bushes around them, or flickering from branch to branch; and the grasses seemed to tremble with the hidden activities of small animals. An insidious pressure that Maerad hadn't noticed until now lifted off her breast. A little farther on, a small stream bubbled down the side of a high ridge and collected in a pool bordered by smooth, flat stones. To Maerad's unutterable relief, Cadvan stopped.

"We're out of the Landrost," he said. "The peak no longer overlooks our path. He can do nothing more to us." He knelt over the pool, splashing water over his head and washing his hands: dried blood and ash swirled out into the water and disappeared. Maerad slumped on the grass nearby, unable for the moment to do anything. It was only three hours after sunrise, but she felt she had lived a whole lifetime since the day before. She was beyond sleep; despite the tiredness of her limbs, her mind was preternaturally alert. For a time she simply listened to the music of the birds and the brook, sounds that entered into her like a balm. By then Cadvan was getting food out of his pack, and she realized with a start how hungry she was.

"We haven't lost all courtesies, at least not yet," said Cadvan, glancing up at her. "You must wash first."

Maerad knelt on the stones and washed the muck off her face and hands. The water was cold and clear. She pulled some dried grasses and, moving with a sudden violent disgust, scrubbed herself as hard as she could, dabbing uselessly at her clothes, which were stiff with filth. Then they sat and ate, Cadvan sniffing the air. Clouds were forming in the east, high dark clouds mounting in the distance. "A storm is coming," he said. "Which perhaps will help us. We need to cover our tracks. More eyes than the Landrost's will be wondering what it was that resisted the wers last night, and perhaps will be tracking us. We're still at least four days from any hope of help, and that's if all goes well."

"I don't know how much farther I can go," said Maerad. Her hands were trembling.

"Nor do I, Maerad. Will has carried us this far. But I too need rest, and that badly. It would be some joke to win through all these perils, only to drop dead of exhaustion within sight of haven."

They munched in silence for a time. I fought the wers, and I wasn't afraid, Maerad thought with a kind of grim gladness. Perhaps now he'll stop treating me like a child. Images of the battle flickered randomly through her head, and she saw again the one that had caught fire, the one who had transformed

into something like a man, and shuddered. I killed him. The
statement struck her like fear. She had slaughtered hens and
rabbits for the table, thinking nothing of it, and once she had
wanted to kill a man, had felt the action stirring in her soul,
a black, implacable rage; but never before had she murdered
anyone. It was kill or be killed, a voice said. What good would
it have done to stand back and let him hack you down? *He
had no doubts.* . . . She knew that was true, but the knowledge
didn't stop a disquiet in her heart, a feeling that, no matter
the justification, killing was wrong, that the act had somehow
wounded her. Shaking her head to rid herself of her thoughts,
she stretched and yawned.

"How I wish there were something else to eat!" she said.
Cadvan looked up and smiled.

"Yes, traveling food serves its purpose, but it palls quickly."

"A roast bird, with roots. And baked apples stuffed with
berries and nuts."

"Mushrooms!" said Cadvan unexpectedly. "Slow fried in
butter. I can almost smell them!" He passed her his bottle of
herbed water. "Drink some of this. Not too much; my supplies
are running low."

"What is it?" asked Maerad, as she drank.

"Medhyl," said Cadvan. "It heals tiredness. It can't erase it,
alas, but it helps. Bards brew it for just such times as these."

"Do we have to keep going now?"

"I think we should rest but briefly. Soon we will have to find
shelter. Look at those clouds! It will be a savage storm, I think.
We shan't get much farther today. There are caves around here,
although we must be careful of what lives in them!"

Presently he gathered up his pack; they crossed the stream
and moved on southward, Cadvan scanning the mountainsides
closely as they went. Maerad was conscious of the storm at their
back; each time she turned, the clouds were closer and darker,

quickening with little tongues of lightning, and she began to hear thunder. The light dimmed as the clouds ate up the sun.

Cadvan halted and pointed to a scarcely visible hole above a ridge, about twenty feet over their heads. "There!" he said. "Quick, follow me." They scrabbled up the steep incline and then, warning Maerad back, Cadvan drew his sword and walked into the cave, bending over because the roof was so low. It was dry, and the floor was sandy. The cave drove in about a dozen feet and then turned sharply. Cadvan cautiously followed it and saw that the cave petered out about ten feet farther in. He emerged where Maerad stood waiting. "It's perfect," he said. "Although something lives there; there are bones. It will be a little annoyed, I fear, to find us here, but I think it is no evil thing. We can light no fire, but at least we will not be wet."

They had found the cave in the nick of time. Even as they entered, a huge clap of thunder broke over their heads, heralding the storm's first heavy drops. Inside, it smelled fusty and close. Maerad sat on the sandy floor where the cave bent, so she could still see its mouth, a circle of light already veiled with rain. "You should lie down," she said. "I'll keep watch. I promise not to fall asleep."

To her surprise, Cadvan did not demur. "Use your listening," he said. "You know how. And wake me if you hear or see anything strange. Anything. I don't mind if it's a false alarm." Then, with the disconcerting swiftness she had witnessed before, Cadvan lay down and seemed to fall asleep instantly.

Maerad sat with her hands clasped around her knees, her cloak wrapped tightly around her for warmth, and listened to the rain and thunder. The sound was oddly comforting, even sitting in a cold cave in the middle of wild mountains. For a time she studied Cadvan's sleeping face, which glimmered palely in the semidarkness under his tangle of dark hair. He had told her he was already old, at least according to normal

reckonings, but he by no means looked it. There was, nevertheless, a sternness to his mouth, a hint of grief or suffering long
mastered, which suggested that he was not misleading her; his
face held traces of long experience. And yet sometimes, and
particularly now, in the vulnerability of sleep, he seemed much
younger, barely older than she was. She knew already he was a
brave swordsman; the toughest of the Thane's men could not
match his quickness or skill, and his endurance astonished her.
She had seen last night how he faced down fear and danger.
Yet he had not once boasted of his prowess and seemed rather
to dismiss it, counting singing and lore the greater skills. She
had never met anyone like him, and all the events of the past
few days hadn't erased her initial astonishment. Perhaps she
would get used to him in time. He trusted her a little now.
Perhaps, even, they could be friends. And what had he said
that morning? "You did well. . . ."

Her mind flinched away from the memory of the battle the
night before, and she remembered that she was supposed to be
watching. It was a fierce storm: the rain was so heavy it now
made a gray, impenetrable wall at the mouth of the cave, lit
every now and then by a flash of sheet lightning. The wind
howled and lashed the sides of the mountain, occasionally
drowned by enormous rumbles and claps of thunder. She felt
very glad they were not out in it; by comparison the cave felt
safe, even cozy. She watched, and saw and heard nothing, and
after a few hours, when weariness began to roll over her, she
woke Cadvan and curled up to sleep on the cave floor, as luxuriously as if she bedded down in feathers.

She woke groggily to the sound of Cadvan speaking. The cave
was now dark, and she blinked and stretched, peering through
the shadows. What she saw made her sit up abruptly and back
close to the wall, clutching her cloak.

Cadvan was face-to-face with an enormous beast. All she could see was the dark shape of it: a monstrous bulk blocking out the light with a long tail slowly lashing, and with it a sharp stink, like nothing so much as a cat. It stretched its nose forward to Cadvan and responded to his words with rumblings deep in its throat. Maerad sat as still as she could. Cadvan gestured in Maerad's direction, speaking as he did so, and gave Maerad a cautioning look. The beast padded forward and sniffed her. She blanched, but submitted to the investigation without protest, although the long, curved teeth and the beast's breath—the hot, pungent breath of a carnivore—made her heart race. She appeared to pass inspection, and the beast turned back to Cadvan and made some more rumblings, which sounded to Maerad a little as if it were laughing at her. It then turned around in circles, padding out a bed for itself, and lay down. Cadvan turned to Maerad, smiling.

"Well done," he said. "It is no easy thing to wake up unexpectedly in the company of a mountain lion, and things might have gone ill if you had panicked. He has decided you are harmless, and will permit us to stay here the night. He assures us he will not eat us and says you wouldn't make much of a meal, anyway."

"Oh," said Maerad breathlessly. "How nice of him."

"He has also told me a few useful things, which if you had had your wits about you, you might also have heard. He has news of our battle with the wers, and claims to be honored to host such warriors. He has been hunting and the land is disturbed. All the beasts are fearful, and he likes not this wind. He says it is not safe for us to travel as we are, southward down the east of the Annova, and has offered us safe passage through the mountains. It will be a shortcut for us, and will throw whatever follows us off our trail."

"Safe passage?" said Maerad dubiously. "And we can trust him?"

"Yes," Cadvan said. "As much as we can trust anything. It is much more than I hoped for."

Maerad had no choice but to defer to Cadvan's judgment— and it was true, the beast hadn't eaten her. Yet. She remembered Gilman's hounds and felt a little less uneasy.

"What did you mean, that I could have heard his news, as well?" she asked, after a short silence.

"When are you going to wake up?" said Cadvan. "Yes, there are things that you must learn. But there are other things that sleep inside you already, as part of your Gift, your inheritance. One of them is the ability to understand the speech of beasts."

"Me?"

"Yes, girl, do you have ears of cloth?"

Maerad felt a new kind of fear stirring within her, a fear of herself, and it pricked her anger. She spoke low, afraid of waking the beast, but with a dark fury.

"That's witchspeak," she said. "You never told me anything like that. It's not true!"

Cadvan didn't react to her anger. "Maerad, the worst thing you can do is deny your own powers," he said. "If you have been kept ignorant, that is not your fault. You no longer have that excuse."

Maerad felt too alarmed to argue with him, and turned sullenly to the cave wall. It was ridiculous for Cadvan to speak of her in this way. She was just what she was, a girl, lately a slave, and yes, she could play the lyre, but . . . Cadvan was quite mistaken.

She took a deep breath and glanced over to the mountain lion. It lay curled up, its nose to its tail, just like a cat on a hearth, taking no notice of either of them. The storm had passed, but still the rain fell steadily outside the cave, a friendly sound, she thought. Night was falling, and she realized she was hungry.

"We're not going anywhere now, anyway," she said.

"No," said Cadvan. "So I might as well have a look at that wer scratch."

He searched the wound on her forehead with expert, gentle fingers, and Maerad struggled not to flinch. "A bruise, and some tearing, but no poison," he said. "You'll have a headache for a couple of days, I'm afraid. I can't fix that up here. But there'll be no scar to speak of. You got off lightly." He pressed his hand hard over her forehead, and some of the pain lifted; he then anointed the wound with a sweet-smelling balm from a tiny jar he drew from his pack.

"We should eat, and then rest while we can," said Cadvan. "We need keep no watch: the mountain lion will guard his own cave, even in sleep."

Maerad nodded. In truth, her bones still ached with weariness, and underneath she felt the aftershock from the fight of the night before, a trembling deep in her whole body. More rest would be welcome.

The next morning Maerad was so stiff with cold she could hardly move; she felt as if she were bruised all over. The day was overcast and drear, and a dim, pale light filtered into the cave, which now seemed inhospitable and comfortless. She turned over with a groan. Cadvan still slept, so she sat up cautiously, looking for the mountain lion. It was nowhere to be seen.

So much for our guide, she thought. What now?

She crawled to the mouth of the cave and looked out. She could see down over the knees of the mountains to the plains, but the forest was hidden in mist or rain. The very world seem drained of color. She was sitting disconsolately, watching the clouds and trying to rub some life into her arms and legs, when Cadvan joined her.

"Breakfast?" he said cheerily.

"The last thing I feel like is food," she said. "Our guide seems to have disappeared."

"He'll be back," said Cadvan. "And you have to eat. We still have a long walk before us, and you can go nowhere on an empty stomach. If nothing goes wrong, we'll dine soon on roast beef and fried mushrooms."

"And roots?"

"Carrots and turnips and beets and anything else you like. Baked, roasted, fried, casseroled, poached, sugared, and smoked!" Cadvan was already back in the cave, dragging fruit and biscuit out of his pack. "And a bath! By the Light, it will be good to be clean again! I haven't had a bath since I can remember."

They were finishing breakfast when the mountain lion returned. Cadvan greeted him gravely in the Speech, and the great beast sat on his haunches and waited patiently while Cadvan packed up. Then the mountain lion lowered his head and made more growling noises in his throat, and Cadvan nodded. "He says to follow," he told Maerad. "Watch his every move. And be quick."

The mountain lion jumped above the cave, onto a ledge, and began to climb up the base of the mountain, following the ledge along the edge of a deepening gorge. Cadvan sprang up after him. Maerad paused, daunted by the height, and then, realizing she had no choice, scrambled up after them, her heart in her mouth. "He's got four feet," she muttered to Cadvan. "I hope he remembers I've got only two."

"Just concentrate!" said Cadvan.

For some time the ledge was wide enough to walk without discomfort, and Maerad began to breathe more easily, although to her left was a deepening ravine and to her right a sheer cliff that became higher the farther they went. There were rough outcroppings of grasses and occasional clumps of hellebore and ladies' sleeves and a fluffy white flower Maerad had not seen before, but otherwise there was very little vegetation, and the way was rough and broken. The rays of the early sun warmed their backs, but soon their path fell into shadow, and Maerad's sweat chilled on her skin. Now they were moving steeply upward again, and the ledge began to narrow and in some places disappeared altogether. Their progress was reduced to a crawl. Maerad felt uneasily like a spider climbing up a wall, without the comforting assurance of a web to dangle from if she fell. When she looked down she felt dizzy, so she fixed her eyes on Cadvan before her and concentrated on placing her feet and hands exactly where he put his. She couldn't see the mountain lion.

She had just decided she couldn't climb another foot when the ledge suddenly turned sharply and changed into a definable path that wound back and forth, still climbing up the mountain. Now they walked, although in single file, and Maerad could see the mountain lion loping patiently before them, his muzzle close to the ground, his powerful shoulders rippling with effortless grace. Higher they wound their way, higher and higher, and the air became colder and colder, and it began to be difficult to breathe. Then the path seemed to stop altogether. The mountain lion turned and spoke to Cadvan, and Cadvan relayed his message to Maerad.

"He says to keep very close now," he said. "Whatever you do, don't panic. I cannot make light, unless we have no choice, because it might attract trouble. Use your ears. And watch for bats."

"Bats?" said Maerad in confusion. What were bats doing on top of a mountain? But then she saw that, instead of stopping, the path led to an opening in the sheer rock of the mountain. It was clearly no natural cave: its sides were regular and smooth, and carved around its lintel were the crumbling traces of runes.

She had no time to wonder; they plunged into the tunnel

and kept walking. Their footsteps echoed dully back from the walls. In the light from the opening, Maerad saw that the floor was straight as an arrow, its way piercing straight into the very heart of the mountain. It was wide enough for two people to walk side by side with their arms outstretched. They had only walked a few minutes when the light was swallowed in utter blackness. The darkness was so complete that Maerad couldn't see her hand if she put it before her eyes. Their footsteps sounded unnaturally loud, and echoed strangely; she could even hear the velvet pad of the mountain lion's paws.

"Cadvan?" she said, in a very small voice, and jumped because her voice came back to her, mockingly amplified.

"Ssshhh," he said. *Ssssssshhhhhhhhhh*, said the tunnel. To her unutterable relief, Cadvan took her hand and squeezed it in encouragement; and he didn't let go. They walked slowly and steadily, dragging the tips of their fingers along the smooth walls for what seemed an eternity, with the slow, steady pad of the mountain lion's paws always ahead of them.

Suddenly Maerad gasped. The side wall vanished, and she nearly toppled into the gap. A chill, rank-smelling draft of air breathed into her face, dispersing for a moment the slight stuffiness of the passage. After three paces the wall returned; clearly a tunnel branched off the main artery. Soon side passages became more frequent, and Maerad realized there must be a network through the whole mountain. Sometimes the air came down from above, sometimes from below, and she guessed they were tunnels leading up and down through the rock. She counted forty-five before they stopped for a meal, and from changes in the air she guessed that a similar number branched off on Cadvan's side as well. The main tunnel still drove straight as a ruler through the mountain.

She wondered who had made this place, and what it was, although she had no desire to follow any of the side tunnels; the thought of being lost inside this mountain, groping through endless darkness, made her shudder. Perhaps it had been a kind of city, though she had never heard of a city built inside a mountain. It felt old, immeasurably old. Occasionally, when her fingers brushed over something that felt like a crumbling carving in relief, or an intricate decoration bordering one of the side passages, she wished that Cadvan would permit them a little light: she would have liked to see what it was they passed through. Surely it had been beautiful once? Perhaps it still was, even in its abandonment?

Despite the darkness, it wasn't a place that inspired fear; if there were ghosts, she thought to herself, they had long departed. As they moved farther into the mountain she began to feel awed by its size. It was many, many times larger than Gilman's Cot; it was maybe as grand as the cities in some of the songs Mirlad had taught her. It seemed to exhale sadness, a pervasive feeling of absence. Had a sickness assailed these folk and driven them away? Or had they simply left, deciding to build another city elsewhere, somewhere warmer? People had lived here, and maybe they had been happy, and now they were gone and the place missed them, missed their laughter and song and light. For she assumed they must have made light here, in these dark places.

She sent her mind ahead of her. She heard the rustlings of small wings, and tiny footfalls, like the spoor of birds, and cheeping and high whistles, and the drip of water on stone, and the whisper of blind fish turning lazily in cold pools that had never heard even a rumor of light; but she heard nothing else.

They stopped for another meal, and then another, and then another. For uncountable hours, they slept on the bare stone: was it a minute they slept, or a whole day? Maerad had no idea. These pauses were the only punctuation in their long walk. Here in the unchanging darkness it was impossible to tell what

time it was outside, in the world of color and light. They
stopped when they were hungry, or when they were so tired
they could walk no farther. They sat down where they were in
the passage. It was strange, eating food without being able to
see it; somehow it tasted of nothing, as if they were eating ash.
They spoke as little as possible, because the echoes were so
unnerving. The mountain lion did not eat anything, though
sometimes he drank from the little streamlets that ran over their
feet, nosing down through the mountain from higher passages.

At one point their guide stopped suddenly and rumbled.
They were so close behind they bumped into him. "He says
there's a pit here," whispered Cadvan, and the whispers ran
along the walls like sinister laughter. "A good sign, he says: it
means we're halfway through. There's a very narrow ledge
along one side. Do not stumble! You go first, and I will follow
just behind you. Lean into the wall."

Hesitantly Maerad followed the mountain lion, who continued his steady pacing, and groped her way along the wall.
Immediately she felt a draft of cold air and a dizzying sense of
appalling depth, so that she almost stumbled. Cadvan hissed
something she didn't hear as she regained her balance and
leaned against the wall, her heart hammering. Then she caught
her breath and concentrated on putting one foot in front of the
other, step by step by step. Passing the abyss seemed to take
forever, but at last she felt the updraft cease and knew she was
past. She took a few paces farther and stopped, breathing heavily, until Cadvan came up behind her, felt for her hand, and led
her on again into the endless darkness.

Time ceased to have any meaning at all. Maerad felt as if she
had been walking through this passage for days, or years, or
eons. It was as if their very minds were blindfolded, as if sight
and color and shape were dreams of another age. Had she been
walking through this darkness for her entire life? Her eyes

played constant tricks: little blooms of red and pink and blue opened on her vision, and when she closed her eyes, they didn't go away, but split into other strange, amorphous shapes. They made the darkness seem even more complete.

When she saw a faint wash of light in the distance, she thought at first it was another illusion. She had ceased long ago to believe in the possibility of an end to the tunnel. She rubbed her eyes, but the light was still there, and then she realized she could see the mountain lion walking in front of them, and turning, could see Cadvan beside her. She felt like crying with relief, or whooping with joy.

They emerged blinking onto a broad ledge high in the side of the mountain. Maerad flinched, as if she had been hit; the light was blinding, after so long in the darkness. She stood for a time, shading her face, while her eyes adjusted. Finally she looked out and gasped in wonder.

Before them stretched a vast green land of rolling hills and dark woods, and the red sun sinking in glory through a wrack of golden clouds threw its light over their faces.

"Behold the beauty of Annar!" said Cadvan. "I thought I would not see it again."

She saw that tears glinted on his lashes, and she looked away, suddenly acutely conscious that he was still holding her hand. But Cadvan spun her around, laughing. "Maerad! We're almost there!"

"Norloch?"

"Oh, no, no, no, that lies many leagues west. No, a bath and a meal! Roast meats! Remember, I promised you!" He let her go and stepped back smiling.

Infected by Cadvan's joyousness, Maerad smiled back. But Cadvan was already speaking to the mountain lion, bowing low as he did so. The beast bowed his head also, and spoke, and then turned to Maerad and made the same gesture. Maerad instinctively bowed in return. Then the great animal vanished into the tunnel without a backward glance, loping with the same slow, steady pace, and disappeared.

"There goes a lord among beasts," said Cadvan. "Thus is the best hope oft unlooked for! Even by my best calculations, we had no chance of being in reach of help so soon. It would have been days, else, and even then uncertain—if we ever arrived."

Maerad shuddered at the thought of the mountain lion's long walk back home through the black bowels of the mountain. "But I couldn't go through that tunnel again, not if all the wers of the Landrost were after me!" she said.

"Don't speak so lightly of such things!" said Cadvan. "You would, if you had to. And we still have to get down off this mountain, and quickly before it grows completely dark."

A broken, narrow path led off the ledge and wound its way eccentrically downward, curling around ridges and gorges and then suddenly switching back on itself. They were not ten feet away from the ledge when Maerad looked up and realized the passage was completely hidden; even from this distance she doubted that she could find it again. After that she had to concentrate on scrabbling down the mountainside. It was exhausting work, and her hands were already scratched and blistered. She gritted her teeth and ignored her discomforts. Cadvan was again displaying his ability to behave as if he had just arisen from a long, refreshing sleep and was now partaking of a gentle stroll, and if, she thought to herself, he could do it, so could she. Once she slipped and slid more than twenty feet down a rocky slope, landing in a small heap of pebbles and dust at the bottom of a gully. Cadvan leaned over the edge of the ridge, anxiously peering through the dusk, and when he saw her answering wave he grinned and slid down to join her. "It's quicker," he said, landing beside her.

"But a sight less comfortable." He stood up, brushing himself off, and peered down the gully. "We could follow this, I think," he said. "There's not much farther before we're off the mountain proper. And then a quick march, and then dinner."

The going after that was not so hard. It was now dark, but it was a clear night, and the swollen moon edged over the horizon, bright enough to cast sharp shadows. For a while they continued in silence.

"Do you know where we are?" Maerad asked at last. She had a strange feeling that she knew this landscape. Were they, perhaps, near Pellinor?

"Yes." Cadvan nodded. "We are an hour's fast walk from Innail, the easternmost of the Schools. It was built in the shadow of the Annova some hundreds of years ago now, and is a strong School that has shaped many fine Bards! I can't say how glad I am. Although, of course, we are not there yet. Fortune so far has favored us; this is better than anything I could have planned. I think our trail was lost in the storm, and I think that none will find it. It would have gone ill with us, if we had been forced to travel the way I planned. More than the Landrost watches over that empty realm."

"And what was that tunnel through the mountain?" Maerad asked, deciding to take advantage of Cadvan's ebullience. "Did you know it was there?"

"No," Cadvan answered. "I have traveled often over this land in my time, and I have heard neither rumor nor tale of such a place. The nearest pass through the mountains, to my knowledge, was at least sixty leagues south from here, through bad country. I don't know who made that place, or who might have lived there in ages past. A great city, it seemed to me; there were hundreds of rooms, empty and forsaken, carved into the rock. Perhaps the whole mountain is honeycombed with them.

I didn't recognize the runes hatched around the door. I wonder who they were, those people! A people of great cunning, they must have been, to pierce the living rock so straightly. There were no bad airs, nor any flaws in that tunneling. Few could do such a thing now."

Maerad was taken aback by Cadvan's cheerful admission of ignorance; it made the world she had just entered seem even stranger and more perilous. She thought of Gilman's Cot: only a few days ago it had been the compass of her entire existence, but to Cadvan it was insignificant, a tiny place in the scheme of things. And now, it seemed, there were things even he knew nothing about. It made her feel very small and unimportant; and she asked no more questions.

The vegetation began to change; there were groves of pine and birch, and beneath their feet, grasses and herbs. The incline became gentler, and the hills were covered with a springing turf that was a relief to their feet after the shingle and small rocks over which they had been picking their way. Cadvan turned his face southward, with the Osidh Annova rearing up like huge shadows to their left, blades of darkness cutting off the stars. The scents of bruised grasses and flowers, spring honeysuckles and bulbs rose about them, and wild briars snatched at their cloaks. In the dim moonlight the countryside was silvered with mystery, but Maerad felt it was unaccountably familiar and walked on as if in a dream.

Then Cadvan cried out and pointed, and in the distance Maerad saw a light. "Innail!" he said. "And only three hours after sunset!"

As they neared Innail, Maerad began to feel nervous. This was a School, and she knew nothing about such places. What would they think of her, turning up with her hair like a mare's nest, stinking and filthy and ignorant? Her apprehension increased as they got closer, and when she saw the outlines of the buildings of Innail emerging, she felt sick with it; proud and noble they seemed to her, towers lit with golden windows that thrust gracefully into the night sky, behind a high wall of smooth white stone that threw back the starlight. Her reluctance increased as Cadvan's step grew more eager, and much sooner than she would have liked they arrived at the tall gates, thick oak stoutly barred with black steel. Cadvan cupped his hands and shouted.

"*Lirean! Lirean noch Dhillarearë!*"

A shutter opened high above the gate and a man looked out.

"*Lirean? Ke sammach?*"

"*Cadvan Lirigon na, e Maerad Pellinor na!*" answered Cadvan, winking at Maerad as he did so. Maerad smiled back uncertainly.

"*Langrea i,*" said the voice, and the window banged shut.

"Will they let me in?" asked Maerad.

"Oh, yes, eventually," said Cadvan. "But they must be careful these days, especially after dark. He goes to tell our names."

After about five minutes, the shutter opened again, and another man thrust out his head.

"Cadvan?" he said. "Is that you?"

"The same," said Cadvan. "Traveling on hard roads, by dark ways, and begging for succor from the Bards of Innail, by the old laws of courtesy."

"What are you doing in this part of the world?"

"Malgorn!" Cadvan threw back his head and shouted. "Come down and let us in!"

"And *who* of Pellinor? I thought they were all dead! By the Light! But wait, I'll get the gate."

He banged shut the window, and Cadvan turned to Maerad. "We are safe now," he said.

"Do you know him?"

"It's Malgorn. I've known him since childhood, and he was

sent here some twenty years ago. They were having trouble in this part of the world and needed someone of his abilities. He is a good man. One of the best."

Then the gate was flung open and a fair, solidly built man came out, his arms wide. "Cadvan!" he said, and gathered him into a bearlike embrace. "How good to see you! How long is it?"

"Too long, old friend," said Cadvan. "And I can't say how glad I am to see you!"

Malgorn stood back, studying his face. "You look somewhat the worse for wear," he said. "I can see there's a tale to this. What have you been doing? But come in, come in."

"This is Maerad of Pellinor, my fellow traveler," said Cadvan, stepping back to include her. "Maerad, this is my old friend Malgorn, a rogue and a scoundrel, and the worst card-player in the Seven Kingdoms. But he has his good points."

Malgorn, smiling, took her hand and bowed over it, suddenly grave. "I am honored to meet you, Maerad of Pellinor," he said. "I thought none of your School yet lived. It has a place in my heart like no other, and was one of the most beautiful in Annar."

Maerad looked up into a pair of warm brown eyes and swallowed. She made an awkward little bob, and Malgorn released her hand. He ushered them through the gates and a small cloister and then into the first courtyard of the School of Innail. There Maerad would have stopped and stared in astonishment, had Malgorn's shepherding permitted her. The moonlight fell on well-tended gardens bordered by huge, smooth flags, and in the center a fountain trembled, a glittering veil. Men and women walking through the courtyard looked at them with cool curiosity. Someone was playing a flute somewhere far off in another building, and from another direction Maerad could hear voices joined together in song. Something within her leaped in recognition.

She had no time to stare, as Malgorn hurried them through curving streets of graceful buildings and across more court-yards to a great stone house with high, narrow windows from which spilled light as yellow as butter. Malgorn flung open the richly chased double doors and strode into the entrance hall, shouting, "Silvia! Silvia! We have guests!" And that was all Maerad saw, before a blackness came rushing over her and she slid to the ground in a dead faint.

INNAIL

Glad was the world, and golden the greenwood
In dawndays of Ulnar, unstained and undarkened
When strode Mercan Goldhand singing in sunlight,
Lord of a proud people, fearless and prescient,
Singers of Maldan, matchless in magecraft,
But master of all was Mercan the Maker:
Deepest in lore among lordly Loresingers,
Arestor's firstling, the archmage of artists,
Tongued with the star speech, speller of seasons,
Singing the spring on Lir's silver waters.
Long were the days then, and bright laughter lingered
Long in the halls where the high people harkened,
Lost now in legend, lamented by Loremen
Reckoning ruins to raise the remembering.
Great grew the houses, gilded with glory
Over the mere where the melt waters murmured.
High then the heart-home, where held Mercan hearth-feast,
Golden the light on the lost land of Lirion.

From *Mercan's Quest*

VI

A BLUE DRESS

MAERAD opened her eyes and blinked away the black spots. Her head was humming, and it was a few seconds before her vision focused and she could see where she was. Someone had lifted her onto a chair, and Cadvan was leaning toward her, holding a small glass full of a golden liquid.

"Drink," he said. She had never touched glass before, and she took it gingerly as if it would shatter; it was cool and light against her fingers. The drink went down her throat like a smooth flame, burning her palate, and she choked as an aftertaste glowed in her mouth like a soft explosion of fruit. Warmth thrilled through her body all the way down to her toes, and for a second she wondered if she was about to be sick. Even feeling as she was, she couldn't have stood the humiliation; but then it passed.

"Another," said Cadvan.

"What is it?" she asked. Despite its initial sting, the liquor was as different from the harsh voka that Gilman's men drank as anything she could imagine.

"It's laradhel, a specialty of the house," said Cadvan, grinning. "Distilled out of selected herbs and fruits, especially apricots, yes, Malgorn?" He lifted an inquiring eyebrow at Malgorn, who nodded. "By this particular connoisseur of the table, no less. Malgorn has a great interest in the arts of brewing and distilling, for pleasure as well as medicine."

She drank again, and didn't choke this time. Sip by sip she

finished the glass, and handed it back to Cadvan. She felt less dizzy now, if a little lightheaded, and she looked around the room.

She was in a chamber that, to her confused perceptions, seemed like a vision or something from a dream. It was high-ceilinged and gracefully proportioned, with a carved mantel on one wall where a fire flickered in the grate. From the ceiling hung a silver lamp shaped like a lily, which diffused a gentle light. The walls were pale yellow, and the ceiling and carved cornices were painted with a pattern of stylized lilies and ivy leaves stenciled in black and subtly colored. Comfortable wooden chairs, heaped high with dark red cushions, were arranged around a huge fireplace, and musical instruments of all kinds were stacked casually against the walls and furniture. There was a big carved shelf of leather-bound books on the wall opposite, and one, with fine black writing illuminated with gold-leafed pictures, was open on a table. She blinked again in wonder.

"She's white as a ghost," said Malgorn. "What have you been doing with this child, Cadvan? Where did you find her?"

"I'm not a child," said Maerad, more sulkily than she intended. "I mean, I'm sixteen summers old!" Then she blushed, feeling graceless, and fell silent.

"She's certainly not a child," said Cadvan, smiling mischievously at Maerad. "She faced twenty wers with only a stick in her hand. But I can't blame her for fainting when she met *you*!"

Malgorn laughed, and then looked speculatively at Maerad. "Twenty wers, eh? Looks at the moment like twenty moths would be too much for her! That must be worth a song or two."

"Not on my own!" Maerad protested, struggling to sit up. "Cadvan's exaggerating!"

A woman entered the room, carrying a tray. "Is she conscious? Thank the Light for that." She put the tray on a small table and bustled over to Maerad, holding out her hand. "Hello, Maerad, I am Silvia. I have the bad luck to be married to Malgorn here, and so have to put up with his nonsense all the time." She smiled, and Maerad smiled back. She thought she had never seen such a beautiful face: kind and merry and wise, all at the same time. "Come, let's leave these two to their own devices," she said. "We'll get you cleaned up. And get some food into you! You're so thin! Has Cadvan been starving you?"

"Why is everyone blaming *me*?" asked Cadvan. "And where is the sympathy for *my* thinness?"

"Sympathy? For you?" said Silvia. "You've been eating her rations, for sure. I've never seen such a stick. Now, Malgorn, stop talking and show this poor man to his room."

"And a bath!" said Cadvan "I crave a bath above all else!"

But Maerad was already being guided out of the room into a long hallway, Silvia's arm around her shoulders. "Are you very hungry, Maerad?" she asked.

"No," she mumbled. "Well, not at the moment."

"If you're not starving, there's a bath being prepared for you. And we'll find you some clothes. These can go in the fire! What has Cadvan been doing with you? Gadding about the wilderness, chasing monsters no doubt. What was he thinking? You're too young for all that business. You should be safe in a school, learning scales and suchlike. Really!" She clicked her tongue impatiently.

"It wasn't his fault!" Maerad said hotly, feeling Cadvan was being blamed unfairly. "Really, it wasn't. He rescued me! I was a slave in Gilman's Cot, and he took me out of there, and I never had enough to eat beforehand anyway. . . ."

"Did he, now?" Silvia stopped and took Maerad's chin in her hand, looking into her eyes with a disconcerting serious- ness. "Don't take our jesting seriously, Maerad. Cadvan is a good friend, an old friend, and one of the most honorable men

I ever met. There are not many Bards like him. Be sure we know that."

Maerad nodded, feeling foolish again; she hadn't encountered this kind of gentle mockery before, and she found it hard to read. Silvia continued her bustling and chatting, and before she knew it Maerad found herself in a steaming room smelling of lavender, with a stone bath sunk in the floor already full of hot water. Maerad had never even seen a bath before. She halted in the doorway, her eyes wide. Silvia looked at her swiftly, and said: "Would you like me to stay? I can leave you, if you like. But it sometimes helps to have someone scrub your back."

"I . . . I don't know," whispered Maerad, almost overcome. "What do you normally do?"

"This time, my sweet, I will stay and help you," said Silvia decidedly. "I should not like it if you fainted in the bath. And you look too exhausted to bathe alone."

Gently she helped Maerad peel off her stinking clothes, throwing them into a basket, and helped her into the bath, pouring into it a sweet-smelling oil from a blue bottle. Then she scrubbed her with a soft cloth and lavender-scented soap, and washed her hair. Maerad was ashamed when she saw how filthy the water was, but Silvia seemed unfussed, and simply tut-tutted over the cut on Maerad's forehead and the bruises and scars on her body. When she was satisfied that Maerad was clean down to the last fingernail, she helped her out, dried her, and draped a soft, warm robe around her shoulders. She smeared a balm on the cut and then took a wide-toothed comb from a cupboard, made her sit down on a low wooden stool in the corner of the room, and patiently combed all the knots out of her hair. It took some time. Maerad leaned back against her, sleepy and luxurious. She had never felt such ease in her body; her skin felt delicious, as if it were made of silk.

"Now, your room should be ready," said Silvia. "Let's go."

She led her down more corridors and up a flight of stairs and opened the door on a small bedchamber. A fire flickered in a grate, and through an arched window Maerad could hear the bubbling voice of the fountain in the courtyard. A bed draped with a brocaded cover stood in the corner, and on it were laid bright clothes. She saw that someone had placed her lyre in the corner. Maerad stood hesitantly by the door, abashed by the rich colors. "Is all this for me?" she whispered.

Silvia looked at her with an unfathomable compassion. "It is, Maerad. All for you. Now, shall I help you to dress? Some of those buttons can be tricky."

Maerad nodded dumbly. She had never seen dresses like this either, of such soft cloth in rich colors, made for comfort and beauty as well as warmth. She felt ignorant and coarse. Silvia chose a simple blue robe with silver embroiderings on the neck and sleeves. "You'll be going to bed very soon," she said practically. "And you don't want to be fussing about. But you must have something to eat first. Are you feeling all right? Do you think you'll faint again?"

Embarrassed, Maerad shook her head. The more kindness Silvia showed her, the less she felt able to speak. She felt as if there were some mistake; soon someone would find out that she wasn't a proper Bard and would throw her out. Silvia picked out some woolen underclothes and passed them to Maerad, who wondered at their softness. She felt that she was dreaming. She sat down on the bed, lost in thought, stroking them with her fingers, and Silvia gently took them from her and, loosing her bathrobe, slipped the shift over Maerad's head. It was like dressing a child, or a doll. Maerad said not a word.

When she was dressed, Silvia led her to a mirror. "Do you think that suits?" she said, leaning her chin over Maerad's shoulder. "You should wear blue, it brings out your eyes. How pretty you are!"

Maerad blinked and stared. There had been no mirrors in Gilman's Cot, apart from the polished metal of a shield or the still face of a pail of water. She couldn't recognize the image in the mirror as herself; only the faint white line on her neck, a hairline scar from some old injury she couldn't remember, seemed at all familiar. Suddenly there came into her mind, at once very vivid and immeasurably distant, a memory of her mother's face bending toward her, perhaps to kiss her. She realized with a slight shock that she looked very much like Milana. It made her feel desolate, and perceiving this, Silvia said quickly: "It's time to eat, before you drop on the floor with exhaustion. I'm sure Malgorn and Cadvan are waiting for us; we should hurry."

She led her down the stairs, which Maerad negotiated hesitatingly, looking around in wonder. She found the house bewildering: there were too many chambers, too many doors, too many passages leading to unguessed-at destinations. She was used to buildings of one room, with beasts down one end and people at the other and no stairs anywhere. Even the Great Hall had been only one big room, with the sleeping quarters attached to one side as lean-tos.

At last they reached a small dining room, where there was a dark wooden table set with candles and fine, plain plates. In the center were dishes piled high with vegetables, and a plate heaped with carved meats. Maerad suddenly realized she was ravenous. Cadvan and Malgorn were already seated, and glanced up as they entered. For a second Cadvan looked a little startled, and Maerad faltered, feeling awkward and self-conscious in her new clothes, but then the men stood and bowed their heads courteously. Silvia bowed her head in answer, and Maerad, looking out the corner of her eye, copied her, and they all sat down.

"Roast beef, Maerad!" said Cadvan, settling in next to her. "Didn't I promise you? And all the carrots and turnips you could possibly want. And they even rustled up some mushrooms, at my urgent request!" He served her generously, and then piled food on his own dish. "Malgorn has told me sternly that I can't keep you up late, and that you mustn't eat too much, for fear you will be ill. I told him it's nothing to do with me!" He smiled, and Maerad began to relax a little.

"I *am* tired," she said. "I can see why you like baths! But it's made me feel so sleepy."

"Have some of this," said Cadvan, holding up a glass decanter filled with a wine as pale as straw. "Malgorn's pulled out a good wine for us, and we can't let it go to waste. Then you'll sleep like a baby!"

He filled her glass, and Maerad sipped cautiously, remembering the laradhel. To her surprise, the wine ran lightly over her tongue, crisp and sweet. Then she concentrated on eating while the others talked. Neither Silvia nor Malgorn were eating, and Maerad guessed they had dined earlier and were simply keeping them company. The food was delicately flavored, as far from the rough cooking she was used to as everything else in this marvelous place; the meat was stuffed with herbs and garlic, roasted so tenderly it dissolved on her tongue, and the carrots were sweet, as if they had been flavored with honey. Cadvan glanced at her, and helped himself to more mushrooms. "You haven't tried these," he said. "You'd better hurry, or there'll be none left."

"I told you he took all the rations," said Silvia, smiling.

Maerad looked doubtfully at the mushrooms, darkly piled on the dish, dripping yellow streams of melted butter. "I don't like fungus," she said.

"But you haven't tasted these," said Cadvan. "Try a little. Just a taste." He put a portion on her plate. Maerad poked it dubiously, picked up the smallest piece she could find, and put it in her mouth. The taste on her palate was pungent and rich, the flavor of woodlands and dark earth simmered in sunshine. "Oh!" she said in surprise. "It's delicious!"

"I told you," said Cadvan. "And nothing tastes so well as a meal well earned. Have some more! But you'd better be quick!"

The conversation was light; for the moment no one mentioned their recent adventures or asked any further questions about where they had been. Although Cadvan had deep hollows under his eyes and his face still bore traces of strain, he seemed wide awake and merry, jesting and teasing with Malgorn and Silvia. Maerad saw the fondness with which they treated him and felt reassured.

Silvia and Malgorn removed all the dishes, and they moved to comfortable chairs arranged around a fire. Malgorn returned with a glass decanter full of cherry cordial, gleaming like a huge ruby, and a platter of sweets. He poured them all a small glass each. Maerad had never seen sweets, but emboldened by her experiment with the mushrooms, she took a candied chestnut. As she chewed it her eyes widened, and she reached for another.

"You won't stay bony for long, if you keep eating those," said Cadvan lazily. He was leaning back in his chair, his long legs stretched before him. "Those are a specialty of Innail, as well. The valley here prides itself on its cuisine."

Maerad felt content just to sit and say nothing, and continued to sip her cherry cordial, which she decided was completely delicious. She made no objection when Malgorn refilled her glass. She was warm and well fed and clean, all completely novel sensations, and the day's weary walk settled slack and heavy in her limbs. Sleepily she listened as the conversation moved to other topics.

"Your timing is impeccable, as usual," Silvia was saying.

Cadvan cocked an eyebrow. "How so?"

"I thought you'd come for the Meet," Silvia said. "But perhaps you have not had news of it?"

"A Meet?" Cadvan sat up and looked a little more alert. "No, I haven't heard. Messengers don't usually visit the Landrost."

"The Landrost?" Silvia's eyebrows arched in surprise. "What were you doing there?" Cadvan made a vague gesture, dismissing the question, and she returned to the subject of the Meet, shrugging her shoulders. "Yes, the biggest in recent memory," she said. "There are Bards here from almost every School in northern Annar. Some from as far away as Gent, and an envoy even from Turbansk, in the south. The Welcome Feast is tomorrow night."

"And what is the occasion?"

Malgorn stirred and leaned forward. "You know as well as I do that rumors of the Dark are increasing in Annar," he said. "Well, you probably know more than I do about all that. Certainly sightings of wers and other creatures are more common, and there's famine and banditry and sickness in many regions. Some say these are but part of the Balance, and will soon right themselves. Others say not. And more than that, there are problems in the Schools: nothing concrete, but a definite unease."

"We've known that for years," Cadvan said. "So why the Meet now?"

Malgorn leaned forward, almost speaking in a whisper. "Some Schools, it is said, are *corrupt*."

Cadvan smiled grimly. "My friend, that is no news to me either. Not all Schools are as noble as Innail, or as faithful to the Light."

Malgorn's brow creased in slight annoyance. "I think you should not make light of these things. There are even rumors . . ."

He hesitated, looking around as if he feared someone might over-hear, and lowered his voice again. "I have even heard there are fears that the Speech itself is poisoned. The wellspring and source of our power! I know, I know, it is unthinkable. But still it is said, though I don't believe it myself."

"Oron thinks that in the past two or three years these rumors have become much more troubling," said Silvia. Kindly, she turned to Maerad and explained: "Oron is the First of the Circle of the Innail, and of great rank in Annar by virtue of her power and learning." Maerad nodded, surprised that they spoke of such things in front of her. But Silvia continued. "Some say that the Dark is gaining on the Light, and that the days of peace are over. And some even say that the Nameless is rising again. Oron has called this Meet to gather together and consider all the rumors and news, to attempt to consider what the situation actually is, and if possible to decide on some action, if it is indeed as bad as people think."

"Which is doubtful," interrupted Malgorn. "Gossips are frogs, they say; they drink and talk. And all fish grow in the telling."

"It's bad," said Cadvan shortly, as if he could say more but would not. He frowned down at the table. Silvia looked at him inquiringly, but did not ask him to elaborate, and changed the subject.

"Maerad, Malgorn tells me you're from Pellinor. That's astonishing news!" she said. "We thought no one survived the sacking. I used to know Milana, First of the Circle there, and her husband, Dorn."

Taken by surprise, Maerad looked straight up into Silvia's eyes.

"Milana was my mother," she said unemotionally, and she heard a slight catch of surprise in Silvia's breath. "We didn't die.

We were captured and sold as slaves. Milana died . . . afterward." There was a short silence.

"There was a little boy, wasn't there?" asked Malgorn. "Maybe I remember wrongly—Cai? Carin?"

"Yes, I had a little brother, Cai," said Maerad. "He was murdered, like my father." Involuntarily she shut her eyes; the memory of her father being cut down before her flashed across her mind.

"Well, you have the Gift, that's clear, which would not be surprising from such a family," said Malgorn, after a slightly uncomfortable pause. "But of what kind? How strange that Cadvan should stumble across you. . . ."

"How do you know I have the Gift?" Maerad stared at them almost belligerently.

"It's a sense that Bards have," said Silvia. "It's hard to explain. . . . You learn over the years. You can tell by a certain light . . . in a person's being. You have that light, Maerad; it's unmistakable."

Cadvan roused himself. "And some Gift it is!" he said. He told them of the power Maerad had revealed when they were escaping the Landrost, and Silvia and Malgorn listened with sudden serious attention. "I've never felt anything like it," he finished. "Not so wholly untutored. It's astonishing!"

Malgorn was looking dubious. "It seems," he said, "a rather neat coincidence. Rather too neat. Think you not, Cadvan?" He looked meaningfully at Cadvan.

"I did wonder." Cadvan reached forward and poured himself another drink. He held the glass before his eyes, admiring the color. "I scried her. I have no doubt she is who she says she is."

"You scried her!" cried Silvia, horrified. "Cadvan, how could you?"

"I felt at the time I had no choice but to ask," said Cadvan, glancing swiftly at Maerad. "I was at my wits' end, wondering what to do. But that's only half the story: she almost scried me, and came close to wiping me out. I am serious about her Gift. What's more, she has a lyre, of Dhyllic ware."

"No!" said Malgorn and Silvia simultaneously.

"Indeed, she has. It must have been the greatest treasure of Pellinor; and there it was, hidden in a miserable cot, as undistinguished as any peasant's harp."

"Are you sure, Cadvan?" said Malgorn. "There are none, after all, with which to compare it—how can you know?"

Cadvan looked across at Malgorn. "I did not study the secret lore of the Dhyllin for so many years without learning the signs," said Cadvan. "Even if they are lost to most knowledge. I have no doubt of it." There was a brief silence. "And there is something else," Cadvan added slowly. "Something has been nagging me—something fated—I think it was not chance that we met. . . ."

He withdrew suddenly into an abstracted silence. "Anyway," he said at last, "I think she's too important to stay here; I think she's a key, somehow. I think she should come to Norloch. I'd like to know what Nelac thinks."

"You can't drag her all over the countryside!" said Silvia, scandalized.

"Nevertheless, I think it might be more dangerous to leave her here than to take her with me," Cadvan replied.

"Dangerous?" said Malgorn sharply. "She'll be safer here than almost anywhere else. Forgive me for saying this, Maerad; but we're talking about a young girl, not a great mage."

Cadvan suddenly grinned. "Why can they not be the same thing?"

Maerad listened silently, feeling slightly resentful. What

were they talking about? What would she be a key to? It was as if she were't there.

Malgorn leaned forward, his face intent and serious. "You're talking nonsense, Cadvan, old friend," he said. "Beware the snares of the Dark!"

"You should know me better," said Cadvan. "I know the snares of the Dark better than almost any in the whole of Annar and the Seven Kingdoms."

Malgorn settled back in his chair. "For all that, she's a child," he said. Maerad stirred as if to protest, but said nothing. "And perhaps she ought to be permitted to grow into her own fate, if fated she is, in her own time."

There was a short silence. A gloom descended on the company, a palpable sense of foreboding.

"If times were different, perhaps it would be easy to know what to do," said Silvia sadly. "But alas, many things these days cannot grow in their own time, and will be cut down in the full flower of their promise." She shivered and stared into the fire, her face troubled, and Malgorn reached for her hand and held it.

"I think all of us will soon know more of the Dark," she said. "The world shrinks, and a bitter winter is coming."

VII

THE WELCOME FEAST

IT WAS late afternoon the following day before Maerad
woke. She was so warm and comfortable that at first she
didn't want to open her eyes. She thought she still dreamed,
and that beyond her closed eyelids waited the grim world she
was used to; but then she remembered where she was and sat
up, tousled and still half-awake, rubbing her eyes. The late
sunlight shafted through the open casement, touching all the
objects in the room with a still, golden light, and she could hear
the various voices of the fountain and behind that, strains of
music. Outside she could see the top branches of a tree burdened with puffs of pink blossom, and a gentle breeze bathed
her cheeks with a delicious smell. The gloomy premonitions of
the night before seemed like a bad dream.

"Good afternoon," said Cadvan. "I trust you slept well?"

Maerad jumped and turned around. Cadvan was sitting on a
chair in the corner of the bedchamber, a big, leather-bound book
open on his lap. He closed it carefully and placed it on a table.

"Someone should have woken me. . . ."

"Woken you up? On pain of death! Silvia is taking your welfare somewhat to heart, Maerad. Be warned! She sat here this
morning, but duties called her, and she wanted to make sure
someone was here when you awoke. And, as I have no duties, I
was given this one."

Maerad felt abashed. "I don't mean to cause any trouble,"
she said. Cadvan crossed the room and sat on the bed, taking
her hand.

"Maerad," he said seriously. "You are in another world now, where it is considered that every human being is worth the trouble of being cared for. No matter who they are. You have a Gift, a special Gift, so people are all the more interested. You must begin to understand this."

She was silent for a time, still looking down. "They are very kind people, Malgorn and Silvia," she murmured indistinctly. "And you have been kind to me."

"I haven't been especially kind," said Cadvan wryly.

"You *have* been kind. You took me out of Gilman's Cot. You didn't have to. But I don't know how to behave here. I don't know anything. I don't belong." She felt tears gathering in her throat, and gulped them back.

"In time you will know how you belong. Be patient. You've only just arrived. You must understand, Maerad, that I belong nowhere either. Music is my home. As it is for you."

Maerad felt she couldn't bear his understanding, and in a way preferred his brusqueness. She gulped again, but a tear was already running down her nose. Before Cadvan scried her, she hadn't cried for years: not after her mother died, not for anyone, not for anything. The world she lived in had been too harsh for tears. She felt as if a grief dammed up in her for years was bursting its banks, about to give way, and each of Cadvan's words loosened further its bulwarks. Cadvan was looking into her face with concern, but she refused to meet his eyes and stared down at the coverlet, her cheeks hot. With all her will, she pushed back her tears.

"I suppose I should get dressed," she said at last.

"Your clothes are waiting for you over there," said Cadvan, pointing to a carved trunk, on which was draped the robe she had worn the night before. He stood up a little awkwardly. "I'll put this book away now. If you like, I'll come back after you're dressed and show you around the School. If you're hungry, we'll go to the kitchens and see what they have for a late afternoon snack. Would that suit you?"

Maerad nodded, and he left the room. She got out of bed and picked up her lyre. As soon as she felt it in her hands, she felt better. It was hers, the only thing that had ever been hers. What had Cadvan said? *Music is my home.* She brushed a couple of chords across the strings, and was about to play when a discomfort she had been feeling in her belly suddenly blossomed into agonizing cramps. It was as if claws had reached inside her and were pulling her innards apart. It took all her will to put the lyre down safely, and then she sank to the floor, gasping. She felt something trickle down her leg. The cramps subsided a little, and she looked; it was blood, great red drops of blood. It soaked through her linen nightdress and onto the polished wooden floor. What was wrong with her? Doubled over, she crawled back to the bed, but couldn't climb onto it. She concentrated on breathing, as she did when she was beaten, to keep her mind off the pain, but it didn't go away. She was sobbing with fright.

Cadvan knocked on the door three times before she heard him, but on the third knock he had already entered, calling her name. When he saw her on the floor he ran, picking her up and putting her on the bed. "What's the matter?" he asked.

"I, I don't know," she said, between spasms. "It hurts so much. I'm bleeding, and it hurts." She gasped again in a paroxysm of pain.

"Bleeding?" said Cadvan sharply. "Where?"

"There's blood down my legs. I don't remember being hurt. . . ." She gasped again and grasped his hand so hard his fingers went white. Cadvan looked at her pale, sweating face and felt her temperature.

"Maerad, tell me," he said. "Has this happened to you before?"

She shook her head. He looked down, and even through her discomfort Maerad sensed his embarrassment. She had thought him incapable of blushing.

"I think it's the menarche," he said, after a long pause. "Do you know what that is?"

She shook her head again. "I should get Silvia," he said. Maerad grabbed his hand in panic, and Cadvan sat irresolute as she doubled over again. It was passing through his head that he would much rather deal with a dozen wers than a girl having her first period.

"Am I going to die?" whispered Maerad, terror naked in her voice. "I'm cursed, aren't I?"

Cadvan took a deep breath. "No, you are not going to die, nor are you cursed. It is a thing that happens to women, all women. It's a bit late for you, that's all. It doesn't mean you are sick."

"Then why does it hurt so much?"

"I don't know, Maerad. It does sometimes. I should find Silvia."

"Don't leave me!"

Cadvan sighed, and sat down again on the bed. "I'll wait a little while," he said. He loosened her hand off his, as he could feel the bones grinding together, and Maerad grabbed his forearm instead. He summoned all his patience and waited. It wasn't long before Maerad straightened up. "It's going, I think," she whispered unsteadily. She realized that she was holding Cadvan's arm so hard that her nails dug into his flesh. She let go. Cadvan was looking a little pale.

"You'll be all right," he said. There was a short silence, and he stood up. "I should call Silvia now. She'll know what to do." Maerad nodded, and Cadvan ran from the chamber.

Before long Silvia arrived, her eyes sparkling with amusement, holding a bottle of elixir and some cloths. She made

Maerad take a dose of the elixir, which tasted bitter but not unpleasant, and then helped her to dress. Her reassuring practicality was a balm to Maerad's distress; by the time she was dressed, she felt almost cheerful. Then Silvia sat down with her on the bed and explained the bleeding of women. Maerad nodded, her face scarlet.

"I thought it only happened to women who were cursed," she confessed shamefacedly. "They used to call it the curse. I always prayed it would never happen to me."

If Silvia had smiled even a little, Maerad would have shriveled inside, but she answered her gravely. "It's no wonder you never bled, considering how thin you are," she said. "Here women think it a blessing, not a curse. Some call it the flowering."

Maerad digested this information in silence. "It means that if you wish, you can now have children, that you are a grown woman coming into her power," Silvia went on. "It is dreadful that any girl should be kept in such ignorance of her own body. But still, you have no mother." She kissed her cheek and then, unable to hold it back, started giggling. Maerad eyed her warily. "I have never seen Cadvan so pale. He came flying into the kitchens as if a brace of wights were chasing him. I thought there must be a fire!"

Maerad began to laugh as well. "I thought I was dying! I think I nearly broke his hand."

"It was a little hard to find out what was wrong," said Silvia, wiping her eyes. "He was speaking with such delicacy I thought there was something wrong with *him*. He hasn't had much to do with women, these past years." She picked up her bottle and stood up. "In any case, you definitely need to eat. Come, we'll find you something."

In the day-lit corridor Maerad had her first chance to look around her. The sandstone walls bore no decoration, save the graceful carvings around the doors and windows, and a level sunbeam shafting through a long window over the stairwell turned the stone a warm pink. "Upstairs are all the sleeping chambers, and a couple of music rooms," Silvia explained as they walked. "And down are just the kitchens and dining rooms and libraries. This is a humble house, but I have grown to love it." Maerad blinked at the thought that this apex of luxury was humble, but said nothing.

Downstairs Silvia took her through to a huge flagged kitchen dominated by a long, scrubbed wooden table. Copper and iron pots and pans hung from racks suspended from the roof, and the walls were lined with jars filled with seeds and oils and flours and rows of preserved fruits and vegetables, and bunches of dried herbs and garlic and onions hung from hooks. Against one wall was a huge hearth, and next to that a big black oven. Men and women preparing food for the evening meal smiled at Maerad, and some greeted Silvia. Silvia nodded back and made for the pantry, where she put some fresh bread and cheeses, slices of cold meat, and salad onto a plate, handing it to Maerad, and then to the buttery, where she poured a tall glass of milk from a high green jug. Then she shepherded her out of the kitchen and through a tiny roofed lane into a courtyard. Maerad realized it was encircled by the entire house, which was square-shaped, and all the inner windows overlooked it. Jasmine and honeysuckles climbed trestles set in the walls, and spring flowers of all kinds, nasturtiums and bluebells and daisies and daffodils and crocuses, nodded in garden beds artfully placed to look as if they grew wild. In the center was a close-leafed lawn of chamomile, and in one corner a small bronze pig stood on a stone plinth, water pouring from its mouth into a little pool in which Maerad could see the silver and orange glint of fish turning slowly beneath lily pads. A flagged path led to a stone table and a bench in the

middle of the lawn, and here Silvia placed the milk and asked
Maerad to sit down.

"You must eat the salad and meats," she said, sitting next to
her. "You'll feel better for them." She settled down on the
bench. Maerad hadn't realized she was so hungry but, chas-
tened by Silvia's presence, ate as delicately as she could. The
food was delicious. The only cheeses she knew were the hard
and oversalted rounds made at Gilman's Cot, and the soft white
cheese Silvia had cut for her melted on her tongue like nothing
she had ever tasted. The salad greens were also a revelation. She
had eaten cabbage, usually boiled into a sour soup, and the
green tops of turnips and kale, again boiled, but had never
eaten raw leaves. She approached the salad with suspicion, and
was enraptured by the sharp, crisp tastes: peppery watercress
and a pleasantly bitter purple lettuce, mixed with fragrant
herbs, savory and basil and mint. As she ate, she asked Silvia
the names of the plants and mulled over the answers. The only
herb she knew was mint.

"I see I've got a lot to learn, about all sorts of things," she
said meditatively, when she had finished. "I do feel better now."
She smiled openly at Silvia for the first time.

"We'll make you into a gourmand in no time!" said Silvia.
"Pleasure is the greatest part of learning, they say. There's a
bit of color in your face, at least. It will keep you going until
dinnertime."

"But I thought that *was* dinner," said Maerad, taken aback.

"No, my dear. Just a snack to stave off the pangs of starvation. You missed out on breakfast and lunch, remember. If you
are up to it, there is a feast tonight, for the Meet. How are you
feeling? Are you tired?"

"I'm all right," said Maerad. "Well, actually I've never felt
better in my life. I feel . . . oh, I feel so . . . happy." She suddenly
felt uncertain again, as if an admission of happiness was also an

admission of weakness, and she glanced quickly at Silvia. "What's a Meet?"

"A gathering of the Bards, as you heard last night. This one is particularly important, called to determine policy in northern Annar. It is Bard business, which is to say, the business of the Light. There will be singing and saying, and much else, over the next few days. No doubt you will be part of the business discussed."

"Me?"

"Yes, my girl. You had better get used to it. News of your arrival has spread through the School like wildfire. I've heard already that Cadvan rescued you from a magic lion, and that he found you in a chicken coop, and that he entered the dungeons of the Shadow King and fought his way out single-handedly, carrying you on his shoulders. There are many imaginative minds here, which in the absence of facts will invent an exciting story to fill the gap. So is our strength our weakness." Seeing Maerad's discomfort, she changed the subject. "But now, tell me about where you came from. Do you remember much of Pellinor?"

Under Silvia's gentle questioning, Maerad told the little that she knew of herself and her family, and talked of her life at Gilman's Cot. Silvia listened intently, her brow darkening.

"Were you beaten often?" she asked, when Maerad spoke of the attempt to drown her.

"Everyone got beaten. Even Gilman's woman usually had a black eye," said Maerad dismissively. "Me less than most. I pretended to be a witch." She glanced sideways at Silvia, wondering how she would react, but her face was unreadable. "They were scared to beat me too much, you see. They thought I would curse them."

"In Innail, no one is beaten," Silvia said.

"No one?" said Maerad, her mouth open.

"No one. And especially not children. To deliberately hurt a child is considered a crime."

Maerad turned this information over in her head. It astonished her. "Then how are people punished, if they don't obey the Thane?" she inquired, and then added doubtfully, "I suppose there is no Thane."

"There is a Steward of Innail, who lives in Tinagel, a town about five miles from here, and then there are the Bards," said Silvia. "Together they govern the Fesse, which is to say, the region and the people. It's a bit complicated. We have laws, but they are not often broken. If they are, there are punishments: a man who murders another, say, will be tried in a court of Bards and townspeople. They will decide what is best. Usually it is some kind of restitution—he might be bound to serve the family that he has hurt for a number of years, for example, or perhaps pay wergild. If he is sick, or mad, as sometimes happens, he will be treated for his sickness. Someone who steals will have to return what is stolen. In the worst instances, people will be banished from Innail. We don't imprison people here."

"But how would that stop murder or thieving?" said Maerad, even more amazed. "If someone's not afraid of being punished, they'll just do it again, won't they?"

"So some people argue. But the fact is, there is very little crime here," answered Silvia. "People sleep with their doors unlocked. There are no hungry people in this valley, and so people are not forced to desperate acts. The law is that the hungry must be fed, and the homeless must be housed, and the sick must be healed. That is the way of the Light."

Maerad was silent for some time, digesting these new ideas. More than anything she had heard or experienced since she had been in Innail, they brought home to her that she was in a different world. She felt frankly sceptical of their efficacy, thinking of Gilman's thugs, but kept her doubts to herself.

Silvia turned the conversation to music, and her interest quickened when Maerad told her of Mirlad.

"He taught you?" she asked.

"Yes, but only music," said Maerad. "I didn't know anything about the Schools or the Gift or the Speech until Cadvan told me. Mirlad said songs were only to pass the time more gently, until death ended all time." A vivid image of Mirlad's face rose before her: his hawklike nose, his harsh mouth compressed by—who knew what?—sorrow or bitterness, his hooded, weary eyes, in which sometimes there gleamed an unexpected gentleness.

"He must have been a Bard," said Silvia. "Perhaps he lost his way. Such things happen. I wonder where he was from, and what was his history? It must be a sad story. And your mother? Did she teach you?"

"She . . . I don't remember much. She taught me some songs. I was only seven when she died." Maerad's face closed, and Silvia waited, holding her breath. "I don't remember her ever telling me about Pellinor. But when Cadvan asked me, I just knew. How is that?"

"Cadvan is a Truthteller," said Silvia. "There are different kinds of Bards, as you will discover. Bards like Cadvan are the most rare, and the path they tread is the most perilous. He can bring the truth out of a person, just by asking, even if they didn't know it was there."

"Yes," said Maerad thoughtfully. "I can see that. He is harsh, sometimes, and distant. But he hasn't lied to me."

"No, nor will he, if he counts you friend, though he is wily too, and apt at the arts of disguise. He is a difficult person to know well. Most Bards are."

They paused, watching the shadows lengthen over the courtyard.

"Are you a Bard, Silvia?" asked Maerad suddenly.

"Yes, I am," said Silvia. "My knowledge is mainly with herblore and medicine. I do not study the high knowledge of peoples long dead or the histories of Annar and the Seven Kingdoms or the great battles of Light and Dark, as Cadvan does. Malgorn's knowledge is that of beasts, the beasts of the farmyard and of the wild. Few know as much as he does of the secret ways of animals, and none more than he of the husbandry of this land. The ways of Barding are many, but all are important in the life of this land, and all meet in singing, which braids together the different knowings into a wide and subtle music, the music of living." Silvia seemed no longer to be aware of Maerad's presence, and gazed into an unseen distance. "It is a great Gift, the Gift of Barding," she said softly. "And a great love, and a great burden. For all that we care for and love so much must die. And is not all our singing a lament for all that is green and fair and must pass, like shadows on a plain, leaving no trace behind? What song, however so fair, can staunch that anguish?"

Maerad perceived the deep sadness in Silvia's face, and wondered what griefs had carved her beauty, so gentle and yet underneath, she sensed, harder than any stone. Silvia shook herself a little and smiled and seemed again the merry, practical woman Maerad was already beginning to love, her starved heart splitting open under the soft pressure of Silvia's smile. Now she saw how profundities moved beneath her laughter, like unmapped depths of water beneath a dazzling surface of ripples, and wondered at the complexities of these people. My people, she said to herself, trying it out. My people. But Silvia was already standing up.

"Alas, we have not time for me to show you the School today," she said. "I thought to show the Singing Hall, and the other Bardhouses, and other things that might interest you, perhaps. Now you should wash. We will eat soon, but not privately tonight: the Bards dine together, for the Welcome Feast. The Meet proper starts tomorrow."

Maerad looked down at her feet, and Silvia clasped her hands. "Maerad, don't be shy!" And she kissed her on both cheeks. "Come, I will help you choose what to wear. Then I must prepare myself. The Welcome Feast is always a joyous time, and no one will be talking business. But if you are tired, or feel that you must leave for any reason, you must tell me. Yes?"

Maerad nodded, and Silvia took her back through the kitchen, where meats were turning on spits over the fire, and the iron range was crowded with pots steaming and bubbling, and breads were being taken out of the ovens and left to cool on clean cloths. A different delicious smell emanated from each corner, and now all the cooks seemed busier and more serious. Silvia put the plate and glass down in the scullery and hurried Maerad up the stairs again to her room, where she drew from the wooden chest a dress of deep crimson, richly embroidered on the neck and sleeves with gold thread, and laid it on her bed. Maerad looked at it nervously.

"Oh, that's much too grand for me," she said.

"No, no Maerad. This is a feast day! It will fit, I promise. It's a beautiful dress; it used to be mine. I loved wearing it when I was little older than you. Wear it as a token of my friendship. But now, you go to the bathroom. I will come back later and help you dress." She pushed the bathrobe into Maerad's hands and hurried off down the hall.

Maerad stood in the doorway and looked helplessly around the room. Since her torment earlier, the room had been tidied: fresh sheets were on the bed, and the fire had been relit. Her hands ached for her lyre, but remembering that Silvia was returning and expected her to be washed, she found her way to the bathroom and washed herself with the soft cloths and soap, thinking she would very much like another bath. She returned to her room, shut the door, and sat on the bed waiting for Silvia. She didn't arrive, so Maerad picked up her lyre and began to play, humming as she did. She slipped from one melody to another, deepening the harmonies and extending the variations as she went, and was completely absorbed by the time Silvia knocked. She stopped, startled, and paused. "Maerad?" said Silvia.

"Yes?"

"May I come in?"

"Oh, yes, of course!" Maerad was halfway to the door when Silvia entered.

"Beautiful!" said Silvia warmly. "Cadvan said your musicianship was extraordinary. You were Bard-taught for sure. You must bring your lyre tonight, but Maerad . . ." and here Silvia's tone was suddenly serious, "you must not tell anyone this is Dhyllic ware. Cadvan knew, because he is versed in ancient lore, but very few Bards would recognize this without being told. And such things are best kept hidden. Now," she went on, "shall we get you dressed? I haven't had such fun since my own daughter was your age."

"You have a daughter?" asked Maerad, a little startled. Silvia didn't look old enough to have grown-up children.

"Yes. I did." Silvia's face was suddenly withdrawn, as if the question hurt her, and something told Maerad not to question any further.

Silvia was in high dress. She wore a moss green robe that fell in rich folds to the floor from a bodice sewn with tiny pearls in intricate patterns of flowers. Her auburn hair, loosed from the band that usually held it, fell in a river of mingled golds and reds, stayed only by a thin gold fillet that dropped a single white gem on her forehead. A gold ring set with a white stone was on her right hand, and on her breast was pinned a curiously wrought golden brooch in the shape of a running horse.

"You look lovely," Maerad said bashfully, and the shadow left Silvia's face. She laughed and picked up the crimson dress she had chosen for Maerad.

"And so do you, and you are not even dressed!" she said. "Now, may I braid your hair? I would like to. Now, you need the slip, so. That's right. As I said, these buttons are a bit tricky." The dress hugged close around Maerad's shoulders and arms and then flared out from her hips in a long, generous fall to the ground. The sleeves opened out from her elbows, like the mouths of lilies, she thought. Silvia was right; the dress felt beautiful to wear, and it swished around her knees with an enticing rustle. She began to feel excited, and turned to make the dress swirl.

"I thought it would suit you," said Silvia. "Now, do you feel all right? Yes? Well then, you must tell me or Cadvan if you do not; I mean if the cramps return. I'm tempted to dose you again, but you might fall asleep—so we will chance it. I shall keep the elixir handy. Now, your hair."

She made Maerad sit on the chair before her and plaited her hair, piling it on her head and fixing it with some small golden combs. Then she let Maerad see herself in the mirror. Maerad blushed; even the rehearsal of the night before hadn't prepared her for this transformation. The cut on her forehead had been artfully concealed with a curl of hair, and by no other sign could anyone have told that less than a week before she had been the slave of a small, crude tyrant, used to pallets of straw and bad food and beatings. Silvia's braiding exposed the fine bones of her face and drew attention to her full mouth. Her eyes stared back at her gravely.

"It is good to dress in fair clothes to dine with friends," said Silvia solemnly. "It honors your host, if you are a guest; and your guest, if you are a host. And both adorn the feast, and so celebrate the gifts of the world."

"What do I do at the feast?" Maerad asked nervously. The butterflies in her stomach, forgotten in the fascination of dressing, had started again.

"Just be who you are," said Silvia, winking. "Remember that people will forgive youth many things. You managed very well last night. And don't forget your lyre!"

Clutching her lyre, Maerad followed Silvia from the room, her heart beating fast. She felt as if she were steeling herself for an ordeal. *The dress helps, the cold, witnessing part of her observed. You can pretend to be someone else. Not Maerad at all.* Pretending to be someone else was an old game of Maerad's; she had often played roles at the cot. She took a deep breath and tried to walk like a fine lady, as her mother might have walked.

They went first to the music chamber downstairs, the beautiful room where Maerad had recovered from her faint the night before. Cadvan and Malgorn sat before the fire, deep in conversation, and both rose and bowed when the two women entered. The men had gone to no less trouble than the women, and were arrayed in fine clothes: Cadvan in plain black, with a long black cloak trimmed with fine silver braiding. He wore his sword openly, and Maerad saw it was sheathed in silver intricately worked with runes and patterns, and that he wore a silver brooch shaped like a four-pointed star on his breast. Malgorn bore no sword, and was like Silvia in moss green; on his breast he bore a silver sign of a horse running. He wore a ring with a white stone on his right hand.

Cadvan smiled at Maerad with no trace of embarrassment. "Two enchantresses!" he said. "If I had to choose, I would be at a loss—who could decide between autumn and spring?"

"Fortunately for me, it is not for you to choose," said Malgorn. "Autumn is all mine." He picked a lute from the wall and took Silvia's elbow. "That is, of course, if she is agreeable."

He nodded gravely at Silvia, and she kissed him on the cheek. "You would grace the halls of Afinil tonight, my love," he said.

"Thank you indeed, kind sir," said Silvia, mock seriously. "But now, you must admire my protégé. And this, remember, is her first Meet!"

"She is indeed very beautiful," said Malgorn, rather primly. For a few seconds all three Bards stopped and examined her dispassionately, as if she were a piece of sculpture. Maerad shifted uncomfortably under their gaze. What was she, a trophy? Cadvan released her from the unwelcome attention by stepping forward and taking her hand.

"If you would do me the pleasure," he said, "I would be honored if you accompanied me to the Welcome Feast."

Maerad hesitated, uncertain of the correct response. "I would be very happy to," she said stiltedly, after a slight pause.

"We are ready, then?" asked Malgorn. "Then let's go!"

"Silvia has worked a miracle!" murmured Cadvan to Maerad, as they left the room. "What would they say at Gilman's Cot?"

"They'd say, 'She was always above herself,'" said Maerad. "I'd get a whipping for my pains. But very likely they wouldn't know who I was!"

"Very likely," said Cadvan. "Though, for all the fine clothes, I see the same girl who gave me a fright in a cowbyre!"

"Thanks!" said Maerad sarcastically.

"I meant, Maerad, that even slavery could not hide who you were. Don't be so touchy!" said Cadvan. "Now, this is your first Meet, and will likely be a little difficult, so grow some armor. Not all Bards are like Malgorn and Silvia. Some, indeed, are so different they barely deserve the name. I'm afraid Malgorn was quite correct in saying that some Schools are corrupt: the only questions are, how corrupt, and corrupted by what? In some places, it is just petty greed and other vices. In others . . ." He stopped and shook his head. "In any case, there will be much curiosity about you, the more since you are turning up looking like a princess. Stay alert! And stay close to me!"

"I'll stick like a burr," said Maerad.

"Silvia has also told me that I am to send you to bed the second you look wan. She is sterner than she looks, and I daren't disobey. Running away once was bad enough!"

"You didn't quite run away!" said Maerad, wanting to laugh but not quite daring.

"I confess to cowardice. Me, Cadvan, unmanned by a young girl! How can this be? But it's true I'm not used to such things." He smiled at Maerad, and suddenly she relaxed and laughed. "That's better," he said. "It's a feast, not an examination. And now you are a grown woman, remember! I may never call you child again."

Maerad flushed with mingled pleasure and embarrassment, and walked straighter. By now they had crossed the courtyard and passed down several streets of houses very like Malgorn and Silvia's, which led to a huge flagged circle surrounded by formal gardens. In the center on a high plinth stood a magnificent white statue of a rearing horse, bearing neither bit nor bridle, its mane flaring in an unseen wind.

"Lanorgrim!" said Cadvan, pointing to the statue. "So he appeared out of the north in the morning of the world, wild and free. No one could tame him, save Maninaë, the Lost King. In battle his mane was fire and his eyes were lances, and the thunder of his hooves put fear into the hearts of all his enemies. I doubt Annar will see his like again. Innail Valley was his feeding ground, and so this School honors his memory. The horse is the School's emblem." Maerad remembered the brooches that Silvia and Malgorn wore.

"Did he fight the Nameless One?" she asked.

"Yes, he was one of the many. In the final battle he was shot with an evil arrow that poisoned his blood, and he died in agony. One of many griefs. A great mound was lifted for him, and his kind have honor throughout Annar."

Dozens of people were crossing the circle on their way to a stone hall on the opposite side, the Great Hall of Innail. Its double doors, three times as high as a man, stood open wide; warm light spilled out from many tapers, and strains of music ventured into the warm air. Maerad had never seen such a diversity of people: men and women, and not a few children, all richly dressed. Most people wore the token of the horse, but she saw many others: a triple clover leaf, a thistle, a rose, an acorn, three linked stars. A few of the crowd were dark and blue-eyed, as she was, but most were fair like Malgorn. She saw with surprise one man with dark skin, arrayed in gold and red, with a golden, many-rayed sun pinned to his robes. She and Cadvan reached the door at the same time as he did, and the man laughed in recognition and clasped Cadvan's hand.

"Well met, old friend!" he said. "I didn't think you were this far south."

"Saliman!" said Cadvan. "Well met, indeed! What brings you here?"

"News, as always, news. To gather and to tell. I am the messenger boy of fate, driven hither and thither on the whim of events." He turned to Maerad. "But you have not introduced me to your fair companion."

"My companion is fiercer than her looks belie," said Cadvan, winking at Maerad. "I would not trifle with such a warrior, myself. This is Maerad of Pellinor." At the mention of Pellinor, Saliman's eyes widened in amazement. "Maerad, meet an old friend, Saliman of Turbansk, far to the south. But be warned: he is a knave."

"I see Cadvan hasn't changed," said Saliman, grinning. "He only accuses to hide his own faults. Of Pellinor?" he continued, turning to Maerad. "Did one escape? That is brave news indeed. I am the more pleased to meet you, Maerad." He bowed his head formally, and Maerad bowed back, grateful for the formality, which smoothed her awkwardness. She had thought all people were fair-skinned like she was, and felt anew the scope of her ignorance.

"Did you know Pellinor?" she asked.

"I only visited there once. It was a fair place, and it saddened me to hear of its fate. Alas, such stories are more common these days, and so shock the less; Pellinor was the first, after all. I went to Jerr-Niken after it was sacked; it was one of the saddest things I have seen in my life. All that beauty in ruin, so much death." He shook his head. "I think it was not simply the work of banditry, myself. Bandits would not have been so thorough in wanton destruction. It had about it the mark of Darkness."

"You are right, I think," said Cadvan. "There is a singular malice that informs these acts. But now is not the time to speak of these things."

"Perhaps you met my mother," said Maerad boldly. "Her name was Milana."

"Milana?" Saliman smiled. "Yes, I do remember Milana. She was First Bard of the Circle, as I recall. A fine musician. Did she live too?"

"For a while," said Maerad, and she fell silent. A clear vision of her mother stood before her: Milana as she was before the sack of Pellinor—tall, proud, and gentle, smiling before a great host of people with her lyre in her hand, a white stone shining like a star on her forehead. Maerad was pierced by a sudden grief, and briefly forgot all about pretense and masks: the world was too cruel for play. The vision passed as quick as thought, and she blinked, aware again of Saliman.

"I see there are stories here," said Saliman. "But stories of sorrow, and I will not darken this evening by pressing for more."

"No, indeed!" said Cadvan "And now we must find our places. Will you sit with us?"

Saliman's face lit up. "With pleasure!" he said. "I know few here."

Maerad now was looking around the hall in wonder, sorting through her confused first impressions of color and movement and sound. The hall was very high, and its plain white walls were pierced with long arched windows with small diamond-shaped panes like those in Malgorn and Silvia's house, only bigger. Through its center marched two rows of tall black columns carved like trees, whose outspread branches held the arched roof. The black polished stonework at the corners of the room and around the window was cunningly carved with twining patterns of fruits and flowers: vines, apples, pears, lilies, plums, roses, and blossoms that gleamed in the twinkling light of the tapers.

Long tables were set in rows the length of the hall, each covered with rich cloths of a deep red and set with fine blue-glazed bowls and plates, and glass and silver. Huge, finely wrought silver candelabras festooned with high tapers stood on each table, and more candelabras hung from the high ceiling, filling the hall with a soft illumination. Every table was adorned with spring blossoms arranged in curiously blown blue glass bowls, and there were bowls heaped high with fruit and nuts, and fresh breads of different shapes and colors, some herbed, some white, some rich and dark; and fragrant cheeses and pickles; and sliced meats, some freshly roasted, some smoked, some minced with herbs and spices; and there were pies and tarts and preserves and condiments. Maerad had never seen so much food.

At the far end burned a fire in a huge stone hearth, and

before that was a raised dais where sat three musicians, one with a lyre and two others playing instruments Maerad had not seen before, a long wooden flute and a dulcimer. She had never heard such music, an intricate play of complex harmonies and counterpoints, and paused involuntarily, enraptured even more by the music than by the sensual shock of entering the hall, until Cadvan jogged her elbow and started her out of her trance.

"We sit over there," he said, nodding toward a table. By now most people were seated, and only a few stragglers were still at the door. They sat, to Maerad's pleasure, not far from the musicians, and Maerad and Cadvan leaned their instruments against the wall. She saw Malgorn and Silvia on the table nearest the dais, and Silvia smiled and waved.

"They are on the high table, being of the Circle of the School," explained Cadvan. "Now, this wine is very good. I believe Malgorn organized the wines, so I would expect nothing less." He poured for Maerad and Saliman, and then himself. As he did so the music stopped and the musicians left the dais and sat down. A tall woman wearing a plain white robe stood up at the high table, and a hush fell over the hall. Iron-gray hair swept back from her stern face, and in her right hand she bore a long staff, which she stamped on the floor three times. "That's Oron, First Bard of the Circle," Cadvan whispered in Maerad's ear.

"Welcome and thrice welcome," she said, in a voice that effortlessly rang over the whole hall. "To those dear to us and to strangers, to those who return and those who enter this hall for the first time, I drink the welcome cup!"

She lifted a silver goblet high in the air, and everyone stood and held their cups high, Maerad scrambling to copy them.

"Let us drink to fellowship. May the Light bless us all, friend and stranger, and make true our tongues, and truer our hearts, and truest of all our deeds."

"May the Light bless us!" the Bards returned, as with one voice, and then all drank from their cups.

Oron stamped her staff three times again and sat down, and it seemed the formalities were over. The talk began again, rising loudly, and people reached for fruit and bread. Cadvan and Saliman were deep in conversation about affairs to the south, and Maerad felt reluctant to interrupt.

"Are you Maerad of Pellinor?"

"Yes." Maerad turned and faced a small, dark-haired woman with blue eyes.

"I thought you must be, when you came in with Cadvan," said the woman. "I am Helgar, here from Ettinor for the Meet. Forgive my forwardness: I heard of your adventures from Silvia. I must say, you don't look like you've been scrambling over the mountains."

"That's thanks to Silvia," said Maerad. "Where's Ettinor?"

"A week's ride west, and more," she said. "I come with tidings, and to seek counsel, like most here, I think. We live in difficult times. All news, these days, seems to be bad news."

"Yes," said Maerad. Again she felt her lack of knowledge keenly; she had been so cut off from the world, she knew nothing. "What news do you bring?"

"You'll hear at the Council," said Helgar, turning the question. "But tell me about yourself. That's more interesting."

"Oh, I don't think so," said Maerad. "Why is everyone interested in me? I don't know anything. I don't know anything about Meets. What do Bards do?"

Helgar shrugged. "We talk, mainly."

"Yes, but about what?"

"Matters of the Light. What affects the Balance. Matters of policy that affect the Schools. That kind of thing."

"But what is the Balance?" Maerad was beginning to feel a little frustrated with Helgar, whose eyes, she noticed, flickered

past her shoulder, as if she were only half listening. She was eva-
sive in a different way from Cadvan, and something in Maerad
bristled with distrust, although she couldn't have said why.

Helgar cross-examined Maerad about her adventures, but
Maerad answered warily, saying as little as possible about
herself and nothing at all about Cadvan. She had noticed that
Cadvan swiftly checked her interlocutor, before returning to his
huddle with Saliman. Despite this, the dinner passed pleasantly
enough. At last, when Maerad thought she could not, to save
her life, eat another thing, the plates were removed. Then to her
surprise Cadvan stood and strode to the dais, amid clapping.

"Cadvan is accounted a great singer," said Helgar. "I have
not heard him, myself. Still, I'm surprised he has first place."
But Cadvan was speaking.

"By your leave, tonight I sing a lay of the ancient days, in the
first years of the lost kingdom of Lirion, when the Ice Witch yet
troubled the world: *Mercan's Quest*." He struck a chord and
began to chant.

"A strange choice," whispered Helgar as Cadvan began, but
Maerad sat spellbound. She didn't know the lay, which told the
story of Mercan's long search for his love Tirian, stolen by the
minions of the Ice Witch. She was found in the snow halls of the
north and brought home, but Tirian's heart had become a splin-
ter of ice, and she spoke no more. Mercan's despair broke his
heart, and when she saw that he was dying, Tirian's heart
melted with pity. She wept, and a tear fell on Mercan's face; his
eyes opened and life returned to him, and the frost melted in
the land, and blossoms leaped to the starved trees, and the long
winter was broken. Cadvan's voice rose and fell, and as Maerad
listened she saw visions of a fair city, of ships setting sail from a
white harbor under a cold sky bright with stars, and the harsh
shores of a far country. The music fell in Maerad's mind like a
sweet rain, and she sighed with happiness, as if she were the

damp earth sighing out the joy of spring. Then the singing
stopped and there was clapping, and Maerad blinked, released
from the spell, and found to her surprise that her eyelashes
were wet with tears.

The Bards were calling for more, and Cadvan looked at
Maerad and beckoned. She shook her head, appalled, but
Cadvan insisted, and at last, pushed on by Saliman, she reluctantly picked up her lyre and walked to the dais. She stared
blindly out on the crowd and swallowed. Cadvan looked to her
for timing and then struck the chords for *The Lay of Andomian
and Beruldh* that they had sung together, years ago it seemed, in
the glade of Irihel. Maerad responded automatically with the
antiphon. As soon as the first notes rang out, her nerves disappeared; in the sanctuary of music, she could be herself without
fear. They sang only the ballad that introduced the story, and
then left the dais amid cheers.

"Leave them hungry, eh?" said Cadvan as they made their
way back to their seats. "And you acquitted yourself charm-
ingly. You have, I might say, an individual style. I expect it will
be all the rage in Innail now, given the response."

"You were horrible to get me to come up there," said
Maerad hotly. "I wanted the floor to swallow me up."

"Now you have done your duty by your hosts, and need
worry no further," said Cadvan, unperturbed. "And you have
proved yourself to be a true Bard of Pellinor. It will be hard to
dispute that now."

When she reached her seat, Saliman was still clapping.
"Where is this cot?" he said. "I must get some lessons there."

Helgar, Maerad noticed, had left her chair and was talking to some people farther away. As Maerad glanced at her,
she turned away. Saliman noticed. "Your friend distrusts
Southerners," he said.

"Oh," said Maerad. "Why?"

"There are not many like me so far north, so I am a curiosity." Saliman spoke lightly, but Maerad saw a hardness in his eyes and a curl in his lip. "And these are distrustful days."

"Take no notice," said Cadvan. "I saw Helgar was pummeling you hard for information. You did well, I thought, under such impertinence."

"She said she was a friend of Silvia's," Maerad said.

"That's using the term loosely," said Cadvan. "I think she was not happy that you sang so well and pleased so many."

"Do you know her?" asked Maerad.

"Let us say there is a history between us. But you are looking a little pale. This will go on all night, but I dare not keep you up late, or Silvia will have my hide."

And indeed, Silvia was coming to their table, her eyes shining. "Well done, Maerad!" she said. "I am proud of you: your playing honored this hall. Are you tired? You look pale."

Maerad admitted that she was tired, and Cadvan led her out of the hall. It took some time: people were smiling and wishing to talk to both her and Cadvan; but Cadvan politely refused to be caught in conversation. When they reached her chamber, Cadvan said, "I know I made no mistake, bringing you here. You did me honor tonight." He kissed her on the cheek, and Maerad, uncertain how to respond, bowed awkwardly and then slipped hurriedly through her door. She put her lyre carefully on the chest, threw off all her clothes, undid her hair, and fell gratefully into bed.

Despite her tiredness, she didn't fall asleep immediately; her head buzzed with wine and the excitement of the evening. She stared up at the ceiling, and images flickered randomly before her mind's eye: Cadvan singing on the dais, and Helgar's displeasure at Maerad's own playing, and Silvia's pearl-sewn dress, and the soft, lovely bloom of the tapers glancing off the pillars of that beautiful hall . . . but above all, Saliman's dark face, angered by Helgar's rudeness. Maerad's skin prickled with some innate animal wariness when she thought of Helgar. "Not all Bards are to be trusted," Cadvan had told her, and now she thought she knew what he meant.

VIII

THE COUNCIL OF INNAIL

THE next day Maerad rose late after a deep sleep. For the first time since she had escaped Gilman's Cot, she woke without fear of the slave bell. She stretched luxuriously in bed, identifying the sounds that floated through her window: the low murmur of people walking through the courtyard and the chatter of some children playing a skipping game right outside her room, the chuckle of birds, a dog barking, and instruments tuning downstairs. Her belly felt much better; the cramps were still there, but well within bearable limits. Throwing on her robe, she padded down the corridor to the bathroom, where she spent a happy hour splashing around with the oils and unguents she found there. On the way back to her room she met Cadvan in the corridor.

"You smell like you've raided the perfumed gardens of Il Arunedh," he said, grinning. "I was just looking for you. There is a Council this afternoon, at the mid-bell, and you are expected to attend. A High Council, I might add, with only those of the Circles admitted. You should be honored."

"Why do I have to go?" asked Maerad. "I can't tell anybody anything; I don't know anything."

"That's not quite true," said Cadvan. "For one thing, you are a survivor of Pellinor: that is great news among Bards in itself. And if you are to learn the Arts, you must become a Minor Bard. That will be little more than a formality."

"A Minor Bard?"

"It should have happened when you were about seven—it's automatic for anyone with the signs of a Bard," Cadvan said. "But also, given your particular circumstances, the Bards must decide how you should best be taught the ways of the Light."

"It all sounds very complicated," said Maerad subduedly. She quailed inside when Cadvan mentioned things like the Knowing; it seemed like a great cloud over her head, obscure but threatening.

"It is and it isn't," Cadvan answered. "And it's not frightening at all, so stop looking like a rabbit. What is important is that the correct decisions are made now. Normally you would have just been instated as a Minor Bard by the Circle of Innail, which is only six Bards, including Malgorn and Silvia; but this time you're going to be grilled by Bards from about ten Schools. So you can count yourself unlucky there! But for now, it's almost lunchtime, and you should eat," he added. "And then I'll show you the School—that is, if your health permits. You look rosy enough this morning, at any rate."

She quelled the suspicion that Cadvan was making light of the Council to take the edge off her anxiety. She dressed, and after they had eaten he showed her the School. He told her that all the oldest Schools, like Innail, were built along the same design. Innail was laid out like a wheel: at the hub was the Circle of Lanorgrim, and from this radiated four major roads, which were linked by circular roads that were the main thoroughfares. The Circle of Lanorgrim was flanked by the finest buildings in the School. On one side was the Great Hall, and to its left stood a huge library where Maerad saw calligraphers at work, and solemn black-cloaked librarians, the Keepers of the Books, who were held in high honor in the town. To its right was the House of Music, where the Mentors lived and the older children and advanced musicians studied. Opposite the Great

Hall itself stood a tall house that Cadvan told her was Oron's dwelling, and the place where the Council was to be held that afternoon.

The senior Bards and their families and students lived in houses like Malgorn and Silvia's, close to the inner circle. Cadvan told her that about two hundred Bards, including students, lived in Innail. "The number of Bards varies from School to School," he explained. "And so too, the number of those who make up the Circles that govern them: in some places six, in some places nine; in some places there are even two Circles, an Inner, or First, Circle and an Outer, or Second, Circle. Here in Innail there is only one Circle of six Bards."

"Then what do the other Bards do?" asked Maerad, fascinated.

"They all do the work of the School," said Cadvan. "Teaching, writing, making, singing, growing . . . there are so many ways of being a Bard! So that too varies from School to School, depending on the people they live among. Innail, you might have guessed already, is especially famed for its herblore and its cuisine, which are held in high esteem here; but much else goes on besides, in the governance of the Fesse. There is not, in all Annar and the Seven Kingdoms, one School that is the same as another. One day, I hope, you will visit them all and see for yourself. Only this they have in common, or should: that they hold the Balance, and keep to the Light."

They walked now toward the outer rim of the School, where there were hundreds more halls and houses. Here lived the many people who were not Bards but made their living from the School or traded in the town, and there also were the crafters: ironsmiths and saddlers and woodcarvers and masons and jewelers. They visited a big complex of stables, for Bards were much traveled and many kept at least one horse, and

Maerad breathed in the smell with a sharp, surprising pang of nostalgia for her former life; despite her drudgery, she had enjoyed tending the beasts.

Innail was full of trees; its houses were set in pleasant gardens, and there were many little squares, sometimes no larger than a room. You could round a corner and there, unexpectedly, was a little fountain or perhaps a statue and stone bench set on a little square of daisied grass, or an ancient lintel, carved in the semblance of a beautiful woman or a strange sprite or a horse, or the image of Lanorgrim leaping out from a window of colored glass that threw back the sunlight in red or blue or gold. Maerad looked and looked, as if her eyes were starving: every street revealed a new marvel. But although Innail seemed busy and prosperous, she noticed that many houses were shuttered and empty.

"That is the way of so many Schools nowadays," said Cadvan, when she asked why this was so. "There are fewer and fewer Bards. Innail is still a great School, and well loved by the valley men, but it is not what it was in its heyday. In some places it's the Bards' fault: they have become arrogant and distant, and despise the people among whom they live, and no longer care as they should for the life of the land. But elsewhere there are other forces at work that blacken the names of Bards and the arts of Barding, sowing lies to plant suspicion where once was trust, and hatred where once was love. To all our loss."

Maerad, overwhelmed by the beauty of what she was seeing, couldn't imagine how one could hate the ways of the Bards. "It's only ignorance, though, of what Bards do," she said.

"Yes, often," said Cadvan. "That and forgetfulness. It is harder than you think to combat such things, particularly in such times, when malice grows apace and even the Bards are divided. But such is our lot."

* * *

When Maerad entered the Council Hall at Oron's house that afternoon, she flinched as if from a blow; she felt that she had walked into a brilliant blaze of light. It seemed that the room was brightly glowing and humming with a strange music, although she saw no light and heard no sound. Some deeper awareness in her mind prickled to alertness. A contested energy, she thought swiftly, as if many different minds strove in opposing directions to no avail.

She blinked and surveyed the room.

At least three dozen solemn Bards were seated at a round wooden table in a hall of austere loveliness, vaulted with a fan of fluted stone that soared over unadorned white walls. The only sign of luxury was a rich red carpet underneath the table, woven with stylized images of horses running over wide fields. The table itself seemed very ancient, carved of dark wood buffed to a high polish. It bore shapely glass decanters of water and goblets and a huge silver centerpiece of a horse rearing, but nothing else. A fire burned in a hearth on one wall, keeping back the chill of the early year.

The Bards looked as if they had already been conferring for some time. When Maerad and Cadvan entered, the entire table turned and looked at them, and Oron stood up. Maerad's stomach lurched with nerves. She turned to Cadvan for reassurance, but he just smiled at her gravely, neither friendly nor unfriendly. She swallowed and let him guide her to a high-backed chair. She stood waiting behind it, hoping that no one could see that her knees were shaking.

"Welcome to this Council, Cadvan of Lirigon and Maerad," said Oron. She introduced the people around the table, most of whom Cadvan seemed to know already. They nodded as their names were spoken, but said nothing. Maerad tried to keep track of them, but there were so many she forgot all of them almost instantly, although she saw Silvia and Malgorn to her right. Helgar, dressed in blue robes, who was a few seats to her left, flashed her a glance of such undiluted malevolence that Maerad was visibly taken aback. Next to her was a man with a long nose whose face Maerad instantly decided she didn't like. Saliman, sitting nearly opposite, smiled warmly. At last they sat down, but Oron remained standing.

"Out of courtesy to Maerad, who has not come into the Speech, we will use now the tongue of Annar," Oron said, with a slight nod to Maerad. "We've been discussing many things this day," she continued, "many of dark and troubling import, and it is pleasant to at last turn our consideration to something that might be thought of as good news. Here is one who claims to have survived the sack of Pellinor, the first and perhaps so far the most grievous of our losses. One Maerad, daughter of Milana, who, perhaps, some of you remember."

There was a murmur around the table. Some looked at Maerad with lively interest, some with open scepticism.

"It was said none survived," said Helgar. "Why have we heard no news before of this? Can we be sure that this woman is who she says she is?"

"Perhaps Macrad can tell her story herself," said Oron unexpectedly, and she sat down.

There was an uncomfortable pause as Maerad looked down at the table as if she could find some help there. Her mind was completely blank. Cadvan cleared his throat and was clearly about to speak for her when Maerad stood up, almost knocking her chair over in her haste.

"I am Maerad," she said, "as you have already heard."

She paused again. She clenched her hands to stop them from shaking.

"When I was little, I lived with my mother and father in a place like this. I remember it, but not very well. My mother was called Milana and my father was called Dorn. But then men came with swords, and they burned my home and killed my father, and they took me away with my mother. We went to be slaves in Gilman's Cot, near the Landrost in the mountains. My mother died there. I was a slave until Cadvan came there seven days ago and freed me and brought me here."

She stopped, and there was an expectant pause, as if all the Bards expected her to say more. Someone sniggered, but Maerad didn't look up to see who it was.

"Cadvan says I am a Bard and that I have the Gift, but I don't know if that is true," she said at last. "I just wanted to be free from Gilman. I was going to die there, in that place. But now that I'm here I don't know what I want. To be a Bard, maybe. Like my mother."

She stopped, twisting her hands, and then sat down abruptly.

"Thank you, Maerad," said Oron. "Now, perhaps some of us here might like to ask you some questions. I understand this might be painful, but I would appreciate it if you could answer them."

Maerad nodded. She felt foolish and out of place and, glancing over to Helgar, she saw again that hostility in her face. She answered as best she could: how old she was, her age when she was kidnapped, who Gilman was, the circumstances of her slavery, how she escaped. She spoke mechanically, wondering why Cadvan sat so silently beside her. Underneath, however, she had a sense of being shamed, and her pride rebelled. Why should she have to prove who she was? She wasn't pretending to be anybody she was not. At last the long-nosed man sitting next to Helgar said with a sneer, "And how are we to know all this is true? None of this is said to us in the Speech, and we all know that lying is easier that way. An interesting ploy, think you not? Some clever young beggar might seek to enter our ranks in such a way. . . . And in these days, we must be wary of the spies of the Dark. . . ."

"I'm not a beggar!" Maerad forgot her self-consciousness, and was for a moment simply furious. "Why should I lie, anyway? I didn't ask to come here."

"Forgive us our questioning, Maerad," said Oron gently. "It is necessary for us to establish in our own minds who you are. The existence of a survivor of Pellinor is great news among us, and we would not have that news mislead us."

Maerad nodded again, slightly mollified. Strangely, she didn't feel nervous anymore.

"The dates fit," said Saliman. "Pellinor was sacked ten years ago, to this month, and Milana did have a daughter."

"As if the Dark wouldn't make it fit," said the sneering man. "It's a likely story. As if one of the Gift, of the House of Karn itself, could stay hidden for ten years, with no whisper."

"There were none left alive to witness their kidnapping," Saliman said. "And the School was burned to the ground. Who would know?"

"And why does Cadvan say nothing?" the sneering man continued. "I'd like to hear *his* story."

At last Cadvan stirred. "I said nothing, Usted, because I was not invited to speak," he said. "If my word and my Knowing mean anything at all, I can vouch for this girl. I am certain that she is who she says she is."

"That's all very fine, Cadvan," said Usted. "But the best of us can be misled by the arts of the Dark."

Cadvan sighed. "I know it is a time of fear, but equally we should be wary of fearing too much and suspecting where suspicion is pointless. The Dark seeks just such erosions of trust, for they serve its purposes. But I will give you my reasons for not doubting Maerad's story.

"Firstly, I have questioned her, and there is no part of what she says that doesn't square with what is already known. Secondly, I have seen where she was, and her circumstances at Gilman's Cot, and I have no difficulty believing that no news escaped from such a place. Thirdly, there is no doubt she has the Gift, and it is an unusual Gift. You all know the signs. Fourthly, in my own doubt, I asked permission to scry her. She consented freely, and I found in my scrying no walls, no inhibitions, no scarred memory, no trace of any dealings of the Dark. Only confirmation that what she has said is the truth."

"But we all saw her play last night," said Usted, a little sulkily. "Where, if she was in such a benighted place, did she learn such playing? For, even if it's allowed that we all know the signs, we also know that playing doesn't come without teaching."

"There was a Bard at the Cot. He taught her. He didn't, however, teach her anything else. There are serious gaps in her Knowing, which will have to be rectified if things are to proceed. She doesn't even have the Speech."

"His name was Mirlad," said Maerad suddenly. "He was a good man."

"Mirlad?" said a woman who hitherto had sat silently, following the debate. "Maybe I knew him. There was Bard called Mirlad at Desor. He was a talented musician, but went to the bad: dabbled a little in the Dark Arts, and was cast out of the School. I never heard anything more of him."

"He was kind to me," said Maerad sadly. "And anyway, he's dead now."

"It seems that he was sufficiently punished, and perhaps redeemed himself, if indeed he was the same man," said Silvia, who had sat without speaking through the debate so far, a small crease between her eyebrows. "I think he was right to teach Maerad the way he did. Perhaps she would have been endangered if she had been taught the Arts. Myself, I believe Maerad's story."

Oron stood again. "Is everyone here satisfied to the truth of Maerad's tale?"

There was a murmur of assent. Usted and a few others still looked sceptical, but said nothing. Helgar stood up, smiling. There was no sign now of the malevolence that had so disconcerted Maerad on her entrance, unless it was in the honeyed tone of her voice.

"Oron, by your leave, I am not satisfied," she said.

The other Bards turned and looked at her gravely. Only Silvia studied the table, as if she did not trust herself to look at Helgar.

"Yes?" said Oron.

"I must say that this is an amusing fairy story," said Helgar. "An ignorant girl, a slave, and you wish to make her a Bard! By Cadvan's admission she is completely untaught. She probably can't even read. And we know nothing about her. Nothing!" Helgar looked around the table, and her face hardened. "Are we really about to admit her into the high circles of Barding, simply on Cadvan's say-so? Cadvan of Lirigon? How trustworthy is *he*, might I ask? Some of us seem to have longer memories than others. . . . I'm tempted to think it's all a bad joke. Or are Bards these days so credulous? Have we really fallen so low?"

A muttering went around the table, and Maerad felt her temper rising inside her. She quelled the impulse to jump up and shout at Helgar. She looked across at Oron, but her face was unreadable.

"Is that all?" Oron asked.

"I think, with the greatest respect, that it is quite enough," said Helgar. "By common consent, we know this is a time for caution. Do we really want a cuckoo in our midst?"

"I would suggest that an argument based on the traducing of a Bard's character is no argument," said Saliman, with an icy courtesy that was more cutting than any rudeness might have been.

"Any other objections?" said Oron.

A few Bards stood and echoed Helgar's sentiments. One, an older Bard dressed in green robes, went on for some length about the declining standards of Barding. Oron listened gravely, her face still expressionless, and at last silence fell. The Bards sat, their heads bowed, seemingly deep in thought. Maerad bit her lip, suddenly afflicted again with nervousness.

"I have heard all that is said," Oron said at last. "Despite the objections voiced here, I take it on myself to overlook Maerad's lack of Knowing. I believe she is as she says, and I know of no reason to disbelieve Cadvan of Lirigon. I here name her Minor Bard of the School of Pellinor. She is to receive the proper teachings and rectify her ignorance of the Three Arts."

An audible gasp ran around the table. For a split second Helgar looked amazed and furious, but she concealed it swiftly beneath a false smile. All the Bards stood and bowed to Maerad. Uncertainly, she stood also, and bowed back, wondering why Helgar disliked her so much. They sat down again, but Cadvan remained standing.

"I have a request," he said. "I ask permission of the Bards to name me as her sole teacher."

Another frisson went around the table, and a few whispers.

"Why do you seek that?" asked Oron. "It's most unusual."

"It's a little archaic, I know," said Cadvan. "But in these circumstances, I think such an arrangement would best serve Maerad. Although she is almost completely ignorant in some areas, she is very far advanced in others. If she stayed at a School, I think it would not serve her Gift."

"Can you take on such a responsibility?" asked Silvia. "I think your duties are already too onerous, and make you unsuitable. We can find a way of teaching that would suit her."

"Indeed, Silvia, I don't doubt that," said Cadvan. "But

Maerad has a Gift of unusual strength, and to reach her potential she requires tutoring that I am uniquely able to give her."

"But can you balance that with her needs as a young woman? She needs to be protected so her Gift can come into its full flowering. And, Cadvan, you are not one who lives a protected life."

"I know that, Silvia. Nevertheless, I have thought long on this. It was not chance, I believe, that I found Maerad when and how I did. I think she is my responsibility."

"But perhaps you read the chance wrong, and take from happenstance what was never meant to be taken. I think, Oron, that Maerad should stay here and be tutored wisely in the Arts in a place where she can learn properly." She didn't say, *instead of gadding about the wilderness with Cadvan*, but it was clearly meant. Their argument had the air of repetition, as if they had been through these same points before in earlier conversations.

"My heart tells me this is the right path," said Cadvan. "The ways of the Light are often beyond simple readings, and we must not dismiss them out of excessive caution. In our fear, we must not forget the strength that lies in trust."

"But trust is a double-edged blade," argued Silvia. "And can invite unwisdom."

"There was good reason for stopping the old system," interrupted Usted, who was still looking annoyed. "Bad training, the indulgence of spoiled students, and worse. I think it's a ridiculous idea." He snorted derisively. "Since when has Cadvan of Lirigon been known as a great teacher? Not in *my* lifetime." A number of other Bards murmured assent.

"Where could she get better teaching than Innail, anyway?" said the green-robed man, whose name Maerad hadn't caught. "We all know the dangers of badly taught Barding. Young Bards overreaching themselves and causing all sorts of trouble.

Cadvan should know better than anyone. No, no, we can't countenance this."

Saliman had been studying the table. He looked up at this comment. "It does not do to speak ill of one of our greatest Bards," he said quietly. "Either we trust Cadvan of Lirigon, or we do not. I know of no reason why we should not trust one who has spent himself in the service of the Light. I believe we should listen to his promptings."

Maerad was beginning to feel like a cow for sale in a market. She was grateful when Oron turned to her and said, "Maerad, what do you think?"

She surprised herself when she said, without hesitation, "I'd like Cadvan to be my teacher."

"And you say that freely, without coercion?"

"Yes."

There was a long silence. Then Oron said slowly, "I think I will grant this. I feel it is correct, however unusual. There is more at play in this than any of us understand, and in such times we ignore the promptings of such as Cadvan, or the freely given decision of Maerad, at our peril. I say this understanding both the risks and rewards of trust. Do you, then, Cadvan, take on the duties of teacher and swear to work always to the good of Maerad's Gift and the Balance, to teach her the Three Arts to the best of your Knowing, and never to betray her trust in you?"

"I do," said Cadvan.

"This then is witnessed by the Bards of Annar, and is binding until Maerad is made full Bard. Thank you for your time, Maerad of Pellinor and Cadvan of Lirigon. We will meet later."

A number of the Bards who had objected to Cadvan were sitting at the table with their mouths open, and Maerad couldn't help admiring Oron's businesslike dispatch. She realized they were dismissed, and she left the Council Hall with

Cadvan. As soon as the heavy door closed behind them, Cadvan laughed.

"Sorry I didn't warn you, Maerad, but I couldn't. It wasn't going to be easy, but we got what we wanted."

"What *we* wanted?"

"Yes. You had to choose me as teacher, out of your heart, and freely. I saw Oron this morning, and those were her terms. I could not take it on without your consent. Silvia will not be pleased with me. She thinks you should stay here."

Maerad felt a sudden pang of regret. "You mean we can't?"

"*I* can't. And you must come with me, if you are my pupil." Cadvan looked at her swiftly. "I think we should talk. I'm hungry after all that business. We should get something to eat."

Maerad opened her mouth to object that she hadn't agreed to leave Innail, but she realized she was very thirsty and thought she could tax Cadvan on that point later. They went to the buttery in Silvia and Malgorn's house, where Cadvan charmed some wine and bread and cheese from the cooks, and took their food out to the courtyard. It was sunny, and the stone bench was warm. They attacked the bread and cheese with relish.

"It went well today, but mostly by the grace of Oron," said Cadvan. "I saw her early this morning, and we had a long discussion. The first thing was to get you named as Minor Bard of Pellinor, which should have happened when you were about six or seven, as I said—though some were implacably opposed to that, more than I expected. . . . I need to think on what that might mean. Nothing good, I suspect. If they had not agreed, you would have been a Minor Bard of Innail."

"What would have been wrong with that?" asked Maerad. She liked Innail.

"Nothing in itself." Cadvan glanced across at her. "But Pellinor is your birthright, and that is your correct assignation.

And now you *are* Maerad of Pellinor, as witnessed by the Bards of Annar, and that is an important step. The second thing, to make me your teacher, is even more unusual, and a bit more complicated to explain. Once Bards always sat at the feet of Mentors, but that was hundreds of years ago. Now more usually they enter a School and take on the name of the School that teaches them, unless they are born into one. Only if you become the First of the Circle, like Oron, do you take on the name of the School you work in subsequently."

Cadvan took a huge bite of bread and chewed hungrily. "By the Light, I was more worried than I realized about that Council. You helped a lot."

"I did?" said Maerad.

"You were very indignant; no one could have faked that so well. And you weren't trying to please, as one who had designs might," said Cadvan. "It convinced those who might otherwise have doubted your name, more than anything I could have said."

"You mean, I was an idiot."

"No, of course not. I mean that you are who you say you are, and you made that quite obvious. You've made friends, Maerad, without realizing it. Enemies also. I've told you that there are Bards who are not to be trusted. You probably don't realize quite how good a musician you are. Your performance last night impressed many people, and that is no small thing among a hall full of Bards. It went a long way to ensuring your placement. But there are always those who are envious of talent. And worse."

Maerad thought of Helgar and Usted, and some of the others. No, she didn't trust them, even if they were Bards.

"So, why did you want to be my teacher?"

Cadvan was silent for a while. "It's hard to explain, Maerad," he said at last.

"But I'm just going to hang off your tail, slowing you down and causing you trouble. . . ."

"Yes, that's true." Cadvan smiled. "You don't know how true that is, Maerad, nor how dangerous the routes I take really are. Silvia is in many ways quite right. You've already had a taste of how I live, and now you've agreed to come with me, instead of sleeping in comfortable beds and learning the Arts with children half your age."

"Then why?" Maerad felt like poking him. Sometimes getting a straight answer out of Cadvan was like pulling teeth. As if he read her thoughts, Cadvan grinned at her.

"Maerad, my feeling on this is sure. There is a fatedness about our meeting, and I believe our fates are bound together in ways I cannot see. And I was speaking truth when I talked about your Gift. It is unusual, and I can teach you better than anyone I know how to use it properly."

"What if I don't want to go? Can I change my mind?"

"Yes, you can. I would not dissuade you, if you think it is wrong. But you should change it now, before it is too late, and only if you are sure in your heart that it is wrong."

"So, if I'd rather stay here, that's not a good enough excuse?"

"Not if you feel it is right that I am your teacher."

"I don't want to leave Silvia."

Cadvan looked at her sidelong.

"Silvia is a woman who is easy to love," he said. "And she already loves you well."

Maerad felt the rush of grief rise up again inside her. She could say nothing for a minute while she fought it down. At Innail, she had discovered a place she had already begun to think of as a home. Cadvan's easy statement that Silvia loved her made her insides flood with a painful happiness. Leave that? It was too hard; she had only just found it.

"Silvia makes me feel . . . wanted," she said in a muffled voice. "I never felt wanted since, since . . ."

Cadvan said nothing for a long time.

"Maerad," he said at last. "I will tell you a little of what I think and fear. I'm not leaving tomorrow; at the very least I'll wait until the Meet is finished. The more I know about what is happening in Annar, the better; it seems at this time, when things are changing so swiftly, news becomes old very quickly. In this week, you will have time to consider what to do, and whatever you decide, I will not impede. I will not take a pupil who resents or mistrusts the burden I place on her. For it will be a burden, make no mistake.

"My feeling is more than that our meeting is fated. I have certain suspicions about who you might be. Perhaps now is not the time to share them, but it's fair to say that I think the Dark, if it knew of your existence, would be very interested in you. It won't be long before some others start putting one and one together and drawing similar conclusions to mine. The merest suspicion would be enough to ensure your death. Your story has already caused a lot of gossip, and these days even the walls have ears. I could have wished more than one Bard absent from that Council. News of your placement will spread fast; there is no stopping that now. I think if you stay here, you will be in more danger than if you come with me, who can protect you better than any other outside Norloch. And I fear that perhaps you could draw danger here, where none might otherwise be."

"Why would the Dark be interested in me?"

"Because you are Maerad of Pellinor."

"But that's no reason."

Cadvan shrugged, and Maerad gave up; obviously Cadvan would tell her more in his own good time.

"What if you're wrong about me?"

"If I am, then at the worst I will have the most brilliant pupil in Annar, and all credit to me," he said. "But I am not often wrong."

"Then where will we go?"

"To Norloch, as I thought when we first met. The High Seat of the Light in Annar. I must go there, and it seems to me that you must, too. There is the business of your instatement and Naming, and on those questions I dearly wish for the advice of my old teacher, Nelac of Lirigon. And in any case, I must report to the First Circle there."

They sat in silence for a while, following their own thoughts. Maerad thought about Norloch, and a sense of excitement began to stir in her. The High Seat of the Light! Like Innail, she imagined, only more so: more wondrous, more pure. Then she wondered again why it was she felt so rapidly at ease in Innail. It was more than Silvia's care for her, more than the beauty around her. Perhaps it was her childhood memories lighting up inside her, a sense of home. . . . And now, somehow, she had agreed to leave it, just as the door had opened, promising delight and friendship, for what Cadvan said frankly would be a life of hardship. Perhaps it's all too much, all this looking at me, she thought wearily, all these curious eyes. She stole a look at Cadvan. She had never met anyone so solitary—well, she hadn't met many people at all, truth be told—but she suspected that Cadvan didn't like eyes looking, either. Not out of wanting to conceal anything, but because somehow it hurt, as if it bruised his soul. Yes, she would leave Innail, although she already loved it, and she would follow Cadvan to Norloch; she knew that was decided, although she didn't really know why.

"I'll think about it," Maerad said at last. She suddenly felt crushingly tired. "But right now, I think I'd like to go for a rest. I might as well use these beds while I can!"

Cadvan gave her one of his sudden, brilliant smiles.

"You might as well," he answered. He watched her go, and then sat alone in the courtyard for a long time, his face dark with thought.

That night Maerad dreamed. She was taken up to a great height over a wide green landscape she knew was the land of Annar. In the distance a sinking sun lit up the eastern mountains and flamed the tall white battlements of a great city in the west, and a wide river ran molten gold between the mountains and the city. As she watched, a black mist crept over the land, obscuring the bright water, and a cold dread gripped her heart. Faintly she heard a sound as of many people weeping. Then came a voice saying, "Look to the north," and she looked, but the mist obscured her view, and she could see nothing. The dream fragmented into a troubled sleep full of dark vague shapes, which after a time resolved into one shape, a shadow on which she couldn't fix her eye; every time she turned to look at it, it dissolved into smoke. It seemed to her vitally urgent that she see it before it saw her, and in rising panic she turned and turned. She felt as if it were already reaching for her, that beyond her perception malignant hands reached out of the shadow toward her, closer and closer. Then she heard a voice speaking a language she couldn't understand. It was a voice she had never heard before, and it was cold and lifeless, as if it spoke from lips long dead. Her heart stopped with fear, and suddenly she was awake, sweating and trembling. She sat up in bed and looked wildly around her, until she saw the remains of the fire glowing in the grate and remembered where she was. She couldn't shake off the dream, and at last, to rid herself of the feeling of dread, got out of bed and picked up her lyre. As soon as she touched it she felt reassured, and climbing back into her bed clutching it, she soon fell asleep again. By morning the dream had vanished, but the new day was stained with a nebulous fear.

IX

DERNHIL OF GENT

FOR the next few days, Maerad didn't see much of her new teacher. Cadvan knocked on her door very early the day after the Council, and, after waiting impatiently for her to dress, dragged her through Innail to the Library at the Circle of Lanorgrim. There they walked as fast as Maerad could go, through labyrinthine corridors to a tiny room that seemed almost to be constructed of books, where Cadvan introduced her to a dark-haired Bard she remembered vaguely from the Council the day before. "This is Dernhil of Gent, Librarian of the Circle," he said brusquely. "Dernhil, Maerad of Pellinor. Dernhil has kindly offered to teach you the basics of script, though what you can learn in less than a week escapes me. Now, I've got to hurry." And he ran out of the door.

Maerad stood in front of Dernhil, catching her breath. Dernhil seemed younger than Cadvan, although Maerad already knew a Bard's age was hard to guess. He was tall and slender, and his face was calm and intelligent, with quick, mobile eyes that now were filled with quiet amusement. He was dressed in the black robes that she had seen the Librarians wearing the day before, slung carelessly over blue breeches and a tunic that looked as if they were woven of silk. To gain time, she looked around the chamber.

Dernhil's room contained a huge, ornately carved desk that was almost covered with tottering piles of books, lengths of parchment, and drifts of paper. In the center was a scroll of parchment, which was clearly half-finished: it was covered with a beautiful flowing script, written in black ink. Next to it was an inkwell made of polished black stone, and next to that an intricately fashioned gilt lamp that cast a circle of warm light over the desk, picking up the azure silk that covered the two chairs beside it. One was clearly where Dernhil sat; the other was burdened with another tottering pile of books.

Maerad sniffed the faint scent of ink with pleasure; it reminded her of something, although she couldn't trace the memory. Despite the mess, the room didn't give an impression of shabbiness so much as chaotically ordered industry. The early light from a high window streamed across the walls, picking out the colors of curious instruments and ornaments on the shelves lining them and highlighting the gilt letters on the spines of rows and rows of books. A small grate held a fire. Maerad thought it the most interesting room she had ever seen.

"Well, now," said Dernhil. "A brilliant young musician who can't read or write, and a week to teach you. What a conundrum! Where shall we begin?" He looked at Maerad as if she could tell him the answer. She looked down, feeling rebuked. "There is no shame in not knowing something," he said gently. "The shame is in not being willing to learn. I can teach you the letters of the Speech, invented by Nelsor in Afinil long ago. That will serve you best, I think, for it is the script most used by Bards. But there are many others, used by other peoples, which it would be an injury not to teach you. I haven't the time, alas. A year would cover the introduction, if you were quick."

He surveyed his silent pupil as if judging her facility. Then he moved all the books off his spare chair, dumping them unceremoniously onto the floor, and drew it up to the desk. He cleared a space on the desk, putting more books on the floor, and invited Maerad with an inquiring tilt of his head to sit next to him. Then he placed two pieces of paper in front of them and handed Maerad a gold pen. It had a long shaft carved with the semblance of a strange flying snake, which wound around the pen and rested its head just above the fine metal nib. Maerad looked at it curiously.

"It's for writing, not for staring at," said Dernhil, and he showed her how to hold it. It felt strangely heavy in her hand. Then he started writing down letters, explaining what they meant and how they formed words.

Maerad couldn't use the pen at all at first, but she gritted her teeth and persisted. As the lesson progressed, she began to see how writing worked, and a ball of excitement began to form in the pit of her stomach. Her memory was trained by years of learning songs and music by heart, and Dernhil was a patient and gentle teacher. Despite her clumsiness, Maerad had an odd feeling, as if an ancient memory stirred in her fingers, that they traced movements familiar to her, if long disused. Dernhil was astonished by how quickly she began to shape letters and then words. By the end of the lesson, she had written her first sentence.

"Time to stop," said Dernhil, and Maerad gave a gasp of disappointment. He regarded her with amusement. "If only all my pupils were so keen," he said. "You've done extraordinarily well for your first lesson, Maerad, but you will be the better for the pause. I would never have guessed you would have come this far."

"But it's such fun!" she said. "I used to wonder if you could do something like this: I mean, write things down, so you could remember them. Gilman kept lists of his sheep and cows and chickens and things; he just marked them with lines and pictures on stuff made of bark, so he knew if any were stolen or eaten. Maybe they taught me some writing at Pellinor, I can't remember. . . . There's so much I've forgotten. But this is amazing! And the script is so beautiful. Well," she added, looking dubiously at her own writing, "it's beautiful when *you* write it down."

"It's just practice," Dernhil said. "A year here, and you'd be scripting like an old Librarian." He looked at Maerad again, and this time there was a hint of trouble in his gaze, a faltering. "What is in Cadvan's mind? That man's a mystery to me, though he has his own reasons. Anyway, you're to have other lessons this afternoon. Cadvan's worked out a schedule for you, but since you can't read it, I'll show you where to go."

He rummaged through his shelves until he found an exquisite little leather-bound book, which he gave to Maerad. "This is for tonight," he said. "I have shown you how to sound the letters. There are some simple poems in here, which I want you to try to read before tomorrow, if you're not too tired. One or two, mind, not the whole collection."

Maerad took the book as if it were a sacred object and opened it carefully. The pages were heavy, dry parchment and made a very faint rustling. She paused at a page that had a vivid picture of bees around a hive, and behind it a landscape of rivers and valleys and, in the distance, snow-capped mountains. The border of the page was a broad frame made of gold leaf, on which the painter seemed to have artlessly scattered some wildflowers: daisies and pinks and others Maerad couldn't recognize. In each corner was a tiny painting that revealed more details the more she looked: a man playing a dulcimer in one, in another a bear lying asleep under a tree, in the third a woman studying what seemed to be a globe of crystal, and in the bottom right-hand corner two people seated at a table, drinking something golden out of a glass. On the opposite page, framed in the same way, was the poem, scripted in black and red letters. She spelled out the title: *The Hive*.

Maerad was speechless. She glanced up at Dernhil, her eyes shining. He seemed embarrassed by her frank joy, and covered it by giving her some sheets of paper and a pen and rummaging through his bookshelves again until he found a small satchel in which she could carry everything. "You can practice writing as well. Try copying a poem. Now, time to go," he said briskly. "I'm late for my next lesson. I'll see you at the same time, the same place, tomorrow."

Maerad's lesson that afternoon was of an entirely different hue: she was being taught horse riding and swordcraft. Dernhil took her to her instructor, a stern-looking man called Indik, with a scar across his cheek which drew the skin tightly under his right eye, making his face curiously expressionless. Maerad felt slightly frightened of him, and unlike Dernhil, he made no effort to make her feel at ease. She was taken first to the smiths, where she was fitted with a small sword, scabbard, helm, and a light coat of mail, so finely forged it almost seemed like heavy cloth. Next she was taken to the stables, where Indik picked out a gray roan mare. "Her name is Imi," he told her. "She's a good mare, prone to be fiery, but loyal and kind. And her breed is fast and sturdy. You'll need a tough mount." Maerad knew enough about horses to judge that Indik had picked exceptionally well; Imi was graceful and strong, and not too big for her. "This horse is now yours," he said. "So you must know how to care for her."

"Mine?" said Maerad in amazement. "How?"

"Cadvan's arrangement. Now, you know how to saddle a horse?"

Maerad's ignorance of animals wasn't nearly as woeful as it was of books, and after she had saddled and mounted Imi, Indik looked at her with an almost approving eye. He mounted his own horse, a large bay called Harafel, and they rode to a yard, where Indik put her through some paces, making her ride with her arms crossed and no stirrups, and running through some commands. Maerad rode mainly by balance which, as Indik acidly pointed out, would do no good if a troop of bandits suddenly appeared out of the bushes and scared the life out of her; but despite all his shouting, he seemed pleased when they finished.

"You'll do fine," he said. "A few months of training, and you'd make a good rider. You know enough to get around. It would be easier if you had the Speech, of course, but that will take care of itself."

They rode back to the stables, and Maerad dismounted and unsaddled Imi. Then Indik asked her to groom the horse and clean her hooves, watching her critically. "You'll need a traveling kit, of course," he said, when she'd finished and loosed the mare into her stable. "But luckily you're not a complete dolt. Two hours' ride every day, to get you fit, and that's all we can manage this time."

Then it was time for swordcraft. This was a different matter altogether, and Indik didn't bother to conceal his impatience. "Mistress Maerad," he said through clenched teeth, as she dropped her sword yet again, "if you do not manage even to hold on to your weapon, you're dog meat. Kindly get that through your thick head. Now, we'll start again."

An hour of sword practice left Maerad dripping with sweat—Indik insisted she wear her mail and helm—and feeling completely inadequate. She had learned, however, how to hold a sword both one- and two-handed, and that flailing wildly was a bad idea. "Intelligence," Indik kept saying. "Intelligence is the key. You're not strong enough to be stupid. *Think!*"

He gave the powerful impression that he thought Maerad would last about a mile out of Innail. When he finally ended the lesson, he leaned on his sword. "*One* hour's riding, I think, and an extra hour of swordcraft. A week might make a difference. By the Light, I hope it does. At the moment my advice is to hide behind Cadvan if any trouble occurs, and don't draw the sword at all. You're just a liability." Then he dismissed her to disconsolately find her own way back to her room.

In the refuge of her chamber she tiredly took off her mail and helm and laid her sword against the chest, where she eyed it doubtfully. It had a simple silver scabbard chased with the design of a snake wound around a tree, with a gleaming red stone for its eye; she had liked the sword well enough when Indik had chosen it for her, but now she wasn't so sure. Her body ached with weariness in all sorts of unexpected places, and after sitting on her bed for a few minutes staring exhaustedly at the wall, she decided to go to the bathroom. Once there, the bath steaming with perfumed oils, she slid in with a sigh and watched the steam coil upward, thinking of absolutely nothing at all. At last she drew herself out, feeling refreshed, and padded back on bare feet to her room, where she dressed in clean clothes and drew her lyre out of the chest. She played it to console herself, and soon was so absorbed that when there was a knock at her door she jumped.

"Cadvan!" she said, letting him in.

"Yes, indeed," he said. He looked a little grim. "How are your lessons?"

"Oh, all right, I suppose. I like Dernhil; he gave me this book—look—to read tonight. But I don't think Indik likes me much."

"It's not his business to like you. He's to teach you what he can, which he will, as he is a gifted teacher and a great swordsman. He does you great honor agreeing to teach you at all."

"I didn't mean . . ."

"The horse is to your liking? And this is your sword?"

"Imi is beautiful; I've never ridden such a fine horse," said Maerad, casting a look of dislike at the sword. "Indik says I'm a liability with the sword and should just hide behind you."

Cadvan laughed, losing his look of grimness. "It is your first day, after all, and he's not used to beginners. But if anyone can teach you to be handy with a sword in a week, he can. You won't learn any great skill, mind, but it's good to know how to hold it, and even an inelegant slash well placed is help in a tight corner.

But this is your sword now: you should give it a name." He took it out of its sheath and examined it closely. "It's actually very fine. He's done you proud." He handed it to her, hilt first.

"A name?" stammered Maerad, taking it. "Why? What sort of name?"

"I asked that you be given a well-forged blade. It's not just a dirk hammered out in some rustic blacksmith's forge, and it deserves the honor. Well . . ." Cadvan considered for a moment. "What about Irigan? Iceblade, in the Speech. It has a chill sheen."

"Irigan," said Maerad, trying it on her tongue. "Yes, that sounds all right. Irigan." She was beginning to feel overwhelmed by owning things; she had never possessed more than the clothes on her back, a pair of boots, and her lyre. Suddenly she had a horse and a sword, like a rich person.

"Silvia's arranging traveling gear and a pack," Cadvan said. "They should be ready tomorrow." He picked up the book Dernhil had lent Maerad and laughed.

"What's funny?" she asked.

"It's Dernhil's own book. His poems. Read it carefully; Dernhil is a great poet, one of the best Annar has seen. I remember when we first met. . . ." He flipped the pages, idly looking through the poems, and fell silent.

"Remember what?" asked Maerad.

Cadvan grinned. "I was young and vain, and I rather fancied myself as a poet then. He was visiting Lirigon for some reason I forget, and he was already famous. He was very young, very talented. . . . I challenged him to a duel, a competition where we both had to improvise poems. I made such a fuss about it, practically the whole School was there."

"And what happened?"

"I lost. For obvious reasons, if you read this book."

Maerad felt a bit taken aback. How was she to know that Dernhil was famous? "But he said they were simple poems."

"So they seem. But what appears simple is often the hardest to understand. Anyway," he continued, "that's not what I came here to say. We are invited to dinner with Malgorn and Silvia tonight, at the next bell. Silvia wants to know how you are, and how you are finding your teaching. She still disapproves of me mightily, but will overlook it for your sake. There's a little time beforehand. Perhaps we could walk to the courtyard?"

"I'm supposed to practice reading tonight," Maerad said uncertainly.

"Dernhil will understand if you can't manage it. I expect you're very tired. In the meantime, you and I should take the air."

Maerad glanced curiously at Cadvan as they made their way to the courtyard in the balmy evening air. Perhaps it was just the growing darkness, which threw shadows across his face; but it seemed to her that he looked strained and even, perhaps, a little upset, although with Cadvan it was hard to tell. He was certainly hurrying her along. They sat down on the bench and Cadvan took a deep breath in and out, as if he were expelling something other than air, and looked up at the sky. One by one, the stars were beginning to open.

"It's peaceful here," he said, and was silent for a few moments, listening to the water trickling from the fountain into the pond and the chirping of birds settling to sleep in the eaves. "Maerad, time is very pressing over the next few days. I've arranged some basic lessons so you can learn at least something of the things you need to know. I wish with all my heart we could stay a few months, so you could get some proper grounding, but we can't. If I could, I'd be off tomorrow."

"Do we have to go so soon?" Maerad asked.

"Yes, the sooner the better. I find myself chafing at this delay, although it can't be helped. I have business in Norloch, and nothing can be done or decided about you until we get there. It's a long journey, and I wish you were better prepared. But need makes the naked man run, as they say." He paused. "I've spent my time better than today, arguing with Bards. It's wearisome and wasteful."

"So it's not going well?" Maerad studied Cadvan covertly; what was bothering him?

"No," he said shortly. It seemed he was going to say nothing else, but then abruptly he added, "Maerad, there is a mort of gossip about my request to be your sole teacher. I thought I should warn you."

"Gossip?"

"I seem to have scandalized half of Annar. Even Malgorn is dubious. They all think I've lost my head over a pretty face." He gestured impatiently. "I guess that if the mean-minded speak ill, perhaps it's all to the good: it conceals any other purpose. But I confess I have no patience with such pettiness; I feel smirched. . . ."

Maerad was staring at him with bafflement, but then she suddenly grasped what Cadvan was saying. "Oh!" she gasped, and then she blushed scarlet.

"It doesn't matter, Maerad," Cadvan said, giving her a satirical look. "It just annoys me; Bards should be above such trivial rumor. What matters is that you do your lessons as well as you can over the next few days and don't let any malicious comments upset your studies. I think you are talented; it's certainly what Dernhil told me, and Indik thought so, even if he wouldn't tell you. I must attend the Councils; the more news I hear the better, especially if we are traveling by hidden paths. I won't leave before it ends. In any case, if we did leave earlier, secrecy would be impossible. So just trust me for the moment; things will be clearer once we leave here. Don't think I've suddenly deserted you!"

"All right. It's fun studying anyway," Maerad said. She looked straight at Cadvan. "I just wish I knew what is really happening. There's so much I don't know, and all this fuss about me, and it all seems very strange."

"I *will* tell you, or at least as much as I know," said Cadvan. "I'm sorry to be so at sixes and sevens, and in such a rush. It needs time, for partly telling is no telling at all. There'll be plenty of time on our journey."

There was a short silence. "I had a strange dream last night," Maerad said abruptly. "I've been thinking about it all day."

Cadvan was leaning back, staring into the sky. "We all have strange dreams," he said.

"Yes, but this was . . . It was odd, Cadvan, not like any dream I've had before. It felt, it felt . . ." Maerad gestured help-lessly and fell silent.

"Well, what was it, then?" Cadvan sat up and gazed at her attentively.

Slowly, trying to find the right words, Maerad told him of her dream. As she spoke on, Cadvan became very still, listening more and more intently. When she had finished, he said noth-ing for a while.

"How I wish you had the Speech!" he said at last. "I think it must have been the Speech you heard there, that tongue you did not understand. At least, it is likely."

"What do you think?" asked Maerad curiously.

"Dreams are strange messengers, Maerad," Cadvan answered. "Some say they come from beyond the Gates, where all that is and has been and shall be is known, for time does not exist there. But we all have different types of dreams, for different purposes."

"So what do you think mine is?"

Cadvan hesitated. "I can't be sure. But I think it was a foredream, a dream telling of what is to come."

Maerad shuddered. "I hope not," she said. "It was horrible. But why would I have a foredream? I've never had one before."

"It's a Gift of some Bards. Not many. Though a good many Pellinor Bards were foredreamers and seers. Lanorgil of Pellinor was probably the most famous, but there have been a few others."

"Do you have foredreams?"

"No," said Cadvan. "Though like all Bards I have a measure of foresight. But foredreams are perilous riddles to unravel; there are many stories of those who seek to avoid their prophecies, only to bring about what they most fear. But this seems to send both warning and hope. *Look to the North!*" He stooped to pluck a blade of grass and chewed it thoughtfully. "What could that mean?"

Maerad shrugged her shoulders. "I don't know," she answered. "That's why I asked you."

"It makes me more certain that I am right to think the Dark would pursue you, if they knew of you," he said. "Perhaps news has reached them already."

With a flash of perception, Maerad realized that Cadvan's complaint about gossip was not the whole reason for his air of strain. She had a uneasy sense, like a boatman who has floated unawares into the deep ocean, of suddenly discovering opaque depths sliding beneath her feet, where she expected to see sunny shallows.

Cadvan stood up, throwing away the leaf of grass. "Now I chafe the more at lost days! But, for the moment, we are stuck here." He checked the sky. "It's almost time for the bell," he said. "We should go in."

X

LEAVETAKING

THE next few days were taken up with the same routine: Dernhil in the morning and grimly comic sessions with Indik every afternoon, which ended with Maerad's jaw jutting with mutiny, when she wasn't on the verge of tears. Indik confined himself to pitiless witticisms on her martial stupidity, although by the third day Maerad no longer dropped her sword when she tried to parry his thrusts, and once almost made it through his defense. On that occasion, he merely doubled his sarcasm, and Maerad's lips set in a grim line. She wished she had the swordcraft to make a fool of him, but he could disarm her as easily as if she were a five-year-old child. Although she always enjoyed her hour's ride on Imi, Maerad much preferred her mornings with Dernhil, which were opening a new and exciting world.

Dernhil was delighted by her quickness; within a few days she could read a short passage or poem with relative ease. It was as if, he said, he were merely reminding her of something she had forgotten, rather than teaching her something she didn't know. He was a very different teacher from Mirlad: not nearly so stern, and more apt to encourage with praise. Maerad blossomed under his tutelage. She would look around his study and sigh. So many books in so many languages, and she could scarce read the smallest of them!

"Maybe I can come back, after we get to Norloch, and learn more," she suggested hungrily to Dernhil the next day. "There's so much I don't know. . . ."

Dernhil looked up from some work he was correcting. "That would be a happy chance," he said. "If you did, I would love to teach you." He smiled, but there was something in the smile that made Maerad's heart constrict; his eyes lingered on her face. . . . She put her head down and drove away the feeling with work.

She didn't see Cadvan at all. In the evenings she ate with Silvia and Malgorn, or in the Hall with the other students, who looked at her either askance or with exaggerated awe. Sometimes she spent an hour or so watching the gis players at the table in the corner of the Hall. She was intrigued by the complex beauty of the game, which was played with black and white counters on a hexagonal table of many squares, but she could never work out the rules. Gis was, she was told, a lifetime's study: at once a game of tactical intelligence and aesthetic judgment. Maerad followed the strange patterns the counters made, how they evolved and vanished in the flow of the game, with fascinated incomprehension.

There was always music, but Maerad didn't play again for an audience, only alone in her room at night, when she needed to. She didn't feel lonely; she was too busy, and at night simply too exhausted. Within two days she had the odd feeling that she had lived there always. The School no longer seemed grand or strange to her, and she wondered at times at how easily she had slipped into this life, as into familiar clothes.

On the second day the clear spring weather broke, and for three days after that it rained almost continuously. Maerad's swordcraft lessons moved to an impressive indoor arena obviously built for this purpose, but the riding continued without concession to the weather. Maerad sometimes felt, wiping her wet hair out of her eyes, that she hated Indik, although underneath her resentment she realized his sternness was impersonal and, in a way, a quality to respect. The lessons did strengthen her determination to learn swordskills, if only to scotch the smug smile that appeared on Indik's face whenever she made a mistake. "That was your throat, young lady," he'd say with satisfaction. "You might as well lie down and offer me your neck, for all the use *that* would be." And Maerad, sweating underneath her helm, would bare her teeth, quietly cursing him as he walked back to battle position. "Don't think I can't hear that!" Indik would say, without turning around. "I can, see. Curses won't do any good if your swordwork's flabby. Now, again!"

Her relationship with Dernhil was quite different, and deepened into friendship. At the end of their lesson on the fourth morning, Dernhil pushed his hair out of his eyes and asked if she was busy that evening. "No," she answered; she was to dine in the Hall that night.

"Would you like to dine with me, then?" he asked. "I could show you some of those books I was telling you about. . . ."

"I'd love to!" Maerad said warmly. She dreaded dining in the Hall; she still couldn't cope very well with crowds.

After the chaos of his study, Dernhil's rooms were surprisingly neat. They were in much the same style as the rooms in Silvia and Malgorn's house, finely furnished with stenciled decorations on warm yellow walls. The dining room was filled with curious objects he had collected on his travels: intricate ivory carvings from the Suderain and silk hangings made by the weavers of Thorold, statuettes of alabaster by unknown Annaren artisans, a huge crystal sphere, strange and intricate metal lamps. . . . The walls, of course, were lined with books.

He served a simple and delicious meal: grilled cuts of spiced meat with tender spring vegetables, and cheeses, nuts, and wine. Then they sprawled on the comfortable cushioned chairs in front of the fire, sipping wine, and Dernhil brought down book after book, pointing out details of the scripting and illumination and reading her poems, and they chatted amiably about many things. Maerad asked him about the duel with Cadvan. Dernhil threw back his head and laughed.

"You should have seen Cadvan then!" he said fondly. "That was before . . . well, when he was younger. He was handsome, charismatic, already a Mage of great power—everyone said he was sure to be First Bard one day, even perhaps First Bard of Norloch—and he was no mean poet, either."

"But not as good as you."

"No," said Dernhil, throwing her an amused look. There was no vanity in his statement. "And Cadvan couldn't bear to play second fiddle. Of course I won. He was furious."

Maerad hadn't missed that Dernhil had edited what he was going to say. "What happened to Cadvan?" she asked curiously. "I mean, why didn't he become First Bard?"

Dernhil's face darkened with sadness. "I think Cadvan himself should tell you that," he said at last. "As no doubt he will, one day. He has indeed become a great Bard. Few can match him. But life seldom turns out as one would expect when one is young and full of hope." There was a short silence, and then he turned to Maerad. "Forgive me for asking such a personal question, but are you and Cadvan . . . are you lovers?"

Maerad blushed, thinking of the gossip Cadvan had mentioned. "No," she mumbled. "No, nothing like that." She looked up and caught Dernhil's unguarded glance. In his eyes was an unvoiced invitation, a tender supplication, something more than admiration; but Maerad went cold. Her life had taught her that male desire meant only violence, and an instinctive, primitive fear overwhelmed any other response. She scrambled to her feet in a sudden panic, her heart pounding.

"I should go," she said. "I must be up early tomorrow."

"Yes," said Dernhil. He stood up also, sighing. "Well, in the morning, then."

"Yes," said Maerad.

She glanced again at Dernhil, but that disturbing look was gone. She took his proffered hand and bowed her head, and left swiftly.

On the sixth day of her lessons, Dernhil told her the following day was a feast day and she need not show up. By now she was able to read her way haltingly through the book of poems, and Dernhil gave it to her. "Come and say good-bye before you go," he said.

"I will," said Maerad, clutching the book. "And thank you, thank you so much." All the things she wanted to say, how a shining new world had opened for her under Dernhil's gentle tutoring, how it filled her with joy and excitement, gathered in her throat and choked her.

Dernhil cleared his throat. "I've enjoyed teaching you," he said. "Cadvan will be able to build on what you've already learned. You can help yourself, also, by practicing reading." He paused. "There are so many things to show you. All the great texts of Annar and the Seven Kingdoms, the stories and songs that make up the Knowing. And that's just the beginning. It seems criminal not to teach them to you." He shook his head regretfully. "You'd make an excellent scholar, with your aptitude and application. All it would take is time."

"I suppose it's not to be," said Maerad. "And we cannot always choose our own paths."

Dernhil looked slightly startled. "No, I suppose not," he said. There was a short, slightly uncomfortable silence. "Well, don't forget to look in before you go." He sat down at his desk, and Maerad realized she was dismissed.

Indik was more abrupt. "At least you can hold your sword," he said. "Which is something. More, I can't say. You'll just have to practice, and hope that you're lucky."

Maerad stared back at him expressionlessly. She didn't feel

like thanking him, although she felt she should. To her surprise, Indik chuckled.

"Nevertheless, a brave heart might prevail where skill is wanting," he said. "Here, give me your sword." She handed it over. "What did you name it? Irigan? A good name . . ." He drew it and inspected it closely. "A fine weapon." He breathed on the blade and then rubbed the condensation in slowly with his fingers, speaking low as he did, so that Maerad couldn't hear the words. Then he sheathed it again and gave it back.

"A charm to aid accuracy, and check breakage or harm," he said. "It will last as long as the blade does. It might help."

Maerad was surprised by a sudden flood of gratitude. She looked up into Indik's eyes, and for the first time saw there an unexpected kindness. To the astonishment of both of them, she flung her arms around Indik's neck and kissed him on his scarred cheek.

"Thanks for putting up with me," she said. "I'll do my best not to disgrace you!"

"You can only do your best," he said gruffly. "Now, off you go."

She bumped into Cadvan at the Street of Makers. He was looking drawn, but smiled when he saw her. "Hail, young warrior maiden!" he said.

Maerad had forgotten she was still wearing her mail, and involuntarily looked down. "Just call me Indik's Despair," she said. "Though he allowed that I might take my sword out if attacked, rather than just run away."

"Then you've passed with flying colors," said Cadvan, laughing. "I've already spoken with Dernhil; he desperately wants you to stay and finish your studies. Not for entirely unmixed reasons, I think somehow. He's clearly quite struck with you."

"Oh, rubbish," said Maerad. "Stop teasing, Cadvan. Although he did give me his book."

"A definite sign of favor," Cadvan countered lightly, but he looked grave again. "But he has a point. As does Silvia. It's not fair to drag you away from this, which should be yours by right."

"Are you having doubts?" Maerad scanned his face, as they fell into step together.

"No. But I'm wondering if you are."

"No," said Maerad slowly. "No, I feel surer. I don't know why, because I really love it here, and I've loved learning with Dernhil, and even Indik. He charmed my sword today, you know."

"Did he?" said Cadvan in surprise. "I was going to do that myself, but he could spell it better than I ever could. It's his special skill, and people travel far to ask him that favor. Sometimes he won't, no matter what they offer him. He's a keen judge of souls, and will help no dark purpose. I'm glad you have no doubts, though. It bears on me that we have little time."

They walked for a while in silence, Maerad turning over Cadvan's words. In the past few days she had forgotten all the dark forebodings of their conversation in the courtyard, and now her feeling of dread returned.

"I want to leave tomorrow night," said Cadvan. "Only the Bards of the Circle here know for certain that we are leaving so soon, and secrets are safe with all of them. The Leavetaking Feast is tomorrow night, and I think we should attend and leave early, so that none will follow us. Otherwise we'll be riding out with close to a hundred Bards, which is not a way to keep close counsel, or be forced to wait another week, which I dislike."

Maerad sensed that, as much as anything else, Cadvan

itched to be free of the demands of society. She felt a little of the same urge. However private she kept herself, there were always clutches of people whispering as she passed or pointing her out in the street, and she didn't like her celebrity; it puzzled and disturbed her. All the same, she felt a pang of regret.

"Dernhil wanted me to say good-bye before I left," she said.

"You'll have time tomorrow," Cadvan said. "I'll come tonight and check your pack; I'm dining with Silvia and Malgorn." He pressed her hand in farewell and hurried off down another street. Maerad thoughtfully made her way home.

Back in her room after a long bath, she placed all her new possessions on her bed. She now owned a small book of poems, a helm, a sword, a suit of mail, a satchel, a pen, and a pack Silvia had given her that she hadn't even had time to open. It was made of black leather, soft but surprisingly tough, and had curious buckles and straps, which she later found meant it could be carried on her back or slung from a saddle. Inside was a leather water bottle, a bottle of medhyl, a stoppered blue vial of the elixir Silvia had used to stay her period pains, and two sets of clothes: soft leather trousers and warm woolen shirts and jerkins, well-made and practical, cunningly woven so they took up very little space when folded. Silvia had also packed some underclothes made of thick silk. Maerad had just opened a package containing the same tough-looking biscuit she remembered eating on her way to Innail when Cadvan knocked and entered.

"Excellent," he said, as she showed him the contents of her pack. "And enough room for your own treasures. I too have a present for you." He handed her a leather cover for her lyre, to protect it as she traveled. It was tooled with a design of flowers like those in the music room downstairs, and in the center was a lily shaped like a slender trumpet, picked out in gilt and silver.

"It's the sign of Pellinor," he said. "You should have a brooch, but I didn't have time to get one made."

Maerad sat down on the bed, holding the leather cover in her hands. She felt more overwhelmed by this gift than anything she had yet received, and found herself unable even to stammer her thanks. Suddenly, to her surprise, she found tears prickling her eyes. She turned away ashamed, but Cadvan sat on the chair and waited for her to gather herself.

"Cadvan, I'm sorry," she said at last. "It's just that, it's just . . ." She shook her head. "It's just that no one's *ever* given me anything before. And suddenly I have all these *things*. And it feels so strange!" She sniffed, and Cadvan silently handed her a kerchief. "I almost wish someone would beat me or call me names," she continued. "I mean, of course I don't really, but this doesn't feel quite real. And I tell myself it is real, and it is, but I can't quite believe it, and I don't know *me* anymore. I feel so *odd*." She stopped, and lifted her hands helplessly. "I can't say what I mean. I'm glad we're going away. I feel sorry at the same time, but glad."

"It's less than two weeks ago that you were sitting in a byre milking a cow, thinking you'd be a slave for the rest of your life," Cadvan said. He was now standing, looking out of the window. "That's not very long. I'm surprised you don't feel more confused. Most people would." He turned around and looked at her straightly. "I'm not promising an easy journey, Maerad. But for a time at least it should be peaceful."

"People keep pointing at me," said Maerad. "I don't like it."

"People are difficult," Cadvan said. "I can never live long in town. But I am perhaps an unusual case." His expression was suddenly unreadable, and he fell silent. After a moment of quiet he said he would meet her at dinner, at the next bell, and abruptly left the room.

* * *

Oron, Dernhil, and Indik were at dinner that night; Oron was there to bid farewell to Cadvan and Maerad, as she said she was not attending the next night's feast. Present also was a short, dark-haired Bard named Kelia whom Maerad didn't know, although she had often seen her in the Hall playing gis with fierce concentration. She was, Maerad knew, the undisputed champion of Innail.

Together with Silvia and Malgorn, these Bards comprised the six of Innail's Circle. As Maerad entered the room, slightly late because she had been over-long getting ready, she felt an electric prickle in her skin. The sense of power in the room was palpable: not troubled this time, as it had been at the Council, but clear and focused, as if the air crackled with a white fire.

Oron had appeared distant and forbidding to Maerad, who had seen her only at formal events in her guise as the First Bard, but in private she had something of the mischief of Silvia, and the meal was a merry affair. Although she didn't realize it, Maerad looked a different girl from the one who had fainted at Malgorn's front door; a week's excellent diet and daily exercise meant that her painful thinness had already become mere slenderness, tinged with a robust energy. There was also a different expression in her eyes: the wariness of one who might be clouted for the smallest misdemeanor was being replaced by a new self-confidence. She joked and laughed with the other Bards as if she had been there all her life.

As they lazily picked at the sweetmeats and sipped Malgorn's cherry cordial, the talk turned to discussion of the Meet. The news, it seemed, was all bad. The prestige of the Schools was the lowest it had ever been, and in some places caused overt resentment. Sighting of wers and other creatures of the Dark were now almost commonplace, even far from the border regions of Annar; worse, a deathly sickness that all but the most gifted Bards seemed powerless to heal was overcoming many of the holds and villages in the west. Also in some western Kingdoms there was the fear of famine, after the failure of crops the year before and a bad winter, promising starvation and desperate violence in the most afflicted regions.

"But that's not what troubles me most," said Malgorn. "It's the tales of the failing of the Speech at the Springturn and harvest. Even Thurl said that when he said the Words of Making this year, they would not live inside him. There are too many reports like that simply to be put down to incompetent Bards or bad teaching."

"Yes, my friend, something is amiss at the heart of things," said Cadvan sadly. "And I think it has no Name."

Silvia looked down, biting her lip. "I have always prayed that I would not live in such times," she said. "And that I would see out my life in peace, in the richness of harvest."

"So have we all, and so have all who live in dark times," answered Cadvan. "But it is not to be."

"Still," said Dernhil, "it is said: fear is but one part of prudence."

"And also, fear hath a quick ear," countered Indik. "The Black Sorcerers have built their fortress in Dén Raven and harried the Suderain for nigh on three centuries now. They have their own Lords and Captains; it seems to me to cast a wide net to say the Nameless rises again."

"Perhaps," said Cadvan. "Still, it does not do to dismiss such fears out of hand."

No one had an answer to that, and a meditative silence settled over the group.

"What do you hope for in Norloch, Cadvan?" asked Kelia. She leaned forward, a slight frown line between her dark brows. "Have you been there in recent times?"

"Not this last year," Cadvan replied. "I am bound there: I

must report to the First Circle. Enkir sent me north to gather news of the Dark, and so I am bound to bring him fair harvest." He spoke slightly ironically. "But chiefly, or closer to my heart, I wish to see Nelac of Lirigon."

"He must be old now," said Kelia. "I have never met him, though I've read some of his work, of course: I liked *The Strange Flowers of Gis*, a minor masterpiece." Some Bards smiled at Kelia's mention of her obsession. "But I should have been clearer: what do *you* hope, for Maerad?"

Maerad pricked up her ears.

"Maerad has yet to come into the Speech," Cadvan answered, "and as you know, that is late for a Bard, though not unheard of; Callihal of Desor, it is said, didn't come into the Speech until he was near nineteen. But of course she cannot be instated, nor will her Name reveal itself until she does. I think Nelac will be able to advise, better than anyone in Annar, what is the best course for Maerad."

"Better than any here?" Kelia lifted her eyebrows, not bothering to hide her scepticism.

"He is deeply read in some matters of lore on which I wish to consult him," said Cadvan.

"Why do you need lore?" she persisted. "This is surely just a question of a latecomer to Barding."

"No, not simply that," said Cadvan, and he refused, despite more prodding from Kelia, to elaborate further. Maerad was disappointed. Kelia was not the only one who wanted to know why Cadvan considered her so important.

"I've finally forgiven Cadvan for taking Maerad away," said Silvia lightly, as Kelia and Cadvan seemed to be on the brink of quarreling. "Though I wanted more than any of you to keep her." She turned to Maerad, smiling sadly. "I was just being selfish, really; it was almost like having a daughter again."

Malgorn glanced at his wife with sudden concern, and Maerad looked up inquiringly.

"Clavila, our daughter, died in an accident almost thirty years ago now," explained Malgorn. Maerad thought she caught an edge of resentment in his voice, as if he disliked remembering old pain.

"Oh," said Maerad awkwardly, unable to think of any graceful response. "I'm sorry." She looked at Silvia with a new understanding, but Silvia's face was turned away toward the fire.

Shortly afterward they all retired to the music room, and the Bards picked up their instruments. Maerad had left hers in her chamber, and on Oron's request ran upstairs to get it. Oron examined it with immense curiosity. "It is Dhyllic ware, I've no doubt," she said. "You are quite right, Cadvan, to keep this from general knowledge. I've never seen one before." She caressed the worn wood and drew her fingers gently over the strings. "What tone it has! How did Milana conceal such a thing?"

"Pellinor was an old School, and had many treasures," said Cadvan. "I don't doubt this was the greatest of all of them; but it looks such a humble object, perhaps it was easier to keep it secret than might be thought. Most folk, even most Bards, would think it a peasant's harp, nothing more."

"That's what they thought at Gilman's Cot," Maerad said. "If it had looked more, I would not have been allowed to keep it." She was still privately staggered that her humble lyre should be such a treasure. "I loved it for other reasons. It is the only thing I have of my mother." She took it back from Oron and struck a gentle chord on the strings. "She sings to me."

"Smart of you to spot it, Cadvan," said Oron.

"If I wasn't smart, I'd be dead," he answered dryly. "Now, what shall we play? An instrumental piece, I think."

Maerad had never enjoyed herself so much, wrapped in the intimacy of music in that lovely room. To play with such accomplished musicians—to her surprise, even Indik was a master flautist, with an astonishingly delicate touch for one of his grim visage—was a pleasure she had never known before. The lamp glow glanced warmly off the polished instruments and glasses of wine, and a joking camaraderie sparkled over the underlying seriousness of a mutual passion for music and song. It was late before Silvia drew the party to a halt and they made their farewells.

As she left, Oron stood and took both Maerad's hands. "I am only sorry our meeting has been so hurried. May the Light bend always to your path!"

"And to yours," Maerad returned, knowing now the polite response. Oron looked her full in the face, and Maerad felt a mind probing hers, keen and merciless, as if a ray of light lanced suddenly into a dark room. She flinched, and Oron laughed gently and let her go.

"I think we will not meet again," Oron said. "The Light blesses you cruelly, and your path will be dark and hard. But a brave heart might prevail where skill is wanting."

Maerad remembered Indik saying the same thing, but Oron's statement had a different weight, as if she were talking of something much more portentous and profound than skill with a sword. A qualm came over her at Oron's words, a presentiment of shadow, and she shivered. "I hope so," she said. "I've much to learn."

"So have we all," Oron answered lightly. Then she gave Maerad a silver brooch fashioned into the lily sign of Pellinor, pinning it on her breast. "Wear it with pride!" she said. "This belonged to Icarim of Pellinor, my old friend, and a great Bard. I think he would be glad to know who now wears it." Turning then to Cadvan, Oron said: "Cadvan, I don't have to tell you to protect this young woman. She is more than worthy of your life. Your path is dark and uncertain, but it was ever so. All I can tell you, old friend, is take care!"

"I am used to taking care," said Cadvan. "But my heart misgives me. I think when next we meet, it will be past the Gates of Unreturn, Oron of Innail."

Oron held his gaze and then bowed her head. "If it be so, I have had a long and joyous life," she said. "I no longer fear for myself. My hopes and fears go with you, and with your task."

She put her hands on his shoulders and kissed his forehead, and for a moment they were still, two tall, grave figures. It seemed to Maerad they stood outside time, like figures in a story told over many centuries: two noble Bards of the Knowing, accounted great in the annals of the land. But the moment passed, and, blinking, Maerad saw just a man and a woman standing in a little room where the fire slumbered over its embers. Oron nodded to the other Bards and left swiftly.

Silvia looked white. "I know not what you saw there, Cadvan," she said. "Oron would be a hard loss to all of us."

"There will be many losses before the end," said Cadvan. "And none can see what that end is."

No one felt like staying longer after that, and shortly afterward Maerad and Cadvan said their good nights to the rest of the company and left.

"Interesting that Silvia mentioned her daughter," Cadvan said, as he walked with Maerad down the corridor. "She never talks about her. You have stirred up old griefs, Maerad."

"I didn't mean to," said Maerad sadly. She thought of her own mother. If she stayed in Innail, she could perhaps restore something of that aching loss. She was beginning to understand a little of Silvia's complex longings.

"It's not to blame you," Cadvan said. "Sometimes new life is painful: the waking limb burns. I think, rather, that it is a good thing, perhaps for both of you."

Maerad felt strangely comforted by his words. They bade each other good night at her door. Inside her room, she curled into bed with the book Dernhil had given her. It took her a long time to spell out the name of the poem she attempted to read: it was called *For Clavila*.

She felt suddenly too sad to struggle with letters, and put the book carefully on her shelf. She would read it tomorrow night.

Before lunch the next day, Cadvan found Maerad sitting glumly on her bed. She had been listening to the sounds of the School: the distant tuning of instruments, the calls of students and Bards elsewhere in the house, the patter of the rain. Today the thought of leaving Innail for an uncertain and uncomfortable journey made for reasons she didn't fully understand seemed less exciting than it had.

"Rain!" Cadvan said, crossing to the window. "Let's hope it doesn't lessen. Though I must say," he added, squinting through the leaded panes, "it looks as if it has set in."

"It's hardly ideal riding weather," Maerad said, a little sulkily.

"So the lesser chance of anyone thinking we are leaving tonight, or stumbling across our path," said Cadvan. He looked cheerier than he had for days. "With any luck, no one will know whether we are here or not for at least a couple of days."

"I suppose not," said Maerad. "Though what difference that makes, I don't know."

"Perhaps none. Perhaps every difference." He walked up and down the room restlessly. "We should check our horses," he said. "And didn't you want to see Dernhil today? We can do both at once."

They donned heavy cloaks and made their way to the stables. Imi snorted in greeting when she saw them, and Maerad cheered up a little; she was already fond of her mare. Cadvan's mount was a big black stallion named Darsor. Maerad had never seen such a proud and powerful beast. "He arrived from the south of Annar yesterday, to my call," Cadvan said. "He is of the race of Lanorgrim. He consents to be my mount; I do not command him. He is my friend."

"He looks as if he is spoiling for exercise, rather than just having ended a long journey," said Maerad in wonder. "What do you mean: you called him?"

"A friend will always hear," Cadvan said inscrutably. "And this is Imi? Indik picked well; she looks perfect for you." He spoke a few words to the mare in the Speech, and she snorted and pawed the ground with her hoof. He laughed.

"A proud and willful mare, like her rider, no doubt," he said, turning to Maerad. "She refuses to be cowed even by Darsor, who is a lord among horses. I asked if she could keep up with us, and she is offended I should ask." He patted Imi's neck.

After they left the stables, they arranged to meet for the Feast in the music room at Malgorn and Silvia's house, and Cadvan went to the Music House on some of his own business. Maerad bent her steps for the last time to the Library to see Dernhil.

Dernhil was, as ever, in his room. Maerad suspected that sometimes he slept there; she imagined him nodding over his books, the fire ebbing in its grate, the pen falling from his nerveless hand. He looked up as she entered. "Maerad! I'm glad you came. Sit down."

Maerad drew up her usual chair, putting on the floor the books that already burdened it, and sat next to him. He was searching around his desk.

"I have something that I thought I should give you," he said.

"It's here somewhere. . . . Yes, here it is." He pulled a piece of parchment out of a pile of books and smoothed it out on the desk. It looked very old: it was worn thin, and the ink on it was so faded that in places it was almost indecipherable. Maerad could recognize some of the letters, but it was written in a strange hand and she could read none of the words.

"I found it the other day, when I was looking for something else," Dernhil explained. "It was in a sheaf of papers and oddments of no especial interest, except to me perhaps—old ballads and lists and so forth. I think it will not be missed, and perhaps it might be more useful to you, and better taken from the Library, where the wrong eyes might see it."

"What does it say?" asked Maerad.

"I'm sorry, I forgot, you can't quite read it yet," Dernhil said. "It's a curious document, written in the Speech of the Middle Years, about three hundred years after Maninaë restored the Kingdom of Annar. It looks like nonsense, but I'm not so certain. . . ."

"Can you read it to me?" Maerad asked. Dernhil looked at her with amusement. On the edge of her chair, fidgeting with impatience, she looked like a ten-year-old child.

"All right. It says something like this: *I, Lanorgil of Pellinor, here set down my dream, so that those to come may know of it when I have gone through the Gates to the Uncircled Open.* Lanorgil was renowned as a seer in his time, which is what caught my eye in the first place. It was odd coming across it, though the Innail library is justly famed, and no one alive has read everything in it."

Maerad shifted impatiently in her seat.

"Anyway, it goes on: *A mist obscures the bright river, a mist on which no eye can fasten its sight, a mist that confuses the brave, and casts down the*—I think—*small in fear and trembling.*" Maerad thought with a sudden pang of the dread of her own dream. "*All is in darkness and despair: corruption assails the High Seats of*

*Annar, and those who truly follow the Light are cast into shadow.
Seek then one who comes Speechless from the Mountains: a Bard
unSchooled and yet of this School. Seek and cherish the Fire Lily, the
Fated One, which blooms the fairer in dark places and sleepeth long in
darkness; from such a root will blossom the White Flame anew, when
it seems its seed is poisoned in the center. Note the Sign and be not
Blind! In the name of the Light and in anxiety for the Speech, whose
roots lie in the Treesong that nourishes all. Thus spake the Voices of
Dream to Lanorgil, on this Dhorday, seventh of the month of Luminil,
in the year 316 in the Annaren calendar.*

"That dates it about six hundred years ago." He looked at
Maerad. "It seems like nonsense. *One who comes Speechless from
the Mountains . . . unSchooled and yet of this School*" His eyes
rested on Maerad's brooch. "An odd locution, though, to say *the
Fire Lily*: that's obviously a reference to Pellinor, though Pellinor
is usually marked by the arum lily. . . ." He trailed off, seeming
lost in thought, and Maerad waited patiently. "You seem rather
to fit this riddle," he said, looking up. "And it might explain
Cadvan's actions. . . . He is learned in the deep lore, and knows
much that has been forgotten."

"I . . . I don't know," said Maerad. "He hasn't said much
to me."

Dernhil looked slightly disappointed. "Well, perhaps you
can just give him this fragment," he said. "No doubt it was not
chance I found it just now; the Light stirs at need, it is said. It
made me think of all those songs about the Fated One. They're
not sung anymore, but not everyone has forgotten."

"The Fated One?" The little pang of dread was expanding in
Maerad's breast; she wished that Dernhil had not found the
parchment, and she had a sudden impulse to tear it up. "What
does that mean? Anyway, what can it have to do with me?"

"It's hard to say," said Dernhil, looking at her with a discomforting intensity. "In any case, speak of it to no one except

Cadvan. I think I begin to understand a little." His face was troubled. "I like not to think of you traveling, so young and so unschooled, over wide and dangerous lands," he continued. "But it may be that you would be safe nowhere, and nowhere less safe than here, where some might guess you are more than an occasion for casual gossip. May the Light protect you!"

There was a short, slightly uncomfortable pause. Maerad didn't know what to say; it seemed to her that for reasons she didn't understand, Dernhil was distressed. She reached out and touched his hand.

"I will be safer with Cadvan than with any other, I think," she said softly.

Dernhil took her hand in both of his, holding it tightly. "I think so too," he said. "Nevertheless, I wish things were otherwise, and that you could stay here, loved as you should be." He kissed her hand and then, very suddenly, gathered her in his arms and kissed her mouth.

Inside her head, a voice screamed *No!* but Maerad could make no sound. For a split second she was consumed by terror: a memory assailed her of hot breath against her skin, cruel hands bruising her body, the brutal gasps of a man aroused. . . . She twisted out of his arms like a snake, lashing out violently with her fists, and stood panting before him, her hands raised to curse, her eyes glaring. She saw that the man's mouth was bleeding. Only then she recalled herself: this was *Dernhil*, not Burk, that thug who had tried to rape her in the cot; and Dernhil had only kissed her. She lowered her arms, speechless with embarrassment and confusion, and turned away. Dernhil covered his eyes with his hand.

"I'm sorry," she whispered. She realized she was shaking. Dernhil stirred and looked up.

"It is not you who should be sorry, Maerad," he said. To her discomfort, his eyes brimmed with tears. "I'm ashamed; I'm afraid I forgot myself. It is sometimes hard to remember that you are so young, and how cruel your life has been. Perhaps we will meet again, and you might then understand something of the ways of the heart. You should go now. Don't forget the parchment! May the Light bend always to your path!"

"And to yours," Maerad mumbled hastily, as she snatched the parchment from the table, where Dernhil sat unmoving, his eyes shaded by his hand. She left the room quickly, her heart pounding, and did not look back.

Maerad went straight back to her room, walking fast through the rain, which now had settled into a steady downpour. She hardly noticed it. Although Cadvan had teased her about Dernhil's preference for her, she hadn't believed him. Had she done something wrong perhaps? Or said something misleading?

In her room she flung herself on her bed. She was filled with irrational panic. At Gilman's Cot she had spent much of her time fending off the attentions of Gilman's thugs and the other slaves; rape was not uncommon. She had only avoided it herself with extreme guile and caution, and because of the virulence of her curses. There had been that one frightening time with Burk—she shuddered at the memory—but after that, no one tried again. He was blind for three days and had boils for weeks, and no one dared to punish her. . . . The only man she trusted at all was Mirlad, and she had been wary even of him; otherwise, the attention of any man, however slight, was to be feared and avoided.

She knew that Dernhil was nothing like those men, yet still she couldn't calm herself. She drew out the parchment he had given her and examined it closely; she could not make sense of it, the writing was so spidery and strange, and it was full of words she couldn't recognize. She pushed the parchment under her pillow and lay on her back, staring at the ceiling. Her feelings about Dernhil were mixed up with her strange dread of the parchment.

Silvia knocked on her door about an hour later to ask if Maerad wanted help with dressing for the Feast that evening. "Are you all right, Maerad?" she asked, with swift concern.

"I'm fine," said Maerad, looking up at her woefully.

"What's happened? Has someone said something? Or are you worried about leaving?"

It didn't take Silvia long to worm out Maerad's encounter with Dernhil. Maerad told her haltingly, almost paralyzed by embarrassment. She didn't mention the parchment, since Dernhil had told her to keep it secret from all save Cadvan. There was a long pause while Silvia turned the words over in her head.

"Listen, Maerad, among Bards it is not quite as it is among most other people," she said. "It is partly because we are so long-lived." She paused again. "One thing Bards learn, and venerate above all else, is to be wise in the ways of the heart, to understand what it is they love. Dernhil is not one of shallow passions. . . . I think he has not been as wise as he should have been. He would not like to think he has so upset you." For a time she was silent. "Why does it bother you so?"

"Did I do something wrong?" She couldn't tell Silvia how afraid it made her, that look in Dernhil's face; she would not understand.

"No, my love, how could you?" She patted Maerad's hand. "I doubt he will be the last. But what do *you* feel?"

Surprised, Maerad considered the question. "About Dernhil? I don't know," she said. "I mean, I like Dernhil very much, he has been very kind to me, but I think of him, well, you know, as my friend."

"And so he is, and so he will remain," said Silvia firmly. She put her arm around Maerad and hugged her close. "You mustn't worry. Dernhil is a grown man and will not blame you for his own feelings. There is no shame in loving: it is the sign of a generous heart, and pain the price of an open soul. He knows that. In any case," she said, changing the subject, "Dernhil asked me to give you this." She handed her a roll of parchment sealed with wax. "He seemed quite distressed; I see why now. Would you mind if I told him about our conversation?"

Maerad shook her head. "Tell him; it's all right now," she said.

"I'll be back later, then." Silvia left the room.

Maerad looked at the new parchment dubiously. After a while, with a strange reluctance, she broke the wax seal and unrolled it. Written there, in Dernhil's clear, firm hand, was a poem, a short *enryu*, which she spelled out slowly.

> *Drunk with beauty, I tore down*
> *Armfuls of blossom.*
> *How desolate the marred sky!*

Underneath Dernhil had written: *Maerad, my deepest apologies for my foolishness. Your steadfast friend, Dernhil.* She studied the parchment for some minutes, and a warm feeling, new to her, stole over her. She wondered whether she should answer it. Of course, she thought. Perhaps one day how I bloodied his lip will be a joke, like the tale of Cadvan's duel. She went to her table and, using some of the paper Dernhil had given her, she laboriously wrote out: *Thank you, Dernhil. From your friend, Maerad.* She would give it to Silvia to deliver later.

Then, remembering the time with a start, she went for the last time to the bathroom, perhaps her favorite room in the house. She had bathed every day, delighting in the warm water and oils, the luxurious sense of well-being it gave her. She spent rather longer there than usual, and by the time she returned

Silvia was already in her room, dressed and waiting.

It seemed almost like a ritual, although they had done it only once before and this time was so different. Maerad felt no sense of abashment at the fine clothes and put her dress on by herself, although Silvia helped her with some buttons at the back. She sat before the mirror as Silvia combed and arranged her hair and realized the cut on her forehead from the fight with the wers was completely healed; the only sign of it was a fine white line near her hairline. She leaned back into Silvia and sighed.

"I will miss you, Maerad," said Silvia, as she stood up. "The risk of all friendship is, alas, a little grief. You have made me remember many things I love, which are now gone. It is a cause of joy, as well as pain, and for that I thank you." She took a small package out of her breast and gave it to Maerad. "I wanted to give you something to remember me by. It belonged to my daughter, Clavila, and I would like you to have it."

Speechlessly Maerad unwrapped the package. Inside was a white stone like the one Silvia wore on her hand. It was suspended from a fine gold chain. "It's the stone we call Starwater, *dhillian*, and it is dear to the Light and has certain virtues," Silvia said. "Perhaps in a dark place, it might bring you healing." She put it around Maerad's neck, and Maerad looked at herself in the mirror. "And in a light place, of course, it adorns you." She kissed her on the cheek.

Maerad turned and hugged Silvia almost desperately, as if she were a small child. She held her tight, breathing in her scent, a fragrant mixture of milk and almond and lavender. At last Silvia kissed the top of her head, and said: "We should go downstairs."

"Thank you, Silvia," Maerad mumbled into her dress. "Thank you so much, for everything, everything you've given me. I wish I could give you something back."

"You have," she answered. "Now, let's go."

* * *

Malgorn and Cadvan were waiting in the music room, and together they made their way to the Great Hall for the feast. Silvia and Malgorn parted with them at the door, because Malgorn was First Bard in Oron's absence. Maerad looked around swiftly for Dernhil, but to her mingled relief and disappointment he wasn't there. The Hall was decorated as before, but Maerad felt a change in the atmosphere of the feast. She thought perhaps it was her own heavy spirits, but when she mentioned it to Cadvan, he agreed.

"Yes, a shadow lies over the Bards," he said. "After a week of talking, all that has emerged are our differences. We are all agreed that something is amiss. There is too much evidence to deny it, or to brush it aside as part of a natural cycle, though there are some even now who seek to do so. But even those of goodwill cannot agree what to do, nor even define what the ill is."

"I have never been at a Meet that was so inconclusive," said Saliman, who was again sitting with them. "I think it is a symptom in itself. And I thought to come north for help!" He shook his head. "Do you know, Cadvan, I think in the south we are closer to the ways and needs of the Light. My people are true and straight: they do not twist the Speech to its letter and so forget its spirit, like some do here. Some in the north have forgotten what Barding means. Not at Innail, of course," he continued. "Oron is a great Bard, and the Light is strong and alive in this School. But those from Ettinor and Desor, and others, I mislike what they say. They come with complaint and leave with anger." He looked over his shoulder, where Helgar and Usted sat at another table, hunched deep in conversation.

"You're right, Saliman," said Cadvan. "That tells us times are amiss as much as anything."

"Why not come south with me, Cadvan?" Saliman asked. "We have need of such as you. Forces build in Dén Raven, and my people arm themselves against the Black Sorcerers. At least there we are prepared to fight."

"I can't," he answered. "At least, not yet. I have other duties, and my way bends west."

"Not all of them so onerous, either," said Saliman, smiling at Maerad. "How are your lessons?"

The talk passed to more general topics, and Saliman entertained Maerad with stories of Turbansk, the great city in the south that was his home. "The sun warms everything there; we do not have this freezing drizzle," he said. "I wish you could see it! The towers are lilies of stone, and inside them are courtyards hung with cool vines, where one might sit and listen to the fountains, eating grapes. And in the streets: the silks of the stalls, and the flower market . . ." His voice filled with longing. "To sit on the walls of the Red Tower, which fall sheer to the silver waters of the Lamarsan Sea, and watch the sun set, listening to the cries of the fruit sellers and the birds and monkeys settling to sleep. . . . There is nothing more beautiful in the whole world."

"Perhaps I will go there one day," said Maerad.

"That's a promise!" Saliman said. "I will take you to the Hallows, the great caves where for thousands of years my people have worshipped the Light. The waters of the Lamar River trickle there into the sacred pool, sparkling in the moonlight like a veil of diamonds. Then you will be amazed. Will she not, Cadvan?"

"No one with eyes could fail to be amazed," said Cadvan, smiling. "I have seen nothing to rival it."

"I am homesick," said Saliman. "I was ever restless, and it is a new feeling to me. I think I have not spent enough time there. Perhaps when the shadows loom, our hearts turn to home and to those we love."

"Are you going home now?" asked Maerad.

"Alas, no. I must go first to Norloch. Perhaps I will find what I seek there, but it seems to my heart that I will not. A long journey, and cheerless to me, although it is long since I saw Nelac, and I have missed him. Nelac was my teacher, as well as Cadvan's," he explained to Maerad. "Perhaps he has spoken of him to you? A great Bard, but even a great Bard ages, and we have need of more like him. I mislike all I hear of what is happening in this land. All that is good and wholesome withers."

"It's unlike you to be so downcast," said Cadvan. "When are you leaving?"

"In a week or so, I think," Saliman said. "I find myself reluctant to hurry away from this haven. It will be all the sweeter if those who slight me for the color of my skin have left." Maerad knew that he meant Helgar and Usted, and others. "I have not had time, either, for proper counsel with Oron, which I hope for before I leave here."

Cadvan did not take the dais this night, and Maerad listened to the other Bards playing the songs of leavetaking. Her sense of foreboding could not abate her delight in the music, and she was so absorbed she jumped when Cadvan told her it was time to go.

Together they said farewell to Saliman and then made their way to the high table where Malgorn and Silvia sat.

"We will come with you," said Silvia. "I begin to tire."

In silence they walked back to Silvia and Malgorn's house, where Cadvan and Maerad changed into their traveling clothes. Maerad took off her finery and put on the jerkin and leather trousers Silvia had laid aside for her, and over all a heavy, dark blue cloak. She kept the jewel Silvia had given her around her neck, hidden under her clothes. Her mail and helm were stowed in her pack. Regretfully she folded the crimson dress and placed it in the chest. She guessed it would be a long time before she wore such fine clothes again. Then, after a last quick look around her room, she picked up her pack and went downstairs.

"Now we are travelers indeed," said Cadvan. He was back in the clothes she remembered from their first meeting, worn and travel-stained, but now clean and mended. "But we won't be camping until we leave the Innail Valley. There are some fine inns here it would be a crime to pass by!"

Maerad smiled with relief; she had been dreading the thought of sleeping outside in this weather. Cadvan offered her a small glass of sweet wine. "We must drink the parting cup." He raised his glass to Malgorn and Silvia. "Peace be on your house, and all who live there," he said.

"And may the Light bring your journey to a safe end," said Malgorn. They drank the wine, and then Cadvan and Maerad embraced Silvia in farewell. Malgorn was to go with them, to show them a private way out of the School.

"Make sure he doesn't eat all the rations," Silvia said to Maerad, smiling sadly. "You still have some weight to gain."

"Now, be fair," said Cadvan. "I can hardly force them down her throat!"

"Good-bye!" said Silvia, and she stood alone at the door and watched them until they vanished completely into the darkness.

They walked quickly through the night streets of Innail to the stables, wrapping their cloaks around them to keep out the cold. It was beginning to rain, a light shower that slowly grew heavier. Their footsteps echoed back from the black walls of the houses, and raindrops glanced off the wet cobbles like flecks of cold light. When they saw a few Bards straggling home from the feast they withdrew into doorways, covering their faces with their hoods. Otherwise they saw no one and passed unnoticed through the shadows.

Already Maerad felt exiled from the life of Innail. Even ten minutes ago she had been part of it, one glowing thread in its complex tapestry. Now sadness dragged her steps. Would she ever come here again? Here she felt safe and at ease. Before her lay hardship and flight, certain danger and an uncertain fate. But a hardening will answered the obscure dread stirring within her; she couldn't say in words why she should leave Innail but, in some deeper part of her mind, she was certain she could do nothing else.

Cadvan helped Maerad strap her pack to the saddle, and then, leading their horses, they followed Malgorn through dark, narrow lanes Maerad had not seen before, until they reached the School wall. He led them to a small, heavily bolted iron door just big enough to admit the horses. Malgorn took out an iron key and opened the door soundlessly. A last hasty embrace and they passed through. The door shut behind them with a dull thud.

Maerad heard the key turn in the lock and the bolts shoot home, and then only the heavy patter of the rain.

RACHIDA

And from his icy throne a king
Rose from his spellbound sleep and saw
A vision of the banished spring,
A form so fair and luminous
That from his frosted eyes the hoar
Ran down like tears and, marveling,
He felt the chains of winter thaw
And years of thraldom ruinous.

Between them stood the wall of ice
And round them barren winter waste,
But each saw in the other's face
The light of summer lingering:
And then like thunder broke the frost,
The chill wall fell, and morrowless
Immortal maid and man embraced,
Their light and shadow mingling.

From *The Lay of Ardina and Ardhor*

XI

INNAIL FESSE

THEY rode through the night in almost total darkness. The heavy clouds meant that little moonlight aided their way, and all Maerad could see was the dark shape of Cadvan, the darker shapes of trees on either side, and the faint glimmer of the road ahead of them. Imi was sure-footed and never stumbled. After an hour the rain lifted, and shortly after that they reached a fork in the road. Cadvan took the western road, and they had ridden for another hour when the dulled sound of the hoofbeats on a track changed to a sharp ring of cobbles, and Maerad saw the black outlines of houses around them. They slowed to a walk and Cadvan leaned toward her, pointing to one of the buildings.

"We're in Stormont now," he said. "That's the Chequers, one of the best inns in Innail Valley. Grall will rise for late travelers, and it's comfortable enough."

Maerad was numb with cold and tiredness, and was grateful for a respite from the rain. It wasn't long before Cadvan had roused the innkeeper, who looked curiously at Maerad but admitted them cheerfully and, after stabling their horses, showed them to a small pair of low-eaved rooms linked by a comfortable sitting room, in which he hastily lit a fire.

"Too late for dinner, by some hours, begging your pardon," said the innkeeper. "You're lucky you came tonight. After tomorrow I'm all booked up with Bards."

"I'd be grateful if you kept quiet about our stay," said Cadvan. "Some are a little too nosy for my liking."

Grall looked sideways at Maerad and put a finger along his nose. "Secrets are safe with me," he said conspiratorially. "As you well know, Lord Cadvan. Can I get you some spiced wine, perhaps? And for the young lady? You look half frozen."

He bustled out, and Maerad burst into giggles. Cadvan threw his cloak on a chair and leaned toward the fire.

"Perhaps it is no bad thing, having a ready reason for discretion," he said, looking at Maerad with amusement. "Grall is a good man; I have reason to know I can trust him. Otherwise, we'd be making camp underneath some dripping trees, with no fire!"

Before long Grall was back with clay cups of hot spiced wine, and Maerad sipped it dreamily, staring into the fire, feeling the warmth thrill down to her toes. The wind threw more rain against the window and howled through the trees outside, and she felt intensely grateful she wasn't out in the night. As soon as she finished her wine, she roused herself and went to bed, yawning.

It seemed only a minute later that Cadvan was knocking at her door. "Time for breakfast!" he said. "I want to get moving straightaway; the Bards from Innail won't be far behind." Maerad realized she was ravenous, and, after a spartan wash, joined Cadvan in the sitting room. Grall brought in a huge breakfast of sausages, chops, black beans, mushrooms, and fresh bread, fussing about Maerad with so much exaggerated tact she had trouble keeping a straight face. It was still dark, but soon a dim gray wash began to lighten the windows. Although it had stopped raining, outside looked bleak and dreary. The last thing Maerad felt like was a long ride, though she wondered hopefully if Cadvan was planning inn stops all the way to Norloch; it mightn't be so bad if he was.

In less than an hour they were mounting their horses. A

watery sun was now struggling to push through the clouds, but with little success. Grall held their bridles while they mounted. "No word, mind, Grall," Cadvan said. "I shouldn't like to hear of my own movements."

"You know me, mum as an egg," said Grall. "Though I'm sorry you're not staying longer. I was hoping to get some news from you, and I know what Lord Cadvan says is more reliable than what comes from some others, if you know what I mean."

"I'm sorry too, and not only for that," said Cadvan. "You've always run one of my favorite stopping places."

Grall's face brightened. "We have a reputation, and that's a fact," he said. "And there's no gainsaying that my beer's been especially good since last you were here. I could wish you visited more often. The Chequers's cellars are famous around these parts now." Then he looked worried again and leaned forward, whispering hoarsely. "I just keep hearing bits and pieces, bad news, and no mistake. Things are out of whack, if I'm not mistaken. I'd sorely like your advice."

"Yes, things are out of whack, Grall," said Cadvan seriously. "May it not touch you! Be sure the Bards are doing what they can. But now, we really must go. A blessing on your house!"

Grall at last let go of the bridles, and they were off.

Stormont was a village of perhaps a dozen houses, all low-windowed and whitewashed and thatched with dark river reeds. Maerad looked around her with wonder; she had never seen such a village before, and in truth it seemed to her as exotic as Innail, although Cadvan was riding through it with scarcely a glance. It was still early and no one was on the road, but she saw rushlights fluttering in the paned windows. Cocks were crowing and dogs barking, and far in the distance she could hear a farmer calling in his cows and the clank of pails. Beyond the village the hills were shrouded in fog, but as the sun rose, it began to disperse and there was even some sunshine, although it brought no warmth, and heavy gray clouds coming in over the mountains portended more rain.

When they were well out of the village, Cadvan turned to Maerad and said, "I might as well disguise us a little. I'm known around here." He simply passed his hands, and Maerad blinked and looked around. She saw no difference.

"You're Bard-eyed, so it doesn't work on you," said Cadvan. "It's only a glimmerspell. But to any casual farmhand ambling along the road, I look like a fat northern farmer from Milhol riding along with his wife. There are many such hereabouts, taking their wares to market or coming to buy. So take care to call me husband, if you need to call me anything."

They continued the rest of the morning at a fast pace, speaking little. They passed a few people on the road, and Maerad looked at them curiously; they were fair-haired and fair-skinned, and dressed in the same fine woolen cloth of which Maerad's clothes were made. They nodded to the strangers with a reserve that was not unfriendly but invited no conversation.

Although she had been in Innail for more than a week, it was Maerad's first real sight of the valley, or the Fesse, as the district surrounding the Schools was often called. When they had first entered it, it had been night, and for the rest of the time she had been enclosed in the School, behind walls, as she had been for most of her life. But the walls of Innail, she reflected, were very different from the walls of Gilman's Cot: Innail protected her and offered freedom, while the cot had been a prison.

Innail Fesse was an almost self-contained region, a thickly populated valley of fertile green hills suspended between two mountainous spurs split from the Osidh Annova, which almost met at their tapering to make a natural sheltered enclosure of perhaps twenty leagues at its widest and not much longer. It had been settled since time immemorial, and its inhabitants regarded themselves as somewhat apart from Annar, though they had acknowledged the Monarch when the High Seat was reestablished in Norloch. They prided themselves on their self-sufficiency and independence, and were famous for their spinning and weaving and for their cuisine. The valley boasted two major towns: Tinagel, where the Steward lived, and the Innail School. There were also many villages like Stormont, of perhaps a couple of dozen houses, and hundreds of small, prosperous farms. The Imlan River ran through its center, fed by many streams that leaped down, fresh and cold, from the mountainsides.

Maerad rode on gravel roads through fields hedged with well-cut rows of hawthorn just now beginning to leaf. She frequently saw farmhouses of the same yellow stone as the buildings of the Innail School, many surrounded by orchards of trees heavy with pink and white blossoms. The flowers of early spring, crocuses and daffodils and bluebells, pushed through the wet grass, and occasionally whiffs of scent blew in Maerad's face on the cold air. It was as if they were riding through a huge bowl; the green hills swept up on either side of them to the sheer walls of the mountains in the distance, which now were hidden in heavy cloud. Even the piercing wind couldn't stop Maerad riding through the valley in a daze of wonder.

They stopped briefly in a copse of ash and had a quick, cheerless lunch. The horses ambled about cropping grass, and seemed as little inclined as they to stop for long. They were soon off again.

"Are we staying in an inn again tonight?" Maerad asked hopefully as they mounted.

Cadvan smiled. "This weather is a bit hard for spring," he said. "Though it is often like this here, being so close to the mountains."

"It would be a sight more pleasant," Maerad said. "And nicer for the horses too."

"I agree," said Cadvan. "We'll have enough of comfortless camps after we leave the valley. Be of good cheer: we're heading for another inn I know, at a place called Barcombe. This time we'll be in disguise. After that, prepare yourself for tree roots!"

Toward dusk the road began to bend into a combe that hid another small village. They clattered past the common to an inn called the Green Toad. This time the innkeeper, a portly man named Halifax, looked at them with suspicion.

"There ain't no market this week," he said. "You got your timing wrong."

"Market was last week," said Cadvan with a heavy northern accent. "We've been seeing my wife's cousin up in Innail. What's it to you, anyway?"

"Pardon me for asking," said Halifax. "I can't be too careful. Strangers come to these parts and are off quick as winking, forgetting the bill, if you know what I mean. Taking us for wetherheads."

"Payment in advance, Mr. Halifax, and I hope that does you," said Cadvan, handing over some coins. "I'd like to see the rooms. My wife and I've had a hard day, and it will be a long road tomorrow."

Slightly mollified, the innkeeper led them to a room with a sitting room. Maerad looked around it, discomforted; clearly she and Cadvan would have to share a bed.

"Dinner, if you please," said Cadvan. "And an early night, my love?" Halifax left, calling for his porter, and Cadvan sat down and took off his boots. He winked at Maerad, and despite herself she blushed.

"I'll be happier when we're out of settled parts," he said. "Then, perhaps, we'll be able to start your lessons. Don't think I've forgotten!" He stretched out his legs to the fire.

Maerad took off her cloak and sat down heavily. She felt sore and exhausted after the day's ride. At the thought of the one bed, she began to feel a panic rise up in her throat again, but she pushed it away.

"There's only one bed," she whispered.

Cadvan glanced up quickly, and Maerad understood that he knew or guessed more than she realized about her doubts and fears.

"That's easily solved," he said. "I'll sleep on the couch. Luxury for a man like me."

"A hard man of the wild," she said, suddenly feeling lighter. "No doubt a stone floor is a king's sleep."

"The finest swans-down. But of course, you are welcome to such comfort, if you desire."

Maerad laughed, her anxiety dissipated. A little later Halifax brought in their dinner on a tray, a thick beef casserole fragrant with herbs and topped with a chewy layer of melted cheese, with fresh bread and a fine local wine. "There's apple tart for afters, if you want," he said. "My wife makes a clotted cream that's famous in these parts."

Cadvan lifted an eyebrow at Maerad, whose mouth was watering at the thought, and when they had finished the casserole they ate the tart, hot and fresh from the oven, criss-crossed with a lattice of pastry so light it dissolved on the tongue, with the clotted cream melting yellow through the caramelized apple.

"That was a lord among tarts," said Cadvan, with an expansive sigh. When Halifax came to take away their plates, Cadvan told him so, and he looked pleased.

"Marta will be grand happy to hear that," he said. "She takes a lot of care over her cooking, so she does, even if some don't care or notice."

"Things have got worse over the past few years, that's for

sure," said Cadvan. "My cousin runs an inn near Ettinor, and can scarce keep body and soul together."

"I hear the Bards is demanding up in Ettinor," said Halifax. "And they leave scarce little for the people to make a life with, living high on the sweat of others with nary a thank-you. Not like our School here, where they run things fair, if you know what I mean. They do the Barding proper here, they do. They're here every Springturn and harvest, and the little 'uns hereabouts all know their letters. And I remember when my daughter had the witchfever, back when she was a babe, and she looked like dying, and Oron herself came and laid her hands on her."

"You can't ask fairer than that," said Cadvan. "But others is not so fair."

"That's the truth, and no mistake," said Halifax. Maerad, who hadn't dared open her mouth during any conversation with the innkeeper, saw with alarm that he looked as if he were settling in for a long chat. "Just the other night, we had a pair here, two shifty types," he went on. "Which was why I was a bit sharp with you, begging your pardon. They left before dawn, and not a farthing did they part with for all they ate and drank. Northerners, they were, and on no good business, if you ask me."

"That's bad," Cadvan said, his interest quickening. "But not all are like that. Some folks are still decent. Where were they heading?"

"They didn't say, not with casting nasty looks around them like we was so much dirt," said Halifax. "But after, I thought they were like Bards; gave me a windy feeling, though. Couldn't look them in the eye."

Cadvan shook his head. "Dark days, Mr. Halifax. Well"—he stretched and yawned—"dark days or no, I have to get some sleep."

"And I've my own business to be getting to, instead of

yammering here like an old woman," said Halifax. "A good
night to you!"

After he left, Cadvan stood up and locked the door. He
looked thoughtful.

"What was he talking about?" asked Maerad curiously.

"Maybe nothing, maybe not," said Cadvan. "I think we did
well to leave Innail when we did. I don't like hearing of shifty
people *like Bards*. Heading to Innail, no doubt. Innkeepers are
not stupid, they are used to meeting many kinds of people, and
their intuitions are often more practiced than most."

"Do you mean corrupt Bards, or something?" Maerad
asked. But despite her probing, Cadvan would say nothing
more of his thoughts.

That night the wind swept the sky clear, whipping the clouds
from the moon and letting her silver light fall over the sleeping
fields and towns of the Innail Fesse. The river glimmered softly,
winding like a silver cord through the gray, dew-heavy fields,
and the wind rushed through the trees, making a sound like the
sea. Underneath the wind there were only small creaturely
noises: the call of an owl, the stirring of sleeping cattle, the
lonely cries of water birds, the shriek of a small animal surprised by a hunter in its nightly wanderings.

Maerad stirred uneasily in her sleep and began to dream.

Far away in the School of Innail, a ray of moonlight slipped
through the casement and fell on Silvia's cheek. She lifted her
hand to her face, murmuring something inaudible, and turned
over. In the street below, the cobbles were white with moonlight
but pooled with black shadows. It appeared peaceful, but anyone watching for any length of time—a bird, say, on a roof—
might have thought, blinking in the deceptive moonlight, that
their eyes were playing tricks. For sometimes it seemed that the

shadows swelled and distorted, as if something black moved stealthily against the buildings, but then, when you shook your head, there was nothing there. If the watcher had been patient, after a time it would have become clear that two darkly cloaked figures moved furtively below, keeping always out of the light, slinking from doorway to doorway.

They moved up the street until they reached the steps of Malgorn and Silvia's house. There they stopped, mounted the steps, and tried the door. There was a brief, intolerably bright flash of light, and they fell back into the road. Swiftly they picked themselves up and vanished into the darkness.

A little while later, Dernhil was sitting in his room as Maerad had sometimes imagined him, his chin propped on his hand, deeply absorbed in a book. The fire was almost crumbled to ash, popping sleepily in its embers, and the light from the lamp fell peacefully across the tumbled books and parchments on his desk. Suddenly he looked up warily, like a deer scenting a wolf, and almost immediately afterward there came a knock on his door.

Dernhil sat very still in his chair and did not get up to open it. There came another knock, as if the door were being struck with a heavy staff, and then the door burst open. Two figures stood in the dark hallway beyond.

Dernhil stood up as the figures walked into the light. They were heavily cloaked and booted in black, and their hoods obscured their faces, although he could see their eyes burning red. A chill, like that of the tomb, entered the room with them and Dernhil lifted his hands as if to fend them off.

"You cannot ward against us!" said one of the figures sharply, making a strange motion with his hands.

Dernhil was suddenly stilled, as if he were frozen.

"We are come for a little information, Dernhil of Gent. Help us, and our master will reward you richly."

There was a long silence. "I know who you are," Dernhil said at last. His speech was thick, as if he were in pain. "I'll not have any dealings with you or your kind."

His interlocutor lifted his finger, and Dernhil grimaced.

"Speak not so hastily," he said. "You know not what you will do in this world or the next one, Bard. Think again. We hear you are teaching a girl. We want to know about her."

This time Dernhil said nothing, but stared at them steadily, and an aura of light, recalling the luminosity of sunlight on summer trees or the radiance of a fountain, seemed faintly to outline him. The other figure hissed, drawing its breath in quickly, and both of them stepped back. The first spoke again through his teeth, his voice tight with anger.

"You will not easily survive such impertinence," he said. "But what is not freely given can be taken." He drew close to Dernhil, who was still unable to move, and took his chin in his hand. Dernhil's eyes widened in disgust and fear as the hand mercilessly forced him to look the figure in the face. He could not shut his eyes nor turn his head, and it seemed the two figures, the Bard and the cloaked one, stood there an age, engaged in a desperate, silent battle. At last Dernhil let out a great cry and collapsed on the floor. The first figure turned, making a contemptuous gesture.

"There was nothing there," he said. "Nothing."

"It's useless now," said the other, and kicked Dernhil as if he kicked the corpse of an animal.

They turned and left the room. Dernhil lay unmoving on the floor where he had fallen, his eyes glassy and wide with horror.

Maerad woke with a start.

It seemed to her that she heard a cry, that from a deep abyss a voice called her name in an extremity of anguish. She sat up in the dark, her flesh goose-pimpling, grasping at the cry; but it had vanished as if it were part of a dream ill-remembered. All she could hear was the wind rattling the shutters. She sat and listened, her heart hammering, struggling with an overpowering sense of despair and loss, but she neither heard nor felt anything more.

It was a long time before she dragged the covers back over herself and fell again into an uneasy sleep.

XII

THE WEYWOOD

THEY were up well before light the next day, and ate in the huge inn kitchen, at the scrubbed pine table with Halifax and his wife, Marta, warmed by the iron range.

"She's a quiet one, your wife, eh?" said Halifax, shrugging his shoulder in Maerad's direction.

"She don't like strangers that well," said Cadvan. "She's sociable enough on her own."

"Well, there's some as never shut up, so I guess it's swings and roundabouts." Halifax rolled his eyes comically, and Marta kicked him under the table.

"I know who doesn't shut up around here," she said comfortably. "Can I do you a lunch? It's a long ways to Milhol, grand horses and all."

They waited while she cut them pieces of a fresh loaf and packed them cold meats and pickles and cheeses and some fresh spring onions. Cadvan stowed them in his pack, thanking the innkeepers, and then he and Maerad went to the stables, mounted, and were off. The dawn was yet a pink streak on the horizon and the loud chatter of birds was beginning to wake up the countryside as they trotted out of Barcombe and back onto the western road.

"We're almost out of Innail Fesse now," said Cadvan. "And right now I'm thinking the farther we get, the better." Silently, still disturbed by the cry that had woken her the night before, Maerad agreed with him. They urged the horses to a canter, and so they continued for the next couple of hours as the sun rose into a clear sky and pulled away the early mists. Maerad saw that the mountains were running much closer on either side of them. They almost met a few miles ahead, where each spur tapered down into soft hills, the opening of the valley called the Innail Let. The road now was wider and straighter and looked much used, but they saw no one else this early on their ride. Within another couple of hours they were again under the mountain shadows, riding along the Imlan River, which rolled broadly between easily sloping banks. On the other side were narrow fields and fewer houses, and pine forests drew away from them up the slopes. Cadvan slowed to a walk.

"We'll be well out of here by lunchtime, I think," he said. "Nevertheless, it's well to be wary now. There could be spies placed along this road; it's the only way out of the valley."

"Spies?" said Maerad. She looked involuntarily up into the sky and saw a black bird circling. Cadvan followed her gaze.

"Yes, of all kinds," he said grimly. As they watched, the bird began to circle down toward them, and Cadvan watched it, halting Darsor. Maerad began to realize the bird was heading toward them.

"What should we do?" she asked, suddenly afraid.

"Nothing," said Cadvan. "It is a raven, if I'm not mistaken."

"A raven?" said Maerad. She waited with Cadvan. The bird flapped heavily down and landed on Cadvan's arm. It opened its beak and, to Maerad's astonishment, spoke in ordinary speech.

"Hail, Lord Cadvan," it said.

"Hail, Lord Kargan," said Cadvan. "What brings you here?"

"Evil tidings. I come from the Lady Silvia, who bade me seek you and tell you this. Last night, two Hulls entered the School of Innail. They tried the door of the house of Malgorn and Silvia, but the ward repulsed them. Then they questioned Dernhil of Gent."

"Dernhil?" said Maerad. Cadvan's face drained of blood.

"And after the questioning, what then?" he asked.

"We know not, Lord Cadvan. He was found in his room first light this morning, and none will know what passed there, unless they journey through the Gates to the Hidden Land."

Cadvan bowed his head.

Afraid, Maerad said, "Do you mean he's dead?"

"Alas, yes, Lady Maerad," said the raven, and nodded its head. Maerad went cold with shock.

"You bear black news," said Cadvan. "Is the Lady Silvia sure they were Hulls?"

"The signs are certain," said the Raven, turning its head to fix him with one of its eyes. "None others of the Dark have the powers to pass hidden through the Gates of Innail. But I also saw them, although they saw not me."

Cadvan was silent for some time.

"Lord Kargan," he said. "You have already done much, but I seek your help still. We need to pass through the Innail Let, and I know not if the Dark has gathered its spies there. It may be that it is yet unwatched, because they think that we are still at Innail. I would be grateful if you could fly there and tell me what you see."

The bird fixed Cadvan again with its unblinking stare.

"I will be happy to do this thing," it said, and flew away.

Cadvan and Maerad continued along the road. Cadvan was ashen, and his hands shook slightly on the reins.

Maerad could not believe the news; it couldn't be true. Dernhil killed! And then, behind the numbness of shock, rose an inchoate fear: They're looking for me. They're close behind. They've already murdered Dernhil. . . . And in Innail, which had seemed so safe, so impregnable.

"This is hard news!" Cadvan said at last. "Alas, he was my friend, and I loved him, and this is a grievous loss."

"I didn't know him for very long," said Maerad awkwardly. She felt too stunned for tears. "But . . . he was my friend also." She stopped, feeling helpless at how inadequate words were to express what she felt. They walked on, each wrapped in their own thoughts.

"I heard Dernhil last night," said Maerad, suddenly remembering the terrible cry that had woken her from her sleep the night before.

"You heard him?"

"I woke up, because I heard someone call me. I heard him call my name. I thought it must have been a dream. A bad dream." Her voice caught, but she continued. "But I know now it was Dernhil."

Cadvan was silent again for some time.

"I spoke of you with Dernhil, Maerad," he said. "I know he loved you. He was one of those who can see clearly into another's soul, and his feelings were true. Such things have little to do with brevity of meeting. And in that lies our hope: for the Dark understands nothing of love. And if, as seems almost certain, the Hulls sought news of you, maybe his love protected you as nothing else could."

Maerad thought of her last meeting with Dernhil, and of the enryu he had sent her. "Perhaps we will meet again," he had said to her, and now there would be no more meetings, no more poems, no more conversations by the fire. She wished, with a sudden fierce regret, that she had not been so afraid when he had kissed her, that there had been more time for them. How carelessly she had assumed there would be a future in which hurts could be mended! And now there was none. . . .

"It's my fault," she said in a muffled voice. "If he hadn't been teaching me . . ."

Cadvan glanced at her. "You did not kill him," he said, with a harsh edge to his voice. "It's not your fault there is evil in this world." He stopped abruptly, as if he feared what he might say, and sighed heavily. "I am thinking that there is a knowledge known only to Bards, which is how to kill themselves without weapons. They might sometimes use it, if nothing else prevails against a forcing of their minds." For a while they both said nothing. Maerad wondered what he meant by "forcing of their minds."

"It is unutterably terrible," said Cadvan at last, "to hope that Dernhil killed himself rather than be murdered by those evil things; yet that is what I hope."

They walked on, saying nothing more. Soon they saw Kargan again, flapping toward them. He landed as before on Cadvan's arm.

"The road is safe, Lord Cadvan," he said. "I have asked the creatures, and they have told me. Two Dark ones passed this way three nights ago, they said, and the forest stirred; but now only the men of Innail disturb the way."

"Thank you, Lord Kargan," said Cadvan gravely. "I shall ever be in your debt. Take news of us to the Lady Silvia, and our thanks and love, and tell her we will be soon out of Innail Fesse."

The raven took off, heading toward Innail, and Cadvan lifted his arm in farewell. Then he turned to Maerad.

"The Dark is at our very heels," he said. "We must fly now like the wind. Imi, *esterine ni*?"

The mare snorted and stamped her feet, and then they were off at a full gallop. The mountains swept in close to them, and the road was before them, straight as an arrow, and then they were through and out of Innail. The wide land of Annar lay before them, and the bright river through it, like a silver snake.

When they were well past the Let, Cadvan slowed down. Imi, for all her pluckiness, was lathered with sweat and beginning to stumble. They paused briefly, going down to the river to water the horses and stretch their legs and hastily eat the lunch that Marta had packed for them that morning. Was it really this morning? thought Maerad to herself, for it seemed an age ago. The landscape stretched before them on a slight decline, and the mountains rose behind, swaddled in cloud. Otherwise the sky was clear and the sun warmed their backs and steamed the sweat off the horses. The Imlan River ran to their left, broad and rapid, sometimes diving into cuttings, sometimes lazily meandering between shallow banks, and to their right was a tall forest of oak and ash. The road ran by the river but more straightly, leaving the river to its wider turns and curls, and here was made of level stone, with low stone markers at the side.

"The Annarens laid this road when the Schools were first built, nine centuries ago," explained Cadvan as they rode along. "Such roads link all the Schools, although some have fallen into disuse and disrepair. The West Road runs all the way to Norloch, and there is the North Road and the South Road and others to all the Seven Kingdoms."

They continued along the road for another few miles, and then Cadvan, looking up and down to make sure nobody saw them, led them swiftly off onto a small track that vanished quickly into the forest. A coolness fell over them; the sunlight fell in dapples, and Maerad saw squirrels vanishing up the trunks of the trees as they passed, and a rabbit propped in a glade, its white tail bobbing into the trees as they drew closer. Many of the trees had massive trunks, and the high crowns of the biggest covered an area the size of a large house.

"This is the Weywood," Cadvan said. "It's one of the oldest in Annar, a remnant of the ancient forests that once stretched from sea to mountain. It is a wild place, and so deserves caution. Human beings have little place here."

Riding through the trees, Maerad had a powerful sense that

the forest shut her out. It seemed to watch with a wariness that was not quite unfriendly. The feeling increased as they moved deeper into the forest and the trees thickened and less light fell through the tangled canopy, but she felt no fear. She thought that if she were not with Cadvan she might feel differently; although he said it was not an evil place, she sensed a power that could be hostile if anything threatened it.

The shadows began to lengthen, and immediately a chill fell around them. Cadvan was looking around as he rode, hunting for something, and at last he nodded and led them slightly away from the track to a small dingle like the Irihel where she and Cadvan had stayed the first night after her escape from Gilman. This one was of rowan trees closely growing in a half circle so their branches met and intertwined above; the smooth grass within shelved down to a spring that bubbled out of a ledge of rock, on top of which grew briars and woodbines. Half hidden by this growth was a smooth cave with a sandy floor, where people had clearly made camp many times before. It even had a rough hearth made of loose stones.

"This is a Derenhel, or Woodhome," said Cadvan, showing her the cave. "It is a Bardhome. There are many such throughout Annar." He spoke to the horses, unsaddled them, and loosed them in the dingle to graze. In all their travels Maerad never saw Cadvan tether his horse, nor had need to tether her own; he asked that they stay close, and they never wandered. Then Cadvan and Maerad took their packs and entered the cave, and there, after they had gathered some dead branches, Cadvan lit a fire, and the gloom that had enveloped both of them since Lord Kargan's news lifted a little. They did not at first speak of Dernhil's death, as the subject was too raw for mere words, but the knowledge lay beneath all their speaking, a shadow of grief and fear.

Maerad felt very stiff and sore after the past two days' ride.

She stretched, grimacing. "Ow! I don't think I'll be able to walk tomorrow," she said. "Let alone ride. I feel like I've been beaten all over with sticks."

"A couple more days and you'll be used to it," said Cadvan. "But I can do some Bardic tricks to get rid of the worst of the stiffness." He told Maerad to stand before him, and then passed his hands around her body without touching her. Where his hands passed Maerad felt a tingling warmth, and the aches lessened. She could then sit down without discomfort, although she still felt exhausted and a little sore.

"Magic!" she said, stretching her legs out in front of her.

"So some call it," said Cadvan. "Bards call it the Knowing. Of which there are certain gaps in your knowledge, young Minor Bard." He grinned through his tiredness. "We'll eat, and then I should start your lessons."

"There are so many things I would like to know," said Maerad. "Oh, lots of things. Why could I understand the raven, if I don't have the Speech? And what is the Speech, anyway? How can I know it without knowing it?"

"The Speech is a lifetime's explanation," Cadvan answered, taking food out of his pack. "As for Lord Kargan, you understood him because he spoke your language. They are the only beast that can speak thus to humans, and so are revered. The ravens of Innail are of ancient lineage, and wise as Bards. But first," he said, tossing her a meat pie, "eat!"

They munched in silence, listening to the crackling of the fire and the sounds of the horses grazing and whickering to each other as the night darkened. Then Cadvan leaned back against the wall of the cave, his eyes following the shadows as they danced on the stone. He looked tired and strained, but his voice betrayed no inner turmoil.

"First, Maerad, is the Knowing. At the center of the

Knowing is the Speech, which all Bards carry within them as their birthright. They say that some Bards are born speaking it, and learn human speech only later, in the normal way; but usually a Bard comes into the Speech as a young child. It is not always so, and you are one of the exceptions. Each Bard comes to the Speech in her own way, and in her own time. It cannot be taught."

"Oh," said Maerad, feeling slightly disappointed. She had thought vaguely that Cadvan might make some incantation, or that she would have to undergo some kind of ritual, and then, all of a sudden, she would be gifted with the Speech. "Then I just have to wait? What if it doesn't happen?"

"It will, in its own good time. In the meantime, the Speech is hidden within you."

"What happened when you found the Speech? How old were you?"

For a second Cadvan's face brightened, and Maerad had a brief vision of how he must have looked as a child. "I remember it well," he said. "I was a very little boy then, about five years old. I was swimming in the river with my brothers and sisters on a hot summer day, and suddenly a fish spoke to me. I was so surprised I jumped out of the water and ran screaming to my mother."

"What did the fish say?" asked Maerad curiously.

"It said, 'You swim like a frog on a stick. Get some fins, leggy one!'"

"And then your mother knew you were a Bard?" said Maerad, laughing. "Was she a Bard?"

"Yes, to your first question. And no, she wasn't." Cadvan's face closed, as if the subject pained him, and Maerad asked no further questions. "So," he continued, "at the center of the Knowing is the Speech. I can teach you some of the Knowing, but it will not make proper sense until you have the Speech. However, you are at an advantage because you do have music, and it is said that at the center of the Speech is the Silence of Light, and that music is the only possible expression of that mystery. Which is why music is so revered among Bards."

Cadvan threw another branch on the fire and poked it, so a trail of sparks flew up to the roof of the cavern. A moth flew in, drawn by the light, and circled clumsily around the cave, throwing huge winged shadows over the stone as Cadvan spoke.

"The Knowing is divided into the Three Arts, all of which are of course interconnected and are, in reality, the one stream. They all serve the Balance, the equipoise of the world, which was determined when time itself was an egg: but these are mysteries that we can talk about later, and are not fully understood even by the wisest. We call the Three Arts the Reading, the Making, and the Tending. The Reading is the knowledge of the High Arts, the histories, the languages, the song, the lore, the tracing of the high forces that shape and bend this land. It's what is most commonly thought of as magic, but it is also as simple as reading and writing. The Making is exactly what it says: it means the making of music, painting, building, jewelery, smithing, writing, dancing. The Tending is the knowledge of growing, husbandry, forestry, childcraft, wilding, herbs, healing, bird lore, and so on." He paused and stared at the ceiling. "There are sometimes debates on where a particular branch of Knowing belongs in the Three Arts. For example, a Bard who makes a thing of power draws on two of them: the Making and the Reading, and if it is a healing thing, a stone, for example, it might draw on all three. But myself, I am not interested in such debates."

Maerad listened, staring into the fire, fascinated. "And what are you?"

"I am skilled in the Reading," he said. "Most Bards find out early what most interests them, what draws them. The Reading is the most dangerous, for it is where a Bard is most easily corrupted. Therefore Bards are required to know about all three; for a Bard who counts power and learning as the highest skill, refusing to understand how all of the Arts inform and nourish each other, is a poor Bard. In the reckoning of Bardlore, all Three Arts are given equal honor."

"And Malgorn is of the Tending? And Silvia, I suppose. . . . And Dernhil, he was of the Reading?"

Cadvan's face hardened again. He looked deep into the fire and was silent for a long time, and Maerad was sorry she had said Dernhil's name. But then Cadvan began to chant:

> "Sweet fall the rains on the mountains of Innail
> Leaping like children down through the pinewoods
> With voices of ice like melodious laughter
> Seeking the harping of Dernhil of Gent.
> But he cannot hear them, his music is ended.
> Where has he gone? His chamber is empty
> And bright are the tears in the high halls of Oron
> Where once he stepped lightly, singing deep secrets
> Out of the heart-vault and into the open.
> Dark are the Gates that opened and beckoned
> And closed on his steps, in the gray twilight fading,
> Folding in silence the weft of his barding.
> No more will he sing in the glory of autumn
> Gilding the birches of Lowen and Braneua:
> The groves of Ileadh will wait him in vain.
> He enters the meadows of music no longer
> To gather us mirth-sheaves and harvests of pleasure.
> His harp is unstrung, his sweet voice is silenced:
> Sad now the streams in the Valley of Innail."

He fell silent, and then he covered his face with his hands and wept. Maerad turned aside, feeling the tears welling in her own eyes, and she let them fall. They sat for an unmeasurable time, each privately mourning, as the fire burned lower.

Cadvan finally sat up and threw more wood on the flames. He glanced over at Maerad. "It is hard to lose such a friend," he said. "Dernhil helped me out of a dark place many years ago. He taught me much about humility. And friendship. And now . . . the Dark has had its revenge. I should have realized the dangers," he added bitterly. "If I had not asked him to teach you, no Hulls would have sought him."

"Perhaps not," said Maerad, remembering what Cadvan had told her earlier that day: *it's not your fault there is evil in the world*. "But I think he might have done the same, even had he known the risks. And I think he did know."

"Dernhil was no fool, but he knew little more about you than that you were my pupil," said Cadvan.

Maerad suddenly remembered the parchment that Dernhil had given her. "No, he guessed more," she said. "He gave me something. I'd forgotten all about it until now, but he said to show it to you."

She rummaged through her pack until she found the parchment, telling Cadvan what Dernhil had told her. Cadvan scrutinized it intently, turning pale as he did so. "Do you know what it says?" he asked.

"Dernhil translated it for me," said Maerad. "But I don't know what it means."

Cadvan read the parchment once more and then gave it back to her. "Hide it!" he said. "I am not certain that we shouldn't burn it, but I wish Nelac to see it."

"Nelac? Who's Nelac?" said Maerad, forgetting that he was Cadvan's old teacher in Norloch; but Cadvan did not answer her at first. His face was dark with thought.

"Maerad," he said at last, "if the Dark knows what Dernhil knew, we are in worse trouble than I thought. By the Light, I wish I knew what happened last night."

"But what does it mean?" asked Maerad stubbornly. Cadvan gazed at Maerad earnestly, as if he were seeing her for the first time. She met his gaze and held it, and at last he laughed gently and relented.

"Maerad, I think you are the Foretold, the one who will come, the Fated One," he said. "Lanorgil was one of the great Seers, and he foresaw you. *Seek then one who comes Speechless from the Mountains, a Bard unSchooled and yet of this School.* He meant you. The riddle is scarcely hard to answer, and Dernhil was right: it is not chance that it turned up at just this time. The Foretold, in the Lore, is the one who will defeat the Nameless One in his darkest rising. It is an ancient tradition, although now mostly forgotten, except by the Wise, who do not forget."

Maerad listened in tense silence, her heart thumping wildly. Cadvan's words filled her with a strange panic, the same panic she had felt when Dernhil had first shown her the parchment.

"It can't be talking about *me*," she said, laughing nervously to cover her confusion. "I'm not . . . I'm not important. . . ."

"It's a lore that is not forgotten by the Dark," said Cadvan, staring at her somberly. "They clearly already suspect you are the One, they know your name, and by now they will know what you look like. They do not know for sure, but that mere suspicion is enough to ensure your death, if ever you came into the clutches of the Dark. But if it is still only a suspicion, they might not seek us so urgently—unless the Hulls were able to steal Dernhil's mind. Or unless they know something that we do not."

"But why? Why would they suspect me?" asked Maerad. "How would they know? It's nonsense, Cadvan." She began to feel angry. "A . . . a silly dream on a piece of paper, and anyway, it doesn't say it's me."

"It might. I think it might." Cadvan paused. "I think Lanorgil, when he speaks of the Fire Lily, means the Name of the One who will come." He quoted Lanorgil's words: "*Seek and cherish the Fire Lily, the Fated One, which blooms the fairer in dark places, and sleepeth long in darkness: from such a root will blossom the White Flame anew.* The lily is of course the sign of Pellinor. But they use the arum lily. The Fire Lily, *Elednor* in the Speech, that is a different flower."

"But my Name's not Elednor!" Maerad stood up in her agitation. "My Name is, my Name is . . ."

"Maerad, you don't know your Name. No one will, until your full instatement as a Bard. And if your Name is Elednor, then you are most certainly the One, as foretold by Lanorgil." Cadvan was speaking with great gentleness, and his eyes were full of a strange compassion.

"What if I'm not? What if you've got it all wrong? What then?"

Cadvan shrugged. "As I said before, then I am simply wrong." He was silent for a while more, and then started to speak slowly.

"You don't realize, Maerad, the greatness of your Gift, nor how unusual it is for a Bard to spring from nowhere in such power, wholly untutored," he said. "I began to wonder soon after I scried you. And no doubt our little adventure with the Landrost alerted others. Even with that power you are dangerous, and better silenced before you come into your own. Until you are instated, it is only a suspicion, a suspicion that in my mind grows stronger all the time. Obviously Dernhil entertained the same thought. And if the Hulls know what Dernhil knew, then our plight is darker still. But I wonder, how could the Hulls even suspect so quickly? What is their interest?"

"Dernhil would not have betrayed us," said Maerad uncertainly. She stood still in the flickering light, her arms crossed. A vivid image of Dernhil's face rose before her, and she saw anew the resolve that underlay its gentleness.

"It's not a question of betrayal," said Cadvan. "You don't know . . ." A spasm of pain passed over his face, and for a while he was silent. "Dernhil was strong, and a pure Bard. And I think the Hulls would have wanted to use him, rather than kill him; they would have sought to make him their puppet, their spy in Innail, the better to get to you. A murder would only alert the School to their presence; they cannot stay there now. Even Hulls cannot face the likes of Malgorn and Oron." He paused in thought.

Maerad looked at Cadvan's shadowed face, and finally sat down again by the fire.

"I think it is likely," said Cadvan at last, "that Dernhil killed himself so they could not enter his mind, and I think it is not only my hope speaking." He shuddered. "Believe me, Maerad, there are many worse things than death."

He stared deep into the fire. "According to Lord Kargan, they tried Malgorn and Silvia's house. I made a doorward, a spell of protection on the house, shortly after we arrived there, and that was no bad thing, clearly. It not only drove them back, but it would have also told Malgorn and Silvia who it was who tried the door. It may be that they believe we are still at the School. But I don't *know*."

Maerad was silent, absorbing what Cadvan had said. It was true that Dernhil was dead. Perhaps it was true that the Dark was seeking her, as Cadvan thought. She felt a black fear roiling in her innards.

"How can we know?" she said at last. "I mean, if I have a Name, how do I know it?"

"None of us *knows* anything," said Cadvan gently. "Which is the beginning of wisdom." He paused. "You must be instated, Maerad, and as quickly as we can manage. That is why we go to Norloch: in no other place can we bypass all the Charges, which would otherwise take years of study. This has always seemed clear to me, but now I see it is imperative."

"What, they'll just instate me?" said Maerad. "As a Full Bard? I can hardly read. . . ."

"In special circumstances they will, yes," Cadvan answered. "And these seem very special to me." He sighed. "If you are the One, Maerad, it is a hard destiny, and one you could only take up willingly. And yet if you did not, if you refused it, or tried to escape it, it would haunt you anyway."

"Some choice," said Maerad dryly. She picked up a twig and pushed one end into the fire, watching until it burst into a little tree of flame. She thought suddenly of her mother. Did Milana know more about Maerad than she had told her? Sometimes she had talked of destiny, but Maerad had never known what she meant; she had been too young. . . . The flame burned down the twig until it almost reached her fingers, and she dropped it back on the flames. "Cadvan, what are Hulls?"

"Hulls." Cadvan hunched forward, and seemed to speak reluctantly, as if against his will. Long shadows thrown by the flames haunted his face. "Hulls are—or were—Bards. They have the powers of Bards. They serve the Nameless One."

He stopped, and in the silence Maerad heard the breathing of the horses outside, the rustle of the trees, and a night bird calling. "The Nameless One, as you know, was once a Bard himself, and in order to conquer death, cast out his Name. That is a great crime, and a crime only Bards can commit. The Hulls are bound to his will, although, unlike many of his slaves, they have wills of their own. They too do not die in the ordinary way, but with this difference from the Nameless One: they can be killed. No one knows what happens to them afterward. They have bodies like ours, but after several lifetimes they become abhorrent to behold, although they can disguise themselves as we can and pass for mortals."

He fell silent, looking into his own memories, and then spoke with a vehement anger that took Maerad aback. "I hate them. They betray everything that makes us what we are, and destroy everything that is worthy of love. I hate them more than the Nameless One himself." Then he recalled himself, and continued more calmly. "No one knows how many there are. It is thought that no Bards have turned Hull in living memory, not since the Silence. But I have my doubts about that."

"What do you mean?" Maerad picked up another twig and set it alight. A feeling of horror was beginning to creep up the back of her neck.

"I mean that I think there are Hulls we have not yet recognized," Cadvan answered. "I've spoken of my fears to very few. Some of the problems of the Schools can be put down to petty vices like folly and greed; but I think not all of them. More often than we like, Bards are seduced by the Dark Arts, which does not mean they become Hulls. Think of your friend Mirlad; it seems likely that he was thrown out of the Schools for practicing the Forbidden Lore, but he was most certainly not a Hull. Hulls are thought to look evil, so people do not question the semblance of Bard, but I have sometimes wondered. . . . So, Maerad, place your trust with care! If there is doubt in your heart, listen to it, even over the voices of reason."

Maerad shuddered, and thought of Usted of Desor. He had seemed merely an unpleasant man, but could he be worse? And how could you tell? She had thought Bards free from evil, even if they were imperfect, but now it seemed no one was. For a wild moment she thought of Annar as a larger version of Gilman's Cot, where no one at all could be trusted; but she remembered Silvia and Dernhil and Malgorn, and Cadvan himself, and quietened her fears.

"Why can't the Nameless One be killed?" she asked.

"He made a binding spell," said Cadvan. "Bards have been trying for centuries to decipher that spell. All that is known is that such an enchantment has never been made before or since, and that its power binds him to the earth so that his soul may not depart through the Gates after death, and may reform itself in another body. It is said that the torment was so great when he said the spell that his cry echoed from the realm of Indurain over the ranges of the Osidh Annova all the way to the Isle of Thorold, from the wastes of Zmarkan even down to the Lamarsan Sea. It is held among the wise that he feels this torment still. For no human body can withstand that agony, and it seems he takes only the shapes that have the will to bear it, and they are all abominable and dreadful to the eye.

"And so the Great Silence came to Annar. But for myself, I think I have spoken too long tonight, and we are both tired. It's time to make a little silence of our own."

Maerad wrapped herself in her blanket, trying to find a comfortable spot on the floor. For a while she was restless, and random thoughts flickered unbidden through her mind: Dernhil's murder, her Name, the great raven settling on Cadvan's forearm, the One, the Hulls . . .

None of it makes any sense, she thought exhaustedly, no sense at all. It was like a bad dream, but a dream from which she couldn't wake up.

Fear stirred in her belly like a cold snake.

XIII

ELIDHU

IN the dark hours after midnight, Cadvan shook Maerad urgently awake. He pressed his forefinger to her mouth so she would make no noise. She was instantly alert and sat bolt upright.

She sent out her hearing and heard at once what sounded like a large animal trampling through the forest, breaking branches as it passed. It was, she judged, perhaps a mile off, and in the direction from which they had come. Cadvan had already cloaked the sleeping horses with a charm, so they would make no sound; and noiselessly as mice she and Cadvan sat and listened as the trampling came closer and closer. Whatever it was stopped every few minutes, as if it were casting about for a scent. Maerad felt uneasily for her sword. It seemed to be following their path, and she wondered what it was—too large, too lumbering for a wolf, and a single animal, not a pack.

It came to within a hundred yards of where they sat, and stopped. Maerad could hear its breathing, a rattling inhalation, and a horrible sound of slavering. She and Cadvan sat absolutely still, caught in breathless suspense. Then the creature lunged forward, away from the glade, and it was as if the blood rushed suddenly in a flood through all of Maerad's veins, and she went limp with relief. They listened as it trampled through the forest, the noise receding farther and farther away from them until they could hear it no more.

"What was that?" she whispered, when the night noises of

the forest began to reassert themselves over the unsettling silence.

"I don't know," said Cadvan. "A goromant, maybe; it sounded like one."

"A goromant?

"A great beast with a tail like a scorpion's and armor plating. They hunt by scent, and are very hard to kill. We were lucky we were in this Bardhome; it protects us."

"Was it . . . was it sent by the Dark, do you think?"

Cadvan squinted at her through the darkness of the night. "No, I think not, Maerad. There are many creatures born out of an older power than the Nameless. And in ancient forests like these they yet live, survivors of an ancient malice. Though it's true they may be used by the Nameless."

"Then how do you know it wasn't sent?"

Cadvan had no answer to that, and simply replied that he would keep watch. Shaken, Maerad lay down again. It was a long time before she went back to sleep.

They rose at dawn the next day and continued through the Weywood. In the peace that now surrounded them, the incident overnight seemed like a strange dream. But Cadvan pointed out the track of the beast's passage: clawed footprints in the soft mud by a stream, and freshly broken saplings and branches. The prints were very deep, and Maerad shuddered at the weight they implied; it must have been monstrous.

Dewlings hung from each twig, sparkling in the shafts of sunlight that penetrated the canopy above the track. Looking to each side, Maerad saw the trees were here more thickly grown, wrapping the forest in shadow. Sometimes in the distance she saw a vagrant patch of sun where a great oak had crashed to the ground and lay twined with ivies and mistletoe, or where gray outcrops of granite rose suddenly out of the forest floor. The ground was thick with patches of bracken, pushing out of the copper wreckage of winter its mild green fronds, and near the track flourished all sorts of plants: celandines and bluebells, ground ivy, clumps of nightshade and hemlock, thickets of nettles and briars. Cadvan identified them as they rode, once dismounting to pluck the modest star-shaped green flower of the oneberry. "Also it is called moonwort or true love, and by Bards, martagon," he told her. "Each flower bears a single red-black berry later in the year, which if powdered has virtues against poison. And some say it has other virtues beside, and if taken as a tea, it gives rise to marvelous dreams."

The track was heavily strewn with rotting leaves, which dampened the sound of their hoofbeats, and was punctuated by frequent stony fords from the many streams that crossed it. They were now deep in the Weywood, heading north. As the day drew on Maerad began to feel oppressed by the silence, and she and Cadvan spoke less and less frequently. She thought often of the great beast they had heard the night before; there was no sign of any such creature now. The only sound she could hear in the forest was birdsong, but the birds remained hidden in the branches. Once she thought she saw the red form of a deer disappearing, swift as thought, between the trees, but it was so brief it could have been a trick of her eye; otherwise she saw no living thing.

Cadvan was turning over in his mind the best route to Norloch. He had turned from the West Road into the cover of the woods as soon as possible, and already they were diverted from their most direct course. He now debated with himself the opposing virtues of discretion and speed. The straightest way was also the most perilous, but to tarry had dangers also. He was deeply disturbed by Maerad's revelation of the night before, and in his dilemma wished he could be certain of the truth of Dernhil's death. He had to decide which way would best suit them, whether to follow the roads to Norloch or to push across wilder country away from habitations. Either route had virtues and risks. He didn't need to make up his mind until they left the Weywood, some days ahead, but then that choice was irrevocable.

That night they stayed at another Derenhel, again planted around a rock face in which there was a cave, and this time with a pool in the center of the dingle. They kept watch in shifts, but they heard nothing sinister. The following evening they made camp under a huge oak near the track, again keeping watch. They lit no fire, for Cadvan would do nothing to arouse attention in the forest, and Maerad slept uneasily, feeling unprotected. She was beginning to find the forest's stillness unnerving.

As they traveled, Cadvan passed the time by teaching her more of the Knowing and the mysteries of the Speech, of the histories of the Seven Kingdoms and the realm of Annar, of the behavior of wild birds, and the properties of plants. He told her the different legends about the appearance on the continent of the Bards, called in the Speech of the Starpeople the *Dhillarearën*, and how none were agreed on their origins; and sometimes he recited lays from the time of the Great Silence about the desperate battles of the Light against the Nameless One. He explained how the Light in that time retreated to the outer reaches, now called the Seven Kingdoms—Culain, Ileadh, Thorold, Lanorial, Amdridh, Suderain, and Lirhan—and was almost driven from Annar altogether. They did not mention Hulls at all.

Most evenings they drew out their lyres and played together. Maerad learned in these days how to listen anew to the songs she knew already by heart, and to understand them in a different way: not simply as stories made to lull away the tedium of winter evenings, but as enactments in which the ancient secrets of the Knowing were brought into the present and made real. After the shock of Dernhil's death, and all the events that had preceded it—everything that had happened since she met Cadvan in the cot—she was grateful for this peace. She wished they were merely journeying, and had no urgent quest; she pushed away thoughts of being the Chosen One, the Fated, all those important words that seemed to have nothing to do with her.

On their third day in the forest Maerad felt the sense of oppression increase, as if they were being watched. Cadvan appeared unperturbed, so she said nothing. They made camp under a tree that night; again there was no fire, and as she huddled miserably in the cold on the verge of an uncomfortable sleep, she started awake with the feeling that she had tripped and was falling into deep water. Her eyes opened on another pair of eyes, gleaming yellow like a cat's, looking straight into hers from less than ten feet away. She sat up in alarm, but they immediately vanished; and when Cadvan asked her what was wrong, she said she thought she had seen an owl, or some other animal.

She was beginning to tire of the Weywood, and longed for a breeze on her face and the clear sight of stars or the sun. For the first time since they had left Innail she yearned for a bath; her skin felt sticky and filthy, and she remembered with regret the sweet-smelling oils in Silvia's house. The next morning she saddled Imi discontentedly.

"How long have we got in these forsaken woods?" she asked Cadvan. "Or do they just go on forever?"

"Not forever," said Cadvan. "I would rather be unseen, and the Weywood is an excellent place for hiding, but I know what you mean." He grimaced, buckling up Darsor's girth strap, and swung up into the saddle. "Another two days, and we'll be in plain sight of the sky again."

* * *

Maerad's feeling of unease grew again throughout the day, and she began to itch to leave the forest and wished Cadvan would pick up his pace. Now she was beginning to feel sure that something was watching them, although she could never see anything. If she looked over her shoulder, she sometimes felt a figure had just flicked out of sight; or she saw movements in her peripheral vision that might have been leaves moving in the wind, had there been any wind to move them. Were they pursued? And if so, by what? By late afternoon she was jumping every time one of the horses stood on a twig.

Then she thought she heard something, a voice that seemed to dance on the boundaries of hearing, so at first she wasn't sure if it was a voice at all; perhaps it was the wind fluting through branches, or the far cry of a bird. It would sound, and then vanish before she could grasp it, and then sound again, all the time seeming nearer. She began to feel afraid and glanced across at Cadvan, willing him to mention it. But he continued on, saying nothing. At last, unable to contain her agitation, she said: "Cadvan, do you hear something?"

"You can hear our fellow traveler?" He turned to her and smiled. "Not all ears can hear that song."

"What is it?"

As if the voice were aware they were listening, it at once carried a new clarity. Maerad began to hear words, although they seemed abstracted, as if they were forms moving beneath the shifting surfaces of water. Then it seemed to her that a focus shifted, as it sometimes does when you gaze into a pool, so that where you had seen only the sunlit edges of ripples dazzling the face of the water, now you see clearly in its depths the still form of a trout stippled with red and gold, its fins waving lazily in the lazy currents. With a slight shock Maerad realized she could understand the words:

Soft as a river is to the sleeping swan
Cold as the moonlight fainting on a stone
Deep as the deathless moss on the singing tree
I am this, and this, and this

Fleet as an unseen star in the dwindling glade
Old as the hidden root that feeds the world
Hard as the light that blinds the living eye
I am this, and this, and this

Imi and Darsor stopped and put up their heads, neighing. Maerad sat still, gripped by the enchantment of the song, which was utterly strange and seemed to echo within her head, rather than be heard. She wasn't aware of Cadvan's swift concern, or that he dismounted and went to Imi, holding the reins and reaching up to grasp Maerad's hands.

It seemed then to Maerad that the woods darkened around them, and there appeared from between the trees a wavering silvery illumination, like light from beneath water, and within the shifting light a figure.

"Hail, daughter," said the figure to Maerad. "I have been watching thee."

Maerad stared back in amazement. The figure was a woman, who would have been naked except for the strange impression she gave of being dressed in light, as if the bright silvery waves covered rather than revealed her. Maerad looked into her eyes, and they were the same yellow eyes that had startled her the night before. She had the wildest face she had ever seen, inhuman and fey, amoral and beautiful as a flower.

"Why?" stammered Maerad. "Why have you been watching me?"

The figure laughed. "How often does one of my kin come

this way? I thought perhaps you were coming to greet me, and make music in the old way. But I see you are with one of these dolts, these humans." She laughed again, and Maerad felt a shiver of ice run down her spine. She shook herself and looked down; Cadvan was staring up at her, but it was as if she looked at him through a veil.

"What do you want of me?" she asked.

"I know thee," said the figure. "I will not hinder thee." She came closer to Maerad, and it seemed that she stepped on the air and stood before her, globed in the aqueous light. "I do not hinder my children." She took Maerad's chin in her hand and lifted it, so they gazed eye to eye. "I loved thy forefather many an age ago, and his head rested on my breast, and such pleasure was a wonder to me."

She let Maerad go and stretched sensuously, like a cat, reaching her arms up into the trees. "But like all mortals, he aged and died. I forgot him. And then I heard your voice, and it sounded like his, and I remembered. So I followed thee, and saw; you are my kin."

Maerad was silent.

"Is he your lover, this human? Forget them; they die like the reeds. Come with me to your own kingdom."

Maerad felt a stab of fear. Was she going to be magicked away? "No," she said, more loudly than she intended.

"No?" The figure shrugged and then smiled. "I understand love. I too loved once. But listen, I'll give thee this. Perhaps you will weary of humans; they soil the world, and poison the root of things." She handed Maerad a little flute made out of a reed. "Play on it, and I'll hear thee."

Maerad blinked, and in that instant the figure was gone and all was as it had been, except that she now held the little reed flute in her hand. She looked down. Cadvan was holding Imi's bridle, staring speechlessly up at her. She shook her head, trying to free herself of the strangeness of what had just happened, and laughed.

"What was *that*?" she said shakily.

"What was what?" said Cadvan urgently. "Tell me, Maerad, what happened?"

"Who was she?"

"She is an Elemental Spirit, an Elidhu. What did she say to you?"

"Couldn't you hear?" asked Maerad in astonishment.

"I could hear her, but no human alive speaks their language. If they want to speak to human beings, which is seldom, they will use our tongue, or perhaps the Speech. Maerad, you spoke a language I do not know when you spoke with her."

Maerad sat very still, digesting this information. "I did?"

"Yes, you did." Cadvan sounded agitated. "I didn't know if you had been bewitched."

"No," said Maerad slowly. "No, I don't think so. She said, *I will not hinder thee*." She then recounted their odd conversation, omitting the Elidhu's comments about Cadvan, and he began to look less worried, if not less stunned. He took the little flute and inspected it thoughtfully.

"I used to make pipes like this when I was a child," he said, and handed it back to her. "But this is of some reed that is strange to me." He looked at Maerad with a new curiosity, not untinged, she felt, by amazement. "There were rumors that there was Elemental blood in the House of Karn. I never believed them. Clearly I was wrong." He shook his head, as if he were trying to clear his thoughts. "What does this mean? It's strange, very strange. . . ."

Maerad looked back at him blankly, still feeling as if she were resurfacing from deep water. Cadvan made as if he was about to ask her another question, but stopped himself abruptly. Instead he handed her the reins and returned to

Darsor and remounted. "We should press on," he said. "There's a Bardhome a league or so from here. There we'll talk further."

At the Bardhome they unsaddled and loosed the horses, and then, as had already become routine, lit a fire in the cavern and prepared a meal. Cadvan seemed distracted and Maerad kept silent, although she burned with questions. When they had finished eating, Cadvan stretched out his legs and leaned back against the cave wall, and Maerad studied him in the firelight. He looked tired; deep furrows ran from nose to mouth, and his eyes were hooded. In such moments he seemed a stranger to her — a dark, withdrawn man, his face lined with thought, toughened and weathered by a life of which she had no knowledge. She waited, and eventually, as the evening darkened, he emerged from himself and looked up at her, smiling.

"Forgive me," he said. "What happened today was wholly unexpected. I had no idea. . . ." He shook his head. "I knew you were full of surprises, Maerad, but this surprises even me."

"It surprises me too," said Maerad. "How can I speak to the Elidhu and yet not know the Speech?"

"I don't know," said Cadvan. "Barding is an ancient knowledge. But there is a Knowing more ancient, as ancient as the waters and the trees and the earth, and much of this is unknown to us, or but dimly guessed. This is the Knowing from which the Barding grows, the root. They are not the same. Barding is the concern of humankind, but these Elidhu walked the earth before we did." He paused, and then continued. "To have the blood of Elementals is, among Bards, not quite considered to be a good thing," he said. "If it was in the House of Karn, it is no wonder it was kept secret."

"Why?" asked Maerad. "She was not evil."

"No, not evil," said Cadvan. "But neither can they be relied on in the human world. You spoke to the Elidhu; would you trust her? The things of the Wild are not as us; they are apt to forget what we must remember, and turn like fire in a trice from benign to deadly."

Maerad was silent, staring into the flames. "And what is the House of Karn?"

Cadvan looked up at her swiftly and then looked down. "It is *your* House, your family," he said. "Some Bards, perhaps about half of them, come from families in which Barding has never been known—I am one of those—others do not. The House of Karn is an ancient family of Bards. They were at the founding of Pellinor, and before that at Lirion in the north, and throughout the Silence their line continued unbroken far in the west, on the Isle of Thorold. Lanorgil the Seer was of that family. Andomian and Beruldh, whose story you have sung so often, are your distant ancestors. Milana, your mother, was the daughter of a great heritage of Barding. As are you."

"Me?" Maerad was more staggered by this news than by the encounter with the Elidhu. Suddenly the tragic story of Andomian took on a new immediacy. It's *my* story, she thought: *my* history. She imagined Andomian dying in the dungeons of the sorcerer Karak, alone and desperate, after rescuing her brothers from slavery, and shuddered. "Why haven't you told me this before?" she said.

Cadvan was silent. "Usted mentioned your heritage at the Council in Innail, but apart from that it hasn't come up," he said at last. "And perhaps I do not trust the idea of inherited Barding. There are those who are not worthy of their ancestry, and who are proud beyond their ability or right."

They didn't speak for some time, each following their own thoughts. Maerad thought she sensed a new distance in Cadvan, a retreat from the intimacy that had begun to grow between them, and this grieved her. It wasn't her fault, she thought, that she came from such a family; she had never chosen it, just as she had not chosen to be a slave throughout her childhood. She was still who she was, whatever rags of history she dragged behind her. But then Cadvan stirred.

"I am puzzling over something," he said. "Can you tell me again the song the Elidhu sang?"

Maerad spoke the stanzas that she had heard, and Cadvan listened attentively.

"Yes," he said. "The *deathless moss on the singing tree*, and also *the hidden root*. And Lanorgil spoke of *the Treesong*. Now, Maerad, I am deeply learned in the Speech, and there is much in that lore that speaks of the root of language, and the Tree of Life, and so on. I guess that these are linked. But I have not heard of the Treesong. I don't know what it is." He poked the fire impatiently. "I think it might be rather important that we find out," he said. "And perhaps the Knowing of the Elementals matters a bit more in our affairs than Bards have reckoned. It is written that the Elementals were often at Afinil, and sang with the Bards there; and much of the Knowing was lost in the Great Silence. There is much that perplexes me here. I wish I could talk with Nelac!" He sighed.

"Your teacher?" asked Maerad curiously.

"Yes, he was my teacher," said Cadvan, glancing across at her. "He's very old now. The greatest of the Readers in this land. He is the main reason I wish to go to Norloch. We need his counsel."

"Is he the First Bard there?"

"No, not the First, although of course he is of the Circle. To my mind he is the wisest there; long ago, after Noldor died, Nelac was asked to be First Bard, but he refused, saying he sought not such eminences. The First Bard is Enkir, another great Reader. The First Bards at Norloch have almost without exception been Readers, although there have been a few Makers. Enkir's intellect is as stern as adamant, and among the wise he is held to be very great indeed; he is a proud and lofty Bard, from another great House, the House of Lenar."

"But Nelac is the greater Bard?" said Maerad.

Cadvan looked up at Maerad and grinned, and her earlier worries suddenly dissolved. "Yes, to my mind, although many would disagree," he said. "For Nelac of Lirigon is also wise in the ways of the heart, which Enkir is too cold, too stern, too proud to understand. But you will meet these people and judge for yourself."

"It sounds as if Norloch . . . well, that it has nothing to do with me," said Maerad.

"Norloch is very different from Innail," said Cadvan. "But you have already withstood more frightening things than old men."

The following day they continued through the Weywood, and at last Maerad thought she detected a subtle thinning of the trees and wondered if they neared its edges. Cadvan confirmed this. "Another's day's ride, and we'll be out in the northeast of Annar, a day or two from Milhol," he said. "And then we will have to decide which way to go. There we could meet the Ettinor Road, and I think it would not be wise to travel that way, although we could go more swiftly; but to wend our way farther north takes us even more out of our way. I am even tempted to go to my own School, Lirigon, and thence south to Norloch. I would dearly like to gather some news. But it is many days' ride northward, and would be little to our advantage in the end, I think."

"Do we have to stick to the roads?" asked Maerad.

"No, not always," said Cadvan. "And I think we will not, although west of Milhol the countryside is rough and in some places impassable. I also fear getting lost!"

They rode on in companionable silence. After her encounter

with the Elidhu the day before, the Weywood no longer seemed hostile to Maerad; and although she still longed to get out of the twilight of the trees into sunlight and wind, she also realized she felt safer here, hidden from prying eyes, despite the dangers of the forest itself. She felt, for no reason that she could trace, as if the Elidhu protected them. The long days riding through the wood had also given her a chance to absorb the events of the past three weeks. She felt less confused in herself, less doubtful, although it seemed the more she found out, the more her questions multiplied. She said as much to Cadvan, who replied: "It is ever the way of the Knowing. I have often thought it is like a light blooming on a dark sea: as it increases, so does the depth and size of the unknown. The most wise are those who know how little they know!"

They made camp in another dingle that night, but this time there was no cave and they could make no fire. The fine weather held, and this night was even a little warm. After dawn the following day they continued, and around lunchtime Maerad saw a light through the trees, and they reached the end of the track.

The forest stopped quite suddenly, and Maerad found, blinking, that they were looking over a land of rolling hills shaded with the purplish bloom of heather. The track wandered over the landscape ahead, and Cadvan told her that if they followed it, in time they would reach one of the Bard Roads that led to Ettinor, following the Milhol River. "For now," he said, "I think we will push on to Milhol. I wish to know how the land lies around here. And then we must decide what to do next."

The landscape they rode through was lonely and bare, swept by strong winds blowing down off the distant mountains, which humped blue on the eastern horizon. No trees grew there, apart from some stunted thorns, and every now and then they passed tumbled outcrops of gray weathered granite blotched with bright lichens, purple and yellow and green and white. There were also other stones, which seemed to have been placed there by human hands: circles at the top of small hills that looked like massive broken crowns, some overthrown and broken, some still upright but leaning crazily like drunken men.

"These were here before Afinil, and date from the earliest days that humans walked this land," said Cadvan. "None now know what they signified; even in the days of the Dhyllin they were ancient and abandoned. They were set here by the hill people who lived many thousands of years ago. Some think that they mark the tombs of their kings and queens, and some think these are the places where they worshipped their gods. Some of them have curious carvings."

"And what do you think?" asked Maerad.

"I do not know," he said.

When dusk began to fall they were still far from habitation, and they found a dell away from the wind under one of the hills and made camp there. There was no sound except the sigh of the wind through the grass and the melancholy cries of plovers, and that night they did not take out their lyres, but talked quietly together. Maerad drew closer to the fire.

"It feels desolate here," she said.

"Yes," said Cadvan. "They call these the Hollow Lands. No one has lived here in living memory."

"It was all so long ago and far away," she said. "But it's as if the land remembers people, nevertheless."

That night Maerad slept restlessly, and it seemed in her dreams she heard the sound of hoofbeats far off in the night, searching for her, and all around were sinister shapes of men cloaked in black. She woke, shivering, and looked straight up into the star-strewn heavens, where the waxing moon rode high in a wrack of cloud. Cadvan lay close by, snoring lightly, and soon she slept again and dreamed no more.

*   *   *

Still they followed the path that had led them through the Weywood, and at midmorning the next day it suddenly dipped into swamplands. Here the going was slow because they had to pick their way through, fearing to lose the path altogether, and often the horses sank into mud past their fetlocks. Clouds of gnats and mosquitoes pestered them, and their discomfort increased as the sun got hotter. They pushed on for several hours, not stopping for lunch, and at last, to Maerad's relief, were past the bogs and back on solid ground. They stopped by a small stream for a late meal, and let the horses graze and drink.

"Now," said Cadvan. "Soon we will be among people again. I doubt that I'll see anyone who knows me, but still, it is worth taking precautions against Bard eyes." He thought for a while, and then said, "How do you fancy being my mute son, and I a . . . boot maker, maybe, from near Pellinor, seeking help for his son's affliction in Ettinor?"

"Why not?" said Maerad, amused. "But do you know any-thing about boot-making?"

"Ar, mistress," said Cadvan, winking in a rascally fashion. "You don't know what I know. My da was a cobbler, and his boots were much prized in Lirigon. And elsewhere, come to that."

Their disguise took a little time. Cadvan attended to Maerad first, making her place her hands on his shoulders, as she had when he scried her, and muttering a charm in the Speech. A brief flash of light passed before Maerad's sight, dizzying her for a second, and when she recollected herself, she looked down and involuntarily cried out. Her body had changed: she now looked like a boy, and her clothes were subtly different, roughly woven of undyed wool. Then Cadvan changed him-self, which Maerad watched with fascination. Her eyes couldn't catch the moment of transformation, but it seemed that

Cadvan's face blurred; she blinked, and when she looked again he was different. His hair was red, and he had a red beard, and his features were heavier.

"Now the horses," he said, and she blinked again, for his voice also was deeper and rougher. "They are altogether too fine for such as us." He worked the charm again, and suddenly Darsor and Imi were two farm animals, Darsor with a walleye.

He turned to Maerad, passing his hands over his eyes. "This will last until sundown tomorrow," he said. "and will do well for us. I don't want to stay more than a night at Milhol. No Bard or Hull will recognize us now. But I must rest a little; it takes more to fool the eyes of Bards than other people. Look well at me, for you must remember what I look like."

That night they stayed at Milhol, a small market town of two or three thousand people, with houses of several stories that almost met above the narrow cobbled lanes, cutting off the light. People looked at them as they walked through the narrow streets, and Maerad didn't like the glances, which she found distrustful and hostile. The streets stank of middens, and their gutters were full of rubbish, vegetable peelings, eggshells, and rotting refuse. It was not, she thought, comparing it to the well-tended gardens of Innail School, a particularly pleasant place. It reminded her forcibly of Gilman's Cot.

She didn't enjoy their stay at the evil-smelling inn either. It was run by a black-browed man in a greasy apron who admitted them surlily; he showed them to a mean little room with a tiny cobwebbed window and two lumpy pallets. To Cadvan's chagrin, he charged them more than twice what they had paid in Innail Fesse. They went to the taproom for dinner, because Cadvan wanted to sound out the locals on the conditions ahead of them, but they didn't stay long. The local talk was that the only real danger on the road was bandits.

Maerad woke before dawn. A cock was crowing somewhere in the distance, but that wasn't what woke her: she itched terribly all over. Scratching furiously, she sat up, and Cadvan stirred sleepily and then woke instantly. "What's the matter?" he said.

"Bedbugs," she hissed. "Or fleas. Or lice. I'm being bitten by *things*."

"Probably bedbugs," said Cadvan. He inspected her dispassionately. "Look, one's bitten your nose."

"I hope they bit you too. Hard," she said, torn between irritation and amusement.

Cadvan sat up. "I don't think they did," he said. "Insects don't like me much. Too tough." He swung his legs over the edge of the bed and rubbed his hair with his fingers, so it stood all on end. "Well, they woke us early enough to get out of this place. So let's go."

Cadvan told her to put on her mail, so she dragged it out of the pack where it had lain since they had left Innail. Her neck prickled as she put it on, feeling its heavy coldness, and she fumbled at the sword that had hung from her hip, unused and almost forgotten, for days. Then they picked up their packs and left the room.

Downstairs the only sign of life was the cook in the kitchen, who was firing up the stove. He was disinclined to serve them breakfast so they left the inn, walking out into the cold air. Maerad felt unutterable relief at leaving that noisome fug and breathed in the fresh air deeply, although it was so cold it was like icy blades stabbing her lungs. She snorted plumes of steam out of her nostrils like a dragon.

They unstabled their horses and found a bakery farther down the street, where Cadvan bought two loaves of bread and some meat pastries. They ate the pastries on horseback as they trotted out of Milhol, their breath curling on the icy air. The gate was just opened, and two grimy guards looked at them suspiciously as they left. Cadvan gave them a cheery wave, to the guards' evident displeasure, and then they trotted briskly down the dirt road by which they had approached the town. In little under half an hour the road ran into another, this one of stone.

"This is the Bard Road to Ettinor. Here we can make up some lost time," Cadvan said, turning in the saddle. Imi and Darsor neighed and pawed the ground, and then leaped forward at a gallop. It seemed they were as glad as their riders to leave Milhol.

The sun rose soon after they met the Bard Road, lighting a dour country softened by heavy mists. They slowed to a trot, and Maerad began to look around her. Behind them the mountains still sat heavily on the horizon, and to their left Maerad could see the purplish hills of the downs in the distance, but all around them the land was flat as a floodplain. The Milhol River ran to their right, and it looked to Maerad as sullen as the landscape, with black reeds poking through its brown surface. There were few trees, and those she saw stood solitary, bent by the prevailing winds. The land was poor and rocky, grown with tussocks of tough grass and thistles and milkweeds. After sunrise they began to pass farmers heading to the markets of Milhol. They passed wagons of produce pulled by tired-looking ponies with rough hair and staring ribs, and the occasional wagon pulled by oxen; two or three times there was a woman walking with a heavy basket strapped to her back, out of which poked the heads of chickens, squawking in protest, or the nodding fronds of turnips or rutabagas. Cadvan nodded to each person they passed, but only once was his greeting acknowledged, by a young woman with a small, grizzling child pulling at her skirts.

"It's hard to scrape a living from this land," said Cadvan. "And it makes the people bitter. It was not always so. A

hundred years ago, this country was green and fertile. The
people here have forgotten how to speak to the earth; they now
take without giving."

The farther they drew from Milhol, the more seldom they
saw people, and by late afternoon they no longer saw anyone at
all and passed no more houses. They moved at a brisk trot, both
feeling that the sooner they left this sullen country the better,
and rode on after dusk until it was almost full night, guided by
the light of the stars and the half moon. Only when they could
travel no more did they draw to the side of the road and make
camp. They huddled in the shelter of a great tree that looked as
if it had been blasted by lightning and lay riven in two twisted
halves. Cadvan sat still, listening, for some time, and then
decided to light a fire. "I hear nothing for miles around," he
said. "I think we will be safe enough. But I think we should
keep watch tonight."

As he kindled a flame with his flint, Maerad saw that
Cadvan had his own face back again. "Cadvan!" she said. He
looked up in surprise. "You're back!"

"And so are you," he said, squinting through the darkness.
"I may say, it's some improvement. I was a little too convincing
in making you an idiot boy." The fire sparked into life and he
tended it, swiftly building the flames. "We'll wear our own
faces for a couple of days. It's risky, but I haven't the energy to
disguise us, unless there is great need."

They continued through the dismal countryside for the next
two days, traveling all day as swiftly as they could and keeping
watch at night. They saw no one else on the road. Gradually the
landscape began to change; the river carved itself into a ravine
that grew deeper and deeper, and ridges began to shadow
them, rising to sharp shoulders of bare rock that dropped to
sheer cliffs. Little waterfalls fell straight down the cliffs, gathering in shallow pools of rock slimed with green, and stunted

pines straggled up the rough slopes. Cadvan looked warily around him, and as they rode, Maerad began to be uncomfortably aware of the sharp clop of the horses' hooves on the road, which echoed loudly off the rocks.

"These are the Broken Hills. Bandit country," said Cadvan. "Use your hearing."

Maerad pushed her awareness out into the hills. She heard the wind whistling through teeth of rock, the scuffle of claws on loose stones, the cries of hunting birds, and the death screeches of little animals, but nothing human. Very high above them she occasionally saw a pair of birds circling on the wind. "Eagles," said Cadvan briefly. "They are not birds of the Dark. They seek their prey." Nevertheless, she couldn't throw off the feeling of menace, which gathered all day as the country became wilder and the road began to push through gorges of rock, the sides leaping sheer from them on either side. But still the land was empty, and she heard neither footfall nor hoofbeat all day. The silence itself seemed threatening.

That night they camped slightly off the road under an overhang of rock. They lit no fire. The horses stamped and circled, cropping the tough, bitter grass, and they sat in silence, looking out into the road and the rocky horizon on its other side cutting off the stars with blades of darkness. They were, Cadvan told her, now less than two days' ride from Ettinor. "If our luck holds, we'll be well past it in three days or so," he said. "But I don't trust these hills. It is altogether too silent here."

"We're not going to Ettinor?" asked Maerad, thinking of Helgar and other Bards at Innail.

"By no means to the School," he answered. "We'll cut around it through the Fesse, and after that we'll leave the road for a while. After Ettinor the road runs along the Aleph River, straight to Norloch. I think we have to stay off roads as far as possible from now on; if the Dark suspects that you are the

One, as I fear it might, it will be using every resource it has to find you."

Just before dawn the temperature dropped sharply and it began to drizzle. Maerad and Cadvan started early simply to get the blood moving in their frozen limbs. In the dismal light before dawn the landscape looked even more dreary than it had the day before. Maerad was beginning to feel exhausted after the punishing pace of the past few days, and she felt a deeper tiredness, which was of the spirit rather than the body, and harder to resist. Imi no longer walked with a spring in her step but plodded on, doggedly keeping up with Darsor, who stepped out as proudly as before. Jogging along on Imi's back, Maerad felt miserable; her hands were numb with cold, her cloak flapped damply around her knees, and her face felt raw with windburn. She tried not to think about a bath or a hot roast, although images of both kept rising in her head; they made the present moment even worse. The drizzle continued through the morning, and then settled into a steady rain. They stopped for a hasty lunch, and after that the rain lifted and was replaced with a freezing wind that cut through their clothes, chilling them to the bone.

Cadvan was still alert, continually checking around them, but Maerad was too cold to care and rode on in a stupor of misery. She was taken by surprise when he halted, lifting his hand to signal that she should stop too. "Listen," he said.

Maerad started and guiltily sent out her hearing. Under the thin whine of the wind she could hear hoofbeats in the distance. It sounded like a single horse, heading toward them. She turned questioningly to Cadvan.

"I think it is about a mile in front of us," said Cadvan. "A solitary traveler in these lands must be a Bard. And I cannot disguise us now; this close, that spell would be sensed." He looked across at Maerad. "We will have to pretend we are simply travelers. If it is a Hull, which is unlikely, don't look surprised or shocked; it will most likely be wrapped in a glimmerspell, and you would not know, if you were not a Bard."

"But won't a Hull know we're Bards?" asked Maerad uneasily.

"He probably won't look that closely, in this weather," said Cadvan. "But it would be well to veil yourself."

"Veil myself?" Maerad stared at him. As she watched, the air around Cadvan seemed to dim. It was barely perceptible, and she felt, rather than saw, the difference.

"Think of a shield around you, hiding you," he said. Maerad shut her eyes and concentrated. She opened them again and looked inquiringly at Cadvan.

"Yes, that's it," he said. He inspected them both, then pulled his hood farther down over his face. "I think we look miserable enough to pass for peasants," he said. "But Darsor will not do." He spoke to the horse, who snorted and pawed the ground but then slumped himself. Maerad blinked in surprise: the proud Darsor now looked goosenecked and swaybacked, and he walked with a slight limp. Cadvan patted his neck. "A master actor, this horse," he said.

"This time I could be your lunatic daughter," said Maerad. "If that would help." She messed up her hair, trailing tresses across her face in witch-locked tangles, and adopted a slack-jawed expression.

Cadvan laughed grimly. "I'm beginning to think that in some respects your education was quite thorough," he said.

They continued at a slow walk. Maerad was now alert, forgetting the cold entirely, and she monitored the hoofbeats until they entered her normal range of hearing. She felt a vague sense of evil, a feeling of desolation and malice that grew as the hoofbeats drew closer. Her heart beat faster and faster. Then, more suddenly than she expected, the horseman appeared a hundred feet or so before them, coming at a slow trot around a ridge of rock.

He was cloaked heavily in black and wore high black boots with sharp spurs. He rode a big-boned bay horse, which continually threw up its head, champing on a cruel bit.

Maerad knew immediately the rider was a Hull. The horse's eyes were circled with white and its sides were flecked with white foam streaked with blood. The Hull's face was entirely shadowed by its hood, but Maerad saw with a shudder that the hands on the reins were shriveled and white and bony, like those of a mummified corpse, and it wore a ring of dull silver that clasped a black stone. She gulped and plodded on with Cadvan, closer and closer to the Hull, although she felt that Imi's steps were full of loathing, and the animal threatened to shy.

After what seemed an age they drew level. Now Maerad's heart was hammering against her ribs, and her tongue was dry in her mouth. She could not have said anything, even if she had wanted to. The rider halted, blocking their way, and her stomach lurched with fright. She looked down at its hands, although the sight of them sickened her, and saw the black stone of the ring was carved into the semblance of a grinning skull. Cadvan stopped, as if it were a courtesy, and spoke. "Good day, sir," he said pleasantly. "Mighty hard weather for a ride."

The Hull stared at him, and now Maerad could see a bony nose and eyes burning like red embers within the shadow of the hood. "It is indeed," it said, and its voice seemed to come from a great depth. "Only the foolhardy venture forth on this route."

"Aye," said Cadvan. "Or the desperate." He indicated Maerad with an inclination of his head. "My daughter, sir, has been mad these last three months, and I go to Ettinor to ask their help."

Maerad obligingly goggled at the Hull. She found that if she unfocused her eyes the Hull looked almost like a Bard or a fine lord in a long cloak, which was easier to bear than the grim figure she otherwise saw.

"There might be help in Ettinor for such as you," said the Hull sneeringly. "Or there might not."

"I seek no favors, sir, that I can't pay for," said Cadvan. His face was blank, eager to please, and a little foolish. "But I wonder, sir: have you seen bandits farther up the road? I feared at first that you were one of them, begging your pardon, but we've seen none so far, though others warned us of them."

"The bandits have been purged," said the Hull. "They became a nuisance."

"Well, then, that's good news, and no mistake," said Cadvan. There was a short pause. "Well, we've a way to go." He urged Darsor on. "A good day to you, then, sir."

Slowly, as if it did so reluctantly, the Hull moved aside to let them pass. Maerad put her head down and followed Cadvan, keeping her mind as blank as possible. She couldn't stop her hands from shaking. As she drew level, the Hull's head suddenly rose, and it hissed as if it were about to say something, looking straight at her. She could feel it probing her mind, as if sickly tentacles crept over her, and the gorge rose in her throat. Without thinking she threw herself forward over the pommel of her saddle, letting out a high, tearing scream, as she had heard a lunatic woman wail once in Gilman's Cot. She filled her mind with nightmarish images of a giant spider, and then of a many-headed snake, and the Hull's fingerings withdrew with a snap, as if in distaste.

"Now, Marta, don't take on so," said Cadvan, riding forward. "Forgive her, sir, forgive her," he said to the Hull. "It's the madness, she has such fits. . . ."

The Hull spat on the ground and spurred its horse on past them, knocking into Darsor. The black horse shied, almost unseating Cadvan. Maerad continued her wailing until the hoofbeats vanished in the distance, and then stopped, hiccupping a few times for verisimilitude. She looked up at Cadvan, who put his forefinger over his mouth to silence her. They continued at the same slow walk for another hour before they dared say anything to each other.

"That was close," Cadvan said at length. "Thank the Light for your quick wits, Maerad. I thought for a second we were lost. It sensed you."

Maerad still felt nauseous, as if somehow she had been poisoned. "He tried to read me," she said shakily. "So I just let myself panic and thought of monsters. It was horrible."

"You're not nearly as fragile as you look. Better to seem weak than to be so." Cadvan grinned wryly, and Maerad wanly smiled back, feeling her nausea begin to subside. "It's rare for Hulls to ride openly through Annar, even these days," Cadvan said. "And it was riding from Ettinor. Perhaps it had been sent to gather news of us, perhaps on other business. I don't know. But I begin to understand some things more clearly."

"About Ettinor?" asked Maerad.

"Yes," Cadvan said heavily. "I've spoken of some of my fears to you already. It seems they are not misled. I have not been in Ettinor these past few years. Last time I did not like it, but did not sense an active evil. But things can change fast." Cadvan seemed deep in troubled thought. "Even if Ettinor is one of the corrupt Schools, I can hardly bear to think of it as beholden to the Nameless One and a haven for Hulls. There are Bards, even there, who have spoken out against the corruption of the Knowing in the Schools, and who work for the restoration of Barding."

They rode on for some time in silence. "The Nameless must feel sure in his power, to be so closely folded in the bosom of his enemy," he said at last. "It is a very bad sign."

XIV

THE KULAG

CADVAN and Maerad reached the Fesse of Ettinor on the afternoon of the next day. The Broken Hills sank gradually down into level plains, and here wild grasses nodded knee-high beside the road in a mild breeze, and willows hung their long leaves in the river beside them. After a few miles the road turned sharply north and forded the Milhol River, and on its other side they rode through farming lands dotted by herds of cattle and sheep, with frequent copses of beech, alder or poplar, or huge solitary oaks. The houses were styled differently from those in the Innail Fesse, built of gray stone with small, high windows and roofs of red clay tiles, and many had bright window boxes with red or pink geraniums. It was a pleasant countryside to ride through, and Maerad felt it as a balm on her eyes after the harsh rocks and scrubby vegetation of the past few days.

They were again in disguise as the cobbler Mowther and his idiot son, this time traveling the countryside seeking work; after their encounter the previous day, Cadvan was taking no chances. They passed several people on the road, but again Maerad noticed that few returned Cadvan's greetings. They saw no Bards. Once they saw a farrier riding along in a big black apron, with his tools jingling on his saddle, on his way perhaps to shoe one of the big working horses Maerad had seen in the fields; and a shepherd with two dogs chivvying along a small flock of sheep; and three barefoot children playing in the road who, when they saw the strangers, immediately ran away and hid. Soon in the distance Maerad saw the walls of the School, and its high gray towers. Cadvan bent their way south of the School, heading west.

"It's pretty country," said Maerad. "Almost as pretty as Innail."

"Yes, but growing poor," Cadvan said. "Not so long ago, you never saw children shoeless around here. Another few decades and it will be like the country around Milhol."

After that Maerad began to notice signs of neglect or poverty; tiles missing in a barn roof or rotting carts and wagons abandoned by the side of the road. Many fields, which Cadvan told her should now be under seed, were growing wild with rank grasses and thistles; and not infrequently they saw farmhouses that had been abandoned altogether, their windows broken, their roofs beginning to collapse, high dockweeds thrusting over the walls of the courtyards. It was not always so, and she still saw many houses with well-tended gardens and orchards, and some very grand houses looking out over big grounds; but beneath the pleasant surface of Ettinor she felt a pervasive sense of slow decay, of hopeless struggle against entropy.

"Despair is in the heart of Ettinor," said Cadvan, as they passed another rotting farm. "It is the worst sickness of all. A betrayal of the covenant of Barding."

"Where do the people go?" asked Maerad.

"Into the towns, sometimes, to try to earn a living there," said Cadvan. "Some become travelers, working for others when they can't make a living on their own land."

"But why is it happening? I mean, it's not like there's famine or anything. . . ."

"It's since the death of Eth, who was First Bard here," Cadvan said. "He was succeeded by Finlan, a proud and ambitious man, fifty or so years ago. Finlan raised the tithes on the landowners, arguing the Bards were ill-paid for their work. Perhaps none would have objected, had the Bards kept up their service; but this he allowed to slacken. And still the tithes rise, and they are demanded with force from those who cannot pay them."

At this, Maerad cocked a questioning eyebrow. Cadvan then explained that the Schools were kept not only by their economies of Wrighting and Making, but by tithes paid by the landowners in the Fesses; and in return, the Bards were considered the servants of the people, and made their skills available.

"They teach the children to read and do their sums, heal the sick, perform the rites of spring and harvest, and many other things," he said. "But Ettinor Bards have become arrogant and believe they are above such service, and they demand payment for much that once was freely given. So the name of Barding in many places has fallen into disrepute."

"Is Finlan a Hull, then?" asked Maerad.

"I don't believe so," said Cadvan. "Although these days it is difficult to be sure of anything. But I have wondered if there are Hulls at Ettinor School, and my doubts have increased with the years. Now I am sure there are."

Toward dusk they entered a small unwalled town named Fort, and there stayed in a comfortable inn called the Brown Duck. To Maerad's delight it even had a bathroom, although it didn't have hot water. With intense relief she peeled off her filthy clothes, washed herself all over, and changed into the clean clothes in her pack. It was peculiar, she thought, washing what felt like the body of a girl but looked like a boy. It had already led to some difficulties: when she wanted to urinate, she thought she ought to stand up, but found this was a little messy unless she stood with her hips stuck out at a very unnatural angle. She had caught Cadvan laughing at her earlier in the day when she was struggling behind a tree and, scarlet-cheeked, she had forgotten her supposed muteness and had shouted at him. Which had, to her fury, only increased his amusement.

She returned to their sitting room to find Cadvan, in the guise of Mowther, slumped by the fire, his boots off. "We need to do some washing," she said, expecting that he would demur that they had no time. To her surprise, he agreed.

"We'll stay here tomorrow," he said. "I think we're safe enough; I doubt anyone will seek us in Fort. I want to buy some supplies and hear what news I can. And we could do with a rest before we go on."

Later, after they had checked the horses—Darsor's report was encouraging, although Maerad suspected that he chafed at any stabling—they went to the taproom for a meal. It was a cheery room with a huge hearth, over which stood copper plates and horse brasses, with whitewashed walls stained by centuries of wood smoke, and clean rushes on the dark wooden floor. A few farmers sat quietly at tables drinking the black local beer, but otherwise it was almost empty. The innkeeper, a pleasant-faced man called Mr. Dringold, was serving drinks, and Cadvan ordered them some wine and a roast lamb with vegetables. A little boy of about four with a black shock of curly hair served the wine, carrying the clay carafe with great seriousness, as if he bore the most precious crystal, and Cadvan thanked him soberly.

Shortly afterward Dringold's wife, a cheerful woman with the same curly hair as her son, brought them their meal. After their thin fare of the previous few days Maerad's mouth was watering, and Cadvan was taken aback by how quickly her serving disappeared. They followed the roast with a mulberry pie with cream, and followed that with some excellent white cheese, made locally, as the innkeeper told them proudly. They had some more of the very passable wine, and they sat without speaking in the nook by the fire, very well content.

"Quiet boy, your son," said Mr. Dringold in passing, as he carried some beers to another table.

"He's never spoke since the day he was born," said Cadvan. "But he's handy enough."

"Just passing through, are you?"

"That's the idea. There doesn't seem to be much call for cobblers around here."

"Mr. Dothan there wouldn't thank you if you stayed," said Dringold, nodding his head at a stocky man hunched over a nearby table. "He has enough trouble holding body and soul together as it is. There aren't that many in these parts who can afford more than one pair of shoes, if any, if you take my meaning."

He returned to their table after delivering the drinks, and he and Cadvan started chatting. Maerad sat sleepily by them, listening to the conversation. It was getting late, and she was looking forward to sleeping in a real bed, with real sheets. The talk was more of the same: the difficulties of making a living, how business was falling off year by year and prices were going up and up. Maerad noticed that Dringold didn't mention Bards. Cadvan nodded sympathetically.

Suddenly the innkeeper's wife rushed into the room, her face white. "Ewan," she said. "It's Lanal! He's got the croup again, but it's bad." Dringold stood up hastily and excused himself.

"I might be able to help," said Cadvan, rising. "This boy had the croup bad as a child, and I learned some tricks." The woman looked at him doubtfully, but didn't protest when he followed them to their private quarters. Unsure what to do, Maerad followed Cadvan.

The little boy was sitting by the fire in the kitchen, cradled by one of the maids. He was clearly struggling to breathe; he made terrible honking noises every time he pulled in a breath.

Maerad saw that his lips were a livid blue. She had seen children in this extremity before. Usually they died.

"How long has he been like this?" asked Cadvan, and Maerad noticed with a slight shock that he wasn't speaking like Mowther the cobbler.

"About half an hour," said the woman. "But he's been getting worse and worse. I don't know what to do." She drew in breath tightly, as if she were trying not to cry, and bit her lip.

"Do you have any coltsfoot in the kitchen? Or borage?" he asked.

"Coltsfoot? I think so . . . and borage too, I think. . . ." She went to a shelf laden with small glass bottles of dried herbs, and picked them out.

"Make a tea, quickly," said Cadvan. "Steep one spoon of each in a large pot."

He took the child gently from the maid and sat down with him. The boy didn't have enough breath to cry but was clearly frightened and struggled weakly in Cadvan's arms.

"What is his name? Lanal?" Cadvan looked up at Dringold. The innkeeper nodded. Cadvan looked down at the boy, and then whispered in his ear: *"Feärnese,* Lanal. *Feärnese."* Immediately the child's breathing eased, and he stopped struggling and relaxed trustingly back into Cadvan's chest. Cadvan stroked his hair and chest, whispering all the time, and a minute later the horrible noise stopped and he began to breathe properly. The frightening blue color ebbed from his mouth. Then, it seemed quite suddenly, the child sat up.

"I'm thirsty, Mummy," he said. "I want something to drink." He looked shyly at Cadvan and reached out his arms for his mother.

"He'll be all right now," said Cadvan, handing him over. "Give him some of the tea, when it has cooled down; it will clear his lungs. If he starts to get like that again, let him breathe

the vapors of the coltsfoot before he gets this bad. And keep him in a warm room."

There was complete silence in the kitchen.

"I thought he was dying," said the innkeeper's wife.

"Children forget pain quickly," said Cadvan. "I've often seen it."

Now that his terrible fear for his son had abated, Dringold almost looked as if he were angry. "That was Bard stuff, that was," he said, a little too loudly.

"Maybe it was, maybe it wasn't," Cadvan answered. "Like I said, I learned a few tricks when mine was a little boy."

"Only Bards are allowed to do the Healing," said Dringold. "A midwife was drove out of town last month for making simples."

"That's not the law where I come from," Cadvan said, and Maerad saw a flash of anger in his eyes. "If someone is sick, someone should heal, if they can. Anyway, the boy is safe now."

They stood in the kitchen watching the little boy, who was now acting as if he had never suffered a day's illness in his life and was nagging his mother for a biscuit.

"So, what do we owe you?" said the innkeeper. Cadvan looked as if he had been insulted, and Dringold blushed.

"You owe me nothing," said Cadvan. "I'd appreciate it if you kept it under your hats, is all. I'd not like to be chased by Bards, if I've done the wrong thing."

"You haven't done the wrong thing," said the innkeeper's wife impulsively. Her eyes were now wet. "Oh, Ewan, I was so frightened. He's never been like this before. I thought of Medelin's little one that was took ill last week, and I couldn't have borne it."

"It's all right, Rose," said Dringold gruffly. "Thank you, then, Mr. Mowther, if Mr. Mowther you be." He gave Cadvan and Maerad a sharp look. "I owe you greatly. That little boy is all the world to me and Rose." He pulled out a large red ker-chief and blew his nose.

"Well, me and the boy had better get to bed," said Cadvan. "And so had you." He nodded good night, and he and Maerad left the kitchen and made their way to their rooms.

"Was that wise?" asked Maerad, as soon as they were in the privacy of their sitting room.

"Wise?" Cadvan shot her a piercing glance.

"I mean, if we're trying to hide that we're Bards . . ." She trailed off. "I mean, Mr. Dringold obviously suspects us. . . ."

"If that is all that matters: no, it was not wise," said Cadvan. "However, what is wisdom, if it means allowing that little boy to die?"

"Would he have?" said Maerad.

"Yes," answered Cadvan. "He would by now be dead." He hunched his shoulders and sat down, brooding. "Maerad, sometimes there are choices that lead to ill, but that neverthe-less have to be made. I could not stand by idly, knowing I could save him. That is not the way of Bards."

Maerad thought regretfully of the washing. "I guess we'll have to leave early tomorrow, then," she said.

"I think not," said Cadvan. "I think Mr. Dringold and his wife will stay quiet about us. We'll wear the risk, for now." Even through his disguise Maerad could see the shadows of exhaustion on Cadvan's face. She thought of the maid and won-dered if he was making the right decision. But she too was tired, and was glad of the prospect of rest.

When they emerged from their beds the next day, the sun was high. They breakfasted generously on spiced sausage and beans and bacon; Mr. Dringold's menu even ran to fried mushrooms, which pleased Cadvan. Dringold also arranged for their wash-ing to be taken to the launderers, where it would be ready by that night. Cadvan and Maerad then made their way to the Fort market.

Maerad had never been in a market before and was fascinated. It was alive with colors and smells. There were huge orange pumpkins and green and gold squashes, and streaky yellow apples, sweet and slightly wrinkled from their winter storage; and she saw greens of all kinds, early spring lettuces and leeks, and dried bunches of parsley and mint and marjoram and nettles, and the purple-green of huge winter cabbages, slashed in half to reveal their intricate white innards. There were piles of dried beans and peas, and yellow lentils and brown grains, and bunches of garlic and onions, and sacks of hazels and walnuts and almonds, stippled the colors of autumn; and great round white cheeses wrapped in leaves or blue wax, plumped fatly on the wooden trestles. Over everything drifted the smells of freshly baked breads and roasting chestnuts, and sausages and onions frying on a brazier, and everywhere were the sounds of donkeys braying and cows lowing and goats bleating in stalls and dogs barking and the chatter of townspeople bargaining.

On the edge of the square two minstrels played pipes and a fiddle, with a hat laid on the ground before them for coins. They were dressed in bright clothes, with scarlet scarves around their necks, and they wore blue felt hats with bells that jingled as they danced. They sang about foolish farmers and lovelorn lassies, and a haunting ballad of a man who fell in love with a river sprite, and a funny song about a drunk blacksmith falling into a well. Maerad stood before them enraptured, until Cadvan told her she looked exactly like the idiot she pretended to be and dragged her off to do some shopping.

He drifted in a leisurely fashion around the market, chatting with the stallholders, and Maerad followed him silently, admiring again his ease with people, how he could make even the most reserved open up and talk. He bought a supply of dried fruits and meats, barley flour and grain, a little oil and vinegar, some tough bread that would keep for up to two weeks, and a small sack of oats for the horses. What struck her most forcibly was the fear that arose at any mention of Bards or Barding; stallholders would look around as if they thought someone listened and would say no more, or loudly change the subject. When Cadvan had finished making purchases, they went back to where the minstrels had been playing, because Maerad wanted to hear more, but there was an argument going on. A woman who was clearly a Bard—she wore the cloak and the clover leaf brooch of Ettinor—was shouting and confiscating the minstrels' instruments. When they protested, she froze them both with a gesture of her hand. Then, with a look of contempt, she scooped up the coins from their hat and left them there, unable to move. Cadvan watched the scene with distaste.

"There is too much that is illegal here," he said.

"What will happen to them?" asked Maerad.

"They will be uncharmed, eventually," said Cadvan. "But they might be left there all night, as a punishment."

After that Maerad didn't want to stay at the market any longer, and they returned to the Brown Duck, where they packed their baggage. Cadvan decided they should eat in their room that night and arranged for a meal to be brought to them. "We'll leave before dawn tomorrow," he said.

"And what then?" asked Maerad.

"If anyone is asking questions, there is beginning to be a trail that the ill-minded could follow," said Cadvan. "We're going to disappear."

"What does that mean?" Maerad lifted a dubious eyebrow; clearly there were going to be no more inns for a while.

"It means we go into the wild," said Cadvan. "For the next

eighty leagues west the country is empty and pathless. It will be hard to find us, if anyone is looking in this direction."

"But in such places live the creatures of the Dark," said Maerad.

"Not only those," Cadvan said. "It seems to me less risky than taking the roads, nevertheless. No way is without peril."

There was a knock at their door and Dringold entered, carrying their dinner. He placed it on the table, and then lingered.

"I should tell you," he said. "There were questions asked this evening."

"Were there?" said Cadvan, seemingly indifferent.

"A Bard came. She was inquiring about any travelers seen coming this way. I said there was a traveling cobbler staying. There weren't no point in saying otherwise," he added hastily, "because they always know already; there's always those happy to run to the Bards. I said you'd already gone, in any case. Then she said she had heard rumors that my son was sick and was healed. I laughed it off. I told her Rose was always panicking about that boy and it weren't nothing serious. She gave me a funny look. Then she said, had I seen the Bard Cadvan, traveling with a young girl. I told her I knew Lord Cadvan as well as any Bard, and would always be pleased to welcome him into my inn; but I hadn't seen him these three years. And then she left."

He paused. Cadvan looked at him expressionlessly. "I am certain the Bard Cadvan is always pleased to stay in such a fine inn," he said. "And is always grateful for discretion."

"So it's not a bad plan to stay in your rooms tonight," said Dringold. "If you take my meaning. I've let the maid know you've gone."

"We plan to leave before light," Cadvan said. "It shouldn't be a problem." He gave Dringold a sudden warm smile, and surprised, the innkeeper grinned back and then bowed.

"I'm sure it won't be, Lord Cadvan. I'm mighty grateful you came," he said. And then he left.

As the door closed, Maerad's stomach churned with anxiety. She had briefly forgotten their present danger, lulled by the small pleasures of the day, and now her fears returned doubly; she remembered the deathly white hands of the Hull and the red coals of its eyes.

"Shouldn't we leave now?" she asked.

"We could, but I doubt it would profit us much," said Cadvan. "Our guise will last until sundown tomorrow. The Ettinor Bards don't know what they're looking for; at the moment they still seek Cadvan."

"Can we trust the innkeeper?" Maerad stood up and walked around the room. "Couldn't the Bards find out from him that we're here, even if he doesn't want to say?"

"It depends how suspicious they are. I think they'll be looking in many directions; there's no special reason why we should be here. I wish I knew what was happening in Innail. . . . There is danger, but I don't fancy entering the wild with short sleep; we'll have enough of that later. I think we must take this risk."

But Maerad leaped to another question. "What about Dringold? Won't he be in danger, if he's covering for us?"

"You're full of anxieties tonight," said Cadvan, frowning. "I think Dringold has enough guile to handle the questions of the Ettinor Bards. Remember their arrogance. It is very easy to underestimate a common innkeeper if you think yourself above him. If we stay quiet tonight and leave tomorrow, they should be safe. But I will make a charm of protection before we leave, to make sure."

Cadvan's answers allayed Maerad's fears a little, but she lay awake long that night, unable to rid herself of the menacing image of the Hulls; and when finally she slept, her dreams were full of black horsemen reaching toward her with pale, bony hands.

Maerad woke in the blackness before dawn to the sound of rain drumming on the roof, and she sighed. Reluctantly she dragged herself out of her warm bed and dressed, shivering in the cold. Especially cold seemed the mail as she dragged it on over her clothes, and she shuddered: it was like putting on a shirt of ice. She and Cadvan made a hasty breakfast, standing up in the kitchen with Dringold and his wife. Rose shyly pressed on them some cold meat pastries for their lunch; she argued briefly with Cadvan about paying for his services for the boy, but he refused point-blank to take anything. Just before they left, Cadvan stretched out his hands before the couple, muttering some brief words; Maerad saw them blink, and then they turned to their work as if Cadvan and Maerad were not there.

"They will remember only what fits Dringold's story," explained Cadvan in the stables as they led out the horses. "Bards usually know when someone is dissembling."

"Wouldn't a Bard sense the charm?" asked Maerad.

"Only if he scried them," said Cadvan. "If they are scried, neither I nor anyone else can help them. But I doubt either Bard or Hull would deign to do such a thing. I hope not, for their sake."

He sat still on Darsor for a moment, listening; but he neither heard nor sensed anything in the night, and led them out into the cobbled streets of Fort. A rainy blackness covered them, and Maerad shivered. The full moon westered slowly in long bands of dark clouds, but gave little light. She looked back at the windows of the inn, glowing golden and welcoming through the darkness, and thought of the little family they had left. The idea of such gentle people in the hands of Hulls did not bear imagining.

* * *

The sun was beginning to tinge the horizon with dull reds and ochers as they passed through villages and towns to the border of the Ettinor Fesse. By the time the rain stopped and the sun climbed over the horizon, shedding a cheerless light over the damp landscape, they were riding through a less-inhabited region, dotted only with solitary farms. After a couple of hours the road wound into a wood. There they slowed down and trotted through the dripping trees, hearing only the sound of birdsong and the dull clop of the horses' hooves.

Maerad was daydreaming, musing abstractedly on some of the things she had seen and heard in the past few weeks. None of her thoughts led anywhere, and she let them drift through her mind, one after the other, as unformed images: the Elidhu in the Weywood; Cadvan still and silent, astride Darsor; the minstrels frozen in the marketplace in Fort; Silvia's merry face, graven with sadness; Dernhil . . .

She was jolted out of her contemplations by a strange noise, a whirring sound like a large bee, and a *thock*, as if something hit wood. She had time to reflect that she had heard such a sound before and knew she didn't like it, when she heard it again; and then she felt as if she had been punched in the back, and was flung forward on her saddle. Without command the horses plunged into a mad gallop, and Cadvan was shouting, "Down! Arrows! Lay your head down! *Down!*"

She obeyed instinctively, hiding her head against Imi's neck, and hung on desperately as Imi bolted wildly, trying to keep up with Darsor. She realized she must have been hit by an arrow, and was grateful for her mail, so reluctantly donned that morning. She dared look back once and saw nothing through the trees; the road had already wound in a loop and hidden their attackers. The horses slowed down to a canter, and then, as they reached a place where a large rocky shelf butted out of the woods, Cadvan halted them with a signal of his hand, his face grave and alert. He led them to the rock, and they stood there, their backs to the stony wall, which stretched upward for about twenty feet with a slight overhang. Maerad could hear the sound of horsemen pursuing them, approaching both along the road and through the trees, cutting through the loop of the road.

"We cannot race on wildly, with such pursuit," said Cadvan. "We will have to stand here. I think there are not many, two or three."

"Who are they?" asked Maerad.

"I don't know," said Cadvan. "Bards, I guess, who noticed us in one of the villages. There is only one road through this part of the Fesse. I have been careless, as I should not have been. I thought the rain would cover us. At least here they cannot come from behind."

Maerad gulped and sat unmoving on Imi, feeling for her sword, and stared at the bend in the road until her eyes started to water. Cadvan waited patiently, as still as stone. It seemed that their pursuers would never come, but nevertheless, sooner than she liked, a figure came trotting around the bend, and then another. They bore arrows set to the bow, and were cloaked in black.

"Hulls," muttered Cadvan, and Maerad heard the sharp intake of his breath.

The Hulls did not see them at first and looked around into the trees, going slowly now as they hunted. Another horseman came over the rise through the woods and joined them. Then the foremost looked up and sighted them and laughed, waving its fellows over. They let down their bows and trotted at their leisure toward them. Maerad began to feel terror screwing up inside her like a vice, and her heart pounded painfully.

When they were about thirty yards away, Cadvan shouted

indignantly, in the accent of northern Annar: "What were you shooting for? You could have killed us. I'm going to complain to the authorities, I am."

The leading Hull halted. "We are the authorities," it said, and its voice could have been the voice of a dead man. The hair rose on Maerad's neck. "You could go squeaking, little man, like a ghost on the wind, for all the good it might do you. No man may set foot in these woods, by order of the Bards."

"I don't know about any law," said Cadvan. The two Hulls behind put their arrows to the string, and Maerad looked desperately at Cadvan, whose face was expressionless. "I can go into the woods if I want, without being chased by Bards and murdered, like as not."

"Death is the price of insolence," said the Hull. "But we will be merciful, and give you a choice. You can come with us, and try the justice of Ettinor." It laughed again, and the Hulls moved closer to them.

"I'm not going anywhere," said Cadvan. "Just on my own business, is all. I'm not doing no harm."

"Everything here is our business," said the leading Hull. It laughed and lifted its bow. "But your time of choice is over."

It loosed an arrow straight at Cadvan, and Maerad's heart almost failed her. Before she knew what had happened, the arrow had exploded in flame and fell to smoldering ashes on the ground before them. Immediately the semblance of the cobbler and his son dropped from Cadvan and Maerad.

Cadvan seemed to Maerad taller and more lordly, his face stern and grim, and he was illumined by a strange light. The Hulls stopped in surprise, and in that second Cadvan stretched his hands out before him and a bolt of white flame arced from his fingers to the heart of the leading Hull. It made a strangled noise and fell from its horse to the ground. At that, one of the other two Hulls spurred on its horse and charged them. Cadvan lifted his hands again, crying out as he did so, and there was a blast of light. The Hull fell, and both riderless horses bolted wildly off through the trees.

The third Hull still hung back, and Maerad saw that it lifted its arms and a strange darkness formed between them faster than the eye could grasp, a form of mist and shadow; and as Cadvan flung the second Hull from its horse, this form raced onward, furious as a striking snake, straight toward Cadvan. Maerad cried out in terror, but just as the shadow reached Cadvan it writhed and boiled and dissipated into the air. Instantly Cadvan loosed a bolt of light toward the third Hull, and it struck; but the Hull simply swayed on its horse and did not fall. It then stood up in its stirrups, raising its arms. Even at that distance Maerad could see the deathly expression on its face.

The Hull began to chant in an even voice. To Maerad the words he used seemed unaccountably familiar; then, with a shock, even in that extremity, she realized she had heard something like them before, in the nightmare of her foredream. A drop of sweat trickled down her back like a finger of ice, and she felt her hands shaking as they held the reins.

Cadvan stretched out his arms, and a white bolt struck the Hull again, but this time it had no effect at all. Maerad watched the Hull, her mouth dry, like a bird trapped in the fascination of terror before the snake that gathers itself to strike and kill.

Slowly it seemed, as a nightmare is slow, but with a frightening swiftness, another blackness began to form between the arms of the Hull, as if shadow coagulated and grew there; but this one was less formless than the first. Cadvan sat on Darsor, who stood unmoved. Maerad glanced swiftly toward him and saw that he was utterly still, although the strange light within him grew in intensity. Then her eyes were drawn back irresistibly to the Hull.

Above it, stretching into the trees, loomed a terrifying form, made of shadow and yet appearing as solid as the trees around it. It looked like a giant man, but misshapen and ugly. Green fire crackled around its brow and its eyes burned with a cold light; it beat dark wings that stretched for many spans, like those of a huge bat, and it bore a black sword that was licked by livid flames. It opened its mouth and breathed a plume of fire, and the flame was cold, deathly cold.

Maerad began to feel dizzy and clutched desperately at Imi's mane as if she were drowning. What was it? It was crude and mindless, like a figure out of a child's nightmare, but its immensity seemed to obliterate the whole world.

Cadvan swayed in his saddle and passed his hand over his eyes. "A Kulag," he said wearily.

He drew his sword, and a white fire flickered along it, answering the flames of the Kulag. Thus they stood for a long second, man and monster, and then the Hull cried out and his arms flung upward, and the hideous thing spread out its wings and dived toward them, letting out an eldritch scream that froze Maerad's blood.

Darsor lifted his head and neighed in defiance, rearing on his hind legs and beating the air with his hooves. There was a blinding flash, and Maerad saw Cadvan's sword raised, brighter than the heart of the sun, gleaming small as a needle against the mighty darkness annihilating the daylight.

Maerad screamed and cast up her hands. She thought a great sheet of flame sprang up before her eyes, white and blue and intolerably bright. There was a crash, as if a vast tree had fallen, dragging in ruin all its companions; and then blackness blotted out her vision, and she knew no more.

XV

THE HUTMOORS

S HE came to a short while later and found Cadvan kneeling beside her on the ground, his hand on her brow, his face tight with anxiety. She sat up, shaking her head, and looked around her. Darsor and Imi stood quietly beside them, and ordinary daylight filtered through the trees. She wondered briefly if she had suffered some strange fit or hallucination; but then she looked up and saw the branches above them were blackened and withered as if a great fire had touched them. Before them on the track she saw the black heaps of the three Hulls, and the corpse of a horse.

"What happened?" she asked.

"I'm not sure," said Cadvan. "Are you all right?"

Maerad rubbed her head, nodding.

"What happened?" she asked again. "Are we safe?"

Cadvan smiled grimly. "For the moment," he said. "All the Hulls are dead." He swung his hand toward the crumpled heaps on the path, averting his eyes in distaste. "I don't know what happened to the Kulag. It vanished when it was cast down."

"What was it?"

"One of the Hulls was a powerful sorcerer," he said. "I don't know what it was doing here. I dare not speculate at what is happening in the School of Ettinor at the present." He grimaced. "That was the last Hull, and it strove with me mightily as soon as it perceived my power. I began to doubt I could prevail against it." He paused. "And then it summoned a Kulag.

Only the greatest sorcerers can command such creatures; they are from the age of the First Evil, from the days of the Wars of the Elementals. They were banished to the Abyss, beyond the circle of the world, long ago. They carry a power more ancient than that of the Dark."

Cadvan paused again. "And then I don't know what happened. I thought perhaps I could destroy the Kulag, but that still left the third Hull, which seemed undiminished in its power, and I was already weary. I thought perhaps that Kulag rushing down on us would be the last thing either of us would see. Then there was a huge flame, and the Kulag crashed down in the path before us. The shock of the flame passed outward, and the third Hull was struck down, and its horse with it. And then you slipped off Imi and fell to the ground. I thought you were dead."

Maerad stared at him in wonder. "Did you make the flame?" she asked.

"It was not of my making," he said, looking at her strangely.

"Then maybe someone helped us, knowing us to be in trouble somehow," she said. "But who could that be?"

"Who indeed?" said Cadvan. "But I think it more likely that the flame burst from you, answering our extremity." He smiled gently at Maerad. "It had something of your wildness."

Maerad sat silently for a while, struggling with amazement and doubt. "But I didn't do anything," she said at last. "I was just terrified."

"No doubt," said Cadvan. "I will take care not to frighten you in the future! In all our minds there are secret places, which we know little of; and in yours most especially, I think." He studied Maerad's face gravely, and with a pang of surprise she thought she saw something like fear in his eyes. She looked down at the ground, unspeaking, and at last Cadvan stood up and looked around them. "We should leave here, and swiftly," he said. "I don't know how many others might be aware of this battle, and what else might pursue us here."

Maerad stood up also, and Cadvan walked toward the dead Hulls. Overcoming a shudder of horror, she followed him. They lay twisted under their black cloaks. Cadvan lifted the edge of one of the cloaks with his boot and Maerad let out a gasp of surprise; underneath the cloak was nothing but dried bones. So it was also with the second corpse. "When the Hulls die, the spell that binds their bodies in this world is broken," said Cadvan. "These should have been dead many hundreds of years ago." He stood up again and leaned briefly against a tree, as if he were afflicted by nausea, and forced himself by pure will to approach the bodies.

He then came to the corpse of the third Hull, which lay farthest back down the track, and lifted the cloak with a stick. Maerad saw the skull grinning at her, and the bones settled down in a heap, making her jump; for a second she thought irrationally that it was still alive. Cadvan knelt next to it without touching the bones, and she saw he was looking at a silver ring on its finger, in which was set a black stone.

"It bears the sick moon," he said. She saw that the black stone was carved in a semblance of a sickle moon, but subtly distorted, so it looked diseased. "The Nameless One has his Circles, even as the Bards. A twisted shadow of the Order. This one was from the strongholds of Dén Raven, and such has not been seen in this realm for many a long year. Not since the Silence." His face was grim again. "It was said there were none left. Many things that the Light thought dead have been, it seems, merely asleep."

He broke off a huge branch from a tree nearby and swept the bones and cloaks off the track until they were hidden beneath some brambles. The corpse of the horse he looked at sadly but did not attempt to move. "The animals that are forced to bear the Hulls suffer greatly." he said. "Perhaps its death was a release for it."

Unspeaking, they returned to their horses. Cadvan stroked Darsor's proud neck, which was rimed with sweat. "Well done, greatheart," he said. "You stayed where many valorous men would have fled." He stroked Imi's neck also, murmuring words in her ear; and the mare, who was still trembling with fright, calmed and snuffled his neck. "Indik chose well for you," said Cadvan to Maerad. "This is a brave animal, of a courage beyond her stature. But now we must leave, and as fast as we can manage. By nightfall I want to be far from this place."

They mounted and pressed forward, galloping swiftly through the woods, and the shadows of branches passed over them like the ripples on a rapid stream.

They did not stop until midafternoon, passing out of the woods into empty grasslands in which sometimes there was the evidence of a farm long abandoned: a row of trees which once made a windbreak, or an orchard grown wild, or even the remains of a house, its roof collapsed and its walls crumbling, overgrown with ivy or weeds so it almost looked like a small hill or natural thicket. The path through the woods faltered and then petered out altogether, and they pushed on westward toward a dark blur on the horizon that looked like a hedge or a wall, picking their way through tussocks of rough grass and occasional dried stands of reeds. Maerad felt very exposed; there were few trees to conceal them. She was still shaky with the aftershock of their battle with the Hulls, and felt a great inner weariness, next to which her physical fatigue seemed almost a relief. Also, at the back of her mind, was a troubling thought. If Cadvan was correct, she had killed a man and a horse. Although she was moved by no pity for the Hull, nor remorse of any kind at killing it, she felt again that strange fear of herself that had nagged her at intervals since Cadvan had first told her about the Speech. It was, in part, because she felt no volition over her powers—if they were so, she added to herself, still dubious. What if something went wrong, and she blasted something she didn't want to? Was it fear she had seen in Cadvan's face? Could he possibly be afraid of *her*? Beneath her doubt was something else, something more disturbing; the sense of her own power, however inchoate, gave her a strange thrill, a sense, even, of *joy*. . . . But her mind flinched away from those speculations, and she concentrated on keeping up with Cadvan and not falling off Imi from sheer tiredness; and she kept her hearing alert for any signs of pursuit. But she heard nothing.

They had gone about twenty miles when at last Cadvan called a halt. They lunched hastily in a miserable copse of trees. As soon as she dismounted, Maerad doubled over with agonizing cramps in her stomach. Cadvan took her hands. "What's wrong?"

"Cramps." Maerad hissed through her teeth. She clutched herself and curled into as small a ball as possible. For a second Cadvan looked worried, and then he laughed with relief.

"Is that all?" he said. "Come, I know Silvia packed the remedy in your pack." He took Maerad's bag off Imi's saddle and rummaged through it until he found the little bottle of elixir. He gave Maerad a dose. She grimaced at the bitter taste, but the cramps subsided, and presently she sat up again, feeling more clearheaded, and looked around. The blur before them had resolved into a stone wall, about ten or fifteen feet high, and they were now riding northward alongside it. Cadvan said the Westwall ran for leagues, marking the border of Ettinor Fesse from the wilderlands beyond. "There are no gates," he said, "but the wall has been ill-maintained for many years, and many parts are crumbled. We should find a way through it soon."

About five miles on they found what Cadvan was seeking;

here a huge, woody ivy had forced apart the stones, and the thick wall had collapsed into rubble. They dismounted and led the horses through, and then looked over a landscape even more desolate than the one they had left: barren moors barely covered with straggly turf, falling away from their feet down into a rocky valley. Through the valley ran a river, and Maerad saw the darker vegetation of trees running along its length. Above them were huge swags of gray clouds, and the wind was turning chilly, presaging more rain. The sun was low in the sky, bleeding long streaks of dull orange along the horizon. Maerad thought of the bright inns they had left far behind, and felt utterly miserable.

"The Hutmoors," said Cadvan. "We'll head down there, to the Usk, and follow it until we are too weary to go farther. Soon it winds westward."

Too tired to ask questions, Maerad followed him down the rocky hill. The rain held off and they crossed the river, here shallow and wide, with many stones trailing long green beards of river weed. They followed it even after nightfall, guided by the light of the full moon, until Imi was stumbling with weariness and even Darsor's head drooped. Then at last Cadvan called a halt, and they made a cheerless camp with no fire under an old willow, huddling against a rocky shelf that offered at least a crude shelter against the freezing wind. That night, despite their danger, they kept no watch.

Maerad was so tired she had trouble going to sleep. She ached all over and her mind hummed like a harp string on the point of breaking. She lay on her back, staring up into the sky. The moon was now vanishing under a shroud of dark clouds, and she could smell more rain on the wind. The fear that was her constant companion rose within her, a blackness flooding through her breast. Who am I? she asked herself again, uselessly. The empty night returned no answer.

* * *

For many days they traveled over the moors, following the course of the river and keeping as close as possible to the trees. They saw no animals of any kind, and heard nothing but crickets and frogs or the harsh call of an eagle high overhead. The going was slow, as the land was covered with little ridges and gullies, and they frequently came across strange pits, as if at some point the ground had been violently upturned. The ground was strewn with boulders of quartz and granite that threatened to turn the horses' hooves.

The weather continued cold and gray, with freezing showers of rain or sleet that passed as suddenly as they appeared. But the wind was constant: a punishing stream of cold air that whistled ceaselessly through the ridges and stones. The endless browns and grays began to fill Maerad's mind with a stupor of boredom. She was troubled by cramps, and was grateful many times for Silvia's elixir, and for the medhyl, which they drank sparingly each morning, to ward off their weariness. Now more than ever she longed for a bath and washed herself shivering at the end of every day in the cold water of the Usk. At night they camped without fire, huddling against the chill, which fell heavily as soon as the sun set, and they spoke quietly to each other, feeling that loud voices would echo for miles in the noiseless wolds.

The silence grew more oppressive each day, until Maerad started to wonder if she could bear it. She began to feel as if they were ants crawling on an endless plain under an endless sky, to some unimaginable, pointless end.

On their third night in the Hutmoors, Cadvan consented to Maerad's entreaties for a fire. It was a laborious task in the damp wind; the wood wouldn't catch, and whenever a feeble flame began to leap from the wood, the wind would blow it out. When the flame had died for the fourth time, Maerad asked

Cadvan why he wouldn't use magic. Crossly, he said, "I will not use what you call magic at my whim, like a cheap magician doing tricks for children. Have you not heard anything I've said about the Balance?"

Maerad subsided, abashed, and at last Cadvan got a fire going, and they had a hot meal for the first time since leaving Ettinor. Cadvan made an herb tea that warmed Maerad down to her toes, and some of the chill left her bones.

"It's horrible country, this," she said. "I doubt that anyone has ever lived here. They'd die of despair."

Cadvan looked at her keenly. "You feel the lament of the earth," he said. "It is heavy with sorrow. But it's not evil, although none will travel here. I have never crossed these moors before, and I have ridden widely from the north to the south, and over the mountains far past the Forsaken Lands. It's said the Dead walk here, questing over the moors for their lost brethren, so tied by their sorrows they cannot pass the Gates."

Then he told her that once the region known as the Hutmoors had been as populous and fertile as Innail. "Then it was known as the Imbral, a great kingdom that stretched across the whole of northeastern Annar," he said. "It was famous for the courtesy and beauty of its people, who made fair towns of whitewashed stone, with arched courtyards in every house, where fountains trembled in the sun under perfumed trees. They still build houses like that in the Suderain, far in the south, where Saliman lives. They have grilled windows of marvelous intricacy, and towers topped with domes of gold and silver and bronze that catch the sun in the morning and evening; but in the north such arts have long been abandoned. This was a country of rich pastures and abundant fertility; Dhyllic vines are still remembered in proverb by winemakers. And here the Dhyllin lived, watching the stars from their towers, or making songs in their great halls, or forging things of great beauty and power, for they delighted in all the arts of the hand and the eye and the ear; and none have yet surpassed their skills."

Maerad looked around her at the bleak hills, rising dark above them under the star-strewn sky. In the Hollow Lands there were still signs of habitation from many thousands of years before, but here there were none: no ruins, no weathered stone bearing the sign of a human hand. There were not even ridges betraying the sunken edges of walls like the ones she had stumbled over in the Forsaken Lands near Gilman's Cot. Cadvan's story was hard to believe, except that it now seemed to her that the wind did lament; at the edge of hearing, she thought she could catch the sound of far-off sobbing, or a thin wail. She dismissed it as fancy. "What happened?" she asked blankly.

"We now walk over the site of a great battle," said Cadvan. "This was the last stand of the Alliance: the massed armies of Imbral, and of the realm of Lirion in the north. They met here with the forces of the Nameless One. Fair and desperate must have been their banners, and bright their swords; the songs say that their spears twinkled in the sun like numberless stars, and their ranks stretched farther than the eye could see. Here gathered the flower of the Dhyllin peoples: Recabarra, the mighty Queen of Lirion, in her chariot sheeted with burnished steel that was said to outshine the sun; and Laurelin, last King of Imbral; and many others whose names are now legends of the distant past. And here they were overwhelmed. Recabarra was taken hostage, to die in torment in the dungeons of Dén Raven; and Laurelin's sword was broken, and the Nameless himself hacked off his head and held it high in the air, and laughed as the blood splashed his face."

Maerad glanced across at Cadvan; his eyes were remote and sad, as if he gazed upon a living memory. Recollections from her childhood, vague as smoke, seemed to stir in her mind as Cadvan spoke.

"The Usk then was a great river called the Findol, famous for the purity and beauty of its waters; in the songs it is said the river ran red for days, and was blocked with bloated corpses that so sullied the waters that none could drink from them. Then it was named Usk, meaning tears in the tongue of Imbral. All the great cities of Imbral and Lirion were laid waste, and their people slaughtered without mercy. The citadel of Afinil was cast down and its power broken, and now even its site has been forgotten. In the Great Silence that followed the victory of the Nameless, a darkness that lasted nigh a thousand years, every sign that remained of the Dhyllin was destroyed. The Nameless especially hated that fair people for their defiance of his power and their courage against him, even in defeat. And now their voices sound no more in Annar, and their cities are forgotten as if they had never been. They are a fair dream remembered by the Bards, but few others.

"How the land was despoiled, I know not: little has grown here for nearly two thousand years. And although the evil has been washed away since Maninaë cast out the Nameless and broke his throne nine hundred years ago, still the earth is hurt. It will be many lifetimes before it is green and wholesome again."

Cadvan stopped speaking, and Maerad sat in silence for some while, caught in the sorrow of the story. As if her mind reflected the images in Cadvan's, there flashed on her inner eye the vision of a beautiful city cast down, its walls in smoking ruins, its towers broken, and all around it the terrible evidence of a great slaughter. She would not have thought the landscape could seem more desolate than it had before; but the recollection of all it had once held made it all the more empty. She wondered again if she heard the sounds of thin voices sobbing, and she shivered.

"Were Andomian and Beruldh of the Dhyllin people?" she asked at last.

"Yes, they were from Lirion, which is where the House of Karn traces back its long line," said Cadvan. "And their story is from some time before the Great Silence, when the war against the Nameless was still a matter of skirmishes and battles, and he had then only despoiled the realm of Indurain, marching up along the mountains to startle the people from their sleep and slaughter them." His voice was harsher now. "Even then, there were those who did not expect him to cross all of southern Annar and even the Aleph River and besiege the proud realms of Lirion and Imbral. Just as now there are those who say his return is impossible, and that the days of the Silence are just a matter of legend and dim history."

Maerad thought of other songs she knew. "Then who was the Ice Witch?" she asked. "Was that before the Nameless?"

"Maerad, I know I'm supposed to be your teacher," said Cadvan tiredly. "But surely I deserve a rest now and then!"

"No!" said Maerad sternly. "You volunteered, now fulfill your duty."

Cadvan laughed quietly and poked the fire. "You're a hard taskmaster. But it helps to pass the time," he said, looking around. "I'm tired. But I'll take the first watch; sleep is far from me tonight." He paused, gathering his thoughts. "Well, the dominion of the Ice Witch was so long ago that the songs reveal little, and there are few of them. It was the Age of the Elementals, when humans were but new in the world. The Ice Witch, the Winterking, who some call Arkan, came from the north and brought with him the storm dogs and armies of hail and snow, and the whole of Annar was covered with ice, down even as far as the Suderain. The Kulags were his creations. The world was a different shape then, although the river Lir still runs as it did then, my home river in the kingdom of Lirhan, once Lirion, in the far north. The Elementals made war with Arkan, and their wars were grievous, and men and women crept into the shadows of the rocks to escape their fury, and many died. Afterward the coastline was changed, and some lands sank forever beneath the waves. But that was long before the Nameless, and even the Ice Witch was the slave of a greater power, as is the Nameless One." He shivered suddenly. "I would rather teach you this beside a warm fire in a pleasant room in one of the Schools than out here in the wilds, where the darkness is all too close. Another time, Maerad?"

Maerad nodded; she couldn't rid herself of the feeling that the wind was crying, like a lost child, and an intolerable melancholy was growing within her. But as Cadvan's voice stopped, so the empty night seemed to creep closer to them. Before Maerad curled up in her blanket to sleep, they spoke together for a while, merely to keep the darkness at bay, of things such as cobbling, and minstrelsy, and cooking.

On the morning of the fifth day on the Hutmoors they reached its western edge. The land suddenly fell sharply some hundreds of feet before them, as if a monstrous knife had sheared it away. The river plunged down in a long waterfall, plashing into several rocky pools on its way down the cliff. A great forest stretched far beyond the horizon, lapping up to the edge of the cliff, and they looked down on the crowns of trees, which looked from their height like little sprouts in a vegetable garden.

Maerad gazed wordlessly out over the forest. She could see no way down the cliff. She glanced inquiringly at Cadvan.

"What now?" she said. "Do we grow wings and fly? And then, how do we get through that forest?"

"I don't know," said Cadvan, unperturbed. Maerad cast him a look of dislike; for a brief second she felt like pushing him off the cliff. They had come all this way, through such lean country, only for Cadvan to tell her he didn't know what to do next? "I can't grow us wings," Cadvan continued. "So there's only one

thing we can do. We can ride north until we find a way down."
He waved his hand out over the void. "This is the Great Forest,
the *Cilicader* in the Speech. If we want to remain hidden, it is as
good a place in all Annar to be."

"Did you know there was a cliff here?" asked Maerad.

"Yes," said Cadvan. "This is the Imbral Cut. It once marked
the western border of that realm. I don't know if it has a more
recent name."

Maerad sighed impatiently. An impatience akin to panic had
been growing on her since the night before, not only because of
the grimness of the Hutmoors, and she begrudged every hour
they spent that morning wandering along the edge searching
fruitlessly for a path.

They stopped at midday for lunch, and Cadvan, as he
munched the tough biscuit, looked warily around.

"Listen," he said.

Maerad cocked an ear. "I hear nothing," she said.

"Neither do I," said Cadvan.

Maerad realized with a shock that there was no birdsong.
She thought back, but couldn't remember when she had
stopped hearing it.

"I like this not at all," said Cadvan. "Pray we find a path
before nightfall. Perhaps at last someone has spotted us."

"Who? A ghost?" said Maerad lightly; but her heart misgave
her. She remembered how the land had silenced around them
near the Landrost, when the wers had been pursuing them.

After that they listened as well as looked, but the silence
continued. The cliff was now bending westward, and she
thought it seemed less high, although still impassable with
horses. Then Cadvan gave a shout and pointed forward. A little
way ahead there had been a rockfall, and a huge slice of the cliff
had slid down into the forest, leaving behind it a rocky slope
down which it looked possible to pick a path.

"It will be dangerous," said Cadvan. "But we might be able to make our way down, if we take care. We'll have to lead the horses."

Maerad didn't like the sound of *might*. She looked dubiously down the slope, which still looked far too steep to walk down. Then she scanned the cliff farther northward. For as far as she could see there was no path more likely than this one, and the sun was already climbing down in the west.

"I suppose it will have to do," she said. "We've got to get off the moors. Hulls on one side, a broken neck on the other. What's the difference?"

"Not Hulls, I think," said Cadvan. "And who is to say the forest will be any better? But at least we will be less easy to spot. Well, hesitating on the edge of anything never made it any easier. Don't follow me too closely, in case one of us falls." He dismounted and stroked Darsor's nose. "Courage, brave one," he said, and led the stallion to the cliff edge.

Darsor looked as dubious as Maerad felt, and followed Cadvan with reluctance, his tail jammed between his back legs. Maerad sighed and dismounted, and led Imi to the edge, trying not to look down. Imi balked and would not even begin the descent. At last Cadvan climbed back up and whispered to her in the Speech, and only then would she follow, climbing down crabwise with her ears pressed flat against her skull, snorting violently each time her hooves slipped.

Slowly and painfully they picked their way, foot by foot, down the steep slope. Every time one of the horses slipped, or Maerad stood on a rock that tilted under her weight, she thought they would go crashing down to the trees hundreds of feet below; in her mind's eye she could see Imi with a crushed leg, or Darsor with a broken back, thrashing helplessly at the bottom. She pushed these images aside with an effort of will and concentrated her mind solely on the present: this step, this next step. She tried not to look down, or, after a while, up; either dizzied her. After an hour her hands were bleeding from falls and she felt utterly spent. She risked a look down and to her surprise the forest was much nearer; what was even more heartening was that not far beneath them the gradient of the slope lessened dramatically, as a huge pile of scree swept against the cliff like the detritus from a giant tide. She pressed on then with less dread, and at last, after what seemed an endless age scrabbling among the rocks, constantly afraid that a horse might strain a tendon or break a fetlock or worse, they made it safely to the bottom of the cliff.

It was already dark there; behind the trees the sun was low in the sky, and the cliff threw a deep shadow over them, although high up Maerad could see where the sun's light struck against the cliff face. The forest came right to the edge, a chaotic tangle of vegetation. Cadvan led them a little way in under the trees, and Maerad looked around in despair. How were they going to pass through this snarl of trees and undergrowth? In places it was an impenetrable wall of briars and brambles higher than their heads, and everywhere, rotting in the dim light, were the fallen corpses of trees, overgrown with moss and creepers. She saw no path. Cadvan was already sitting down on a log, breathing heavily.

"Well, we're well out of that," he said. "Whatever that was. But I think eyes would have marked where we left the Hutmoors, and we can't stay here tonight. We'll have to go back south, toward the Usk."

"Won't they guess that's where we're going?" asked Maerad; but she quibbled no further. The alternative was to get totally lost in the bewildering woods. It added up to no choice at all.

After a very short rest they started the exhausting task of battling through the undergrowth. They kept the cliff to their left, fearing that if they moved farther away they might lose their direction entirely. This was difficult, as their way was often impeded by narrow gullies filled with brambles and dead and broken branches, and sometimes they had to wander many hundreds of yards out of their way before they could find a way to cross and then retrace their steps along its other side. Once Imi stumbled crossing a gully and gashed her leg on a stick, high up near her chest. By the time dusk began to draw in, they still had not found the Usk. Maerad was uncomfortably conscious of the rustle of creatures in the leaves above them. Sometimes she saw dark shapes in the branches or the small paired lamps of yellow eyes.

"We have to stop soon, or we'll get lost," she said, wondering uncomfortably what creatures haunted the nights in this wild forest.

As if he heard her thoughts, Cadvan turned and spoke. "Look to your sword, Mistress Maerad. There are strange beasts in these parts."

"More goromants?" she asked, with a lightness she didn't feel.

"This is as old as the Weywood; parts of this forest are supposed to have been here since the first foundations of this land were laid, long before the Wars of the Elementals," Cadvan answered. "And as in the Weywood, creatures survived here when the kingdoms of Lirion and Imbral drove back the woods. It remained untouched by the Silence, but it was not always so broad. Since the Silence it has stretched almost as far as Lirhan, and far to the west. Many things might live here beyond the knowledge of the Nameless himself: more ancient, and with a malice more profound."

Maerad reflected briefly that it might have been less dangerous to take the open highway to Norloch, even in the face of the

Hulls, but kept her thoughts to herself. Nevertheless Cadvan caught the tenor of them and gave her a piercing glance.

"Better to face that which has no particular reason to notice us, than to run in broad daylight before foes whose first desire is to hunt us down," he said. "Or so runs my reasoning. May it prove to be sound!" He looked around impatiently. "Darkness will fall soon," he said. "The days are short in this forest! I think tonight we will have to stay by the cliff; if we have our backs to the rock, at least we can't be attacked from behind."

Before the light failed entirely they found a suitable place. At one point the cliff drove slightly in, making a hollow that was not quite a cave, but offered at least some shelter. The horses stood glumly by; they were thirsty, and apart from a brackish puddle, Cadvan had not been able to find water for them all day. They were not cheered even by Cadvan's whispering, although Imi relaxed a little when he attended to her cut and eased it with a salve. They passed an uncomfortable, if uneventful, night, and found the next day that they had been only two hours from the Usk, which fell into a wide pool as it splashed down from the Hutmoors. The horses waded in, drinking deeply, and Cadvan and Maerad refilled their water bottles gratefully.

"Now at last we are back where we were two days ago, only several hundred feet lower," said Cadvan, squinting up the length of the waterfall, which arched gracefully down in several steps, spraying the sunlight into trembling rainbows. "We've lost a lot of time. And if the forest continues to be so difficult to move through, we will lose much more, and we have not enough food to last more than three weeks. I can hunt, at a pinch, but it takes time and energy; and speed is our friend, not this endless delay. I was told the forest was not impassable and that you could ride a horse here, at need; but perhaps the western end was spoken of. At any rate, we can't stray far from the river."

"Perhaps it will clear the farther we get from the cliff," said Maerad, not very hopefully. But it proved to be the case; it seemed the briars and rough ground hugged the edge of the cut, and under a mile away they found the trees much bigger and better spaced, opening sometimes to wide glades where broad yellow beams of sunlight pierced the gloom. Some trees were clearly very ancient, huge oaks with trunks as broad as a small house, whose lofty crowns stretched more than a hundred feet; and there were beeches and elms and blossoming groves of rowan and crab apple. The river ran lazily between shallow banks, eddying into little pools in which grew yellow water lilies and crowsfoot and cresses and tall green reeds; and dragonflies hung there shimmering like winged emeralds and sapphires. The forest briars and brambles shrank to bushes rather than impassable shoulder-high thickets, and here they saw bluebells and daffodils pushing brightly through the long grass; and at last they mounted their horses and began to move at a better pace, feeling more hopeful than they had in days.

They traveled for almost ten days without incident, covering, by Cadvan's calculations, some forty leagues, which he reckoned meant they had crossed half the forest's length. Their nights were disturbed by nothing worse than frogs croaking in the pools or owls floating almost soundlessly down through the trees or the squeaks of mice hunting crickets. Still they remained wary and always kept watch, and did not play or sing in the evenings when they made camp. At night sometimes, struggling against sleep, Maerad thought she saw eyes watching them from the branches, although when she rubbed her eyes and turned to look at them, they vanished. Once during the day they surprised a huge red stag standing in a glade; it turned to them with a proud sweep of its head, and then slowly, moving with a lordly contempt, cantered off through the trees. For the most part, although the forest seemed to quiver with life, it remained hidden, and they moved through it like strangers or shadows, having no part in it.

Cadvan was cautious about lighting fires and only did so well away from trees. "Those who live in the forests do not trust those who wield fire," he said. "And I would not inadvertently rouse them." This was no great hardship, for the weather continued clear and almost warm, although it remained cool beneath the eaves of the trees. The horses began to gain a bit of the condition they had lost in the soul-eroding tramp through the Hutmoors, and both Maerad and Cadvan looked less drawn.

"I wonder," said Maerad one day, "why they say the Great Forest is such a dark place? For it seems fair and wholesome to me."

"It does feel as if some spirit presides here, or once did; for it seems distant in time, as if only its memory lives here," Cadvan answered. "Perhaps I am mistaken, but the light seems rich and gentle, as the wilds never are."

"Maybe it is just that no one has been here, and so strange stories have grown out of ignorance," said Maerad. "After all, there are evil stories told about Bards."

"Yes, there are," said Cadvan. "But, alas, you have seen how they are based in fact. And I do not doubt that there are parts of this forest that are dark indeed and are the lairs of nameless creatures. But perhaps we ride through a part in which fair memories of the Light live still. I don't know."

That afternoon, just before dusk, there was a light rain and they sheltered under one of the great oaks waiting for it to pass. They had just urged on the horses when a voice spoke suddenly from the tree above them.

"*Lemmach!*" it said.

Maerad looked up wildly, but could see nothing through the leaves. Startled, Imi moved forward one pace. There was a *whir*, and an arrow appeared in the ground before her, quivering.

"*Lemmach, Oseanë*," said the voice again.

Maerad stared at Cadvan, her eyes wide.

"Don't move," he whispered. "Whatever you do." He looked up and called, "*Ke an de, Dereni? Ile ni taramsë lir.*"

"*Ke an de, Oseanë? Noch de remanë kel de an ambach.*"

A man sprang down from the tree, a jump of easily twenty feet. He landed lightly on his feet, as if he merely leaped from a log. He bore an intricately carved bow almost as tall as he was, and a white-feathered arrow was set in the nock. The arrow was pointed directly at Cadvan's chest.

Too startled at first even to be afraid, Maerad stared at the bowman with wonder. He was tall and fair and long-limbed, dressed in motley green designed to conceal him among leaves.

He stared back at Maerad and Cadvan, his face utterly expressionless. Only his eyes betrayed any feeling, and they were unwelcoming and cold.

XVI

LADY ARDINA

CADVAN again told the bowman they traveled in peace, holding out his bare hands as he did so. Although he didn't lower his bow, the man seemed to regard them less coldly. They spoke for some time, and Maerad shifted uneasily in her saddle; she knew enough of the Speech to know they spoke that tongue, but she understood nothing of what was said. She heard Cadvan mention her name, and he turned to her with a gesture of his hand; she nodded then, and smiled with what she hoped was a guileless and open expression. Still the stranger did not lower his weapon, and at last, after more talking, Cadvan turned to her.

"He says we have to go with him and he will brook no disobedience. He says he has friends close by, and that if we move in any direction save that he says, we will both die instantly with an arrow in our throats. I think we have no choice."

"Who is he?" said Maerad. "Is he a Bard?"

"No," said Cadvan. "And I have never heard of Bards in the Great Forest. But these are not evil people, and I think we will be safe enough, or at least I hope so."

The bowman was impatiently indicating they should move forward, so they ceased speaking and moved in front of him. Immediately four other bowmen, as tall and graceful as the first, jumped down from the oak and joined him. They all had arrows to the string. Maerad and Cadvan were told to dismount; the bowmen seemed wary of the horses, and consulted privately before they ordered that they must lead them. Then

they were marched away from the river, deep into the heart of
the forest. Even if they had tried to escape, it would have been
fruitless; soon they had lost their bearings entirely.

The bowmen led them for hours, long into the night. Maerad
looked up through the trees and saw there the stars shining
bright and cold above them. How many times had she cast up
her eyes to the stars for succor? she wondered to herself; for as
long as she could remember she had found a comfort in their
chilly beauty, so remote from human suffering. She was tired
now and very hungry, and her legs felt numb; she moved by
sheer will. At last, when she felt as if she really could not walk
another mile even if an arrow was pointed at her breast, their
captors led them through a thick ring of trees into a Bardhome.

This one was bigger than any Maerad had seen: a grass
arena of perhaps two hundred feet across, so the night sky
looked down unimpeded at its center, and the crescent moon
and stars let down their shadowless light over the grass. At the
far end of the glade a stream fell silver and pearl in the moonlight down a small rockface. Here they were allowed to rest,
and the horses were unsaddled to drink and graze. Behind the
veil of the waterfall was a large cave. To Maerad's surprise, it
concealed a large and comfortable chamber lit by flickering
torches set into the rocky walls; there were even beds, made of
branches thickly twined. Two of the bowmen then left on some
urgent errand. The one who acted as the leader spoke to
Cadvan, and Cadvan told Maerad that here they would eat
and rest before pressing on again the following day.

"Where are they taking us?" asked Maerad fearfully.

"They won't say," said Cadvan. "But I for one am grateful for
a bed and a hot meal." He walked to where the stream gathered
in a small pool, before it flowed away through the Bardhome

and out through the forest, and splashed water over his face. "Now perhaps I might stay awake long enough to eat!"

In a little while they were given steaming herbed stew in bowls made of glazed clay. Maerad looked at the workmanship curiously; the bowls had a purity of line that caught her eye. She ate hungrily and then lay down on one of the beds and instantly fell asleep.

The bowmen woke them early, and once again they began their weary tramp. Soon afterward Maerad realized they were following a path that wound through trees that seemed, she thought, even bigger than those they had seen over the past few days. Despite being on foot they went swiftly and covered perhaps twenty miles before they stopped at another Bardhome, very similar to the first. Cadvan and Maerad spoke very little during the day, although he chatted with the bowmen, who were called Farndar, Imunt, and Penar. Their conversation revealed very little. They would tell him neither their destination nor who they were beyond their names, and did not ask Cadvan of the reason for their journey, or where it began. Maerad didn't feel afraid so much as apprehensive; she wondered how they would ever get out of the forest, if these strange folk let them leave. They were less hostile, but it was clear that Cadvan and Maerad were their captives. How were they to get to Norloch now?

At lunchtime the next day they reached a broad river that flowed swiftly in a rocky course, hurrying between high banks. "This might be the Cirion, which flows uncharted through the Great Forest," Cadvan said to Maerad. "It flows from the Osidh Elanor through Lirhan, and then vanishes into the forest, where it disappears from the maps. I begin to remember stories from my childhood of the wild people, the Deridhu, who live in the

heart of the forest; they are supposed to come out and bring
nightmares to children who do not do as they are told, and ride
the cows so they come to the morning stare-eyed and milkless.
Perhaps they are a hearthside memory of these folk. Many forgotten things live still in children's tales." Maerad glanced at
the bowmen; they looked altogether too grim to take cows on
wild rides.

The path ran along the banks of the river for some time and
then turned left. Here it was possible to cross; there was no
bridge, but the banks were less steep and the water spread
shallowly. A small stream split off from the river and wandered
lazily off through the trees. The crossing was not quite a ford,
but Penar waded across and tied a rope to a tree on the other
bank. Using this as a guide they crossed safely to its other side.
They followed the smaller stream, noticing that the golden light
grew steadily more intense and that the trees were even more
broadly spaced, so at times it seemed they moved through
meadows densely treed rather than a forest. They didn't stop
for lunch, and the sun was just beginning its slow descent when
they suddenly left the trees and found they overlooked a long
green valley cleft into the very heart of the forest.

Maerad gasped with astonishment. Before them stretched a
city made wholly of wood. All the buildings were low, with
high, curiously carved gables and doors that opened out to
wide porches, and their shingled roofs gleamed bright silver in
the sunlight. Around them were fair gardens and lawns, and
blossoming trees—rowan, plum, almond, and apple—were
everywhere thickly planted. They were just now coming into
leaf and the blossom mostly fallen, and the ground was strewn
with pink and white petals, as if it had snowed.

The bowmen spoke to Cadvan, who had halted, his face
bright with wonder.

"They tell me this is the city of Rachida," Cadvan told

Maerad. "I have heard of a place with that name: it was one of the havens of the Dhyllin and was thought destroyed many years ago. I think I begin to understand. But how could so fair a place go so long unmarked by the Bards of Annar?"

He shook his head, as if he did not quite believe what he had said, and they walked on, following their escorts through the wide streets of the city. The bowmen had at last laid aside their arrows, and they walked freely, turning their heads from side to side to look at the buildings as they passed. They were fairly and strongly made, all with curious carvings around the doors and lintels and eaves. Maerad saw nowhere any glass; the houses had wide windows which were shuttered at need with thick wood, and behind them were stretched white screens that admitted a gentle daylight, which she found out later were made of a strong paper. The inhabitants were fair-haired and tall like the bowmen and nodded courteously to the strangers, although after they had passed many stood and stared after them. Maerad and Cadvan, being both dark-haired, stood out; but of even more interest to the people they passed were the horses, which seemed to be completely unknown in that land. As they progressed through Rachida they began to gather a curious entourage of small children who followed them in an increasing throng, wide-eyed and laughing, calling to each other and pointing.

At last they reached a broad hill, covered by a smooth lawn dotted with small blue flowers, and there Imunt and Penar left them and the children dispersed. Farndar told Cadvan the hill was called the Nirimor, the Navel in the Annaren, and at its top was the Nirhel, the hall of their ruler. The horses were told to stay at its base and Cadvan and Maerad followed Farndar up shallow steps cut in the turf to the top of the hill. There stood a large house, made like the others they had seen, but loftier. Its doors were fashioned of silver wood, intricately carved and strangely unweathered, and they stood open to a wide, light corridor. They were led inside and off to the left into a pleasant room in which stood a low table of hard black wood surrounded by broad, richly dyed cushions. The screens were drawn back from the windows, and they could see through the casement to a small grassed courtyard in which blossoming trees hung black branches into a pond. Petals floated on the clear water, and they saw flashes of gold where carp swirled lazily under lilies.

They were told they could wash if they wished, and were shown another room in which were laid basins of water and fresh towels and clean clothes. Maerad, ravenous after their missed lunch, was relieved when they returned to the first room to find breads and cold meats on the table. The food tasted strange to her tongue, herbed with fennel and horseradish and a strange kind of mint, but it was fresh and delicious.

"What is this place?" she asked Cadvan as she ate. "I don't think they mean us any harm, at any rate not now."

"No evil place, at least," Cadvan answered. "Yet it has a strange feeling. It's steeped in some powerful enchantment."

Yes, it does feel strange, mused Maerad, looking out through the casement to the courtyard. It was as if they had been transported back in time, or even taken out of time itself. All sense of urgency had vanished. She settled back into the cushions, content for the moment to do nothing at all but eat and rest.

Shortly afterward Farndar came back and took them to a large hall in the center of the house. The ceiling rose high, supported by many beams carved ingeniously into writhen shapes of branches and leaves. The walls were of the same silver wood made to look smooth and jointless, hung with richly colored tapestries woven in the semblance of a woodland. In the center was a shallow pool blooming with white and yellow lilies. A light radiated from the water, illuminating the hall with a soft, golden effulgence like the sun of early spring.

At the far end was a dais on which was placed a single chair, carved simply out of a polished black wood that Maerad thought at first was stone, and in the chair sat a tall woman. She was robed in white, and her hair fell freely down her shoulders almost to her feet, like a river of silver. Her face seemed at once young and infinitely ancient, as if she were the painted image of a queen who had reigned in ages long past which, by some enchantment, lived; and her glance pierced Maerad with a strange thrill, as if she had stepped into a cold river. She bore no circlet or jewel or staff of authority, yet Maerad knew at once she was a queen of great power.

Farndar led them before the woman and bowed his head and spoke. She nodded, and then turned to face them.

"Welcome to the city of Rachida," she said, and her voice was as musical as water. "Few from the outside world have ever gazed on this place and lived."

To Maerad's relief, she spoke in the tongue of Annar, strangely accented but still understandable. "I have been told your names, and that you are of Annar; and indeed you are fortunate that Cadvan of Lirigon knows the Speech, for otherwise he would surely be dead. But we seek not to kill needlessly; and so you are brought here to know my edict."

"I will tell you willingly of us, Lady of Rachida," said Cadvan, bowing. "But it seems a lack of courtesy not to know who I am addressing, and who reigns over this enchanted place."

"You wish to know who I am?" The woman seemed to ripple with amusement, although she did not laugh. "I am called many things. To my people I am the Star of Evening, and the Song of Morning, and the Sap That Feedeth the Tree of Life;

and once I was called the Child of the Moon, and the Jewel of Lirion, and many other names. I have wandered beyond the Gates to the Meadows of Shade and returned whole, and so am encumbered with a doom alone of all my kind, and am also called the Alone. What is a name?"

Maerad, glancing at Cadvan, saw that he was struck speech-less with amazement. He bowed low.

"Lady," he said, when he had recovered his composure. "Do I have the honor, then, of addressing the one known among Bards as the Queen Ardina?"

She gazed at him, and Cadvan held her glance for a long time before he looked down and aside. "I see you are one of deep lore, and one whom the Speech inhabits, rather than one who learns it tongue-wise," said the Lady. "Such are rare in my realm." She paused. "I did not think my name was still spoken in the wider world."

"Your beauty is still sung in the Halls of the Bards of Annar and the Seven Kingdoms," said Cadvan. "But the songs do you scant justice. They say also that you passed long ago to the vales of the stars, and dwell there yet; and so I am abashed, meeting here one I thought I would never meet, no matter how far and long I wandered in this world."

"Long ago I hid from the world, passing from the memory of Annar," said Ardina dreamily. "But I did not leave this world. I may not." A shadow passed over her face, briefly as a bird's wing eclipses the sun. "But come; it is dull to speak of me. I wish to know who you are, and why you are here." She turned to Farndar and addressed him, and he brought them two chairs and a small table with drinks, and then left them with the Queen.

The Lady questioned Cadvan about his direction, and why he was in the east of the Great Forest. He told her of their journey and of their intention to go to Norloch, but did not mention the reason for it. Ardina seemed satisfied with his answers. She asked for news of the realm of Annar with a distant curiosity, as if they spoke of something that had nothing to do with her, but was quaint, like travelers' tales of distant regions. "I have heard there is a new fear abroad," she said indifferently. "For news comes even here. But this has as little to do with us, as we with it."

For a long time Maerad sat bored, kicking her ankles against the legs of the chair and wishing she could be dismissed if she was going to be so ignored. At last the Lady turned to her, and said: "Now I wish to speak to Maerad of Pellinor. For I perceive that she is one of my kindred, and I am curious to know from whence she came; for in the Darkness much that I loved was extinguished beyond the hope of the hither realm."

Maerad looked up, jolted out of her boredom, and met Ardina's eye. She was, Maerad realized, perplexingly like the Elidhu: her face had a similar wildness, although the regard she turned on her was gentle and thoughtful. With a shock, Maerad realized that Ardina's eyes were not human. They were the same as the Elidhu's: within the white was a golden iris with a pupil like a cat's eye. Again she felt as if she were plunged into cold water, and a strange shiver went all the way down her spine.

"I am the daughter of Milana of the First Circle of Pellinor," she said, with a kind of defiant pride. "How could we be kin?"

"By the strangest of chance, if chance you call it," said Ardina softly. "Often what you humans call chance is instead the workings of a deeper pattern, which the casual eye cannot easily perceive. In the past I have seen you with my inner dreaming, which does not lie. But in such dreaming it is often hard to know what is seen: whether it is the future, or the past, or something that only may be. In you I know my own blood. But there is more. . . ."

Maerad felt goose bumps rising on her skin, and the grip of a strange dread. What did she mean? She couldn't meet the Queen's strange gaze, and she stared down at her feet, deeply unsettled.

There was a pause and then Ardina stood up, as if thinking better of what she was about to say. "I tire you, importuning you with my questions," she said. "Go then in peace, and rest, and savor the delights of my realm; and when you are rested, we will meet again and talk further. And then you shall know my mind."

Cadvan and Maerad both stood and bowed their heads. It seemed a golden light increased around Ardina, growing brighter and brighter until they were forced to blink; and in that moment the Queen vanished, and the chair stood empty before them, and the beautiful room was suddenly desolate with her absence.

Wordlessly they left the hall. Farndar was waiting for them by the door, and he took them to a house not far from the Nirimor, which he said was theirs to use as they liked, and he left them there. The house was arranged around a central courtyard and surrounded by a wide porch, furnished in the same style as the Nirhel. The floors were polished wood, well covered against the cold with rich rugs, and little braziers of iron warmed each room. A meal and wine were set out on a low table in the main room. There was a walled lawn where Farndar said the horses might stay, for they had no stables. Afterward the horses walked freely through the streets of Rachida, where they were given sweets and carrots by the children, and caused much wonder.

By now it was twilight. Both Cadvan and Maerad felt strangely exhausted after their interview with the Lady Ardina, as if they had sat long in talk and been questioned deeply, although in truth their interview had lasted less than an hour.

"This is the strangest of many strange things that have happened to me," said Cadvan as he poured them some wine. "The Lady Ardina! Now legends come to life and walk the earth!"

"Who is she?" asked Maerad. Cadvan said nothing at first, seeming lost in thought; and then he pulled his lyre out of his pack, and began, almost randomly, to strike a few chords. After a while they modulated into a melody, and his voice rose in song:

"When Arkan deemed an endless cold
And greenwoods rotted bleak and sere,
The moon wept high above the world
To see its beauty dwindling:
To earth fell down a single tear
And there stepped forth a shining girl
Like moonlight that through alabaster
Wells, its pallor kindling.

A wild amazement fastened on
The Moonchild's heart, and far she ran,
Through all the vales of Lirion
Her voice like bellnotes echoing:
And from the branches blossoms sprang
In iron groves of leafmeal wan,
And Spring herself woke up and sang,
The gentle Summer beckoning.

"So, long ago, sang the Bard Tulkan, in the tongue of his own country," said Cadvan, laying down his lyre. "It's a difficult measure to render in our speech; I've done my best, but this is only a shadow of the song. It tells of the birth of Ardina, the Moonchild, before the world was changed forever in the Wars of the Elementals, and of her love for Ardhor, who was a mortal king. She rescued him from the trammels of the Ice Witch, who cursed him when he would not do his bidding and froze him deep in the mountains for many years. The full tale is long and sad." Cadvan poured himself more wine.

Maerad listened, enraptured; now she thought she understood something of Cadvan's awe. "Are there many songs about her?" she asked.

"Yes, very many," he answered. "It is one of the great tales. Yet Ardina passed out of our knowing an age ago. The world tonight is a different place for me." He shook his head. "To think I have gazed on her living face! But I wonder what she meant, when she spoke of her doom. The Lady Ardina was one of the Elementals, and she alone of all her kind attempted to die as a mortal and to follow her lover through the Gates. The songs say that they walked together past the Meadows of Shade to the Starry Groves that overlook this world, and there at last they could be together as they wished. But it seems the songs are wrong."

Cadvan was silent then for a long time, pensively sipping his wine, and Maerad, content to say nothing, contemplated him curiously. He seemed wrapped in some fair memory that nevertheless filled him with deep melancholy. She could see now what he must have been like as a young Bard, as Dernhil had remembered him, and it stirred within her an obscure feeling that was like pain. At last Cadvan sighed and looked across at Maerad.

"No power, not even love, can overcome the ban against Return, save that binding chosen by the Nameless One," he said, smiling sadly. "Alas! The world is cruel. More wine?"

Maerad proffered her cup. "I wonder what the Lady Ardina was going to say to me," she said.

"I wonder too," said Cadvan. "There are mysteries here beyond my power to understand. And you, Maerad, not the least of them!" He lifted his cup to her and drank.

"Well, I'm a sore puzzlement to myself," she answered ironically. She leaned forward and poured herself another drink. It
was a light golden wine, but surprisingly strong, and she felt it
going to her head. She wanted suddenly to break this aura of
enchantment; Cadvan's odd mood disturbed her. "For all that,
it all seems a bit, well, a bit *remote* to me. If she has little to do
with us, we have little to do with her. We still have to get out of
this forest; we can't stay here, however beautiful it is. How will
we find a way out from here?"

"I don't know," said Cadvan, frowning. "I am full of doubts
and fears; wise she is, but perilous, this Lady of Rachida, and I
fear she will prove as stern as the very mountains. She does not
care for the travails of our world. Although," he added, "it
occurs to me that perhaps many things that have been long
sundered from each other may now have cause to look beyond
their borders." He stretched and yawned lazily, and drained his
wine. "At least we'll sleep safely tonight, as we haven't since
leaving Innail."

Shortly afterward they retired to their chambers, where they
found couches heaped high with blankets woven from a soft
cloth they did not recognize. The night was mild, so Maerad
kept her window open, pulling back the paper screens. She
went to sleep laved by scented breezes from the garden, where
water from a small channel trickled in a little fall, down into a
stone pool. Its gentle voice ran underneath her dreams all night.

For the first time since she could remember, Maerad
dreamed of her mother. Not as she had last seen her, twisted
with illness, crippled by anguish and despair, her light
extinguished; but tall and proud and strong, as she barely
remembered her. In the dream she had stood in a high crystal
tower playing her lyre, and, as she played, birds of fabulous
colors—sapphire, gold, emerald, crimson—flew out of her lyre
and circled her in a graceful dance. Maerad ran up to the tower

wall, calling for her mother; but there was no door in the tower, although she searched and searched. She came close to the glass and called her—"Mamma, Mamma,"—but her voice was small and pathetic; her mother did not hear her and kept playing, absorbed by the music. Maerad beat her fists on the hard, cold walls until her hands were bruised and bleeding, but still Milana would not turn to look at her, and at last Maerad sank to the ground, exhausted. "How could she abandon me?" she sobbed to herself. "How could she forget?"

She woke to find her cheeks wet and cold with tears. She turned over and looked out of the window into the garden. It was still deep night and the stars blazed in the cold sky, casting shifting shadows on the cool grass, which was gray with dew. The image of her mother burned in her mind, bright and immeasurably far away. If she was First Bard of Pellinor, she thought to herself, why did she not free us? Why couldn't she run away with me, like Cadvan did? Maerad couldn't remember Milana ever mentioning her father, but suddenly she knew with adamant certainty that his death had destroyed her mother. She wondered what it was like to love someone like that, like her mother had loved her father, like Ardina had loved Ardhor. She never would: it was too dangerous. It had killed Milana. And even Maerad hadn't been enough to save her. Why not? A pain she had never acknowledged opened and flowered in her breast. Why couldn't *she* have saved her mother? Why did Milana die, so miserable, so broken, in a place so far from the bright world that was her right?

Maerad sat up and stared sadly in front of her, hugging the blankets around her shoulders. She no longer felt sleepy. There were so many things happening to her, and she didn't know what to think about any of them. Her mind ran restlessly through the events of the past weeks; all she felt was confused.

She thought of Silvia, of how deeply she already loved her, of how in that short time at Innail she had been more of a mother to her than anyone. Except Milana before Pellinor burned, she loyally added to herself; but the truth was she could scarcely remember Pellinor. And the Elidhu had called her *daughter*. What did that mean? And how could Ardina tell? She looked ordinary, the same as everyone else. What marked her? And what was the flame that killed the Kulag and the Hull? Did it really come from her? Was that why the Hulls were hunting her? A vision of Dernhil suddenly rose vividly before her inner eye, his face alight with enthusiasm, his forefinger on the page of a book. . . . She wondered uneasily what Cadvan and Silvia meant when they spoke so easily of love, of the ways of the heart. He died because of me, she thought miserably. Why? What am I? How am I ever going to know?

She wondered restlessly if they would ever reach Norloch, and if they did, whether it would answer any of her questions. Her feelings about Cadvan were entirely enigmatic. She knew she trusted him as she had trusted no man in her life, except perhaps the father she could barely remember, but she didn't really understand why. Perhaps it was because Silvia had trusted him too; but inside she knew it was more than that. She remembered how he had first stood before her in the cowbyre, years ago it seemed, though it was only a couple of months: how his face then was gray with exhaustion, vulnerable, and, she thought now, sad. Even then it hadn't really occurred to her to doubt him. She thought of his stern, mobile face, how driven he seemed, how isolated; but then he would light up with that vivid, warm smile. . . . What was she to him? A tool of the Light, a thing of mysterious power . . . not merely that, surely? What was she doing, fleeing through such perils with this man, to Norloch, a place of which she knew nothing? What if he was wrong? Would he then abandon her?

Feeling restless, she wrapped the blanket around her shoulders and got out of bed. She wandered in the darkness to the room where they had eaten, feeling her way slowly along the walls, and then to the front door, which gave silently under her hand. She stepped barefoot out onto the porch. A half moon swung high above her among the stars. A few dark wisps of clouds hurried high above, but she felt no wind. She curled into a cushioned couch that was set there, wrapping the blanket tightly against the chill, and looked up into the sky, greeting the stars as if they were old friends: the swinging belt of Melchar, and the Great Boat, and the single star Ilion, burning like a brilliant crystal low over the horizon. Their wordless beauty eased her anxiety, and she stayed there until, without realizing it, she fell fast asleep; and there Cadvan found her early the next morning, with her hair fallen in cobwebs across her eyes and mouth. If she had been able to see his face, she would have perceived there a tenderness that he had never shown her. He bent over her and gently brushed back the hair from her face. She stirred, mumbling something, and did not wake. He gazed at her for a few more seconds and then he smiled and went indoors, leaving her to wake when the sun rose high enough to strike her face.

Later that morning Farndar, one of the bowmen who had captured them, arrived and told Cadvan he was leaving Rachida again to go south, to the borders of their realm. He spoke with a new respect. "You have the Lady's favor," he said to Cadvan. "Strangers are uncommon here. There have been none in my lifetime."

Maerad stood by trying to follow their conversation. The words of the Speech slipped strangely from her memory; she didn't feel she could learn it, as these people seemed to, in the normal way. Somehow that made her feel even more exiled, as if she were foreign even to herself. At last Farndar turned to her and bowed courteously. She bowed in return, and then he left.

"I wish I could understand these people," she said to Cadvan after he had gone. "Why can't I learn the Speech? They're not all Bards, are they?"

"No," said Cadvan. "I haven't yet met one who is. The Dhyllin were the only race that used the Speech as their own language; these people must be a remnant of those folk. In the mouths of those who are not Bards the Speech hasn't the virtues of Barding. In truth, they speak an odd dialect of it here; but I can still understand them."

"Then why can't I learn it?" Maerad sat down, frowning. "I don't have a problem learning other things. But I forget a word as soon as I hear it. It slips out of my mind."

"No one understands how the Speech springs in the minds of Bards," said Cadvan. "But perhaps it's closed to you, until it arrives of its own accord."

"I don't think I'll ever learn it," said Maerad.

"You will," Cadvan said. "It yet sleeps in you."

"What if you're wrong?"

Cadvan gazed at her dispassionately and then sat down next to her. "I can always be mistaken," he said. "But that is for neither you nor I to worry about. We must do what we can, knowing or guessing what we can; and if it is any comfort, my guesses are not often far off the mark. I believe you are the Foretold, and I have good reasons for thinking so; perhaps the best are those that I cannot explain, which link to an inner Knowing of which I am not completely aware. It does not do to be impatient with any part of the Knowing, and most especially of the Speech, which is one of its chief mysteries."

"You didn't know about the Elementals," Maerad said pugnaciously.

"No," said Cadvan. "I don't know everything. No one does,

and only the foolish seek to." He searched her face and then
said gently, "Don't sit so glowering and sad, Maerad. It's hard
to be thus picked out, beyond your own choice and will, for a
life that makes you separate from others. Even to be a Bard is
difficult, if your own people are not Bards; to be the Foretold
must be so much the harder. Still, how it opens the strangeness
and beauty of the world!"

Maerad said nothing for a while. I've always been separate,
she thought. That's not what bothers me. At last she asked, in
a muffled voice: "Was it difficult for you, when you found out
you were a Bard?"

Cadvan sighed and looked down. "Yes," he said. "My
people were simple folk. As far as they knew, there had been no
Barding in my family. It is often so. My father was, in fact, a cobbler in Lirigon. If need be, I could still make a fine pair of boots!
I was the youngest child, and it was hard for them to see me
leave them for a world of which they had little understanding.
And it was hard when I did not grow old as they did. My parents died when I still felt young. My brothers and sisters died
long ago. I couldn't cure them of old age."

"But even among Bards, you're a bit separate," said Maerad.
"I mean, you seem more at home with innkeepers, somehow,
and marketers, than in the Schools."

Cadvan gave her a sharp glance, and then laughed. "It's odd
for me, to be observed," he said. "I like to think of myself as the
eye that looks but goes unseen. Not true, of course. . . . Yes, perhaps part of me wishes that I had been allotted an ordinary life,
and had been a cobbler, like my father was. My parents were
good people. But it wasn't my fate! And I don't regret it,
although sometimes it has made me sorrowful."

"Then why . . ." began Maerad, but Cadvan cut her off.

"I'll be answering questions all day, at this rate," he said,
standing up. "I think we should go out and look at Rachida. We

have the freedom of the city, so Farndar tells me, and I am impatient to see this place. We can't run away; we'd be utterly lost in the forest, so we might as well take advantage of our stay."

Maerad had been about to ask him why his Barding had led him to search out the Dark. She remembered the flash of a face that she had seen when he had scried her, and Dernhil's hint of a tragedy long ago, when Cadvan was young, and she could begin to guess. . . . But on reflection she thought it better she did not ask him. She doubted he would tell her.

After the discomforts and perils of their journey, Rachida was a welcome haven. They spent their days resting and eating, or walking through the town. During the day they noticed that the sky seemed to be veiled by a golden mist, and a strange sense that they walked through a time that was at once present and yet irredeemably distant began to grow on them. Cadvan believed Rachida was gripped by a powerful concealment charm created by Ardina. It was a place of rare beauty; every object, from pots and bowls to children's toys to fabrics, was remarkable for its fineness. The Rachidans ate from fine glazed clayware, with perhaps a single detail of a flower or a snake or a bird, and dressed in garments subtly dyed and exquisitely cut. Even a meal was presented like a work of art.

The people of Rachida were friendly and generous, and Cadvan and Maerad had no trouble in making friends. They were invited to eat at many houses and were shown many marvelous things: a rowan tree, true to every detail, carved from a single piece of alabaster, and a necklace of many intricately carven links made from a single piece of deer bone, and a robe of silk, dyed all the colors of the sunset spilling on a river, woven from a single thread. The Rachidans delighted in such feats of skill and cunning, but in their delight was no sense of greed. Cadvan and Maerad refused the offers of many precious things, given simply because they admired them, with the plea that they could not carry them home. Even so, more than a few turned up in their house.

If they didn't eat with others, food was brought to their house by a young man called Idris. Unusual for a Rachidan, he was very curious about the world beyond Rachida, which no one he knew had ever seen. Despite their isolation, most people they met had little interest in anything that lay beyond their borders. They called Rachida the Navel of the World, and believed their city held everything they could rightly want. Idris listened intently to Cadvan's tales of far cities, his eyes glowing. But when Cadvan asked him if he desired to travel, he simply shook his head. "I don't want to," he said. "What treasure could I find richer than this?" Maerad and Cadvan both saw his point; but after a couple of days they began to chafe at the delay. They had still not had word from the Lady Ardina.

"I've never been in a place so withdrawn from the world!" Cadvan said, after Idris had left. "I begin to wonder if we will be allowed to leave. Perhaps the price of trespass here is that we must stay; and we cannot."

Maerad counted back and figured it was just over two months since she had first met Cadvan, which made it now late April or early May. So short a time! she thought to herself in astonishment. Her time in Gilman's Cot seemed like another life altogether, an evil memory dulled by distance, and even her stay in Innail seemed an age before. And here they were, caught like flies in amber outside time itself. She looked out through the window to the fountain, which plashed softly in the warm air. The room was utterly peaceful, but she felt no answering peace within herself. She didn't belong here.

"I hope not," she said. "It's time we left."

* * *

On the seventh day they were again summoned to the Nirhel. This time they made their way unaccompanied to the great house. When they entered the hall the Queen Ardina awaited them, seated in her black chair.

Maerad blinked. She had already forgotten the impact of Ardina's beauty, the potency of her glance. This time Ardina's hair was braided in a long silver twist wound with pearls, and she wore a plain silver circlet in which was set a single moonstone.

"Cadvan of Lirigon and Maerad of Pellinor," said the Lady, standing to greet them. "I trust you are rested, and have tasted the hospitality of my city?"

"Our thanks, Queen Ardina," Cadvan answered. "We are indeed rested. And we have been shown much courtesy and have seen many beautiful things. Rachida is a place of marvels, in which a sore heart might rest content."

Ardina indicated they should sit down.

"Rachida is truly named the Navel of the World," she said. "But the sight of these marvels comes at a price. The law of Rachida is that none who wander here might leave. So we preserve in secrecy the purity of this place, which otherwise might be injured by the evils of the outside world."

Maerad drew in her breath. This was what Cadvan had feared. She stared at the Lady, seeing there an immovable will; she was beautiful, yes, as fine alabaster welling with imprisoned moonlight, but stern and implacable as adamant.

Cadvan seemed unshaken. "I guessed as much. And yet I ask that the law be set aside for Maerad and me. If we were only concerned with ourselves, it would be no punishment for us to while away our lives here among your generous and openhearted people. But we are not merely concerned with ourselves. We carry with us a deadly doom that concerns each of us alive in this time: and we cannot tarry here. If you forbid us to go, we should have to leave against your will."

"Then you would die," said Ardina. Her eyes were stern and cold.

"Even so, we should have to make the attempt," Cadvan replied. "Such is the urgency of our quest, that we have no choice. Would you have it said that the Lady Ardina aided the Dark?"

The Queen gave Cadvan a proud glance. "You ask a great deal of me," she said. "So great, that it is a discourtesy to ask. In granting this, I risk destroying all that I love. Rachida is precious to me, and my people I value above all others. Why, then, should I grant this to you? What is this doom you speak of?"

Cadvan paused, as if gathering up his resolution. Maerad felt the force of the Queen's will strongly; she was almost ready to abandon their journey merely at Ardina's request.

"Lady Ardina, I trust you remember the Nameless One, who destroyed all Imbral and Lirion," said Cadvan.

The Queen stirred, and seemed to look deep into her memories. "I remember Sharma well, before he came into his power," she said. "A secretive, unpleasant man, I thought him, unworthy of the favor of the great Bards of Afinil, for all his talent. I told them so. And so it proved. Why think you I withdrew into the heart of the Cilicader? Why think you I made such a ban as I have made?"

"I do not know if you have heard the foretelling, that his last victory was not the worst," said Cadvan. "It has been long said among the Bards of Annar that the Nameless will return, and his next coming will be his darkest, destroying all that is beautiful and free, withering all forests, drowning in shadow all the havens of the Light that yet remain. For think you not that he has learned from his defeat? And do you think, Lady, that even you, in your great power, could preserve here such Light as you have done, if all Annar was laid desolate and the Bards were utterly defeated?

"His last victory was not complete. The Light held havens not only here, but hidden in the Seven Kingdoms; and so at last his reign was destroyed, and his power overthrown. But it is said that if he next prevails, his malice and might will be absolute until a time beyond the ability of mortals to perceive. And I say to you, Lady Ardina, the Dhyllin were ever those he hated the most and most sought to destroy. I think if he achieved such power, this time he would not overlook Rachida."

Such was the power and urgency of his plea that Ardina looked down at her lap, and her face was shadowed with doubt.

"Say on," she said. She glanced at him keenly. "This foretelling may be true. But what do you know of this uprising of the Nameless? You speak as if he rises now."

"I believe he rises now," said Cadvan heavily. "I have been shown so." He took a deep breath before he continued. "Before this winter, I was sent by the Bards of Norloch on a mission far to the north, and on my return I was captured by one of thy kin, one who inhabits a mountain some know as the Landrost. He was long ago snared and corrupted by the Nameless. He is a sorcerer of great malevolence and strength, and even so he is but a slave of that Dark power."

"I know of whom you speak," said Ardina. "I do not say his name."

"He cast me into his dungeons." Cadvan was silent awhile. "I will not speak of what I underwent there. But in his pride he boasted to me of the coming of the Dark. In his throne room he hath a pool, like to yours, Lady, but an evil reflection of it. No Light lives there, but an unspeakable Shadow. And in that mirror may be seen things that are. He thought to make me die in despair; and he showed me the building of forces in Dén Raven and the gathering of corruption in the places of the Light and an evil creeping over Annar like a poisonous smoke, and lastly he revealed to me that the Nameless returned again."

"The tools of the Dark have ever lied," said Ardina swiftly.

"Aye, Lady," said Cadvan. "But I am said among Bards to be a Truthteller, and have the gift of knowing what is a lie and what is not; and I am long used to the deceptions of the Dark. What he showed me was not a lie. He could not have hoped to have tormented me with a falsehood or a meretricious shadow; and he well knew that."

For a long time there was silence, while Ardina sat pensive. Maerad looked at Cadvan with a new wonder; he had not spoken of the Landrost, except briefly in their first journey together to Innail. Now Maerad saw more clearly what Cadvan had meant by the strange chance of their meeting. She wondered how he had survived, and how he had escaped; but the Lady did not ask.

"You have not told me of the burden you bear," said Ardina at last.

Cadvan, who had been sitting staring at his hands, looked up. His face was overcast with painful memory.

"There is another prophecy, a memory preserved in song by the Bards, although it has fallen into forgetting and now is little known," he said. "It speaks of one who will appear when the Nameless increases in his power for his darkest rising. This one is the Foretold, the One. And it is said the Foretold will defeat the Nameless, and will cast him down from his strongest assault on the Light."

"Is it said how this will happen?" asked Ardina.

"No," said Cadvan.

"And who is this Foretold?"

"I believe that Maerad of Pellinor is the Foretold. And therefore together we journey to Norloch by untrodden and hidden ways, so we might not be perceived by the Dark, which pursued us almost to the borders of your realm. For in Norloch there is wisdom and lore that might better understand this riddle."

Ardina looked searchingly into Cadvan's face. This time he held her gaze. At last she looked away and sighed.

"Almost you remind me of the King Ardhor," she said sadly, "for such is your courage and verity. I would it were not so: for you place me on the edge of a razor, and no matter whither I step, there lies danger."

Then she turned to face Maerad, and looking up into her inhuman eyes, Maerad saw with astonishment a fathomless compassion and sadness. Suddenly Queen Ardina seemed not a distant figure stepped out of legend, but mortal and frail, like herself.

"I see a Fate on thee, sister," said Ardina. With a thrill, Maerad realized that Ardina was speaking to her in the tongue of the Elidhu, not in the language of Annar. "I sensed it when first I saw thy face. I know not what to say to thee, for thou art yet asleep, like the lily that sleepeth under the ground in winter; and yet within thee there dwells a fire of unsurpassed brightness, which will blossom in its own time. I know not what it means and what it tells; and I fear in my heart that it spells an end for my people, no matter how I construe it."

"Say not an end," said Maerad in the same language, surprising herself, for she felt as if another voice spoke within her. "Say rather another beginning."

"Perhaps," said Ardina. "But an ending, nevertheless. And it may be that the doom we all fear will overtake us, no matter how we struggle against it. But better to fight than to be overwhelmed without resistance." As Ardina spoke, it seemed to Maerad that her vision wavered, and she saw again the shimmering Elidhu in the forest laid over the image of the mighty Queen. She realized with sudden wonder that Ardina and the Elidhu in the woods were one and the same. She gasped, and looked up into Ardina's yellow eyes.

"Aye, sister," said Ardina, who was studying her closely. "You see aright. I am both Queen and Elidhu, here and there, wildfire and hearthfire, forgetting and remembrance. But do not yet speak of this, for men are impatient with such things and do not brook contradiction."

Cadvan was looking between the two women with incomprehension, and the Queen glanced toward him and rose.

"Cadvan of Lirigon," she said, in the tongue of Annar. "I know you speak truly to me. How you have increased my sorrow! Do not believe that my isolation means I know little of the fortunes of Annar; I have my own mirror on the world, as you guessed. I hoped yet to remain unseen. Like all false hopes, it was comforting. But it has never been said that the Lady Ardina was faint of heart, or took refuge in the excuses of cowards."

She paused, as if considering again her thoughts. "I will now say my resolution to you. You alone of all who have wandered here may journey from my realm without hindrance. I grant you this because I know you speak truth, and because you travel here with my kin, and because we must make ourselves strong against our common enemy, and not be divided. I ask only that you speak to no one of your sojourn here. And further, I will give you what help I can and will offer you guidance to the borders of the Cilicader, for there are many dark places in this forest it would be well to shun."

Cadvan rose and bowed his head. "I thank you, Lady Ardina," he said. "I know what it costs you to grant us this. Truly you are a mighty Queen, and your law is just." He looked as if he wished to say more but could not.

"Farewell, then," said Ardina. "Maerad of Pellinor, my

good wishes travel with you. May your Doom be not as hard as mine! And as a sign of our kinship, I bid you take this." She took from her finger a thin band of gold fashioned into the semblance of lilies, each flower twisted into the next in miraculously fine workmanship. Maerad received it awkwardly, taken aback by surprise.

"Wear this in memory of Ardina," said the Lady. "It was given me long ago by one I loved. Your future is uncertain, and I can tell you nothing that can help you. You are singular and dangerous, and so it is that you are sought by both the Dark and the Light. Perhaps you will find that your Fate has nothing to do with either of them. It may be that you will find that your greatest peril exists already within you. Only this is clear: you have a great heart, but will only find it to be so through great pain. This is the wisdom of love, and its doubtful gift. Yet I have endured much suffering and still remain unbitter and unclosed."

Maerad looked again in the Queen's eyes, and it seemed to her that Ardina's glance pierced her where she was most tender, hurting her; and yet she welcomed the wound. She couldn't hold the Queen's gaze for long and bowed her head, puzzling over Ardina's words, which she did not understand.

"To you, traveler and Truthteller," Ardina said, turning at last to Cadvan, "I give nothing but my blessing. Your road will be dark, but I doubt that is unknown to you. And Light blooms the brighter in the darkest places."

"The blessing of Ardina is no small thing," said Cadvan. "I thank you again, Lady. Well your people praise you as the Sap of the Tree of Life!"

Ardina raised her hand in farewell, and then the golden light gathered around her, and they blinked, and when they looked again she was gone.

"Such was the glory of the days of the Dhyllin," said

Cadvan, sighing after a long silence. "I will be grateful all my life to have been vouchsafed this glimpse. And yet its gladness is mixed with great sorrow."

When they returned to their house, Maerad realized that her period had started again. She cursed the inconvenience and took herself to her room to deal with it. While she was digging through her pack for cloths, it suddenly struck her that she had no cramps. She sat back on her heels, thinking, Had Ardina eased them? She thought of her profound glance, which had seemed at once a wound and its mending, as merciless and compassionate as the knife of a healer. Certainly the pains had gone, and they never troubled her again.

She pondered what Ardina had said to her. Despite its ominous portents it was strangely comforting. It seemed to her that Ardina had understood, as no one else could, her own doubts and fears, and her loneliness. That single moment of perception illuminated her confusions and somehow made her feel less isolated. She would always wear the ring, as she wore the jewel that Silvia had given her, as a token of love.

The following day they made ready to leave Rachida, not without mixed feelings. Ardina's decision had clearly been made known; it seemed the whole town knew they were leaving, and early in the morning they found a pile of fresh supplies waiting on the porch. Many gifts were pressed on them, but Cadvan refused them smilingly, saying they could take only the barest minimum for fear of overloading the horses.

That evening, despite many invitations, they stayed at their own house and ate alone. They felt an unspoken need to prepare themselves for the journey ahead. Idris arrived with the food and made his farewells, looking very downcast. Seeing this, Cadvan gave him his silver brooch, the star sign of Lirigon. Idris embraced them both and left in tears.

"I don't want to leave," said Maerad gloomily, as they sat down to their meal, "although I know we must."

"I've never been welcomed with such warmth among strangers," said Cadvan, pouring them both a cup of wine. "I have been in many places with more majesty than this, but none so enchanting. It's one more thing imperiled. Think of what Ardina has already done to protect her people! But I doubt they can preserve their isolation for much longer, even if they capture every wayfarer who strays into these forests." He picked at his food moodily. "There is already too much to fear for."

The next morning they woke early and dressed in their traveling clothes, and shortly afterward met their guides, who were their early captors Imunt and Penar. "Since we brought you here, we have the task of releasing you," said Penar, grinning as he embraced them.

They led the horses through the town, a heavy reluctance weighing down their steps. Maerad looked hungrily around her, wishing to imprint its beauty on her memory. Rachida lay unstained before them, damp still with the morning dew, and as the horses clopped through the streets, windows opened and people waved and fair-haired children ran out to give the horses some last dainties and to run alongside them laughing and shouting. They felt as if they were the occasion for a festival.

They climbed the western side of the valley, leaving the houses behind them. At its rim Maerad turned around for one last look before Rachida vanished forever behind her. The rising sun struck the roofs so they shone like burnished silver, and the light fell gently in a honeyed mist onto the streets and gardens, picking out the fresh colors of tree and flower and home so they seemed newly minted. Yet already it seemed to her that a shimmering veil lay between her and Rachida, as if, even at this distance, it lay only within her memory, a golden dream of untouchable beauty.

NORLOCH

Grows a Lily on the Briar
Grows a Briar on the Wave
Triple-tongued its voice of Fire
Edil-Amarandh will save

True and false the cunning Flame
Burning in the darkest Night
False and true the secret Name
Quickened in the womb of Light

Where the Briar on the Foam?
Doth the Lily stemless stand?
Who will bring the Singing home?
Where the Harp? And whose the Hand?

From *The Canticles of Pel of Norloch*

XVII

THE VALVERRAS

THEY followed a path that led west, walking at their ease through flowering meadows that slumbered beneath broad stands of trees. The sun shone warmly, and Maerad thought it would not be long now before summer. Now the perils of their journey, which in the serenity of Rachida had receded, began again to press on Maerad's mind, and for the first time for many days she had dreams of being hunted by Hulls.

They were not far, Imunt told Cadvan, from the borders of their land. He was taking them to the river they called the Cir, which Cadvan was certain was the course he knew as the Cirion. The river split to the north into two streams, the Cir and the Ciri, and met again farther south. The two streams enclosed between them a large leaf-shaped island, of which Rachida was the center, and roughly marked the borders of the realm, although Rachidan outriders also went south as far as the Usk. Once they reached the Cir, their guides would leave them; if they followed it south it flowed into the Usk, which, thus augmented, continued through the forest and then out into the plains of western Annar. From there, it was a journey of some eighty leagues south to Norloch.

Later that day they met the river, which ran swiftly between steep banks, with many falls into wide pools. Their guides gave them final advice and warnings on what they might expect to find on the other side: bird spiders as large as two fists, giant leeches, wild cats, and other perils. But they knew of no wers or goromants at this end of the forest.

"There is an old path that runs alongside the Cir. It meets the Ciri within a day's walk and joins to the Usk after about three days," said Penar. "Mind you stay on this bank on the Cir, for it becomes deep and is uncrossable farther down. The path should avoid such perils as we know of, but after you meet the Usk, you move beyond our knowledge. We do not venture past the Cir now. It may be that wers now live there. You will need vigilance."

Their guides bid them farewell, holding their hands high in salute before they turned and vanished with a startling swiftness among the trees. Maerad and Cadvan stood for a time looking after them, and then with a sigh turned their faces west. For the first time in days they mounted Darsor and Imi and quietly forded the river. The light, although it was no less bright, seemed less rich on the other side of the river, and this, more than anything else, told them they had now left the protection of Ardina's haven and were again alone in the world.

A few hours later they reached the meeting of the two waters, Cir and Ciri, and after that the river began to dig itself between steep banks and their way became less easy to follow. In places there was scarcely a trace of a path at all and they simply followed the river, hoping to find a clearer track farther on; eventually a shadow of a path would appear between the trees, only to peter out again. Despite this they were moving swiftly; both Maerad and Cadvan felt strongly the need for haste, and they urged on their horses.

Three uneventful days of riding and they came again to the Usk, which met and mingled with the Cirion and thereafter leaped down strongly between rocky banks, breaking into frequent rapids that roared unseen beside them. The path still continued vertiginously between the trees, but the going was a little slower. If it had not been for Maerad's abiding anxiety, the ride would have been peaceful, so removed did they feel from human affairs of any kind. They saw no sign of bird spiders or wild cats or goromants, and they heard nothing at night save frogs and crickets and the rustles of small animals. The forest seemed deserted and shabby, even a little forlorn; the trees were thickly overgrown with moss and creepers that dangled shaggily from the branches, further obscuring the light. Even sound was muffled: their hoofbeats fell dully on a bed of dead leaves, and their voices seemed to die on the damp air. They moved through the trees like ghosts.

Maerad looked somberly at the river running beside them. "When do you think we'll get out of these woods?" she asked.

"I think maybe a couple of days," said Cadvan. "It seems to me the forest is thinning a little."

Maerad brightened at the news; the endless trees were beginning to oppress her. And as Cadvan had guessed, late on the fifth day after they had parted from Imunt and Penar, having encountered nothing more sinister than wood spiders, they emerged from the western edge of the Cilicader.

The forest ended messily, gradually thinning out until the trees vanished altogether. Maerad and Cadvan looked over wide plains that fell away from them to the horizon, pocked by frequent dips and hollows and by outcrops of rocks that now and again gathered into huge tors that cast long shadows toward them. The sky seemed huge. Drifts of rose-and-purple clouds hung lazily over the horizon and veiled the westering sun, which sent down great shafts of light that spilled red on the travelers' faces. The Usk still ran to their left, tumbling between broken piles of granite, which looked as if they had been tossed there long ago by giants, blotched with livid lichens and cushions of moss. They saw no sign of habitation. It was, in its own way, a country as lonely and empty as that they had left, and Maerad felt suddenly vulnerable, exposed by the light and space.

"Every time I'm in a forest," she said to Cadvan, drawing to a halt beside him, "I can't wait to get out. And then once I'm out, all I want to do is get back in! I feel like everything is watching me." She squinted at the sky. "Even the clouds."

"We've reached the Valverras Waste," Cadvan said. "It does feel like that here. They tell strange tales of this place."

Maerad stared at the desolate landscape and shuddered. "Don't tell them to me," she said. "I'm sure they're horrible."

The Valverras, Cadvan said, was a desert place that stretched between the forest and the coast, falling to a maze of fens and marshes nearer the sea. It divided that part of north Annar. If they now went farther north about a hundred leagues, they would strike the Lir River, about which clustered the hamlets and towns of Lirhan. Closer south ran the Aldern River, which was also thickly inhabited. Norloch was almost due south, about eighty leagues distant as the crow flew. The Kingdom of Ileadh, Dernhil's birthplace, was almost directly ahead of them, a broad peninsula to the west; slightly to the north of that was Culain.

"If we were not so urgently bound, it would be pleasant to visit the Schools there," said Cadvan, as they sat astride their horses looking over the waste. "Culor in Culain and Gent in Ileadh are beautiful in the way Innail is, and noble centers of the Light, but different each from the other, as all Schools are; I think you'd like them. Then we could take a little boat from Gent and journey to the Isle of Thorold; there we could visit the silk markets of Busk, and walk through the pine forests on the mountains—which are like no other place—and taste their freedom and silence. And after that, perhaps, we could beg a ride on one of the noble ships of Annar and sail to Mithrad Bay, arriving at dawn so you could see from the harbor the rising sun strike the white towers of Norloch. It is one of the greatest sights of Annar, and no matter how many times

I see it, I always catch my breath. Norloch leaps up from the sheer cliffs, wall upon narrowing wall, until at last the high tower of Machelinor rises tallest of all, the Tower of the Living Flame. Its tip is as graceful as the summit of a fair tree and is roofed with gold and crystal, so the sun catches there like a pure fire."

He sat silent for a time, and Maerad looked across at him. Cadvan's eyes were distant, as if he saw far visions.

"And what then?" she asked.

"What then?" He turned to her and smiled, and he was suddenly present again. "First we must do what we must do in Norloch. That is our quest. If the doom of Annar and the Seven Kingdoms hangs in the balance, the fulcrum, I believe, is you; but until you are instated as a full Bard, we cannot know for sure. And how to instate you? That is the first step, the first puzzle. Who knows what will happen then?"

Who indeed? Maerad thought to herself. And what if she wasn't who Cadvan believed her to be? Was that the end of her tutelage? What would she do then? But Cadvan continued to speak.

"Perhaps, if fate was kind to us, we could afterward travel to Lanorial by pleasant and leisurely roads, and I could show you the gardens of Il Arunedh, which are planted on terraces so they cascade down the mountainside in great swaths of color. They are one of the marvels of the world. In spring the perfume is as heady as wine." He sighed. "I have many friends in these places whom I have too long neglected. Always I have been driven hither and thither and must go forth along dark roads, instead of lingering in the fair places of the world."

There was a yearning in his voice that Maerad hadn't heard before, and she made no answer; she wondered, with an unexpected pang of jealousy, who it was he so missed. They stood silent for a while, letting the horses crop grass, and Cadvan sighed again. "But I think we will not travel there, unless all foresight fails me," he said, a little harshly. "Our paths are more perilous. Perhaps in some far morning yet unseen beyond the shadows of the world, we will ride there and wander the perfumed gardens of Manuneril and Har. Well," he said, gathering up his reins, "we should find a place to spend the night. Tomorrow we'll ponder the riddle of crossing the Usk. There is a Bard Road forty or so leagues hence, where there is a ford; it skirts the marsh and then forks to Lirigon on the one side and Culor the other, and southward goes straight to Norloch. But it would irk me to go so far out of our way, and I would rather avoid roads, if we can."

The following day they followed the Usk westward, searching for a place where they might cross. It ran too fast and deep to risk swimming the horses; in some places the banks were too steep to even consider going down to the water. Maerad found the Valverras hard going: dreary, empty, and dispiriting. She couldn't shake off the sense of watchfulness, although neither she nor Cadvan saw any sign of living things, save the kestrels that soared high above them and the rabbits that startled and thumped into the distance.

Halfway through the morning, Imi picked up a stone in her hoof and started limping. Maerad swore and dismounted, picking up the mare's foot to inspect it. She picked out the stone with her little dagger, but Imi's foot was bruised; she continued to limp, and Maerad was loath to push her in case it became worse. When they came to a place where the banks shelved more gently, they stopped for lunch. Cadvan tended Imi's hoof, easing the pain, and afterward Maerad bathed the mare's legs in the running water. Even so, she still walked with a limp, and Maerad began to worry she had hurt herself badly. A lame horse would slow them down seriously, and they had

already lost more than three weeks in the Great Forest.
Maerad's sense of urgency was, if anything, greater than
Cadvan's; she chafed at any delay, fuming with impatience,
while Cadvan accepted the trials of their road with imper-
turbable calm. Cadvan's serenity only increased Maerad's
impatience. Then, late in the afternoon, it began to drizzle, and
they traveled only a little farther before the light became too
bad to see. They made camp in the shelter of a granite tumulus,
still on the wrong side of the Usk, and by then Maerad was
smoldering with suppressed bad temper.

"How long are we going to be scrabbling around like dogs
in the wild?" she grumbled, dishing out a barley stew. "I've had
enough of it. And Imi's had enough of it. She needs a rest."

"Until we reach the end of it," said Cadvan. "Which
shouldn't be that long, all being well." He stretched out his
long legs, regarding Maerad with tolerant amusement. "We've
done very well to cross the Great Forest with no injury. Nevertheless, the wilds pall, I agree."

"Pall is not the word," answered Maerad. "I wish I'd stayed
in Rachida. It's not as if there's any home for me to go to, anyway. I might as well have stayed there."

"No, we can only go forward now." Cadvan leaned forward
and looked at Maerad intently. "You know we must go to
Norloch."

"I don't want to," said Maerad. "I don't want to go anywhere."

"You've had choices," Cadvan answered mildly. "If you had
wished to stay in Innail, or in Rachida, I would not have
stopped you. I couldn't have stopped you. You listened to your
inner voice as much as I did. You knew that your fate, the fate of
many others, was at stake. Think of your dream. Or have you
forgotten all that?"

"Some choice." Maerad was picking irritably at tufts of grass and throwing them on the ground, her eyebrows drawn down in a straight, angry line.

"You know it's the truth."

"What difference, being a pawn for the Light or a pawn for the Dark?"

There was a short silence.

"There is a great difference," said Cadvan. "One difference is that for the Dark, certainly, you *are* a pawn. For the Light, you are a free human being, free to make mistakes, to do wrong, even. You are free to choose, whether or not you believe it."

"Funny idea of freedom."

"It is the difference between commitment and slavery," Cadvan said. "Between working for what you hope for and believe in the depths of your heart, and what someone else forces you to do."

Maerad, who had been a slave and knew that her present life, however difficult, was very different, had nothing to say to that. She didn't know why she was trying to pick a fight with Cadvan, but he refused to get angry with her and after a while fell silent and stared into the fire. She sat glowering just out of its circle of light, kicking a bit of turf with her toe; and then, because it was Cadvan's turn to watch, curled up in her blanket and, surprisingly rapidly, went to sleep.

The next day was equally fruitless, although the weather began to clear and at last some sunshine warmed them. Imi's limp was not so serious, but they went anxiously for fear they would delay its healing. After a while Maerad forgot her black mood in the rhythm of the riding, but the feeling of being watched never left her. She didn't mention it to Cadvan, but she often felt a prickling on the back of her neck, as if there was a presence behind her, and she would turn sharply, only to find nothing there. She began to feel that the stones were playing tricks, transforming into rocky monsters that stalked her, only to instantly turn back into innocent boulders whenever she looked back. They didn't ford the Usk until the third day, and then at last they turned their faces south.

Thus began days of toiling through the Valverras. Cadvan guided them by the sun and the stars, and they watched the moon growing thinner until it waned to a nail paring and disappeared, and then witnessed its gradual return. The weather continued to get warmer, although there were days when it was overcast and their journey was made more unpleasant by brief bursts of rain. Each day Imi was less lame, but it made their progress no faster. They could travel at the most ten miles in a day, and it was more than thirty leagues before they struck the Aldern River. The land prohibited swift movement; the ground was uneven and strewn with small rocks, and treacherous with holes that might turn a horse's leg or even break it, if they went carelessly. The turf was poor, thick with burrs and small thistles, and everywhere grew a creeping plant with small grayish leaves that stank like old fish. If they stepped on it the smell rose up and clogged their throats, and if they camped over it they couldn't get the stench out of their clothes. Frequently there were small dips or hollows, in which gathered brackish water and swampy plants, and in these sheltered places they camped at nightfall. Sometimes at night, Maerad saw strange lights in the distance, fey blue wisps that shimmered and vanished, only to tauntingly reappear a short distance from where they had been.

"Marsh lights," Cadvan told her. "Take no notice. And never follow them!"

"Why?" she asked curiously, as they watched them. They were strangely hypnotic.

"They'll lead you into a bog. Or worse. There are old

mounds here, graves of ancient peoples, and not all of them are empty."

The Valverras eroded the soul in a different way from the Hutmoors, Maerad thought. The Hutmoors were haunted by despair, an endless lamentation. The Valverras felt strangely hostile, and although she never saw anything sinister, the farther they traveled, the jumpier she felt. She began to get a sore neck from constantly looking over her shoulder.

Cadvan resumed Maerad's lessons, as much to distract them as for any other reason, although they did not take out their instruments; the watching silence of the heaths around them seemed to forbid music. Cadvan also began to train her in swordcraft. Maerad found him a less harsh teacher than Indik. He told her she was an apt pupil; her reflexes were swift, and her accuracy and skill grew with her confidence, so that one day, to his delight, she disarmed him.

"You're no elegant fighter, but you're fast, and very strong for your size," said Cadvan, breathing heavily and picking up his sword. "In a pinch you'd have a chance. Perhaps more than a chance. The thing is not to overestimate what you can manage."

"And not to be afraid of running away," said Maerad, smiling.

"It is always smarter not to have to fight at all," Cadvan said. "But if you must fight, you must know how to defend yourself. You'll be a warrior yet! Now, let's start again."

They had traveled in this way for about a week when one day they saw a thin line of smoke rising on the horizon far in front of them. It puzzled Cadvan.

"Unless I am very much off in my reckoning, we are still at least two days from the Aldern," he said. "I know of no settlements this side of the river, and it's not yet dry enough for wildfire, which sometimes sweeps these parts."

"Perhaps others travel in the waste, like us," said Maerad.

"Perhaps," said Cadvan. He altered their course slightly east, and that night they lit no fire and kept more careful watch. The next day they saw the smoke again briefly at lunchtime, a little closer, and as dusk began to descend it rose again to their right, perhaps three miles away.

"Whoever they are, they're not hiding," said Maerad.

"Anyone who is in this waste is hiding," Cadvan replied. "Why else are we here? No doubt they think there is no one to see them."

That night they camped in a deep hollow, in the shelter of two huge rocks that leaned together at a rough angle, making a natural roof. Maerad was on the first watch and sat at the edge of the dell, looking out over the silent hills and the stars burning over them. She was very tired, but she was well used to fighting her weariness, and to pass the time sent her mind out over the wastes, wondering if she could hear anything of the other fugitives in the Valverras. She heard nothing. Over everything was a huge silence, save for the wind stirring the grass stems and whining over the stones, but an undefinable sense of dread began to plague her. She shifted on the hard ground; it was becoming very cold, and the dew was falling, and her legs cramped with stiffness.

Three hours after sundown the half-moon rose and cast a chilly light over the landscape. Maerad was thinking that it was time to wake Cadvan, when she heard something. Immediately she sharpened her mind and sent it out to follow the noise; it was barely distinguishable from the wind, but she thought she heard the sound of men shouting, and perhaps a child crying. It grew louder, and she listened, unable to move, her hair bristling on her skin. Then she heard screaming—a woman's scream, she thought—and the faint clash of metal, and more shouts.

Quite suddenly, Maerad had an overpowering sensation of

suffocation, as if she were enclosed in a very small space like a coffin, and her sight went dark. An unreasoning terror possessed her, as if her life were directly threatened, now, by something malign that sought her, which was a mere arm's length away. . . . And behind the terror there was another feeling, much harder to define, a mixture of despair and longing and intense tenderness, which seemed to well up from the deepest levels of her memory.

The scream grew higher and higher and then stopped, and there was nothing more. Maerad found she was cowering against the ground, her hands over her eyes, her heart pounding. She sat up, breathing hard to regain her composure. Gradually her sight came back, and she found she was staring at the hard, bright stars over the empty, broken landscape. She listened, frightened, for some minutes, straining for any sound that might tell her what had happened, but the silence seemed if anything deeper than before.

She woke Cadvan and told him what she had heard. Immediately he put his ear to the ground. He lay there so long she thought he had fallen asleep again; but at last he sat up.

"There are horses," he said. "A number, eight or ten perhaps, maybe five miles away, and they are drawing away from us. They are not in a hurry. I can hear nothing else."

"But what's happened?"

"I don't know," said Cadvan. "We can be sure it is nothing good."

Maerad felt a wave of exhaustion sweep over her and she realized she was shaking. The terror of the scream still echoed in her mind. Cadvan studied her face and said, "Sleep now, Maerad. We can in any case find out nothing until the morning."

She stumbled to the bottom of the hollow and lay down, looking at the roof of stone over her. A little moonlight glimmered grayly on the rocks at the edge of the hollow, but otherwise all was in blackness. After a while she sank into a restless sleep troubled by vague, disquieting dreams.

She opened her eyes as the sun rose. Cadvan hadn't roused her for the third watch, letting her sleep through the night. She sat up, immediately awake, and saw him preparing breakfast a few feet away. The horses stamped sleepily in the hollow, cropping what grasses they could find, and their breath steamed in the early air.

"Cadvan, what are we going to do?" she asked, coming toward him.

"Do?" he said. "What do you mean?"

"We have to find out what happened. Those, those people . . . someone was hurt."

"There is no fire this morning," said Cadvan. "And I think there will not be. I heard nothing else all night."

They ate their breakfast in silence, each deep in thought.

"We have to see if there's anything we can do," Maerad said at last. "Maybe we can help."

Cadvan squinted up at the sky. "I think we will not," he said. "We would lose half the morning at least, finding the camp. And we know nothing of these people, or why they were attacked. They may have squabbled among themselves. Perhaps, to my mind most likely, they were a camp of bandits, and we might walk into a hornets' nest. We can ill afford any trouble."

"Maybe not," said Maerad rebelliously. "But we still have to go and see. Maybe someone's still there. Maybe someone is hurt." Maerad shuddered as she remembered the night before. She couldn't articulate to Cadvan why she had to find the camp; she just knew, with an iron certainty, that she must. Some echo of the strange longing she had felt in the midst of the terror still reverberated within her, like the aftertones of a bell: but a bell that, instead of ringing to silence, swelled louder and louder, until it drowned out all other sound.

"I told you, I heard nothing all night. I think any who yet lived have long gone. There is no hoofbeat or footfall for miles around."

"All the more reason to check," said Maerad. "If no one is there, there is no risk."

Cadvan looked at her steadily.

"Yet I think we will not. The risk is too great, Maerad."

"I heard a woman screaming," Maerad said.

"I think nothing is alive within miles of us," Cadvan said. "And if there is, what can we do? Strap them to the saddle-bags? Maerad, I say we cannot do this; it will do no good, and may do harm."

"And I say we must." Maerad squatted on the ground, chewing the hard biscuit. "What did you say to me when you cured that little boy? *Sometimes there are choices that lead to ill, but that nevertheless have to be made.* That's what I feel."

Cadvan let out his breath impatiently. "Maerad, I know what you are saying. But I cannot permit this risk. It's too great."

"What risk?" Maerad stared at him steadily, and Cadvan looked down at his hands, and at first did not answer her.

"Maerad, the air here is thick with evil. Have you thought that spirits might have tricked you, and made you hear what has not happened, to draw you into a trap?"

"It was real." Maerad knew that with certainty.

"Still, I counsel against this. I sense a great danger if you go."

Maerad stood up. "So I'll go on my own," she said.

"You will not." Cadvan also stood up, and she saw his rare anger. "Mark me well, Maerad. If I have to tie you to Imi, I will."

"Then you'll have to carry me screaming all the way to Norloch," said Maerad. She had now lost her temper, but her voice was low and dangerous. "And I'll never, ever forgive you. All this talk about choice. It's talk, just talk. We do what *you* say, when *you* want. Well, I say now what *I* want. And I don't care what you say, because you're *wrong*."

She started to saddle Imi, her hands shaking with rage and her eyes so blind with tears she could scarcely fasten the buckles. Cadvan stood motionless and watched her.

"Maerad," he said.

Her back was turned, and she didn't answer.

"Maerad, I'm sorry. I still counsel against this; I feel a great foreboding. But I was wrong to speak against your heart. I will come with you. I will say only that we cannot look for longer than one day. We have lost too many days as it is; I feel it in my heart. Time is running out."

Maerad paused and nodded, and then continued to saddle Imi. She didn't feel able to speak to him, although the gust of fury had passed. Now she just felt very tired and despondent. She didn't know why she felt such a compulsion to investigate the noise she had heard the night before, but it was overwhelming.

Together they mounted the horses and began the slow job of picking their way to where they had seen the smoke rising. They had nothing to guide them except their memory of where it had been, and there were no landmarks. After a few hours Maerad began to feel the hopelessness of the task of finding a small camp in all this waste; they could easily have passed it, in one of the many hollows, and they could wander around in circles for hours, searching fruitlessly in the wrong direction. She felt more and more uneasy and startled at any sound, infecting Imi with her edginess, but she set her jaw and kept looking. Cadvan said nothing at all.

Maerad was on the point of giving up altogether when Cadvan called out and pointed. She looked over her shoulder to the left and saw two unpainted wooden caravans a few hundred yards away, pushed against the shelter of one of the great tors of rock. One was tipped on its side, and the other was half collapsed. There was no sign of life. They dismounted and walked slowly toward them, Maerad with a sudden deep reluctance.

It was definitely the camp. Between the caravans were the remains of a fire, and underneath the ashes the earth was still warm, with blackened cooking pots smashed and scattered around it. Then Cadvan wandered behind a big rock that jutted out from the tumulus and returned quickly, his face grim.

"They are there," he said. "I would not go there, if I were you."

Maerad gulped and then, strengthening her will, stepped slowly behind the rock. She had to see for herself. Cadvan didn't stop her.

The sight hit her like a savage blow to her stomach. Even the brutality of Gilman's Cot had not prepared her for this kind of violence. She gagged, breaking into a cold sweat of shock. There were four of them: two men, a woman, and a small child. They had been dragged and lay where they had been left, all facing the sky. They were horribly mutilated and already flies gathered about them. Maerad averted her face and walked quickly back.

Silently they looked about the camp. "Perhaps we should look in the wagons," said Maerad shakily.

Inside, the caravans had been thoroughly ransacked. They did not enter the caravan that had been tipped over, but looked inside. Utensils and belongings were thrown everywhere, and bottles of oil and grains and pickles had been smashed on the floor. At the far end were narrow bunks; the mattresses had been slashed and the floor was covered with their stuffing of horsehair and straw. The caravans had clearly once been cozy; there were bright cloths, now torn and soiled, and hand-carved ornaments, and wooden toys. Maerad picked up a little cat made of black wood and held it in the palm of her hand.

"Who would do this?" she asked.

"I don't know," said Cadvan. "I will never understand this. I never have."

An image of Hulls rose in Maerad's mind, their eyes flickering a baleful red. "Do you think it was . . . Hulls?"

"Hulls enjoy the suffering of others." Cadvan's face was expressionless. "It answers some lack within themselves." Maerad shuddered, thinking of the corpses. "It's possible they were looking for us," he added. "I think we should not stay."

They were bending their heads to leave the caravan when they heard a small noise, like a sneeze. Both of them were instantly alert. It came from somewhere inside the caravan. They returned and looked again; in such a tiny space it seemed impossible that anyone could hide. They went to the back, where the beds were, and could see no likely hiding place; and there was no more sound. It was as if everything held its breath. Cadvan stood very still, listening. Then he went to one of the beds and threw the remains of the mattress on the floor. Underneath was a plank of wood. It seemed to be merely the base of the bed, but he examined it carefully and finally found a little catch near the head, which he sprang. He then lifted the plank, which revealed underneath a narrow space as long as the bed and no more than a foot high. Out of the darkness stared two terrified eyes. It was a boy.

They stared at each other in shock, and then Maerad leaned forward to help the boy out. He made a noise like a frightened animal and cowered back into the darkness.

"We won't hurt you," said Maerad softly. "We've come to help." She reached forward again and tried to pull the boy out of the space, but he clung desperately to the edge of the bed. He made absolutely no sound. Maerad kept making soothing noises, and at last he let go of the bed and allowed her to bring him out. He fell on the floor before them and began to sob violently, shaking uncontrollably. There were no tears. He stank of urine, and his face was filthy and streaked with dust. Cadvan lifted him up and they took him out of the caravan into the light.

Outside, they saw he was probably about twelve, darkhaired and blue-eyed, with dark olive skin. He was painfully thin and his face was shadowed with hollows. Cadvan found a pan and a cloth and collected some water from a small pool nearby. Gently he washed the boy's face. Then he went back into the caravan and found some clothes: a shirt and some trousers and a jerkin knitted of raw goat's wool and a cloak, stoutly woven in the Zmarkan style, with curious animals embroidered around the cuffs and hood. Carefully he took the child's clothes off one by one and dressed him, washing him as he went. The boy still said nothing, accepting Cadvan's ministrations passively, protesting only when Cadvan tried to undo a cloth bag on a string that he wore around his neck; but gradually, as Cadvan tended to him, the shuddering stopped.

"Can you speak Annaren?" Cadvan asked, when the boy was clean.

"Yes." The boy stared down at the ground and would not look at them. He spoke so quietly they could scarcely hear him.

"Good, then. My name is Cadvan. This is Maerad. We were traveling nearby, and last night we heard screaming, so we looked for this camp; and that is why we found you. We mean you no harm."

The boy gulped hard. "Were there only five of you?" Cadvan asked.

The boy nodded. He looked utterly vulnerable: his young face was twisted by grief and terror. The clothes they had found were too big for him; his bare feet stuck out the bottom of the man's trousers, which they had rolled up and tied around him with a piece of rope.

"What is your name?" asked Maerad.

"Hem," said the boy. He stirred and sat up straighter. "My name is Hem."

"What happened here?"

The boy looked down at the ground again, and Maerad, biting her lip, was sorry she had asked. But after a while he spoke. "Men came on horses," he said. "I hid under the bed, but there was no time. . . . They came out of the dark. They took everybody somewhere, and I heard them crying and screaming, and then . . ."

There was a long silence, and Maerad and Cadvan exchanged glances. The boy shuddered again convulsively and took a deep breath. "I don't know what happened," he said. "I heard Sharn and Nidar fighting, and then Mudil screamed and screamed. I think they killed the baby first. I think everyone is dead." He spoke blankly, with no expression at all. "I don't know how long I was in the bed. I didn't know if they would come back. I thought you were come to kill me."

He put his face in his hands and began to weep, curling himself into a tight ball. Maerad crept forward and put her arms around him. He didn't push her away, letting himself lean into her, and she felt his thin body wracked with sobs. She shut her eyes and held him for what seemed like a long time. Like her, he was an orphan; like her, he was alone in a harsh world, homeless and kinless; but something within her that was deeper than pity was stirred by this strange boy.

At last Hem's sobs subsided and he sat up and moved slightly away from her, rubbing his sleeve over his face. Maerad looked around. Cadvan was nowhere to be seen, and Darsor and Imi were grazing a short distance away. She looked up at the sky. It was already midafternoon, and they would soon have to move, or be forced to stay the night. She wanted to leave this place as soon as they could. She wondered if she should look for Cadvan, but she didn't want to leave the boy on his own.

"Are you hungry?" she said.

Hem nodded and sniffed. Maerad went to Imi and took some biscuit and fruit out of her bag. She gave him some medhyl, and then watched as he ate hungrily. As he was eating, Cadvan returned and sat down cross-legged with them. His face looked grim, but he spoke gently.

"Hem," he said. "We must leave very soon. We'll take you with us, if you wish. All your family is dead. I haven't been able to bury them, but I have done what I can, so at least they will not be disturbed by crows or wild dogs."

The boy stared at him and said nothing.

"Would you like to see?" Cadvan asked.

After a slight hesitation, Hem nodded. "They're not my family," he said, standing up slowly.

"Who are they, then?" Cadvan said; but the boy didn't answer.

Maerad followed Cadvan and Hem around the rock, steeling herself. Cadvan had put the bodies into a fissure between the rock and the earth, which shelved in about four feet underneath. The boy looked at them wordlessly.

"What were their names?" asked Cadvan.

"Mudil," said Hem. "And Sharn and Nidar. The baby was called Iris."

Cadvan bowed his head. "Here then lie the remains of Mudil, Sharn, Nidar, and Iris," he said. "May the Light protect their souls, and may they find solace beyond the Gate."

The three stood silently, their heads bowed, and the only sound was the thin whine of the wind over the rocks. Cadvan began to roll a boulder toward the fissure, to wall it over, and Maerad helped him, and last of all Hem; and before long they had covered it completely.

After that, there was nothing else to do. Hem went into the caravan that was tipped on its side and shortly afterward emerged, pushing some objects into the bag on a string that he wore around his neck. There was no food to salvage, and Maerad thought in any case she would have felt odd, eating the food of dead people. She kept the little wooden cat. Cadvan mounted Hem in front of him on Darsor, and they moved off.

They rode long into the night, moving quietly as shadows in the uncertain light of the moon. They all wanted to get as far away as they could from that lonely place, made ghastly by violent death. Maerad thought of Dernhil, murdered by Hulls, and her mind flinched. She could not get out of her mind the sight of the slain family, flung behind the rock like so much rubbish. She wished she had not seen them.

XVIII

THE BROKEN TEETH

HEM was the most silent human being Maerad had ever met. He rode with Cadvan, because Imi was not big enough to bear two, and all day he said nothing. Cadvan was often silent, but his silence seemed calm, the wordlessness of abstraction or deep thought; Hem was tense, a jangle of nerves, watchful and wary behind his roughly cut hair. At times he seemed much older than his twelve years; his face was at odd moments world-weary, like an old man who'd seen too many horrors, and yet at other times he was disconcertingly a little boy. At night he twisted and kicked, and would wake sometimes out of a nightmare with a cry, until Maerad or Cadvan stilled him by stroking his forehead. He accepted their help and caresses, but passively, with no sign of gratitude; he ate what he was given to eat, and spoke when he was spoken to, but volunteered neither question nor information.

Maerad found Hem fascinating; he disturbed and attracted her. For the first time in her life she was in a position to help a human being more wretched than herself, and that made her feel stronger and more certain; but he was full of strange gaps and tensions she didn't understand, and that sometimes, in their sheer bleakness, frightened her a little. She wondered what he dreamed about, and sometimes she asked him, but he would never say. She pitied his fearfulness, the wariness in his eyes that told of a harsh history. But more than anything, there was about him something she couldn't define, a kind of *glow*, she thought, that puzzled her.

Tacitly Maerad and Cadvan agreed to keep quiet about Barding, and Maerad had no lessons the next nightfall. It was difficult to talk while the boy sat by them, and impossible to talk about him while he was there. Maerad tried to ask him about his life but he was not especially forthcoming. They learned that the people in the caravan were a family, two brothers, the wife of one of the brothers, and their child; and that they were Pilanel, the traveling folk who settled nowhere, but lived in their caravans and went from town to town working as minstrels, tinkers, cobblers, or farmhands. Cadvan had already guessed this. Hem said he had been living with them for about a year but would say nothing of his life beforehand, except that he was an orphan and they had taken him in out of kindness, because he had nowhere to go.

"What were you doing in the middle of the Valverras?" asked Maerad.

The boy said nothing and simply stared ahead of him, chewing the end of a piece of grass.

"How did you get there?" Cadvan asked him. Maerad had wondered this herself: how did they manage to drag two caravans over this trackless waste? Hem glanced sideways at them. "We had strong horses, four of them," he said scornfully. "It wasn't that hard. The raiders stole them."

"Do you know who those men were?"

The boy glanced at them again through his eyelashes and looked as if he would not answer. At last he said, reluctantly, "Yes."

"Who were they?"

"The Black Bards. They were hunting us down. Sharn thought we'd be safe in the Valverras." He spat on the ground. "Sharn was a fool."

"The Black Bards?" repeated Maerad, looking at Cadvan and thinking of Hulls. "Who are they?"

"People think they're lords," said the boy, with an edge of contempt in his voice. "But those with eyes to see can tell what they really are."

"And what are they really?" asked Cadvan.

Hem turned and looked him in the eyes, and Maerad saw in his drawn face a bleak memory of horror. Cadvan winced slightly and then leaned forward and took the boy's hand. "*Ke an de*, Hem?" he said gently.

Hem jumped violently and leaped to his feet. If Cadvan hadn't moved more swiftly than Maerad could see, he would have dived off into the darkness and perhaps still have been running an hour later. Cadvan caught and held him, and Hem fought him desperately, kicking his shins and biting his arm; but Cadvan would not let go. Finally Cadvan said, "*Lemmach!*" and the boy stopped as suddenly as he had begun, and hung limp and panting in Cadvan's arms. All this time he had not made a sound. Maerad watched the whole scene in astonishment.

"We're not going to hurt you, Hem," she said. "I promise. I *promise*." She stretched out her arms and took the boy from Cadvan. He was almost as tall as she was, and she sat awkwardly with the child in her lap, her arms around his waist. "I promise," she said. Hem twisted his head away from her hand, but didn't get out of her lap.

"Then why do you speak like that?" said Hem viciously. "That's witch's cant."

Cadvan was still standing, rubbing his arm where he had been bitten. "Nay, Hem," he said. "I think you understand it, yes? Perhaps it is a little frightening, when the beasts speak to you?"

The boy shook his head violently, but Maerad knew he lied.

She looked at him again. With a shock, she realized that the "glow" that had so puzzled her was the sign that the boy had the Gift, as she did; and like her, he knew almost nothing about it. Cadvan was shaking his head and pacing up and down restlessly.

"If I find any more baby Bards in the wild, I shall give up traveling," he said at last. "I'm not running a School." He sat down by them and looked hard at Hem. "Hem, believe me, we are not Black Bards. I think you mean those we call Hulls, and if so, I don't know why you were being hunted by them. I've never heard of them kidnapping child Bards, though I suppose that's not impossible. I have no idea at all why they would be hunting Pilanel. Just be sure that they are hunting Maerad and me as well, and we have as little desire to run into them as you. And if our danger is increased by helping you, I would like to know why." He rubbed his hair so it all stood up on end, and then hid his face in his hands.

For a while all three were silent. Then Hem got awkwardly off Maerad's lap and sat cross-legged. He looked at Cadvan, who was watching him closely now, ready to move quickly if he ran.

"You don't feel . . . bad," Hem said. He paused, and then said with a rush, "The witch's cant came to me two years ago. I had to keep it secret, or else I'd be drowned. And then the Black Bard was at the house and he knew and he tried to make me, tried to make me . . ." He stopped, and his face twisted with the effort to speak. At last he whispered: "He tried to make me come with him, and when I wouldn't he said he would tell them so they would kill me, and when he laughed at me it was like knives going in. And I ran away."

Maerad looked at Cadvan, totally perplexed; but Cadvan's face was dark. "You don't have to tell us about it now," he said. "Later, if you wish to. But, Hem, I am very anxious to know where these Hulls, these Black Bards, came from, and why they were hunting the Pilanel family. Were they hunting you? Or were they after something else?"

The boy bent down over himself. "No, they weren't hunting me," he whispered. "Sharn stole something from them, and they wanted it back. And then he was afraid, and that's why we came out to the wilds. They didn't know about me."

"Are you sure?"

The boy nodded. Cadvan took his chin in his hand and forced Hem to stare him in the eyes; the boy stared back with an air of defiance, and at last Cadvan let him go, his face shadowed.

"What did he steal, that the Hulls so wanted?"

"I don't know."

Maerad knew again that Hem was lying, but Cadvan didn't pursue the point. Hem told them that the Hulls were at Imrath, near the Aldern, and that there were five of them. They had arrived a year or so before, and lived like lords in the house of Laraman, the mayor, and went about in the guise of worthies. There was much sickness around, and other problems, so little notice had been taken of them; but Hem had seen them and recognized them. What Sharn had taken from them, or why, he wouldn't say; and he would say nothing more about his earlier dealings with the Hulls. His answers troubled Cadvan, but he didn't press him. Maerad, watching anxiously, said abruptly, "Why don't you just scry him?"

Cadvan looked up swiftly. "Against his will?"

"Why don't you let Cadvan scry you, Hem?" Maerad looked directly into the boy's face, but he wouldn't look at her.

"I'm not letting any smutty witch scramble my brains," hissed Hem, tensing up as if he were about to run again. "I've heard of what they do."

Cadvan looked eloquently at Maerad, and she gave up the idea. "No scrying then, Hem," he said gently. Hem seemed to believe him, and relaxed.

They talked little more that night, and soon Maerad curled

up with Hem under her blanket and went to sleep. The boy lay very still until he slept, but in his dreams he turned and twisted and cried out until Maerad put her arms around him to hold him still; and at last he relaxed and breathed quietly against her.

They spent most of the following day toiling uphill, and at last reached the crest of a mighty ridge. On its other side the land fell away in a wide valley, and through the middle of the valley ran the silver thread of a broad river. To reach the river they had to leave the shelter of the rocky tors and descend a hillside bare of anything except short turf and heather punctuated by large boulders. They stood in the lee of a big rock, and Cadvan surveyed the country. Nothing moved before them, and if a rabbit had run across that expanse, they would have seen it.

"We must cross this valley, and it will be hard to do so unseen if anyone is watching," said Cadvan. "This is the Aldern River. On its other side, over that ridge, we will strike people again. It is, or was, rich country with many farms and towns. The only way across is that bridge."

Maerad squinted down and saw the tiny span of a bridge across the river and a road that wound through the valley and then ran along the river on the near side. She heard and saw nothing in that empty country except the high cawing of crows, but she was assailed by a fresh sense of menace.

"I think the bridge is watched," said Cadvan.

They retreated back off the ridge and ate a meal behind a rock. It was late in the day; shadows were already drawing in, and a chill was in the air. Cadvan looked at the clouds.

"It may be we're in luck," he said. "I think it's going to rain."

They finished their meal and waited for the sun to go down. Just as it sank beneath the horizon, the rain started: a heavy, driving deluge that soaked them almost instantly and then froze them through their clothes with a cruel wind. Before long it was completely dark; there was no moon this early and the sky was only a lighter darkness over the black hill. Cadvan waited another hour, while they huddled miserably against the rock trying to escape the worst of the downpour, and then led them over the ridge into the valley. A blast of wind nearly knocked them over as they crossed the top.

They went slowly, leading the horses, fearing to lose each other in the darkness and worried that a horse might stumble on one of the stones. Hem sat on Darsor, miserably huddled in his cloak, his bare feet like ice. It was so dark they almost had to feel their way. Gradually Maerad's eyes adjusted and she could make out dim shapes and outlines before her feet. After about an hour the wind eased and it was not as bitter, although the rain continued in a steady cascade. Maerad was so tired she felt dizzy, and all her senses were dulled by the punishing cold.

They reached the bottom of the valley, and Maerad could hear the river rushing before them, although she couldn't see it. They had lost their direction slightly in the dark and had to turn right to find the bridge; but at last they were walking on a road again, which was less hard on their legs. Then the sound of their steps changed, and Maerad knew they were passing over the bridge. She looked to her side and saw the water rushing beneath them, a faint gray glimmer between the utter blackness of its banks. The wind blew chill off the surface of the water.

It was a broad stone bridge called the Edinur, made centuries before in the great days of building in Annar. The road was now little used and if Maerad had been able to see it, she would have perceived that it had fallen into disrepair. At the highest point of its span was carved the image of a woman's face, her hair rippling off into stony waves of water down the wide arch; but her face had almost crumbled out of recognition and the ripples of her hair were mere runnels in the stone. Despite this, the Edinur Bridge was sturdy, and they crossed safely to the other side and followed the road up along the other side of the valley; the first Maerad knew of this was that the road surface changed again, and then they were going uphill. It was easier going up than down because they had a road to follow, and they stumbled less often. Halfway up the valley the moon rose, waxing toward full, and the clouds tore open and released a wavering light, easing their way, although Cadvan looked anxiously up and hurried them on.

They reached the top of the ridge after midnight, and the rain ceased altogether, but it became colder and the wind blew bitterly again, chilling them to the bone.

Before them Maerad could see the black shapes of trees. They went off the road a little and found a copse, dripping and black, and rested there; but it was so cold and they were all so wet that none of them could sleep except in short, fitful dozes. The horses stood shivering close together, their tails jammed between their legs. Hem was so stiff with cold that he had to be lifted off Darsor, his teeth chattering. Cadvan rubbed his feet until a little life came back into them, and they all drank some medhyl, which warmed them; but they could do nothing about the wind, which whirled about the copse loosing showers of water onto them from burdened leaves.

"Welcome to Edinur," said Cadvan. "Perhaps things will improve when the sun gets out of bed. But perhaps not. I am not sure what we will find here."

The sun rose, reluctantly at first, sending pale glimmers of light that only made the world look more desolate and cold. But then it swung clear of the clouds, and bright rays fell and sparkled on the wet land, throwing up a blinding shimmer from the puddles. They looked around them. They were in a small beech wood, and the road was visible from where they had huddled the night before. Cadvan moved them deeper into the woods, finding a broad glade where the sun shone unimpeded. There they stripped and changed into dry clothes and stretched out their wet clothes to dry in the sun. Hem huddled in a blanket; he had no spare clothes, and he looked ill. Cadvan examined him with concern and gave him some more medhyl; after that the boy's teeth stopped chattering, and a little color came into his face. They were all gray with exhaustion and ate their meager breakfast wordlessly. Maerad felt too tired to chew. She ached all over, and the chill was set so deep in her bones she thought she would never get rid of it. But it seemed the sun was determined to make up for its absence the day before and strengthened until it was hot. Their clothes steamed on the grass and Maerad relaxed, feeling the sun's healing warmth on her shoulders. Hem began to look a little better, but he had a bad cold and could not stop sneezing.

Cadvan asked Maerad to watch, and disappeared with Darsor in the direction of the road. She sat drowsily in the sunshine, happy to do nothing and move nowhere. Hem got dressed again, hiding behind a shrub in an agony of modesty, and then stretched under a blanket and slept all day in the sun. After an hour or so Cadvan returned.

He and Maerad talked quietly so they would not wake Hem. Cadvan had ridden down the road to a village some five miles away and had spoken to a few people. Strangers were unwelcome, greeted with distrust and suspicion, and he thought it would not be wise to stay in any inn. Maerad's heart sank at this, as she had been looking forward to a bed. They were to travel through Edinur by night, avoiding people as much as possible. He wanted now to use the road, rather than risk further delay. And the boy complicated matters.

"I thought at first we might find some farmhouse that might be glad to take him," said Cadvan. "But now that we know he has the Gift, we can't leave him; he should be trained as a Bard, and we should take him to a School, to be healed and taught. And now, also, he knows we're Bards, and if he went his own way, word might spread to the Hulls, for I've no doubt what he calls the Black Bards are Hulls. For the meantime, I think we're stuck with him. The nearest School from here is Norloch itself."

"No, we can't leave him," agreed Maerad, looking at the sleeping huddle. "He should stay with us."

"Maerad, it's been exercising my mind that we should have found him; it was something that called to you, not to me, and I can't think it is chance," Cadvan said. "Somehow he is bound up in our fate. He looks as if he were of the Pilanel; if that is true, his people came a long time ago from farther north, from Zmarkan past the Lir River. They are an ancient race of great wisdom and nobility, though they care not for stone houses and riches. They used to produce many fine Bards, although much has fallen into forgetting, even among them; if they drown any with the Speech, then they are indeed decayed in their Knowing." Cadvan lay on his back, clasping his hands together behind his head. "I think Hem's story is a hard one, and he has suffered more than any child should; and I fear he is so scarred by it that trust will be hard to make between us, if we can make it at all. It was hard enough with you, Maerad." He smiled across at her.

Maerad smiled back, and the hurt of their quarrel, which she had been nursing like a bruise, dissolved within her. Suddenly she felt lighter than she had in days since they had entered the Valverras.

"He lies, I know," she said. "But I like him; there's something about him; it's like I *know* him. . . . And I feel so sorry for him. He's so lost, and so young."

"Yes," said Cadvan, reflecting privately that in ways Hem wasn't so different from Maerad. "But even so, there is a blackness in him that it would be well to be wary of. I would like to know what he was doing with the Hulls. I think he has not been honest with us about them, and I fear that he might put them on our trail. Or that, in hunting him, they may find us."

"But he's running away from them too," said Maerad.

"But why?" said Cadvan. "I'm deeply troubled, Maerad. I can't help but believe he somehow means peril for us."

A little later they woke Hem and made a meager repast of dried meat and fruit. Cadvan had bought some fresh bread at the village, and this was a welcome addition; Maerad thought hungrily of the meals they had eaten in Innail and Rachida, and wished again they could stay at an inn and enjoy some comfort.

Cadvan told Hem of their plans for night travel, and Hem nodded, seemingly indifferent. Once the sun slipped below the horizon they stowed their packs and mounted the horses, Cadvan again putting Hem in front of him. They were all refreshed after their rest, but Hem was miserable with his cold and wiped his nose constantly on his sleeve, until Cadvan gave him a large kerchief to use instead.

It was a beautiful summer evening and no trace of the previous night's storm now troubled them; the air was balmy and gentle, and the stars blazed overhead, casting faint shadows on the road. They were the same stars that Maerad had so often looked for, on lonely evenings in Gilman's Cot, when she had played her lyre for comfort in the squalid kitchen yard; but how differently she saw them now, with the free wind rippling her hair! Hunted and homeless though she was, when Maerad remembered Gilman's Cot she couldn't suppress the thrill of her freedom; it still seemed miraculous.

They cantered gently down through the sleeping village and past fields and isolated houses. Under the starlight it looked like a peaceful country: lamps were lit in many shuttered windows, and cows and horses grazed in the fields, and dogs barked as they passed gates. The scents of grasses and flowers rose from the ground, released by the cool night air and the falling dew, and Maerad relaxed into the rhythm of their riding.

They traveled in this way for three days, covering about thirty leagues, and Cadvan was pleased with their progress. "We're nearing the end of our journey," he said. "We will come soon to the Vale of Norloch, and there we will be safer. The Light is strong there, and Hulls dare not ride openly on the road."

Maerad felt the mixture of apprehension and excitement that stirred within her whenever she thought of Norloch. Would she be found wanting by this lofty citadel of the Light? And if the Bards of Norloch did agree to make her a full Bard, would she be alone in the world again? Beneath her questions was a deeper fear she could barely articulate to herself: the same sick terror that gripped her every time she thought of her *fate* or the *doom* Ardina had spoken of, the dread that haunted her foredream, and that had risen within her when Dernhil gave her Lanorgil's parchment. Am I afraid of myself? she wondered, or of what I am not and cannot be?

As they rode farther south and the relief of moving freely at last wore off, Maerad began to realize that all was not well in Edinur. Sometimes they passed through villages that had a sense of melancholy emptiness, as if no one now lived there, though she thought at first it was simply that everyone slept. Then on the second night they rode through a hamlet in which every second house had been burned to the ground. It looked as if it had been the site of a battle. Dismal drifts of ash eddied through the charred skeletons of the buildings, and the smell of burning still hung in the air, although the fires had been long cold. Packs of dogs, half mad with hunger, scavenged among the ruins and set up a volley of barks and howls when they saw the horses, snapping at their heels until Cadvan warded them off with a few words of the Speech. They passed as quickly as they could through the ruins, galloping at last into the sweet night air of the open meadows.

"What happened to the people?" asked Maerad. "Was there a war here?"

"Of a kind," said Cadvan. "Of a kind." He seemed disinclined to explain further, as if his heart were too heavy for speaking, and Maerad, feeling the increasing sense of despair that seemed to gather in the very air around them, did not press him further.

Through the shadows Maerad had seen the symptoms of a land sorely troubled. By day it would have been clearer. Cadvan had not told her, but the townspeople he had met had told him that Edinur was afflicted with the White Sickness; and this, more than his fear of encountering Hulls, was the chief reason they traveled by night and spoke with no one. The ruined houses were those in which the illness had set itself. They had been burned by their neighbors in fear, to scorch out the disease, or by their surviving inhabitants, fearful to touch or bury the corpses inside, or even by those diseased, in their final madness and despair.

The White Sickness had entered Annar only some twenty years before, first appearing in the south. There seemed no pattern to it: the disease would flare in a region and wipe out many of its inhabitants in a brief but terrible holocaust, and then disappear altogether for years until it sprang up again elsewhere. It was becoming more common, and Cadvan thought privately it was an illness brought by the Hulls, who used it to weaken the strength of Annar. Those most prone to catch it were the young and strong, and sometimes in a town in which the sickness had raged, none were left alive between the ages of eighteen and thirty. All those afflicted by the White Sickness withered away in fever and madness. It was so called because, as the disease overtook the sufferers, their sight became misted over as if with cataracts that silvered the entire iris. In those far gone, their eyes were terrible sightless balls set in ravaged faces. The chances of surviving the illness were very small, and most of those who did were afterward blinded, unless the sufferer was lucky enough to be treated by a great healer. And there were very few healers of any kind in Edinur, even though Norloch was only a few days' ride away.

Hem kept his own counsel. He seemed content to ride with them, though his eyes flashed with fear when Cadvan mentioned Norloch. Cadvan and Maerad both noted this and tacitly kept a close eye on him; they did not want him to run off while they were distracted, making camp perhaps or looking for a spring to fill their water bottles. Maerad especially didn't want him to flee; she had begun to feel that Hem somehow belonged to her. As Silvia filled the gaping hole left by her mother's death, so Hem replaced her dead brother, Cai. Cadvan pitied the boy—who sat so silently within the circle of his own arms each day, his head bowed in inscrutable reflections or memories—and when he spoke to him, he addressed him gently. But he found out no more about Hem's childhood, and by dawn each day was too tired to probe; he was pushing the pace hard, anxious to reach Norloch as soon as he could. When Maerad slept, she always took the boy in her arms as she lay down. Hem never objected, and was less restless cuddled against Maerad, as if her touch reprieved him from his nightmares.

When he was keeping watch, Cadvan often turned to contemplate his two charges: the fair-skinned and the dark, their black hair mingling in the grass, two waifs of the Light, brought together by a destiny that was impossible to guess. Although they were both very different, there was something about Maerad and Hem that was kin, and a wordless understanding had arisen between them. It wasn't only that they were orphans and had been forced to survive alone in worlds where no one cared whether they lived or died, nor was it simply the marking of the Gift.

Their kinship reinforced Maerad's youth; as they lay together, it was clear that the child had not altogether left her face. Looking at their sleeping forms, a sadness would gather in Cadvan's eyes and his face became tender and abstracted, as if he saw simultaneously some other vision now far off, or gone forever: a memory of his vanished childhood perhaps, when he slept in innocence with his own brothers and sisters and knew nothing of Hulls, or hardship, or grief.

On the fourth day in Edinur they camped again in a dell, sheltering under some trees. They were now passing through a less-populous region, where the southern edge of Edinur petered out into uninhabited downs. They saw the black shapes of houses less often on the brows of hills, and the hamlets were more widely spaced. This was a relief to Maerad; those they did pass through oppressed her spirits. The downs continued for ten leagues or so before the great Vale of Norloch, which stretched from the Aleph, the widest river in all Annar. The city stood proudly on the coast, looming high over the fertile deltas of the Aleph, which split into many broad streams at its estuary and ran into Mithrad Bay through waterlands thickly overgrown with mangroves. The next night's ride would take them onto the downs and, all being well, they would ride into Norloch Vale at dawn the following day.

Cadvan did not explain this to Maerad, afraid that Hem would run off if he knew they were so close to Norloch. Hem seemed to regard anything to do with Bards with the deepest dread. But Maerad knew that they drew close to the end of their long journey, and her fear began to dominate her excitement. If Innail had been daunting to her, coming from slavery and petty tyranny, Norloch, the high city of Barding, was even more so, no matter what she had learned in the past three months.

When they set off the next evening, the wind shifted. The clear summer weather seemed to be turning and a chill wind began to blow from the west, bringing clouds hurrying into the sky. The moon rose huge and swollen on the horizon, swathed in dark rags of cloud. Cadvan sniffed the air and wrapped his cloak around him, clasping it so it covered Hem, and Darsor stamped at the ground restlessly with his forefeet.

"It will be a hard night," said Cadvan. "The farther we get, the better." He stood silent for a while, sending his listening out into the night; then, satisfied he heard nothing sinister, he urged Darsor on, and the great black horse sprang forward, and Imi followed.

A couple of hours later it began to drizzle, but the rain didn't impede them and the riding kept them warm. Maerad didn't draw her hood over her head; she enjoyed the smack of the cold wind in her face and her hair streaming behind her as they rode at speed. Now they were well onto the downs and no longer passed any houses. Sometimes on the crests of hills Maerad saw the shapes of single standing stones pushing up into the sky like ominous fingers, but otherwise the downs rushed past like a black ocean rolling with dark waves. The moon crept higher and hid altogether under the clouds, and they saw only the faint glimmer of the road in front of them, pushing broad and straight through the undulating emptiness. Maerad began to feel that she was not moving at all, but rather that she sat on Imi still as a carven statue, and the downs whirled past her in a great rush of wind.

They didn't speak. Around them seemed to crouch a listening silence that forbade chatter. Maerad shivered: the cold was beginning to bite, and she drew her hood over her and huddled her cloak more tightly around her. She could feel that her period was imminent, and this made the cold less easy to bear; her body felt strangely fragile, as if she were made of glass. Cadvan was now pushing them faster. It rained again, a heavier shower, and then the moon emerged from hiding so the road shone silver before them, a path of wet moonlight that stretched endlessly into the distance between the dim shoulders of the hills.

At the darkest hour of the night, Maerad saw that the road cleft through a high down, so it ran narrowly between two tall shoulders of stone and plunged into shadow. At the entrance of the cleft, on the top of each shoulder, stood a standing stone. They rose like two broken fangs, seeming to form a gate with no lintel. As they approached, Cadvan slowed down and drew level with Maerad. She saw Hem's pale face poking out of Cadvan's cloak, his eyes dark and sleepless.

"They call these the Broken Teeth," Cadvan said. "It is an evil place, and there is no time to ride around it. Better to ride through in daylight, though even then it is grim enough. As always, we choose between bad chances. Be wary, and keep your hand on your sword, and your mind quick and clear."

As they approached the gate Maerad felt her loathing increase, and her hair prickled. Cadvan stopped altogether and listened; Maerad listened with him, and could hear only the wind.

"I think the Teeth are held against us," said Cadvan quietly. "We come to an ill choice: to dare whatever awaits us, or to await it here." He drew Arnost and the blade rang faintly in the silence. Maerad hesitated, and then took the hilt of Irigan and held its weight in her hand. She heard the words of her swordmaster Indik echo sardonically in her mind: *hope you're lucky.* She didn't feel very lucky.

They paced slowly toward the gate. Imi snorted, trembling beneath Maerad as they drew under the black shadow of the hill. As they passed the standing stones, it was as if a scarf were tied over Maerad's eyes; she could see nothing in front of her, not even the dark shape of Cadvan and Darsor. She took a deep breath to contain her fear and paced on steadily. Gradually her eyes adjusted and she could see dim shapes, shadows among shadows. All around her she could feel an evil watchfulness, as if she were a mouse creeping past a cat that waited, still and malevolent, for it to come within reach of its claws. The cleft was charged with the desolate horror she had first felt in the battle with the wers of the Landrost; but it was worse, much worse.

Maerad listened in an agony of alertness, but could hear nothing except an oppressive silence. The walls rose higher on either side, and their hoofbeats echoed dully, as if sound itself were afraid and cowered against the stone.

When the attack came, it was swift and without warning.

There was a sudden flash, but it seemed to be a flash of darkness rather than light, a rush of black energy that came at once from above and before them. Instantly there was an answering stab of light from Cadvan, intolerably brilliant in that dark place; and for a second Maerad saw that before them the road boiled with shadows, wolf shadows whose eyes gleamed red with malice. In their midst stood a tall form, cloaked and high-helmed, and behind it were cloaked and hooded riders, with the pack swirling around the knees of their horses. They roiled back before the blast of light, and Cadvan, now shining with a white fire, lifted his sword high. Darsor reared and screamed, beating the air before him with his hooves. In that moment Imi, who had stood frozen with terror, sprang sideways and reared, and Maerad fell to the ground. She heard Imi bolting back along the road. Maerad scrambled back against the side of the rock wall, panting with fear.

Cadvan never brought down his sword. Although he still blazed with a pure, unconsuming fire, he sat motionless on

Darsor, transfixed, and with a thrill of terror Maerad realized he was unable to move. The dark shape moved toward him; and, as it approached, Maerad saw that its face was not dark, but glimmered with a fell light that illuminated nothing except itself.

It was not a Hull, but something older, more chill, more deadly.

Maerad shrank into the rock, panic-stricken. This thing was infinitely more menacing than the Kulag, which was merely monstrous. She was acutely conscious of an evil intelligence, a vicious will. She felt its awareness brooding on Cadvan, gathering all its might to strike him down. Her mind reeled and she cringed, almost fainting, overwhelmed by a sense of enmity and malevolent pride, tempered over countless years to a sheer, focused point: immeasurably bitter, immeasurably cruel, colder than any ice.

It was a wight, summoned from the Abyss. Its face had the livid hue of something that had been long dead, and in its face were no eyes, only empty holes opening to impenetrable darkness. And yet it seemed to see. A stench of the grave breathed through the cleft, cold and foul. Maerad heard Hem give a little gasp.

It moved close to Cadvan, level with his eyes, although he was on horseback. It stopped and spoke with a deathly voice, and as it spoke a loathing came so thickly over Maerad she thought she would be sick.

"Who disturbs the sleep of Sardor?" it asked, and then it laughed, and its laughter was more terrible than its voice. "What miscreants dare enter my chamber, thinking in their folly and vanity that I lie in chains?"

Behind it the horsemen moved in closer, and Maerad saw they were Hulls. There were five of them. They kept the wers behind them, whipping them back with cruel thongs, so they yelped and howled.

"I think I know," said a Hull, mockingly. "It is the great Cadvan of Lirigon. I hear he has been riding around the countryside as he pleases, snapping his fingers at our Master, for he believes he is a great Bard, and may flout even the authority of the Great One. He has ridden so in his arrogance for years; but alas, he cannot be allowed to continue."

"Nay," said another. "And now he hath stolen something of mine. There is no end to his insolence. Well, might we ask why the great Cadvan, Norloch's pampered darling, keeps such company? He has fallen very low in the world, methinks."

At this, all the Hulls laughed, but the tall one stood motionless and did not laugh.

At last Maerad heard Cadvan speak, although he still did not move. "I may have fallen low in my time," he said thickly. He sounded as if he were speaking under water, but as he spoke his voice gathered strength. "But my memory differs from thine. Methinks I fell lowest when I knew thee, Likud, once of Culain, and that now I move so far beyond thee thy muddy imagination cannot reach there."

The Hull hissed and flinched, as if Cadvan had hurt him. "You will regret that, Cadvan of Lirigon," he said, with a malice that made Maerad's skin crawl. "I will make plenty of time for regretting."

The light within Cadvan grew brighter and brighter, but still he did not move. Maerad, pressed against the stone as if she wished it would swallow her up, willed him to move, begged in her mind, in a panic; but he sat arrested, his sword arm high, and Darsor stood as if he were carved of stone.

"I will have my own thing back," said the Hull called Likud, and rode up to Cadvan. Maerad saw Hem twisting in Cadvan's frozen arms, but he was locked there and could not escape; and then, with a desperate contortion of his body, he wriggled out and fell off the horse. Scrambling to his feet, he fled down the road and casually the Hull lifted its hand and sent a bolt of darkness after him, hitting him in the back so the boy stumbled and fell, and then lay still.

"The rats are easily dealt with," said the Hull contemptuously. "But the King Rat? Well, that is a different question." He lifted the whip and struck Cadvan viciously across the face. Cadvan swayed in his saddle, a livid welt rising on his cheek. Arnost fell from his hand and clanged on the stone road.

"Such spawn of filth should be dealt with at leisure, think you not, friends? What is sufficient punishment for this renegade, this murderer, this treacherous spy? Do you think we have forgotten, Cadvan, how eagerly you studied the secrets of the Dark? Think you that such treachery will be easily answered? The torment of a single night alone is not enough. No." The Hull moved closer to Cadvan, his eyes gleaming with cold hatred, and spat into his face. "Not a single night, but countless nights of agony, until the mind is flayed into madness and can bear itself no longer and cries alone in the darkness, forbidden the Gate forever. And even that is not sufficient." He struck Cadvan again savagely across the face, and the light within him dimmed. He struck him again, the thongs whistling and cracking as they hit, and Cadvan's light went out utterly, and he fell senseless to the ground. And then the Hulls loosed the wolfwers and they leaped forward with chilling howls.

Maerad watched helplessly, cowering in the shadows, numb with horror and despair. She saw Cadvan fall from Darsor and, with the sickly inevitability of nightmare, the arc of his fall seemed to take hours; at last he hit the ground and lay still at Darsor's feet, his face glimmering palely in the darkness, streaked with blood. And as he fell, she seemed to see another sight: her father also falling, his head staved by a mace, and behind him the towers of Pellinor collapsing into a roaring torrent of flames.

With that a great grief and despair rushed into her. Now there's only me, she thought. What can I do? Cadvan was unconscious or perhaps even dead, and Hem lay dead behind her. And now her own death stood before her. Desperate and alone, she stood up with tears running unnoticed down her face; and as she stood, she saw with a vision other than sight that the wers were leaping toward Cadvan and Darsor and would be on them in a moment. Suddenly the torrent of grief became an all-consuming anger, and as if her anger tore aside a veil, a new awareness blazed inside her. Despite her extremity, she was possessed by a fierce, wild joy. Her blood sang through her veins like a silver fire. At last she understood her power, and she knew, with a clarity like that of a dream, what she had to do. She stretched out both her hands and shouted: *"Noroch!"*

The road lit up instantly with white flames, throwing the faces of the Hulls into ghastly relief, and there was a chaos of howling and yammering from the wers. All the wers were ablaze, with white fire running along their backs and lapping down their sides, and they snapped and howled like mad things and bolted away from the flames. The Hulls' horses reared and screamed in terror and backed along the road, away from where Cadvan lay. The Hulls sawed viciously on the reins, so bloody foam dripped from the animals' mouths, and they fought the horses back toward Maerad. They peered into the blackness behind the flames, trying to find the source of the fire, but Maerad was small against the stone wall, hidden among the wild shadows thrown out by the inferno. Before they could catch sight of her, she sent out a great sheet of white flame, knocking all the Hulls and their horses down.

Maerad had no time to feel amazed by what she had done. The wight still stood unmoved, a huge malevolent shadow, and in that instant it perceived her; and she felt the might of its evil will, even as it had bent Cadvan against his own iron resolution. For a second she thought she was lost, and her head was forced down beneath the deadly strength beating against her; but as her eyes lowered, she saw Cadvan lying pale and limp on the ground, and her anger again overcame her. Quicker than thought, she struck out wildly, with all the power within her; and she saw for a second the wight blasted as with lightning, and it let out a terrible high wail, writhing in the flames before vanishing before her appalled eyes. And suddenly everything was silent, apart from the faint crackle of twigs burning high above her, and the harsh sobs of her own breathing.

She fell to her knees, and for a while everything went black. Then she remembered her friends and crawled toward Cadvan lying on the road; her legs were shaking too much for her to stand up. Darsor still stood next to him, lathered in sweat and trembling violently; but he would not leave his friend, and nosed him gently.

"*An de anilidar,* Darsor?" she asked. The Speech came as naturally as breathing, as if she had always spoken it.

The horse turned his great head toward her and blew out of his nostrils against her hand. He spoke, it seemed, into her mind, and she understood.

I am well, he said. *My friend is not. I think he lives, but he breathes only faintly.*

Maerad stroked Cadvan's brow. It was clammy with sweat and blood. One of his eyes was bruised and swollen shut and there were savage welts on his left cheek, where the thongs had bitten deeply into the flesh. She didn't know what to do. She desperately wished she had Cadvan's skills of healing. For a brief second she wondered if she could use her new powers to ease him, but nothing within her stirred in response; she felt utterly emptied. She felt gently over his face and body, but nothing seemed to be broken. Please, she pleaded in her mind, please wake up. She sat there for a long time, stroking Cadvan's face, but he didn't stir, and in the dim light she thought his face looked ghastly. She was glad for Darsor's presence; she had never felt more lonely. She wasn't afraid. But she was still out in the wilds, and Cadvan was insensible, and she did not know where Imi was, and Darsor could not carry all three of them alone.

Like a thunderbolt she remembered Hem. In her anxiety for Cadvan, she had forgotten all about him. She stood and looked back down the road and saw his small shape on the ground, his limbs splayed out with the force of his fall. She stood and walked to him shakily, wondering if he were dead. She turned him over and his head fell back, hanging limply, and she was briefly certain that he was; but she pressed her ear to his chest and heard his heart still beating faintly. She shook him gently, as if he slept, and to her relief the boy opened his eyes. He looked up into her face, his eyes widening with dread, and then cringed away from her.

"No, Hem, it's all right," she said. "The Hulls are all dead. Everything's gone." Despite herself, tears brimmed over her eyes.

"Gone where?" said the boy faintly. Then he sat up. "You lie," he said. "You can't kill Black Bards."

"Yes, you can," said Maerad. "I just did."

Hem stared at her in disbelief and then looked down the road. It was too dark to see anything clearly, but there were faint shapes on the road, past Darsor—the corpses of the Hulls and their mounts. He turned back to Maerad and gaped at her with wonder.

"What happened to Cadvan?" he asked.

"He's hurt," said Maerad. "The Hulls hurt him." Again she found herself weeping, but dashed away the tears impatiently. "We have to get out of here. And I don't know where Imi is. She ran away. Can you walk?"

Hem stood up slowly. "Yes," he said.

"You have to help me," said Maerad. "I can't lift Cadvan on my own."

Together they walked back to Cadvan and Darsor. The horse looked at them inquiringly. "We're going to lift Cadvan onto you," said Maerad in the Speech. "Can you help us?"

I will kneel, said the horse. *And you will need to hold him, so he does not fall.*

Cadvan was heavy and a dead weight, and even with Darsor kneeling it took a long time to hoist him onto Darsor's back. Maerad bit her lip, fearing all the time that they might hurt him more. They laid him across the saddle like a corpse, his head down one side and his feet the other; and then Darsor heaved to his feet. Maerad picked up Arnost, uncertain what to do with it; in the end she found Cadvan's scabbard and put the sword back. Then, with Maerad on one side and Hem the other, they moved off slowly down the road. They passed the Hulls, and Maerad averted her face so she could not see them; she knew without looking that they were all dead, and she had no desire to know any more. But Hem stared at the shapeless cloaks and the scattered bones, and kept turning his head when they were past, as if he did not believe such a thing was possible. They saw no sign of any wers.

In less than half an hour Maerad saw the gray night sky in front of them, at the other end of the cleft. Then at last they were out of it and in the open downs, and a clean wind blew in her face. The moon was sinking beneath bars of cloud, and she thought it would not be long now until dawn. She was very tired, but she felt a new sternness in her bones and thought that she could walk all night and all the next day if need be, no matter what her exhaustion. When they had gone about a mile down the road she called a halt, and gently she and Hem lifted Cadvan down from Darsor and laid him on

the grass. They took his pack down too, and Maerad found a
jerkin that she used as a pillow. As she laid his head on it, she
saw with a clutch of fear that his face seemed to be growing
more pale, and she thought he was dying; but then she realized it was the beginning of dawn, which was just now
sending its first outriders into the fields of night, lightening
the downs to a pale gray.

"Darsor," she said. "Imi ran away."

No one can be blamed for being mastered by fear before such foes,
said Darsor.

"I don't blame her," said Maerad. "But I wonder how she
can be found. Could you find her?"

Darsor stood very straight and looked back over the downs,
sniffing the air.

She ran far in her fear, he said. *She will be ashamed. I will call her
back, if you will care for my friend.*

"I will," said Maerad. "He is my friend also."

Darsor pawed the ground, and then nudged Cadvan gently
with his nose, as if whispering something private to him. Then
he was off, and Maerad saw at last how swiftly he could run; he
sped like a black bolt down the road, and the fall of his hooves
sounded like thunder.

Maerad and Hem sat by the side of the road and watched the
sun rise over the downs. Gradually the world filled with color,
and a chorus of birdsong rose around them, and the horror
ebbed away. Still Cadvan did not move. Maerad took out some
food, and she and Hem ate, and then Maerad took the water
bottle and soaked the edge of her cloak so she could wash
Cadvan's wounds. They looked nastier now; his face was badly
bruised and cut. One of the lashes had just missed his eye, and
the skin around it was torn; but at least his wounds no longer
bled. She was frightened by his continuing unconsciousness;

she thought it must be four hours at least since he had fallen, and he had not stirred nor made a sound. She scrabbled through his pack and found the unguent he had used on her own cut and smeared his wounds with it.

"Why don't you give him some medhyl?" said Hem.

She took the bottle, and propping Cadvan's head in her lap, she tipped the bottle between his teeth and wet his mouth with it. Most of it dribbled out of his mouth and down his chin. As she leaned, the jewel around her neck swung forward and touched his face. She shook her head impatiently to get it out of the way, but Hem said, "Look, it's glowing."

She looked down and saw that the jewel was bright with a white fire that seemed to burn in its depths. She thought of Silvia, the gentle healer who had given it to her. She wished with all her heart that she was there.

"Try rubbing it against him, or something," said Hem. "It might be a healstone."

Maerad laid the stone against Cadvan's forehead, and then gently rubbed it over his face. Please, she said again in her mind, please wake up. She wasn't sure if it was a trick of the increasing light, but it seemed there was a faint flush in Cadvan's face. Encouraged, she tried again. After a while she was sure it wasn't a trick of the light; and then, to her joy, Cadvan's eyelids fluttered open and he looked up into her face.

"Maerad," he said. Then his eyes fell shut.

"Cadvan?" she said, her voice wavering.

He opened his eyes. "By the Light, my head hurts," he said. "I suppose that means I'm not dead." He shut his eyes again. "Where are we?"

"Somewhere on the downs," said Maerad. "On the other side of the Broken Teeth. Darsor's gone to look for Imi." She felt like weeping with relief, but thought she had already wept too much that morning, and therefore bit back her tears. Cadvan was silent, lying with his eyes shut. Then, groaning, he sat up and put his head in his hands.

"Do you want some medhyl?" asked Maerad, offering him the bottle. He took a large sip, and this seemed to ease him; then he turned to his pack, took out a small bottle, and took a sip of that. "Woundwort, and other herbs, to staunch pain," he said, looking across at Hem and Maerad. Then he felt over his face.

"I see you've already salved me," he said.

"I remembered that you used the salve on me," said Maerad. "But I didn't know how to wake you up." Her voice wobbled again. "But then Hem said this might be a healing stone, so I tried to rub it on you, and then you woke. . . ." She trailed off, willing back her desire to break into tears.

Cadvan looked at her and tried to smile, and then winced. "Well, I am awake now. As awake as I can be. The last thing I remember is being whipped by a Hull, and behind the Hull a wight of the Abyss, and behind the wight a phalanx of wers and more Hulls; and the wight had stilled me, and I could do nothing. It looked very bad. And then I remember a lot of evil dreams." He shuddered and fell silent. Hem and Maerad exchanged glances and waited.

"I suppose you saved my life again?" Cadvan said at last. "That's three times now. I'm beginning to wonder how I survived without you."

"How did you?" said Maerad, beginning to laugh.

"Luck, I suppose," he said. "Though it could be that life is more dangerous around you. So tell me, Maerad, what did you do?"

Maerad then told them what had happened and Cadvan sat up, his eyes brightening. Hem listened in silence, his face in shadow. When she had finished, Cadvan clasped her hands.

"So you've come into the Speech at last!" he said. "And in the nick of time, I may say. Maerad, I never heard of a Bard blasting a wight to pieces. Not a wight of the Abyss. You have some power I know nothing of; think of the Kulag in the woods near Ettinor. And it seems the Dark doesn't know of it, either." He sat then awhile, lost in thought.

Maerad and Hem gave him some food and water and he chewed cautiously, trying not to move the skin on his face, and took some sips from the water bottle. "Thinking back, we were ambushed," he said as he ate. "The Broken Teeth are considered evil, but the place is just a rallying place for wers and they're easily dealt with. Well, fairly easily. Even Hulls we could have faced. I did not expect to find a wight there, and we all know what happened when I did." He smiled ruefully. "We didn't pass through Edinur as unseen as I hoped," he said. "The Dark has many servants. Unless, of course, there was one who laid a trail for the Dark to follow." He looked at Hem, and suddenly his face was stern and cold. "Do not think you can lie to me. You cannot. I think, Hem, it is time you told me who you are."

XIX

HEM

HEM'S head was bent, and Maerad saw his cheeks burned with shame or humiliation.

"I don't think Hem would have—" she began, but Cadvan cut her off.

"Neither you nor I know anything about Hem," he said. "Now I would like to know. And I would like to know the truth."

Hem sat silently, his head still bowed. Maerad looked at him with pity and then turned away.

"Speak!" said Cadvan harshly.

"I ran away from the Black Bards," said Hem, so quietly Maerad could hardly hear him.

"I know that," said Cadvan impatiently. "What I want to know is what you were doing with them. And why they were hunting you. I want to know who you are."

Hem's story emerged haltingly, bit by bit. He was, as he had said, an orphan, and until two months before had lived in an orphanage in Imrath, the major town in Edinur. He said little about his life there, but Cadvan's face grew even more grim. He knew these places; there children whom no one cared for were taken, and kept in filthy conditions. If they were crippled or simple or weak, they were not given enough food, and usually died of some illness brought on by their starveling condition. When they were old enough to work, they were farmed out as laborers for a fee paid to the orphanage, or sold as slaves. Once children with no family to care for them had been looked after by Bards, but in places where Barding had retreated these small stinking prisons had sprung up to deal with orphans; and now, because of the White Sickness, there were many such children.

As Hem spoke on, Cadvan's questioning gradually became less stern. Hem told them that when he was two years old, he had been brought there on horseback by a man dressed in a black cloak. That was the only thing he knew about himself. He knew nothing of his life before the orphanage; but he had comforted himself with the thought that perhaps he was the son of a prince or a great lord, and one day the cloaked man would return and claim him. He was a proud child and would not admit to his sufferings, but as he spoke, Maerad saw opening before her a vista of bitter, loveless days and lonely nights full of fear, and her heart was wrung with pity.

The Speech had come to him when he was ten years old. A cat had hissed at him when he tried to steal its food. "What did it say?" asked Maerad curiously, and Hem replied: "She said I was a pile of mouse dung, and that she would scratch my eyes out when I was asleep." He ran away and hid, frightened, but afterward he became used to it and started to speak to the birds, who were the most friendly to him. They told him of lands far away in the south where the sun shone warmly all day and the trees were heavy with marvelous sweet fruits. Hem dreamed of going to these magical places, and he thought that when he was old enough to be hired out to a farm, he would run away. He no longer dreamed of the horseman returning for him; he dismissed that as a childish fancy of his infancy. Others noticed him talking to the birds and began to call him a witch; and there was talk of drowning him, of binding him with heavy rocks and throwing him in the river, as happened to others who had the Speech. So he was forced to hide, and he spoke to the birds less often, because it was hard to find privacy in the orphanage, and he became more lonely.

Then one day he had been called to Malik, the cold-eyed woman who ran the orphanage, and standing next to her was a man hooded and cloaked in black. It was Hem's old daydream, but he was frightened and drew back against the wall, because the man's hands were white and bony and he could not see his face. But Malik was not afraid, and treated the man like a lord. She smiled at Hem for the first time he could remember.

"Hem," she'd said. "This is your uncle. He has returned at last from the far lands, and he claims you for his own. You're a lucky boy."

Hem looked up, but he could not see past the hood.

"Get your things, boy," said Malik. "You're going home now."

Hem had nothing to get, so he had stood silently before the two adults, nervously shifting from foot to foot. Then he was taken on a horse to the house of Laraman, the mayor of Imrath. It was a grand house, the grandest in Imrath, and for a while Hem was happy, because he thought his daydreams were coming true. For the first time in his life he had enough to eat and a comfortable bed to sleep in and he wasn't beaten.

Laraman treated him coldly, but tolerated him in the house, as long as he didn't have to speak to him. He was the most important man in Edinur and treated the region as his private fiefdom, exerting heavy taxes and harsh laws. It seemed the five black-cloaked men were his servants, although Hem thought Laraman feared them and that it was more likely that they told him what to do.

"They told me they were Black Bards, and that I could be a Black Bard too," said Hem. "They said they were the most powerful of all the Bards, and that if I were one of them I would never die, and I would be a great lord. One day one of them stabbed the other right through with his sword, and the one who was stabbed stood up as if nothing had happened. They asked me if I had the witchspeak, but I said I didn't, and

I never told them. They seemed happy enough with that, but then . . ."

Hem had been talking freely; it was as if, once he started, it was a relief to unburden himself. But now he stopped, and his face crumpled, and he looked very young and vulnerable.

"Then?" said Cadvan sternly.

"They wanted me to begin my lessons."

There was a long pause while Hem stared at the ground. Then he began to speak in a monotone.

"They woke me in the middle of the night. It was a dark night, the last dark moon, two weeks ago. They took me downstairs to the courtyard outside. There was a fire there, but it was a funny color; it had green flames, and the flames burned straight up and they didn't flicker. And one of the Bards had a, had a . . ."

He stopped again, and Cadvan said, more gently: "Don't call them Bards, Hem. They are not Bards. They are merely Hulls."

"He had a little boy. I knew him; it was Mark, from the orphanage. He was younger than me, but sometimes we played together." He sniffed. "I liked him." He paused again. "He was crying and twisting in the man's arms, and he had no clothes on. And they gave me a black knife, and told me to kill him."

There was a short, shocked silence. At last Maerad asked, almost in a whisper: "And did you?"

"They tried to make me," said Hem. "They said they would beat me, and they said I would have nothing to eat and be locked in my room. And then they laughed at me, and it was horrible, and they said they would stab me instead, and they put the knife to my throat. But, but . . . I couldn't. And then they . . . no, no, I can't say." He hid his face in his hands. "They killed him. It was horrible. And then they said next time, unless I did it, it would be me." Hem was crying now, and the tears ran down his face, making little rivulets in the dirt. Maerad and

Cadvan waited, and after a while he stopped crying, although his chest still made little jumps and hiccups.

"They locked me in my room. And I didn't have anything to eat that day, nor the next day. And then the next day the Bar— the Hulls and everyone went out, and someone robbed the house. It was Sharn. And he found me in my room, and he took me away with him."

"What else did he steal?" asked Cadvan.

"Oh, money, and some things he could sell. Stones."

"What kind of stones?"

"Precious stones that he could sell. He said he would hide until the fuss died down, and then he would go south and sell them at the markets and make his fortune. And I thought that was good, and that I would go south with them, and maybe find the places that the birds talked about. And that's why we were in the Valverras." He paused, and his face creased again with sorrow. "They were kind to me. They said I was one of their own."

Cadvan now took the boy's chin in his hand, as he had once before, and Hem looked up straightly into his eyes. After a long time, Cadvan smiled; and Maerad relaxed with sudden relief. She was sure Hem was not lying this time.

"Why didn't the Hulls find you, when they attacked the Pilanel?" asked Maerad.

Hem shuddered. "I heard them coming from far off," he said. "I knew they were coming to the camp. I told Sharn, but he told me I was being stupid and imagining things. So then I hid, and the Pilanel thought I had run away into the wastes; and then the, the Hulls came. . . ." He trailed off, and his face was haunted with black memory. "I heard everything," he said, whispering. "They wanted to know where I was, and Sharn said they had sold me, then he said I'd run away; and then they, they killed the baby and tortured them, and Sharn kept screaming I had run away. But I think the Hulls did it for, for fun. And they said they would find me anyway, and they laughed and rode off."

The three sat silently for a while, and Maerad thought of the pitiful bodies they had seen, and then tried not to think of them.

"Hem," Cadvan said, and his voice was no longer stern. "I don't suppose you have any of these stones with you?"

Hem reluctantly took out the little bag he kept around his neck and fumbled with the drawstring. Out tumbled three polished black stones carved with grinning, malicious faces, and a tarnished silver trinket. "I thought," he stammered, "that I could sell them at the market, like Sharn said he was going to, and then I could go south. There were other stones, but the Hulls must have taken them back." He looked at the objects in his hand, and gave the stones to Cadvan. "The medallion is mine," he said, with an odd defiance, as if he thought he wouldn't be believed. "I didn't steal that." He closed his fist tightly over it.

Cadvan took the stones and rolled them in his hand, laughing softly. "Oh, Hem, Hem, Hem," he said. "You do not know what these are. Yes, you might be able to sell them at a market, but only to those who know how to use them."

"What are they?" asked Maerad curiously.

"They're warestones. The Hulls must have left them there in case anyone came back to the caravan. Probably they thought you would, Hem. I doubt they would have believed their luck when we turned up. They're useless now; there's no power left in them. I think last night you blasted everything of the Dark within miles, Maerad. But I tell you, Hem, that if we had gone through Edinur in broad daylight with trumpets and heralds proclaiming our presence, it still would not have been as useful to the Hulls as having these little spies traveling with us. Everything we spoke of, everything we did, was open to the Hulls, as long as these stones were with us; and they knew exactly where we were, and who we were, and where we were going. They set a nice trap for us, and this time Cadvan of Lirigon was not to escape." He threw the stones one by one far into the downs.

Maerad thought back uneasily to their conversations over the past few days. "We haven't talked much about anything lately," she said uncertainly.

"No," said Cadvan. "Fortunately. Well, Hem, all's well that ends well, but it almost ended very badly. Almost in disaster."

Hem looked down, and his cheeks flushed. Cadvan patted his shoulder. "I forgive you for almost getting us killed, or worse," he said. He tried to smile, and winced with pain. "But remember: the things of the Dark are best left alone. They are made only for evil reasons." Hem nodded, swallowing, and there was a pause. "Do you mind if I have a look at that medallion?"

Hem reluctantly handed the object over to Cadvan, and he examined it closely. Maerad peered curiously at it; it was so tarnished it was almost black, with a design she couldn't make out on one side and some script on the other. She looked questioningly up at Cadvan, and saw his face go still with shock. He glanced swiftly across at Maerad with an odd expression, and then looked down at the medallion again. He turned it over and over in his hands, saying nothing.

"What?" demanded Maerad, after the silence had lengthened unbearably. Hem was watching them both with a mixture of bafflement and fear.

Cadvan didn't respond at first. "Maerad," he said at last. "Do you remember your father very well?"

Maerad was taken aback by the question. "No, not really," she said. "A little. Why?"

"Do you remember what he looked like?" Cadvan was gazing at her with a strange intensity, and she flicked obediently through her memories, wondering what was bothering him.

"He, he was tall. And he had long black hair. I think he had gray eyes, or blue eyes, I can't remember. . . ." She pushed her hair out of her face and stared around her at the empty downs. Her blood was beginning to pound with a painful sense of expectation. "Why?"

"Did you know Dorn was of the Pilanel?"

"Of the Pilanel? No, I . . ." She looked back at Cadvan and then at Hem, her heart constricting.

Cadvan was still looking at her with that strange intensity. "Maerad, did you *see* Cai being killed?"

"Everyone was killed," she said, beginning to feel panicky. "Everyone except me and Milana."

"But you didn't actually see Cai murdered?"

"Nnnno. . . ." Maerad's hands twisted painfully together. "No, I didn't actually *see* him . . . killed. . . ."

Cadvan handed her the medallion.

She held it in her palm and rubbed her fingers over it. It didn't seem to be anything special at first; it was so dirty. But as she looked more closely, she saw it bore an intricate design of a flower: a lily. An arum lily. The same lily, even the same design, as on her brooch.

"It's the lily of Pellinor, Maerad," Cadvan said softly. "This is an ancient thing, an heirloom. The signs of the Schools have not been made as medallions like this for some five hundred years."

Maerad turned the medallion over. On the back was writing in the Nelsor script, but in her agitation she couldn't read it.

"What does it say?" she whispered.

"It says: *Ardrost Karni. Minelm le caraë.*"

"*The House of Karn. Minelm made me.*" Maerad sat back on her heels, her face blank. "The House of Karn."

"Can I have it back?" Hem reached out his hand. "You've finished now? It's mine."

Startled out of her reverie, Maerad automatically held out her hand toward him.

"What's the matter?" he said.

"The House of Karn is *my* house, Hem," Maerad said. She stared at him, her thoughts running so fast she could barely catch them.

"So? It's *my* medallion." He snatched it from her and put it back in his drawstring bag. "It's *mine*."

"Yes, it's yours," said Maerad, not knowing whether she wanted to laugh or cry. "But it's mine too. You see, the House of Karn is *my* family."

Startled, Hem stared back at her.

Cadvan had been watching in silence. "You both have the same eyes," he said. "It's easy to see, when you know." He passed his hands over his brow. "I wish I were not so hurt. Or so tired. I think I see now."

"See what?" Hem's face was strained and pale, his anger ebbing into confusion. "Are you playing me some trick?" For a second his face creased up, as if he were going to cry, and he put his fists to his eyes like a little boy. Maerad wanted to hug him, as she had without self-consciousness since they had found him, but felt herself constrained by an odd shyness. For a while all three sat in silence.

"No one is playing tricks here," said Cadvan. "I think you could be Maerad's brother. You're the right age. And it would explain why the Hulls wanted you. They could have taken you after they sacked Pellinor."

Maerad was coming out of her daze. "That's why I had to go in the Valverras. I had to." She shook her head, trying to rid herself of her stupefaction. "Hem, I *know* it's true. It means you're my brother and Hem isn't your name at all. Your proper name is Cai." She was still staring at him. "I thought you were dead."

Maerad didn't know what she felt; disbelief, anger, joy, exhilaration, grief were all whirling into chaos inside her. Cadvan's face was stern, and Maerad remembered with a start that he was injured. She took a deep breath to calm herself.

"I did wonder," Cadvan said at last. "I wondered why I should find two child Bards in such circumstances. In all my travels I have never even stumbled across one. It felt to me much more than the workings of chance. And I often pondered what it was that called you to that caravan. An evil force, I thought for a time; certainly it boded ill for me, and I wanted to stay away almost as much as you wanted to go there. But maybe it was a deep thing, a calling of kindred; and even if the Dark had a hand in these events, as I suspect, I have told you that the Dark understands nothing of love. Such callings are beyond their calculations. I remember Dorn, Maerad; and Hem is unmistakably Pilanel. It would explain why the Hulls were interested in him. But I might be wrong."

"You're not often wrong," said Maerad with a wry smile, echoing something he had said to her long ago in Innail.

"No." Cadvan smiled very slightly. "I'm not often wrong. Mind you, when I have been wrong, I've been very wrong indeed. So I am the less eager to make rash judgments. The lily token seems to confirm what I strongly suspect, something maybe you already knew, underneath. But still, we should be wary; it could be a trap. We don't know if that medallion really belongs to Hem."

"A trap?" Maerad looked distractedly over at Hem. "I think we know what the trap was. And it didn't work." Hem was hunched over, turned away from them, and he was very still. "I *know* he's my brother," she said, fiercely. "Why did the Hulls take him? Is he the One?"

"Hem isn't the One," said Cadvan. "His Gift is nothing like yours."

"But you still don't know for sure if it's me," Maerad said.

"No," said Cadvan. "I feel all but sure. A little surer, in fact, if Hem really is Cai. It would mean that the Hulls knew something that we didn't know, plainly. It could mean that they guessed that the One was to be born to Milana and Dorn. I don't know how they knew that. But I believe they picked the wrong child."

Maerad shivered. It might have been her. . . . Compared to Hem's life, Gilman's Cot had been merciful. She had never had to deal with the horrors of the Hulls as a child, and, for a short while, she had had her mother. But Hem—Cai—had been little more than a baby when their lives were destroyed. He had never known any gentleness.

She crept over to Hem and put her arms around him, and he clutched her convulsively, hiding his face in her cloak. They sat silently together, beyond words. Cadvan turned away. After some time, Hem let Maerad go, and he noisily blew his nose.

Cadvan was standing, shading his eyes, looking into the distance. He glanced at Hem and Maerad.

"We still have to get off the downs, and the day is passing," he said. "I would not like to pass another night in the open, even with Maerad the Unpredictable to protect us; and my head is sore as a bear's. Where's Darsor?"

As they had talked the sun had risen high, and it was now already midmorning. It was a warm summer's day. The downs stretched green and peaceful around them with a faint haze of heat, and everywhere was a warm hum of bees. There was no sign of Darsor. Hem had black shadows under his eyes and looked ready to drop with weariness.

"You two Pellinor folk should rest while we are waiting," said Cadvan. "I couldn't sleep if I wanted to, with this headache. I'll watch for Darsor."

"Pellinor?" Hem said, with the ghost of a smile. "I can't remember all these names."

"You're going to have to," said Maerad, with mock sternness.

"Make me, then," said Hem, flashing her a look of mischief she hadn't seen before. "I bet you can't."

My brother, Maerad thought in wonder.

They lay down and Hem was asleep in less than a minute. Maerad's mind was too agitated for sleep; she finally sat up again and watched Cadvan, who turned to her with a faint smile on his torn face and then resumed scanning the horizon. Maerad sat in silence, reflecting on what had happened in the past twelve hours. She was still dizzy with the successive shocks: first the ambush, then coming into the Speech, then discovering her brother. Her thoughts couldn't rest on anything for long, but leaped ahead of her, flashing a kaleidoscope of images into her mind: Cadvan falling senseless from Darsor, the deathly face of the wight, Hem's medallion. . . .

She remembered with a strange unease the exhilaration which had possessed her when she had come into her Gift in the battle at the Broken Teeth. For those moments she had felt invulnerable and immeasurably dangerous; the power that surged through her seemed infinite, as if she merely had to crook her finger and entire cities would crumble at her whim. It was a heady feeling, but it also frightened her. Ardina's words in their last conversation came back to her: *Perhaps you will find that your greatest peril exists already within you.* Was this disturbing joy what she meant?

After about an hour they saw Darsor emerging from the Broken Teeth, closely followed by Imi. The great horse cantered up to Cadvan and put his head on his shoulder.

I feared for you, my friend, said Darsor. *I thought perhaps we had ridden together for the last time.*

"I thought so too," Cadvan answered him, and he caressed the horse. "But it was not so."

The girl is a great mage already, said Darsor. *And she is but newly foaled. What will she do when she is grown?*

"Only the Light knows," said Cadvan.

Darsor bent down and blew in Maerad's ear. Imi still hung back behind Darsor, and her head drooped. She was marked all over with white lines of dried sweat and looked entirely disconsolate. Maerad went up to the mare and flung her arms around her neck. Imi snuffled her, her ears pricking upward.

"It's all right now," Maerad said to the mare.

At last you can speak! said Imi, standing back and blowing out of her nose. And then she dropped her head low. *I'm sorry I ran away.*

"It was better so," Maerad said, stroking her. "What could you have done? And now you're back; that's all that matters."

I had to search long to find her, said Darsor, *and then she would not come, because she was so ashamed. But she is here now.*

"There is no shame in running from such foes," Cadvan said. "Even the mightiest might be excused for quailing. All is well, and now we must go away from here. Tonight we will all dine well, yes?"

Darsor put up his head and neighed loudly, waking Hem, who sat up, rubbing his eyes. Almost at once they mounted and cantered slowly down the straight road.

After an hour their path started to incline upward, and then they saw that the downs ran up, like a green tide, against a high ridge of jagged stone. They reached the ridge, called Raur na Nor, the fiery Crown of Norloch, two hours after noon. The road pierced the stone, continuing the undeviating course laid many centuries before by the Bards of Annar. Here they rode into a narrow gorge, and the heights of the Crown soared a hundred feet over their heads, casting them into deep shadow. An hour later, very suddenly it seemed, they rode out blinking into the afternoon sunshine.

They stood high up, looking over a wide valley that stretched for many leagues to the south and west. The road plunged down its sides into the fair Vale of Norloch, which fell in rills and terraces away from their feet. They saw beneath them the tiny shapes of houses and barns and haystacks, and sometimes the darker clumps of unwalled towns and woods.

"Down there is an inn, the Hardellach," said Cadvan, sounding exhausted. He pointed to a town that nestled into the side of the hill some five miles away. "It's been many years since I traveled this way, but it used to be run by Colun of Gent, and I sorely hope it still is. Farther on, by the sea, you can just see the light of the Tower of Machelinor, the highest tower of Norloch. All we need do now is ride there, and then we can rest."

Rest, thought Maerad. It was the most wonderful word she had ever heard.

Far to the south they could see where the Aleph River wound lazily through the farmlands, glittering in the afternoon sun like a huge golden snake dozing on a green sward. Hem peeked out of Cadvan's cloak with a dazed look, as if he thought he had reached the fabulous realms of the south. With an obscure feeling of dread, Maerad picked out far in the distance a white flash of light, tiny but bright as a star, and beyond that a glimmering blue mist, which she thought must be the sea. It was her first glimpse of Norloch, Citadel of the White Flame, the High City of Bards; and her heart beat fast in her breast.

XX

THE HOUSE OF NELAC

FOUR days later they reached the wide meads of the Carmallachen at the center of the Norloch Vale. Now at last they saw Norloch rising tall and white out of the fields, and Maerad gasped; even at this distance it was bigger and more lordly than she had imagined. The citadel flung up, battlemented wall within battlemented wall, and its high towers thrust into the sky as gracefully as lilies, but proud and puissant and stern. At the very top, the Tower of Machelinor threw back the sunlight like a crystal, and the city seemed like a bright crown surmounted by a living star. Beyond the citadel stretched a blue distance that might have been the sky, but might also have been the sea slumbering under a summer haze. Maerad thought that she heard the faint sound of a bell drifting over the meadows toward them.

They had ridden hard since the ambush at the Broken Teeth. Maerad was exhausted after the battle with the wight, but there had been no time to rest. They'd spent one night at the Hardellach Inn, where the Bard Colun stitched the wounds on Cadvan's face. Then early the following morning they set off on a punishing trek through the Vale of Norloch.

If Maerad had not seen everything through a blur of weariness, she might have enjoyed the ride. The weather was fine but not too hot, the sky a deep clear blue, and above them she could sometimes hear the faint twittering of a lark borne high on the summer thermals, although she could not see it. Around them stretched a peaceful and fertile landscape slumbering in a faint haze of heat; they passed many stone houses edged with over-flowing gardens, set in the hills overlooking the vale.

The road pushed steadily downhill, winding past meadows of rich grass growing in wide terraces, which were often divided by silver streams and treed with fine stands of beech or birch or elm. White herds of cattle or black-faced sheep grazed there, or perhaps a few horses drowsed in the sun, flicking away the flies with their tails. Around the gray stone houses were small hedged fields planted with barley or oats or wheat, their seed heads fattening in the ripe sunlight, or dark green rows of beets or cabbages, or peas flowering cheerfully in pinks and whites, and everywhere were green orchards of apples and almonds and soft fruits. Sometimes the road passed through a small forest and the cool, dappled shade fell on their faces, a welcome relief from the heat. They saw many people: farmers with carts, or children skipping or intent on some errand, or women walking with big wicker baskets, and once a shepherd with his dogs, the sheep filling the road like a bleating cloud. Sometimes they passed cloaked riders who Maerad thought must be Bards.

When they reached the straight road through the Meads of Carmallachen, on the morning of the fourth day, they went at a fast canter. Occasionally they could see the Aleph River winding many miles to their left, glittering in the sun. Cadvan squinted at the sky. "I think our fine weather is going to break," he said. "The wind is changing."

By the time they drew close to the walls of Norloch, late in the afternoon, a dark bank of clouds had spread over most of the sky and a chill wind was blowing. As the sun dipped to the horizon it fell beneath the clouds, loosing a rich golden light that seemed to etch every object with a surreal clarity, and it seemed as if the world held its breath. Close up, the city stretched dizzyingly high above them; Maerad craned back her neck to look, feeling as if the whole thing would topple down on her, crushing her with a vast weight of stone. The road led to high gates of black iron, featureless apart from huge silver hinges in the shapes of curling flames. Above the gates was a tower with a belfry of white stone, in which hung an enormous bronze bell.

"The gates shut at the sundown bell. We're just in time," said Cadvan. "I sent a message by bird to Nelac, but we may have arrived before it. I hope he's expecting us." He turned to Maerad, unsmiling; the marks of the whip still slashed lividly across his face, and his eye was bruised black. She was shocked to see how pale and strained he looked. "There will be a savage storm tonight, if I have any weatherlore."

They passed through the gate arch, and its dark shadow fell over them. The sun was already beginning to disappear. Before them stretched a wide thoroughfare, edged with big stone buildings of many kinds: the Ninth Circle of Norloch. On its other side the Circle was bounded by a great stone quay that stretched beneath black cliffs, but Cadvan led them away from the quay, upward to the Eighth Circle. A few large raindrops began to splash on the road, and Maerad shivered and gathered her cloak close around her.

Cadvan began to hurry them down the street, anxious to reach Nelac's house before the storm broke and, it seemed to Maerad, driven by some other urgency she couldn't guess. There was no time to stop and stare, but she had a confused impression of wide streets lit by huge lamps that cast a broad, steady light over grand houses and buildings and inns. The dusk was vanishing swiftly, and as the sun finally disappeared she heard a great tolling; the bell of Norloch was signaling the coming of night and the closing of the gates. Then, almost instantly it seemed to her, it was deep night. The isolated raindrops were now falling more swiftly and she could hear distant rumblings of thunder. It would not be long before the storm broke over their heads.

The horses rode swiftly up the nine levels, climbing each time, winding back and forth from gate to gate. Norloch had been built many hundreds of years before on a pinnacle of rock that thrust straight up more than seven hundred feet from a harbor enclosed by steep cliffs. On one side the rock dropped sheer to the sea, and on the other it inclined more gently down to the plains of the Carmallachen. It was on this incline that the city had been built. The Circles of Norloch were in truth half-circles, becoming less regular the nearer they fell to the plains, and their walls stretched from cliff to cliff. In the Ninth Circle the wall stopped at the harbor, a small cliff-bounded inlet with a narrow mouth, bordered on the city side by a wide stone quay.

The original up-thrust rock had been strengthened and extended, and it was now fashioned into an almost impregnable fortress, protected on one side by the sea and on the other by the swamps and waterlands of the Aleph River. The one clear approach to the Ninth Gate was from the north, and the only other entry to the city was by sea through the narrow heads of the harbor, which were risky to navigate and would admit only one ship at a time. Beneath the city there were delvings and caves that reached deep into the rock, with provision for supplies to keep the city alive for many months if it came under siege. The city's garrison lived in the Third and Fourth Circles, companies of stern warriors numbering in the thousands. Even in the days of Maninaë, when Norloch had long fallen from its greatness, it was proud and strong.

They went unquestioned until they reached the Fourth Circle, where a man in the silver and blue livery of the citadel challenged them. Maerad concealed herself in her hood, suddenly fearful they would not be allowed through, and she noticed that Hem was completely hidden inside Cadvan's cloak. But when the soldier recognized Cadvan, he bowed low and drew aside, and they passed through; and so it was at each higher gate. As they walked through the final gate into the First Circle, the storm finally broke. A brilliant flash of lightning illuminated the High Citadel starkly, for a brief second, before the rain started to pour down. Maerad saw glimmering white walls reaching high into the darkness and streets edged with trees, now boiling and thrashing in the gale, and high plinths on which were set figures, some leafed with gold and gleaming brightly, some black in the darkness, before the rain came down like a blinding sheet.

"We haven't far," shouted Cadvan over his shoulder. "But hurry! Don't lose me!" And he set off at a brisk canter. Imi, skittering nervously at the lightning, followed Darsor almost at his tail; although the streets were well lit, it would have been easy to lose him in the heavy rain and flailing shadows. At last, with water streaming off their cloaks, they reached the house Cadvan was seeking. It gave a blank, high wall to the street, in which was set one high door with carvings about its lintel. Cadvan dismounted and pulled a small iron lever in the wall, which Maerad guessed must be attached to a bell. They waited, sheltering against the side of the wall to try to escape the savage wind, for what seemed an age. It was in reality a short time before the door opened and before them stood an old bearded man heavily cloaked in gray, bearing a lamp.

"Who's there?" he said, peering out into the darkness. "By the Light, Cadvan! What are you doing here? Come in, come in, this weather isn't fit for rats!" He waved them in, and they led the horses through the door into a wide stone-flagged courtyard. They were at last out of the wind, although the rain still poured down in a deluge, coming off the roofs in great spouts. The man locked the door behind them.

"Nelac," said Cadvan, embracing the old man. "How good it

is to see you!" Maerad saw that Cadvan suddenly looked exhausted and gray, as if he'd been holding himself together by sheer will and now, having reached his goal, was on the verge of collapse. The old man stood back, his hands on Cadvan's shoulders, and inspected him sharply.

"And good to see you, Cadvan, my dear friend. I've missed you. But you've been ill-used, I can see." He nodded at Maerad and Hem. "Let's get out of this weather before we talk. Come." He led them across the courtyard toward some stables. "We must attend to the beasts, first."

In the shelter of the stables it was suddenly quiet and calm, and Maerad breathed in, comforted by the warm smell of hay and horses. They said nothing more as they hastily unsaddled and groomed the horses, leaving them comfortably housed, snorting at full mangers. Then Nelac led them at a run across the courtyard and through more high doors into a wide hallway.

It was made of plain stone and dimly lit by a silver lamp suspended from the roof, but it gave an impression of richness; there were gold hangings of heavy brocade on the walls, and Maerad saw that many rooms ran off it. Some doors were open and their light spilled onto the stone floor, and she heard voices talking and, far off, the trilling of a flute. They put off their cloaks in the hallway; they were all so wet they stood in little puddles. Cadvan leaned against the wall, swaying slightly.

"Well!" said Nelac, surveying the dripping group. "And who are these two?"

Cadvan gestured vaguely, too exhausted for formalities. "They're Maerad and Hem, I mean Cai, of Pellinor." Nelac's eyebrows rose in surprise, and his gaze rested for a second with a strange intensity on Maerad's face. "Maerad, Hem, this is Nelac. My old teacher and a good friend."

"We'll have to get you dry clothes," said Nelac. "Brin!" He called down the hallway and a dark, stocky man appeared out of a door. "Brin, we have some unexpected guests. Can you get their rooms ready? Three. And I need clothes for three, urgently. One woman and a boy." The man nodded and disappeared. "Come into my rooms while we're waiting," Nelac said. "It's warm in there."

Like Malgorn and Silvia, Nelac lived with his students; his rooms were downstairs off the huge entrance hall, behind a high, plain wooden door. Nelac led them into a large sitting room that seemed very bright after the dimness of the corridors. Here it was not so grand; the room was full of tables and comfortable chairs and shelves laden with books and instruments of various kinds, and a fire blazed in a large iron grate. One wall, free of any shelves, was painted curiously, so that it seemed to look out on a woodland inhabited by marvelous beasts and birds. On its other side the room had windowed doors that opened out onto a garden, but there it was all blackness and storm. Maerad looked around, her mouth open, and saw a tall, black-skinned man standing to greet them, his face blank with astonishment. She blinked in surprise: it was Saliman.

"Cadvan!" he said. "What on earth are you doing here? You keep close counsel; you didn't tell me you were coming this way. We could have traveled together. And Maerad too? And who's this?"

Cadvan swayed in the doorway. "Well met, Saliman," he said quietly. "I thought you might be here." He staggered across the room and fell into a deeply cushioned chair by the fire. Maerad saw that he was shaking badly.

"And very much the worse for wear, I see," said Saliman, swiftly covering his shock at his friend's state. "You're white as a sheet. Who punched you in the eye? Not to mention those whipstings. Let me get you a drink!" He raised his eyebrow at Nelac, who nodded, and went across to a sideboard on which there were several glass decanters. "Laradhel, perhaps?"

Cadvan nodded. Saliman poured a glass of the golden liquor, then looked across at Maerad and Hem, and poured another two.

"Sit down, sit down," said Nelac. Maerad and Hem were still standing uncertainly in the doorway. Maerad, with Hem sticking close behind her, walked to a sofa against the painted wall and sat straight as a bolt on the very edge. Saliman gave her the glass, and she sipped, looking sideways at Hem, who at first spluttered wildly and then drained the entire glass. A glow of warmth ran through her body, and she began to relax a little.

"That's a little better," said Nelac. He looked at Maerad. "Did I hear aright?" he said. "Cadvan said you were Maerad and Cai of Pellinor? Brother and sister, I guess?"

"Brother?" said Saliman, staring at Hem, who stared boldly back.

"Yes, my brother," said Maerad. She still had a feeling of unreality in so claiming him.

Nelac shook his head in amazement. "Pellinor! Though now that I look, I can guess who your mother was, Maerad. Surely she was Milana of the First Circle? You're alike as two peas. I didn't know Dorn so well, but Cai takes after him. You both have your father's eyes."

Hem wriggled, in discomfort or pleasure, Maerad couldn't tell. "My name's Hem," he said abruptly, and then gulped nervously, as if he thought he'd be clouted for speaking.

Nelac lifted an eyebrow, but didn't comment. Instead he looked across at Cadvan, who was staring into the fire and didn't appear to be listening. Maerad followed his gaze, beginning to feel alarmed. She had never seen Cadvan like this before. Even when his wounds were stitched at the inn, and in his agony she had thought him at the extremity of his endurance, he hadn't seemed so wraithlike, so gray. He looked deathly. Nelac seemed to share her concern; he went over to Cadvan and knelt before him. Cadvan looked up heavily.

"What has happened to you, my friend?" Nelac asked gently. He cupped his hand under Cadvan's chin and looked straight into his eyes. To Maerad, Cadvan suddenly seemed ten years old, a child in pain pleading wordlessly for relief, and she flinched at the sight. She had no idea until then of the extent of Cadvan's suffering: over the past four days he had been grimmer than usual, but she had put it down to the whiplashes and weariness. What she perceived now was his wounded mind, broken in the battle on the downs. She realized with a rush of distress that he had been in constant anguish ever since, and she had never guessed.

"It was a wight," Cadvan said hoarsely. "A wight of the Abyss, Nelac. It struck me down. There was nothing I could do."

Maerad heard the sharp intake of Saliman's breath. "A wight!" He looked at Maerad and Hem, marveling. "How is it that you're still alive?"

Cadvan waved his hand. "Maerad . . . ," he mumbled. Nelac, who seemed deeply worried, looked up sharply.

"No time for questions," he said. "They can be answered later."

Nelac put his hand on Cadvan's brow, and, as Maerad watched in wonder, she saw a silver radiance gather around him, growing in intensity. He shut his eyes. After a short time, Nelac's hand was brighter than anything else in the room, and the Bard himself seemed to be a form of sheer incandescence, a being of air and light rather than flesh. Very far away, or very deep in her mind, Maerad could hear an ethereal music; she thought it was like bells or pure voices, but it was really like nothing she had ever heard before. Cadvan's eyelids fluttered closed, and a deep peace flooded into his face.

Hem was sitting beside Maerad with his mouth open, his glass forgotten in his hand. They watched, entranced, for an immeasurable span of time; and then Nelac breathed out and drew his hand away from Cadvan's brow, and the radiant music softened and dimmed and disappeared.

Sighing, Cadvan opened his eyes and leaned back in his chair, gazing at the ceiling. Nelac stood up slowly, and Maerad realized properly for the first time that he was an old man; how old she couldn't guess. He suddenly looked intensely weary. He poured himself some laradhel and sat down again without speaking.

"What was that?" Hem's voice squeaked with astonishment and alarm, and Maerad jumped. "What did he do?"

Nelac looked up at Hem, amused despite his evident tiredness, but it was Saliman who answered.

"Young Hem, you have just seen the greatest healer in Annar and the Seven Kingdoms exercise his full powers. Take note! It is a rare sight. And something for a young Bard to aspire to. An old Bard too," he said, lifting his glass toward Nelac.

"Will Cadvan be all right now?" Maerad asked in a small voice. She still felt cold with distress: why hadn't she noticed how ill he was? She wondered again at Cadvan's powers of endurance; he had led them all that way.

Nelac sighed. "Yes," he said. "It was almost too late. Even another few hours and perhaps not even I could have helped him. I had to go deep to heal him. But yes, he will be all right now. For the rest, he just needs sleep." He looked at Hem and Maerad. "I would say that you two do, as well. Maerad, I don't know what has happened. I see already it is a cruel story. For the moment we'll leave that be; we can talk tomorrow. Perhaps you would like a bath, and dinner, and a long sleep?"

"A bath!" Maerad was overwhelmed with a sudden physical longing. "That would be so lovely! I haven't had a bath since . . . since Innail."

There was a knock on the door, and Brin, Nelac's housemaster, entered. "The chambers are prepared, Master Nelac," he said.

"Good!" said Nelac, standing up. "Then you shall have a bath straightaway, if you wish, young Maerad. And you too, Hem."

"A bath?" said Hem, looking alarmed again. "What's a bath?"

"Or not, as the case may be," said Nelac, smiling with great gentleness. He seemed to find Hem very amusing. "It's not compulsory, if, perhaps, advisable. Saliman, could you take these young people upstairs? I need to sit for a while. Cadvan can go up later, when he's ready."

Maerad took her pack from the hallway, and then Saliman led them up several flights of stairs to their guest chambers. She blinked as they walked through the dimly lit corridors. Nelac's house was big and grand, the ceilings high enough to be lost in shadow, and everywhere, carved into the lintels of doors and windows, were runes and symbols: ancient charms, Saliman told them, for the prosperity and wisdom of those who dwelt there. It was sparsely but richly furnished, and Maerad saw often the glint of gold or a bright tapestry, or they would turn on a landing and confront an exquisite statue glimmering whitely through the shadows. They passed many doors through which they could hear the murmur of conversation, or the tuning of instruments, or a lone voice practicing scales; and often they passed people on the stairs, Nelac's students, she supposed, some of whom turned and stared at their wild state. Maerad wondered how many people lived there. She began to understand what Silvia had meant by calling Innail a "humble house"; privately she thought she preferred

Silvia's friendly abode to this grandeur, which she thought cold and gloomy.

"So, Hem of Pellinor, or Cai of Pellinor . . . what really *is* your name?" said Saliman as they walked along.

"Hem," said Hem firmly. "It's Hem."

"Did Cadvan find you too? What is going on here?"

Maerad didn't know how to answer, wondering what Cadvan would want her to say, and Saliman glanced at her and laughed. "It's all right, Maerad, don't feel you have to tell me anything. I'll find out from Cadvan later. But I can't get over it! *Two* from Pellinor!"

"And where are *you* from?" demanded Hem rudely. "Not from around here, I'll bet."

Saliman seemed to find Hem as amusing as Nelac did. "No, Hem. I'm from Turbansk, to the south."

"The south!" Hem's face brightened with wonder. "Are you really from the south?"

Saliman's mouth twitched. "Indeed I am. From the land of pomegranates and monkeys and oranges bigger than your head!"

This seemed to temporarily silence Hem, whose eyes were now as big as saucers. They went on without speaking until they came to another wide corridor. Saliman opened the first door and poked his head in. "This looks like your room, Maerad. Make yourself at home."

Maerad's chamber was bigger and higher than her room at Innail, with white stone walls draped with plain blue hangings. The stone floor was warmed by an intricately patterned crimson carpet. A curtained bed was let into the wall, and by the window was a cushioned window seat, on which were laid a rich red dress and other clothes. A fire crackled comfortably in a small grate.

"The bathroom's down the hallway," explained Saliman. Maerad walked in the door and turned to thank him, but he was already farther down the hall, showing Hem his room. Hem was now chatting away freely; he seemed to like Saliman, or at least was not as awed by him as he was by Nelac. Maerad shut the door quietly, put down her pack, and sat motionless on the window seat. Her hair fell over her face, still damp from the storm, and she flicked it back, watching the rain beat on the black window pane. She would have a bath and change, but first she had to unpack.

She took out her possessions, leaning her lyre against the chest and placing the small cat and the reed flute on the mantel. As she lifted the flute, the ring wrought of golden lilies flashed in the firelight, and she thought of Ardina, who in her different guises of Elidhu and Queen, had given her both gifts, rustic flute and exquisite ring. She wondered, for the first time, what they might mean. Ardina, she felt sure, had very little to do with the Light; but she was most certainly not evil. She was somehow outside these human laws—free and strange and dangerous—and yet she called Maerad her kin. Feeling unsettled by her thoughts, and too tired to follow them, Maerad put Dernhil's book on a small table, next to a lily-shaped lamp that sat there. For a second she gazed at it sadly, suddenly vividly reminded of Dernhil's serious face, bent over his desk, writing something. Saddened, she turned back to her unpacking. She didn't know what to do with her fighting gear, but when she looked into the chest, she saw there was plenty of room to stow it. The chest contained more soft, warm raiment like that she had worn at Innail, and the wood smelled sweet, imbuing the clothes with its scent.

She took the crimson dress, which was made of a fine, very soft wool, from the window seat and hurried down the hallway to find the bathroom. No one was there, and she drew a hot bath, pouring generous amounts of oil into the water, and lowered herself in with a feeling of bliss. For a while she allowed herself simply to relax, emptying her mind of everything except the sheer pleasure of the warm water. She thought she had better not dawdle and, long before she was ready, dragged herself out, dressed in the crimson robe, and returned to her room.

With the tempest raging outside it seemed very cosy and welcoming. After the punishing ride of the past few days she didn't feel like moving at all; she sat by the fire and listened to the storm hurling fistfuls of rain against the window, lighting up its blackness with white flashes of lightning. At last she was at Norloch, but she felt too tired to think, or even to feel any sense of triumph; more than anything else, she felt a strange, persistent unease. Norloch was grand and noble, and that daunted her; on the other hand, she liked Nelac very much. Why, then, this feeling of doubt?

Saliman led Maerad and a yawning Hem downstairs to Nelac's dining room, where food was set out on a table. Hem was now wearing a plain jerkin of dyed blue wool and blue breeches of heavy cotton, instead of the ragged garments in which he had arrived, but they were too big for him, and he still went barefoot. Clearly he had not bathed.

"We'll have to get you clothes that fit, eh, Hem? And some shoes," said Saliman, inspecting him. Hem looked up, surprised; he was pleased enough to be dressed warmly, and Maerad had the impression that he had never owned any shoes. "And I shall introduce you to a bath, as well."

"Not for me," said Hem, shaking his head vigorously. "I'm fine as I am."

"You're probably quite a different color under that dirt," Maerad said reflectively.

"Yes, white as the driven snow," said Saliman mock seriously. "His hair is probably blond."

Hem hunched his shoulders and walked on ahead without answering. Maerad looked laughingly across at Saliman. "You've a challenging task ahead, if you really want to clean him up," she said.

"I am undaunted," said Saliman, throwing back his head heroically. "Not even Hem cows Saliman of Turbansk!"

Cadvan was not at dinner; Nelac said he had gone to bed. Maerad was very hungry, but black waves of exhaustion kept breaking over her; she felt that if she didn't lie down soon, she would simply pass out at the table. Hem ate ravenously, and he couldn't hide his look of disbelief when he was offered a second helping. When he tentatively asked for more and wasn't refused, his incredulity became comical. He consumed, Maerad thought, an unfeasible amount of food: he would probably be sick. He ate at least four times the amount Maerad did, in the time it took her to finish a single plate.

While they ate, neither Saliman nor Nelac asked them about their adventures. Saliman told them tales of his homeland; his strong, slender musician's hands sketched pictures in the air, his teeth flashing white as he laughed. Hem sat enraptured, chewing noisily, his head full of images of golden-roofed towers and fruit markets and silk stalls and strange, exotic animals. He couldn't keep his eyes off Saliman, and when the Bard intercepted his stares and smiled he blushed furiously and looked around the room instead.

Nelac's dining room contained many curious things: a crystal globe carven with strange runes; curious, intricate instruments made perhaps for measuring or observation; and a shelf of big leather-bound books with their titles stamped in gilt on their spines. Parchment scrolls and paper manuscripts were piled high on a table against the wall. On one shelf was a collection of different kinds of stone: crystals of quartz and amethyst, polished agate, jade, and amber. Another held huge exotic seashells with strange spikes and horns, blotched with freckles of brown and pink, and one perfect nautilus, with intricate whorls as delicate as paper. A gilt lamp overhead let fall a gentle light. Maerad thought of Dernhil's study: this room seemed even more disorderly than his, but in the same way, as if a hidden purpose lay beneath the chaos.

"Forgive the disorganization of my private quarters," said Nelac, noticing Hem's glances. "I never seem to have enough space for all my work, and it spills into every room."

"It doesn't look disorganized to me," said Maerad, and then, despite herself, she reddened. She couldn't rid herself of her reticence in the presence of Nelac, although he didn't frighten her. He was like no one she had met before, and she felt how far he was beyond her experience; even Ardina had not abashed her so. Maybe it's because Ardina was a bit like me, she thought. And that's what she meant by kinship. But still, she wanted to know what had happened to Cadvan.

"Is Cadvan all right?" she asked, when she finished eating.

Nelac's eyes were dark and somehow ageless, and the glance he turned on Maerad was almost as deep as Ardina's. "Cadvan will be well in a short time," he said. "I had to use all my powers of healing, but I have made whole what was broken in him, as if it were never wounded. That is more than a spell of mending. All that ails him now is exhaustion, and a long rest will heal that."

"But what was wrong with him?" She gazed at Nelac, the distress rising within her again. "I didn't know anything was, I mean, beyond being tired, and the whips . . ."

Nelac's glance was full of gentle understanding, and Maerad looked down at the table. She found his acute perception discomforting.

"Cadvan is a Bard of unusually strong will," he said kindly, smiling briefly, as if at some far memory. "If he seeks to keep something hidden, it is near impossible to find it out. When you arrived here, he was on the brink of death. He was struck down and broken by an evil will, even as he opened his full power. In a Bard, that is a grievous thing; the greater the Bard, the more grievous. And Cadvan is a very great Bard. Even as the physical wounds healed, he was sickening and wasting away."

Maerad sat in silence, shocked at the thought of Cadvan dying. She had thought of him as somehow invulnerable.

"I must say that I am full of curiosity," said Nelac, after a pause. "How is it you were not all killed outright? And who was the wight, I wonder? It's been many centuries since one was heard of in Annar."

A trembling overtook Maerad, as the wight's baleful figure loomed vividly in her memory.

"It said it was called Sardor," she said.

"Sardor?" Nelac's face was suddenly grim. "He was chained long ages ago. He once haunted the Broken Teeth in the Edinur Downs, his barrow; but the Bards cleansed it after the Silence, and only his shadow remained. A black memory of former evil, but a memory nevertheless. I guess it was there he assailed you? He was a mighty king once, in the dark times. It is ill news that such an evil walks again in this land."

"I don't think it does anymore," said Maerad faintly, and now her hands were shaking, and a roaring rose in her ears. "I blasted it, and it all burned up and disappeared."

Nelac and Saliman stared at Maerad in astonishment.

"You *blasted* it?" said Saliman, incredulity straining his

voice. He looked across at Nelac, who was staring at Maerad somberly from beneath his heavy brows.

Maerad felt suddenly that she couldn't bear the Bards' disbelief, not now, not here, not tonight. She clasped her hands together to stop them from shaking.

"Nobody saw it," she said. "Cadvan was unconscious. I thought Hem was dead. Nobody saw me do it. But I *did*. You can believe me or not." She looked up defiantly and caught Nelac's steady gaze. She held his eye, refusing to be intimidated. At last he stirred, looking away and passing his hand over his brow. To Maerad's surprise, he looked immensely sad.

"I believe you," he said.

XXI

A COUNCIL OF FRIENDS

FOR what seemed a long time, Maerad floated through the mists and fogs of dream: nonsensical images rose up before her of a citadel like Norloch, but tiny and enclosed in glass like a child's bauble, and trees walking toward the sea, and Hem eating a supernaturally large bunch of grapes. But suddenly she gasped in her sleep; a Hull appeared before her and reached out its hand toward her wrist. It clasped her, and she could not move or speak. Then the Hull vanished and she dreamed, as she had long ago in Innail, that she was taken up like a bird over the realm of Annar. In the distance a sinking sun touched the eastern mountains and the battlements of a great city in the west, a city she knew now was Norloch; the Aleph River ran through its center, a snake of molten gold. Again a dark mist crept over the land and she heard lamenting; and then the voice cried, "Look to the north." She felt a rising panic as a dissolving shadow sought her; and then, as before, with the sickly dread of nightmare, came the dead voice. She understood, with a numbing sense of shock, that it was using the Speech, but the Speech subtly turned and distorted so that it was no longer a language of high beauty, but evil and empty, its potency inverted. "I am again," said the voice, "but none shall find my dwelling, for I live in every human heart." It started to laugh, and the laughter hurt her; and then, twisting and turning in her bed, Maerad escaped the tentacles of the nightmare and woke up. She sat up in bed, trembling all over, and looked around her. Her room was still and peaceful. A little faint light

came through the casement and illuminated the room with silver. She looked around, reassuring herself; there was her lyre,
there her book, there was the pipe the Elidhu had given her . . .

As she sat in bed, trying unsuccessfully to rid herself of an
overwhelming feeling of dread, there was a quiet knock on her
door. Maerad almost leaped out of her skin.

"Maerad?" It was Hem.

"Yes?"

Hem's pale, sleep-tousled head peeked around the door.

"Maerad, can I sleep with you? I'm getting bad dreams. . . .
The room's so big and dark. . . ."

Maerad nodded, and wordlessly Hem crept into bed with
her. She lay down, putting her arms around his thin, bony body.
He was snoring within seconds, and it wasn't long before
Maerad too slid back into a black, dreamless sleep.

Maerad opened her eyes. All she could see was an expanse of
white, and across it danced a golden ripple of light. She
watched it, fascinated, for what felt like a long time, and slowly
realized she was looking at a ceiling. She must be in Innail, she
thought; but the ceilings there were stone, not white. Then suddenly everything rushed back, and she sat up abruptly.

Hem was sitting in the corner, eating a bread roll.

"You sleep like an old dog," he said. "I've been waiting ages
and ages for you to wake up. I've been up for hours."

"What's the time?" Maerad pushed her fingers through
her hair.

"Three hours after noon." Hem took another bite of his roll.
"You snore too."

"How's Cadvan?" Maerad swung her legs out of bed, looking for her clothes.

"I don't know." Hem shrugged. "He's probably asleep
like you."

"Go away so I can get dressed."

"All right." Hem shrugged again. "There's food downstairs if you want any. I have to come back and show you; Saliman's worried that you might get lost." Maerad threw her pillow at him, and he ducked out of the room.

After she was dressed, Maerad went to her window and looked out. The day was clear and beautiful, as if the sky had been scoured clean by the previous night's storm. She could see over the rooftops of the lower Circles, right down to the Carmallachen and beyond, over the Vale of Norloch, and she was admiring the view when suddenly she remembered, with a shock that went right through her body, her dream of the night before. It struck her with a wave of nausea that started at her toes and went all the way to the top of her head, and she clutched at the table, feeling dizzy and sick. It was a somber Maerad who joined Hem ten minutes later and wended her way downstairs.

Cadvan and Saliman were already in Nelac's sitting room, deep in conversation. They looked up when Maerad and Hem entered. Cadvan was still very pale, with deep shadows haunting his face: the whiplashes, covered with tiny herringbone stitches, stood out vividly on his skin, and his black eye was now spectacularly fading in a blaze of sunset colors. But the deathliness that had so troubled Maerad the previous night was gone.

"Good morning," said Cadvan. "Or I should say afternoon. I'm but lately up myself!"

"Hello," said Maerad. She was so relieved to see Cadvan looking almost normal that tears started in her eyes. She blinked them away and looked toward the dining room. "Hem said there was food."

"Hem and food!" Saliman rolled his eyes. "I've never seen a

human being eat so much. I don't think he's stopped chewing since he got out of bed!"

"I'm hungry," said Hem. "What's wrong with that?" He disappeared into the dining room.

"How are you feeling?" Maerad asked shyly. Cadvan smiled at her for the first time in days.

"Very fine, my young Bard," he said. "Apart from a few itchy stitches. I'm sure I look worse than I feel, for a change. Go and get something to eat. Nelac's going to come soon; he's doing some lessons at the moment. We all need to talk."

Maerad ate her breakfast—with Hem, who unashamedly explained that she needed some company—and returned to the sitting room, where Cadvan and Saliman were talking of Saliman's journey to Norloch.

"Not quite so eventful as your traveling," Saliman said, glancing at Cadvan's wounded face. "I saw no wights. But three Hulls attacked me at the crossroads, and although I drove them off, they killed my mare, Dima. I still mourn her. She has borne me these past seven years. I didn't expect such dangers in the heart of Annar! So it took me longer to get here than I wished. I bought another horse, but it was not so fine as mine, as I was pressed and in no position to bargain."

As he spoke, Nelac returned. The sunlight streamed through the large windows, and he pulled them open to let in the fresh air. Maerad looked out; she saw a bower of bright blossoms spilling over an emerald green lawn, and gasped in delight.

"My blooms survived the storm, mostly," said Nelac from behind her. "But not the windflowers, alas! The merest breath will dislodge their petals; and they were so beautiful this year."

She turned to Nelac, smiling, and suddenly her shyness of him fell away. Rather than his nobility, she perceived his gentleness, and beneath that the sadness that seemed a quality of all

Bards and that confused her at times, because so often it modulated without warning into joy. He was, she realized suddenly,
very similar to Cadvan; and then she remembered they both
came from the same School.

The Bards then talked for some time. Hem sat on the floor,
listening and nibbling morsels of food, which he occasionally
vanished into the next room to replenish. He seemed to be afraid
that all the food would disappear in the next hour if he didn't
immediately consume it. Nelac and Saliman sat on the big chairs
beside the unlit fireplace, and Maerad sat next to Cadvan on the
couch by the painted wall, with Hem near her feet.

Cadvan told Nelac of his discovery of Maerad in Gilman's
Cot, their flight from Innail, and of Dernhil's death at the hands
of Hulls, which Nelac already knew of from Saliman. Saliman
shook his head sadly. "Dernhil is a grievous loss," he said. "And
so strange! All Innail was in mourning when I left; Silvia was
inconsolable." Maerad's heart jumped at the mention of Silvia,
and she saw her face in her mind's eye, darkened with sorrow.
"Why would Hulls attack Dernhil?" said Saliman. "Is it revenge,
perhaps, Cadvan? Or think you it's to do with Maerad?"

"Both, perhaps," said Cadvan grimly. He then related their
encounters with the Hulls and the Kulag, and lastly their
ambush by the wight. Because of his promise to Ardina, he
didn't mention Rachida. Hem listened in silence, chewing
thoughtfully. Neither Nelac nor Saliman interrupted; they listened intently, their faces grave. Sometimes Saliman looked
over at Maerad with an expression of wonder on his face.

"The Kulag is strange enough," he said, when Cadvan finished his tale. "But to destroy a wight!"

"We don't know that it was destroyed," said Nelac.
"Though it does sound as if it were. I've never heard of a Bard
doing more than banishing a wight to the Abyss."

"And even that takes a strong will," added Cadvan. "Yes,

there is something here that we don't quite understand." They all looked at Maerad.

"Then why couldn't you banish it?" she asked Cadvan. "Everyone says that you are a great Bard."

Cadvan sighed. "I should have been able to. But I was taken, I confess to my shame, by surprise. I was in a hurry and made the wrong decision; I thought I could deal with Hulls and wers. Even if there were five Hulls, it seemed to me not impossible; a risk, but not a great risk, if I was wary. A wight was something else." He grinned wryly. "Even if it might seem but a little thing to you."

"Well," said Maerad, blushing slightly. "It didn't seem little, so much as . . . as I didn't think about it. It sort of just came out of me. I've been very tired since," she added with a rush.

"No wonder," Saliman said, smiling. "I would have been laid out for a week, myself."

"I wondered . . . ," said Maerad, and then stopped.

"What, O my Deliverer?" said Cadvan.

Maerad blushed again at his teasing. "I wondered if the Landrost had hurt you, and that was why . . ." She faltered and stopped again.

"The Landrost did indeed hurt me," said Cadvan. "And I was less in my power than I could be. But that is no excuse for rushed decisions and the mistakes that come from them. I judge myself at fault, and so I am; and it is a severe judgment, Maerad, because things very nearly were otherwise, and the result would have been terrible for many more than us." Maerad saw for an instant an implacable harshness in Cadvan's face, and she shivered; she thought she would not like to be judged by Cadvan, if she had done any real wrong. But then it passed, and he kept speaking. "If the cloud is golden-edged, it is that it made you come into the Speech; and perhaps only such extremity could do that. You were very deeply veiled."

"The deep veiling can be a sign of a great Gift," put in Nelac. "There was Thorondil of Culor, say. He didn't come into the Speech until he was twenty-one."

"There is more," said Cadvan. He spoke then of the parchment that Dernhil had given Maerad, in which Lanorgil had spoken of his foredream, and told Nelac about Maerad's lyre, the hidden treasure of Pellinor. At Nelac's request, she ran up to her room and fetched them both from her pack. The old Bard took the lyre with reverence, turning it over in his hands.

"Yes, Cadvan, you are right," he said at last, brushing his fingers lightly over the strings so they sang faintly through the room. "Dhyllic ware indeed. A beautiful, a perfect thing. Such balance!"

"I was hoping you could read what the script says, around the rim," Cadvan said. "I don't recognize the lettering at all."

Nelac looked at it closely. "No," he said at last. "There were many scripts in use in Afinil, and I do not know all of them. These are runes, and such scripts can hold a whole poem in a single symbol. They are very difficult to decipher if the key is lost. But perhaps it says nothing more than the name of the maker and a snatch of verse."

He stroked the lyre again, then gave it to Maerad, who slipped it back into the case Cadvan had given her. She handled it with more than usual care; it was precious to her, as it had always been, but these Bards regarded it with a kind of awe.

"This is the parchment Dernhil gave me," she said, holding it out to Nelac. He scrutinized it thoughtfully.

"I read it as telling the Truename of the One who was Foretold," said Cadvan, looking inquiringly at Nelac. "What do you think?"

"Seek and cherish the Fire Lily, the Fated One, which blooms the fairer in dark places, and sleepeth long in darkness: from such a root will blossom the White Flame anew, when it seems its seed is poisoned

in the center," said Nelac, reading from the parchment. "Hmmm." He glanced up at Maerad and back to the parchment. "It is certainly not the lily of Pellinor he speaks of, and it does seem plain that he talks of a Truename, sometimes that is said to come 'from a dark place.' *Note the Sign and be not Blind! In the name of the Light and in anxiety for the Speech, whose roots lie in the Treesong, which nourishes all.* The Treesong? Now, it is long since I have thought on that. . . ."

"You know of it?" Cadvan leaned forward, his eyes brightening. "It's a clue; it's something to do with the Elementals. There is something else. Maerad, tell them of the Elidhu."

Maerad then told them of the meeting with the Elidhu in the Weywood, and recited the song she had sung to her. Saliman and Nelac listened in absolute silence, and she enjoyed the telling, sensing their amazement. Hem looked up, his mouth open, for once forgetting to eat. Maerad thought about the strange knowledge that Ardina and the Elidhu were one and the same. But they were forbidden to mention Rachida, and she had not even told Cadvan of Ardina's revelation.

"Elemental blood in the House of Karn! That surprises even me!" said Nelac at last. "But I'm sure you're right, there is a connection. I shall have to go deep into my memory to find it. The Treesong is an ancient tradition, dating from Afinil, long fallen into shadow; it's to do with the Speech. It does link, somehow, with the Foretold; I can't quite remember . . . there are so many songs about the Foretold. And they are all riddles."

A beautiful tenor voice suddenly filled the room:

> *"Grows a Lily on the Briar*
> *Grows a Briar on the Wave*
> *Triple-tongued its voice of Fire*
> *Edil-Amarandh will save."*

Maerad looked up in surprise. It was Saliman, whom she had never heard sing before. "What was that?" she asked.

"That's from Pel's *Canticles*," he told her. "Written down just after the Great Silence. The Fire Lily seems clear enough, if we take Lanorgil's prophecy as a guide. As for the Briar, that's the House of Karn."

"Is it?" she asked in astonishment.

"Its sign is a rose," said Cadvan. "A wild rose." He was frowning in thought. "I hadn't thought of the *Canticles*," he said. "Triple-tongued? Surely that means the Speech, the Annaren, and the language of the Elidhu?" He looked at Nelac, his face alight with excitement.

"Are you suggesting that Maerad is the Foretold?" asked Nelac, his eyebrows almost disappearing into his hair.

"Yes, yes, yes, of course I am." Cadvan was musing again, abstracted. "The wave. What's that? The wave means so many things. . . ."

"Cadvan, this is a great claim!" said Nelac. "Are you serious about this?"

Cadvan stared straight into Nelac's eyes. "I'm as serious as I've ever been," he said. "Need wakens the Light, it is said. Can you doubt there is need now?"

Nelac gazed back unblinkingly. Slowly he nodded, then sighed. He turned to Maerad, and his eyes lanced deep into her mind, much more searchingly than he had looked the night before. She flinched, taken by surprise. There was a sudden silence in the room. He then made a curious gesture: slowly his head sank down to his chest, and his right hand crept to the back of his neck and clasped it. He sat like that for some time while Cadvan and Saliman stared at him, the words arrested on their lips.

Finally Nelac looked up. "Yes, I believe that Maerad is the One," he said. "I think you guess aright." He sighed again, gazing at Maerad with an immense compassion. She stared back speechlessly, wanting to ask how he knew, feeling her blood singing in her ears.

"You have more to say, I think," Nelac said.

"Yes," said Cadvan. "But I wonder what the wave signifies?"

"It's a sign of the Light, of course," said Nelac. "And also it is a symbol of music and, as it happens, of the School of Amdridh. It might just mean the sea. It's too many-sided to make sense of."

"It says 'foam' later in the *Canticles*," put in Saliman.

"Hmmm. Yes, it does." Nelac frowned. "The Elidhu were associated with wave foam, being able to take different forms. That's drawing a long bow, of course." He paused, frowning in abstraction. "I remember what the Treesong is now. It is an ancient word for the Speech, from the days of Afinil. It signifies that which is beyond words. And it is also a song, supposedly written when the Bards first appeared in Annar, in which the mystery of the Speech is held, but the Lore maintains that it is a riddle that no Bard has been able to unravel. And it is long lost. Even in the first days after the Silence, when Bards began to find again much that had vanished, many said that it never existed."

There was a blank pause.

"Then how do we find it?" asked Maerad.

Nelac shot her a sharp glance. "I don't know," he said. "But I think you must." He looked inquiringly at Cadvan. "So, what else?"

"There's the question of Hem, or Cai," said Cadvan.

Hem stirred as if he were going to say something, but thought better of it.

Cadvan plunged into the story of their discovery of Hem, telling of his life in the orphanage and their discovery of his medallion. Nelac and Saliman this time cross-questioned Cadvan more closely, and then questioned Maerad.

"I *know* he's my brother," said Maerad, unconsciously moving protectively toward Hem. "I think I knew before I knew — underneath, I mean."

"It could be that your understandable desire to have your brother alive is here read wrong," said Nelac gently. "So far the only proof we have is his medallion and a passing resemblance to Dorn. The Hulls could have placed the medallion on him, to fool others."

"No, it's mine," said Hem vehemently. "I had it when I went there. I've always had it." And Maerad recognized the passion of one who had nothing; she had felt exactly the same about her lyre, her one precious thing, her sole token of identity in Gilman's Cot.

"That still doesn't mean that a Hull couldn't have put it there," said Saliman. "And in the absence of other proof . . ." Maerad put her hand on Hem's shoulder, clasping it tightly.

"Yes." Nelac's head lowered in deep thought. "Yes. And we know, of course, that memory can be inlaid into a mind. Hulls are fond of that. The only way we could be sure would be by scrying."

"*I'm* not scrying him," Cadvan said. "It was bad enough scrying Maerad."

"Then I will," said Nelac. "That is, if Hem agrees."

Hem was scowling down at the carpet. "I'm telling no lies," he said thickly.

"I know," said Nelac. "What I doubt is not something you can do on purpose. But you must know, Hem, that no one here is scried against his will. It would help us a lot if you did agree."

There was a long pause.

"All right then," said Hem angrily, sounding as if he were about to cry. "Scry me, if you don't believe me!" He stood up and ran out into the garden.

"You've frightened him!" said Maerad, glaring at Nelac,

and followed Hem outside. He was standing underneath a blossoming tree, glowering at the flowerbeds.

"Hem," she called softly.

"What?" He didn't turn around.

Maerad was at a loss. "Nelac . . . Nelac doesn't mean to hurt you," she said at last. "Cadvan scried me. It doesn't hurt. You know, when he did it to me, I hurt him!"

"I'm not lying," he said in a muffled voice. "It's all right for you; nobody says they don't believe *you*."

"That's not quite true," answered Maerad, thinking back to the Council in Innail. "Anyway, he's not going to do it *now*. Come on, come back in."

Sulkily Hem turned around, his eyes lowered. Maerad took his hand and he shook it away, but he followed her back into the room. Cadvan, Saliman, and Nelac were sitting in silence.

"Hem, I am sorry if I have frightened you," said Nelac gravely. "And I am sorry also that I seem to doubt you. What we are speaking of here is so important that we cannot be less than certain of what we believe."

Hem nodded, swallowing hard.

"I can promise, however, that the scrying will not hurt you," Nelac continued. "And I will order a special feast afterward, just for you, to make up for it."

Hem nodded again, looking a little cheerier.

"I'm not *scared* of it," he said with scornful bravado. "Do you want to do it now, then?" he asked, after a pause. "My brains are ready."

Saliman grinned and gently cuffed him. "What would you not do for food, rascal?" he asked. "We have yet to finish here, anyway."

"Later will be quite soon enough," said Nelac, hiding a smile. "And then, of course, we must decide what to do with you."

"Do with me?" The alarm instantly returned to Hem's face.

"You must go to a School."

"Oh."

"But alas, I do not think that Norloch will accept you."

"No, probably not," said Cadvan. "I had forgotten that. . . ."

"Forgotten what?" Maerad looked up sharply.

"Somehow those of the Pilanel do not seem to get places here," said Cadvan, with a trace of contempt in his voice. "A School is supposed to accept all those with the Gift, but here it is argued that, as Norloch is the Center of the Light, only those of proper birth should have the honor of being taught here."

"But Hem's of the House of Karn!" said Maerad. "You said that was one of the noblest families there is!"

"Yes," said Cadvan. "But even if we are completely sure of it, it's going to be difficult to persuade anyone else of Hem's claim. Especially here. I think also that Hem might be happier in another School."

"What about Turbansk?" asked Saliman.

"Turbansk?" Hem's face suddenly lit up. "Could I really go there?"

"If you wish," said Saliman. "I could take you. I must leave here soon."

Maerad felt a sudden pang: would she lose her brother so quickly? Hem seemed to have the same thought. "Would Maerad come too?" he asked.

"Perhaps," said Cadvan. "If not, she could certainly visit you." Hem looked a little reassured.

"We can think on Hem's future in the coming days," said Nelac. "There are several possibilities. One of Hem's, ah, *unusual* background needs to be placed carefully. I agree that Norloch is not the place. But how time rushes past! Already the sun is westering. I need to digest everything we have said today. It is clear, then, that we believe that Maerad is the One."

Cadvan nodded.

"It is a big claim," Nelac went on. "And we do not have a hope of convincing others until she is instated and we know her Name. I accept the prophecy of Lanorgil; he was one of the greatest Seers we have seen. I would be now very surprised if Maerad was *not* the One, but we must give thought to what is best for her. For all of us. For she is still very young, and untested in her powers; and she has not had the schooling that one of her abilities should have. And that can be a dangerous matter." He paused, and his eyes again passed over Maerad's face and she shivered, suddenly abashed; she remembered, with a qualm, the strange joy she had felt when she had destroyed the Kulag and the wight. "I think also," Nelac added, "that we will have serious problems getting the First Circle here to agree to her instatement."

"Even with all that has been said here today?" said Saliman in astonishment.

Nelac looked at him from underneath his brows. "How long since you have been here, Saliman? Five years? And you, Cadvan? At least a year?" They both nodded. "I must tell you, then, that Enkir has banned the teaching of women here."

"What?" said both Bards, at the same time. Maerad, forgetting that Cadvan had already told her, asked, "Who's Enkir?"

"Enkir is First Bard," Nelac explained. "You both know that he has been writing against women for some time. Three years ago he forbade the teaching of swordcraft and unarmed combat to women. Late last year he published the edict that women should not be taught as Bards."

"But that's not fair!" Maerad burst out.

"It is a measure of his power," Nelac continued. "Since Nardil died, four years ago now, there has been no check on him. I do what I can, of course, but I and a few others are consistently outvoted on the Council. It's been more than a lifetime since there was a woman on the First Circle. I like it not. Something is wrong in the Balance here, and it slips always more awry."

"Enkir is proud and ambitious," said Saliman. "I well remember. But I think he is not an evil Bard."

"Not evil, maybe," Nelac answered. "But a man of iron will. He is certain that he does right, and so convinces others. And it can be costly to oppose him."

"I find it hard to believe him corrupt, even though I have no love for him," said Cadvan. "He has done much in service of the Light." There was a silence as the Bards brooded on their own thoughts, and Maerad felt her uneasiness returning.

"I had a dream last night," she said abruptly. "It was . . ." She stopped; the nausea rose inside her again, and she waited for it to go away.

"A dream?" said Cadvan quickly. "I forgot to mention her foredream in Innail," he said to the other two.

Nelac looked up. "Is there no end to this girl's abilities?" he asked.

"It was the same one. Only this time I understood it," Maerad said. She related the two dreams, fighting down the sickly sensation of nightmare, and again the Bards listened with absolute attention. Nelac's hands gripped the side of his chair as she spoke, and his knuckles whitened.

"I see," he said quietly, when she had finished.

"What do you see, Nelac?" asked Cadvan swiftly.

"It is certainly a foredream, and it has too much in common with Lanorgil's prophecy for my comfort," he said. Maerad looked down to hide her expression; she felt queasy. *"Look to the north!* I wonder what that means. It appears to me, Maerad, that if indeed you are to search for the Treesong, you must look north. But it's also a warning. There is much amiss here. It seems to me imperative that Maerad be instated as soon as possible, so we know for sure if she is the Fated One. I will ask for a Council tomorrow."

"That is what I think too," said Saliman soberly. "But it grows late, and all this talk has made me tired. I think it's time for some wine."

After their conference Maerad wanted some fresh air, so Cadvan showed her the First Circle. She stared at the buildings, marveling at the graceful towers. They were mostly round, although some were oddly shaped, with nine or seven sides, and many were roofed with gilded tiles. Around the windows and doors were carved strange faces, some grotesque, some of surpassing beauty, and inscriptions in ancient runes. They were built of white stone joined with such skill that some looked as if they were carved from a single block, and against the white walls flowered anarech trees, which grew in few places elsewhere in Annar. The anarech were tall and graceful, with black bark and long leaves silver beneath and dark on top, so when they rippled in the wind they looked like fountains of moving light and shadow. They were now in full flower, and after the previous night's storm the streets were crimson with fallen petals.

There was little other vegetation in the streets of Norloch: the citadel was austere, eschewing mere prettiness. There was something that bothered Maerad, but at first she couldn't put her finger on it; it took her a while to work out what it was. She couldn't hear the voices of children anywhere. No child laughed in the hidden courtyards or played in the lanes; the people who walked the streets were adult and grave, and she saw very few women. Like Nelac's house, Maerad thought Norloch was grand and beautiful; but it also seemed cold, more conscious of its majesty than of the living beat of human life.

Cadvan, however, who was used to the glory of Norloch, was deep in thought. "I'm glad that Nelac and Saliman agree with what I think about you," he said as they walked. "It eases me. I am all but convinced, but to some it might be such a mad idea that it could take more than all the signs we have. It gives me hope that the First Circle will instate you."

"What if they do, and I'm not the One?" Maerad said hopefully. The thought lifted a weight off her heart.

"Then I am wrong, that is all," said Cadvan, smiling. "I could take you to a good School, maybe to Gent, since that is not far from here, and you could complete your learning."

Maerad thought for a while, remembering what Dernhil had said to her about continuing her studies. She would like to see his School. "Would you stay there?" she asked, knowing the answer already.

He glanced at her quickly, his face unreadable. "For a time, until you were settled in," he said.

"I'd like that best of all," Maerad said meditatively. "Not to be the One, and to learn reading and writing properly. Maybe Hem could come too. All that other stuff still seems ridiculous to me." She remembered the rhyme Saliman had sung: *Edil-Amarandh to save*. "What could *I* do?"

"None of us know what we can do," said Cadvan. "Perhaps you are not the One, though even Nelac now is certain that you are. Perhaps it *is* ridiculous. We will know for sure soon, one way or the other." They walked on in silence.

When Maerad returned from her walk, Hem asked if she would come to his scrying. She was curious to see what scrying looked like from the outside, and she eagerly assented.

"It's not usual for anyone to be there," said Nelac dubiously. "Scrying is a very private thing. But neither is it usual to scry a child." They were again in Nelac's sitting room, the late afternoon sun streaming through the windows. Hem was standing with his back turned to Nelac, looking out into the garden.

"I'd like it better if Maerad was there," he said. Despite his cocksure veneer, Hem was unable to conceal the nervousness in his voice, and Maerad's heart lurched with pity. What if the scrying revealed that Hem was not her brother, after all? She'd still feel the same about him, she thought. Somehow they belonged to each other.

"Of course I'll be there, if you want," she said warmly, glancing sideways at Nelac. He nodded.

"That's fair," he said gently. "And now is as good a time as any. Waiting is usually the worst part of any ordeal. Yes, Hem?"

Hem nodded dolefully, looking as if he were being led to his execution. Nelac took them to a room Maerad hadn't seen before, which she thought must be Nelac's study. It was much bigger than Dernhil's, lined from floor to ceiling with books and laid with a richly dyed blue carpet, and it looked out on the same garden as the sitting room. In the corner was a huge gilt harp, carved in the semblance of a dragon, and next to that a big oak desk. As in every other room in Nelac's quarters, parchments and scrolls and papers were piled everywhere, and among them were more curious objects: figurines of alabaster and jasper, and models of ships and musical instruments carved intricately out of polished wood and stone. But then her attention turned to Hem and Nelac.

As Cadvan had done in the Irihel with Maerad, Nelac asked Hem to stand in front of him, and they placed their hands on each other's shoulders. With a slight shock, Maerad saw that Hem was almost as tall as Nelac. Hem glanced nervously over to Maerad, and she winked at him encouragingly. He gulped, and then looked into Nelac's eyes.

"Now, Hem," said Nelac in the Speech, "relax." He muttered a few words that Maerad could not catch, and began to glimmer with the same silver light as when he had healed Cadvan. This time it was not so intense; it was a gentler radiance, as mild as starlight. It seemed to Maerad that light gathered around Hem as well, only the luminosity around him was slightly different: more golden. A beam of light seemed to link their eyes, though when she blinked she wasn't sure if she really saw it at all, or just imagined it from the intensity of their gaze.

Hem seemed to fall into a trance; his eyes went completely blank, as if he saw nothing around him. Then his hands clutched Nelac's shoulders, and for a second he seemed to struggle, and then his face went completely white. She couldn't see Nelac's expression, as he was facing away from her. Maerad bit her lip with anxiety; was Hem all right? Then, much more quickly than she expected, Nelac leaned forward and kissed Hem's brow, and he let go of his shoulders. Hem's hands dropped away from Nelac, as if he were exhausted, and the light in both of them died away.

"Well done, Hem," said Nelac softly. "It is a hard thing."

Hem sat down abruptly on the floor. His face was still pale, but his expression was more open than Maerad had ever seen it. He looked up at her and then, to her surprise, blushed.

"I saw you," he said. "I mean, I remembered you. I didn't before. You were a little girl, but you looked big to me. You looked just the same." He halted, an intolerable grief gathering in his eyes. "Father was holding me." His face crumpled, and he covered it with his hands, and Maerad saw that his shoulders were shaking. She felt suddenly the truth of Nelac's admonition about the privacy of scrying; this was a sorrow more intimate than even a sister could share.

She turned away from Hem to Nelac, feeling a glow of relief spreading through her body. Now all doubt was gone; Hem was her brother, beyond question. She hadn't realized how anxious she had been.

Nelac looked weary, as if he had labored long in thought. "Yes, it's true. Hem is your brother," he said, catching her eye. "I am very glad that Hem agreed to this. It makes me much surer in my mind. The more we are sure of in these doubtful times, the better." He fumbled around for a chair, and sat down, passing his hand over his eyes. "I'm not as young as I was," he said. "It's a tiring business, looking into another's soul. I can quite see why Cadvan didn't wish to scry Hem. There is much anguish there." He sighed heavily.

Maerad stood awkwardly before both of them, feeling like an intruder. "Can I get you something?" she asked at last. "A drink, maybe?"

Nelac smiled wanly. "A glass of laradhel would be most welcome, thank you, Maerad."

Maerad left the room with a feeling of release. She brought back two glasses of the laradhel, leaving one by Hem on the floor, and then left them alone. It didn't feel right to be there.

At dinner that night, Hem was absent: he had gone to his chamber after the scrying and had not reappeared. Saliman arched an eyebrow. "He *must* be tired, to miss a meal," he said. "Cadvan tells me the scrying went well?"

"Yes, it confirmed everything we discussed earlier today," said Nelac briefly. "There's no doubt now." Maerad thought he still looked weary.

Nelac said then that he had arranged a Council for the following afternoon. "Enkir was curious to know what you had to say that was important enough for a full Council," he said, glancing at Cadvan. "I told him you had news from the north."

"That's true enough," said Cadvan. "Important news, as it happens."

"And I also said that Saliman bore messages from the Circle of Turbansk, which require the deliberation of all the Bards. It was a little trickier to get permission for Maerad to attend. If I had said we wanted to bring a girl, he would have refused outright. In the end, I told him that Cadvan wished to bring his student. Even he wouldn't dare to throw her out, in front of the whole Circle."

"Do I have to go?" asked Maerad, her heart sinking. She had hoped that she would be excused.

"It's crucial that you are there," Nelac answered. "They need to sense your Gift for themselves. So, yes, I'm afraid you have to go."

Maerad made a face. She didn't like the sound of Norloch's First Circle at all.

"I strongly suggest that we omit any mention of the Elementals, and of Maerad's lyre," Nelac continued. "I think that, for now, we should speak just of our surmise that Maerad is the One, and say why."

"I agree," said Saliman, wiping his plate with some bread and chewing it with relish. "Any suggestion of a connection with the Elidhu, and the more doubtful Bards would instantly balk. I see no reason, either, to mention Hem. Only we three know who he is, and only those of this house even know he is here. I think it would complicate our case."

"There are no spies in this house, if that is what you are suggesting," Nelac said. "But I take your point."

"The Hulls' interest in Hem strengthens our argument," objected Cadvan.

"Yes, but do you think they're going to believe that you've found *two* Bards of Pellinor?" said Saliman. "The Kulag, the wight, and that little episode with the Landrost should be enough to give pause. Some of the Circle would think we were gilding the lily already; presenting them with too many marvels at once would be a mistake. One thing at a time."

"And no mention of the Treesong?" said Cadvan doubtfully.

"No, I think not," said Nelac. "Definitely not. That can come later, when we can prove Maerad is the One. For the moment, we must just argue for her instatement under these

special circumstances. That will be difficult enough. She is a
woman, for a start, and she has none of the correct training."

"It's about factions," Saliman explained to Maerad. "We
have to be careful. If it's Nelac, Cadvan, and me presenting an
argument, it will be seen as a bid for power by Nelac."

"Why?" asked Maerad, bewildered.

"Because Nelac was mentor to both of us, when we were
young Bards," said Saliman. "So we're seen to be on his side.
There's the question of the One being a woman, to begin with.
Enkir will see that as a direct attack on him. And for some, that
will be enough to discount our arguments altogether."

"But isn't it more important than that?" asked Maerad.

Cadvan sighed impatiently. "How I hate these politics!"
he said.

"You, my friend," said Saliman, pointing his bread at him,
"have never been politic. That's your main problem. I, however,
come from the south, where politics is an art. It would be better,
Nelac, if another Bard were to present our plea."

"I've thought of that," said Nelac. "But I daren't mention
Maerad's claim to anyone else in the Circle. Caragal, perhaps,
but I can't guess what he would say. I cannot be sure enough of
their discretion. It is likely that it would instantly be known to
everybody, and would be dismissed before we could even get
to the Council. We must present it fully and fairly, before all the
Circle, untainted by gossip. That is our only chance."

For some time they all sat in contemplative silence.

Cadvan nodded. "All right then, I agree," he said. "The most
important thing now is Maerad's instatement. Tomorrow,
then!" He lifted his glass, and the rest followed.

Maerad raised her glass more slowly than the others. She
felt sick with apprehension at the thought of the Council.
Tomorrow her fate would be decided, and she didn't feel ready
at all.

XXII

THE FIRST CIRCLE
OF NORLOCH

HEM was busy all the next morning; after breakfast Maerad didn't see him at all. Saliman was taking him in hand. "A bath, a haircut, and some proper clothes, and you won't recognize him," Saliman murmured as they ate breakfast.

"You're taking his welfare deeply to heart," Maerad said, smiling.

"Yes, I am," said Saliman, suddenly quite serious. "I like your Hem, monkey though he is. He'll make a good Bard one day, if he learns the right things. He might as well start now."

As the day wore on toward the Council, which was to be convened at the midafternoon bell, Maerad became more and more agitated. She had nothing to do: Hem, Saliman, Cadvan, and Nelac were all out. She walked around the First Circle, but found she could take nothing in; she wandered to the Library, but felt too daunted by the stern looks of the librarians to look around properly, and, in any case, it conjured memories of Dernhil, which confused her already disordered feelings. Brin, Nelac's housemaster, brought lunch to her room, as everyone was still out. Afterward she tried to read some of the books in her room, but she couldn't concentrate at all. Half an hour before the Council, she was in such a state she could hardly speak.

Cadvan had advised her to dress formally and to wear her sword and brooch. Alone in her chamber, she put on the long crimson dress and tied her hair back in a braid, her fingers trembling. She could scarcely pin on the brooch, and when she tried to strap on her blade, Irigan, she dropped it, the clatter of the scabbard making her jump. When Cadvan knocked on her door, arrayed in black and silver with his sword at his side, he took one look at her white face and clasped her hand.

"Maerad, even if we get nowhere with this Council, it will be no failing of yours," he said. "Remember that! Not everything hangs on the First Circle!"

Maerad smiled weakly in reply. Cadvan looked at her a little more closely.

"They're only Bards," he said gently. "Why so afraid? You've dealt with Bards before, and much worse. Come, this isn't the Maerad I know!"

Maerad nodded and tried to look braver. She looked at Cadvan's marred face: he had faced death without quailing. A lot of old Bards weren't nearly as frightening. She felt slightly reassured, but she still couldn't control the deeper apprehension in her breast, or the trembling in her knees. She hoped that her shaking legs were completely hidden by her robe. Wordlessly, with a feeling of doom, she followed Cadvan down the corridor. When they passed Nelac's students on the stairs, she turned her face away so she didn't have to greet them. She didn't feel able to speak.

They met Saliman downstairs, and together they bent their steps to the Tower of Machelinor, the highest and fairest in that city of high and fair towers. At its base was a single domed building, the Crystal Hall of Machelinor, and this they entered through wide, gold-embossed doors, just as the hour bell tolled in the tower high above them.

Maerad gasped when she walked in; her first impression was of a blinding blaze of light, a surge of mighty power. This was the center of the Light in Norloch, in all of Annar, and its force pounded in her ears, making her dizzy. She shook her head, trying to clear it, and looked around.

It was the most beautiful hall she had ever seen. The floor was of polished stone, pearl white and rose and black, with gold runes inset all around the perimeter. The zenith of the ceiling was crystal, and light also streamed in through windows set high in the plainly adorned white walls, filling the airy space with radiance. Around the walls were black plinths on which were set curious statues, some clearly of Bards, some of figures of an unearthly beauty that seemed barely human. They were made of bronze or marble or carved of a solid rock of crystal, and all were leaved with bright gilt that threw back the light in flickering beams. At the far end of the room were more golden doors wrought in intricate designs of birds dancing amid trees of flame. These were shut; beyond them lay the winding stairs to the Tower of Machelinor, which rose in a single leap so that one who climbed to its loftiest height stood a thousand feet over the Meads of the Carmallachen. The Bardsighted could gaze eastward over the entire realm of Annar to the Osidh Annova, or turn westward and look over the measureless expanse of the ocean; and thus the First Bards of Annar saw much of what passed in the realms of Annar and the Seven Kingdoms. For this reason the tower was also known as Dancsel, or Farsight, although in the northern speech that phrase could also mean the Cold Heart.

But Maerad's gaze was pulled to the center of the hall, where the floor was raised in a circular dais on which was placed a huge round table carved of black stone. The table and the stone chairs around it were completely plain, without decoration of any kind. On it were placed goblets of gold and a golden ewer, and in its center was a huge natural crystal of adamant that, alone of all things there, was unshaped by human hands; the light in the hall passed through it and broke around the walls in flickering rainbows, and in its center dwelled a white fire.

Maerad's feelings of dismay deepened as the three of them walked slowly toward the table. It seemed a very long way, and her feet were heavy with reluctance.

She saw that nine figures were seated there. They would have seemed dwarfed in that huge space but for the sense of power that emanated from them, which grew stronger the closer she approached. There were far fewer people sitting than there were chairs, so each Bard sat alone, with empty chairs on either side. Maerad gulped and glanced at Cadvan; his face was unreadable. Her mouth had gone completely dry. She fought a sudden strong impulse to run out of the Hall, out of the First Circle, out of Norloch altogether. Steadily she paced on.

At last, Maerad reached the High Table of the First Circle of Norloch. She and Cadvan and Saliman stood by the table while the Nine Bards of the First Circle regarded them in silence. Maerad was sure, in the absolute silence that filled the Hall after their footsteps had ceased, that her thumping heart must be audible to everyone there. She looked down at her feet, desperately trying to gather together her scattered wits. It was as if the force beating through the Crystal Hall wouldn't let her think or see; all her awareness was dissolved in the pulsing heart of the Light.

She heard someone stand up and speak. It must be Enkir, the First Bard, she thought. His voice was icy and clear.

"Welcome to the Council of the First Circle of Norloch, Saliman of Turbansk and Cadvan of Lirigon," the voice said. And then it was edged with a barely concealed spite or anger. "And who is this other you dare to bring here, into the very inner sanctum of the Light?"

Maerad heard Cadvan's voice ring out confidently beside her.

"My Lords, Bards of the First Circle, I wish to present to you my student, Maerad of Pellinor."

As Cadvan said her name, Maerad relucatantly dragged her eyes up from her feet.

Directly before her, on the other side of the table, stood a tall, thin Bard dressed in white robes. He was staring straight at her, and his nostrils were pinched white with rage. He had a fierce, hooked nose set between dark, flaming eyes, and deep lines furrowed between his nose and his mouth. His brow was high and white, and also deeply lined. It was a proud, intelligent face, pitiless as a hawk at the moment that it stoops for a rabbit; but it was cold, as a beast never is, and beneath the coldness Maerad sensed a bitter cruelty. So Maerad first perceived Enkir, First Bard of Norloch; and as her eyes met his, her dizziness overbore her and she felt her knees buckle beneath her, and her sight went black.

She knew that face. She had seen it before.

The world shattered into pieces around her, whirling into a storm of confused images. Maerad collapsed to the floor, but she was not aware of Cadvan and Saliman bending over her in alarm, nor of the murmured consternation of the other Bards.

The towers of Pellinor were burning.

The darkness itself seemed to be screaming. There was a chaos of noise: the roar of flames, the crack of stone and wood buckling and crashing, yelling, the clang of metal on metal. Maerad squeezed her eyes shut, but still the noise went on and on and on. She sobbed with terror.

Someone was carrying her. Her mother. She pressed her face into her shoulder, breathing in her warm scent to block out the acrid stench of smoke and another smell, unfamiliar and much worse, the reek of blood. She was being jolted up and down; it hurt.

"Don't cry, Maerad," her mother whispered in her ear.

"There's my brave girl." She looked into her mother's face, glimmering whitely in the darkness. Milana was not afraid. Her face was smirched with ash, grim with despair and grief. But she was not afraid. She was as hard and beautiful as adamant. Maerad swallowed her tears.

"What happened to my daddy?" she whispered.

Milana's face twisted with anguish. "We'll tell later," she said.

But Maerad knew what had happened to her daddy. She had seen him hacked down just inside the walls of Pellinor, as the cruel men had burst through the gate with brands of fire and black swords.

"And where's Cai?"

"Cai's with Branar," Milana said, between gasps. Branar was a friend of her father's. "We'll meet them in the Linar Caves. Just be brave, my little one. We must be very quiet."

Soon they were running through the outer streets of Pellinor: tiny cobbled lanes that were eerily empty. The sound of the flames was now muted, but they still cast flickering red shadows over them; Pellinor's topmost tower was on fire. Milana's feet sounded too loud; her footsteps echoed off the walls. After a while, Milana said: "I have to put you down now. My arms hurt. Can you run?" Maerad nodded, and Milana clutched her hand, and they ran together. Maerad's chest felt as if knives were going in, but still she ran.

They turned and twisted around the corners, Milana always stopping sharp and peering around, and then dashing down the street, but they saw no one. Where was everybody? Maerad was too frightened now to cry. Milana's hand bit into hers, and she shook it to loosen the grip, but Milana didn't notice.

At last they reached Milana's goal, a small, stout door in the outer wall of Pellinor that Maerad had never seen before. It was completely hidden by a veil of ivy, and hastily Milana pushed the tendrils back and, fumbling at her waist, brought out a bunch of iron keys. She sorted through them, panting, and at last found the right one, which she thrust into the keyhole and turned with both hands. She shot back the bolts and pushed it open. It swung out with a loud creak, and she started and looked around. Nobody was there. She dragged Maerad through and pushed the door shut behind her.

But somebody was waiting for them outside the door.

"Where are you going, Milana of Pellinor?" A tall shape loomed in the darkness. Milana gasped and pulled Maerad close to her. She heard the whisper of metal as Milana drew her sword. The voice laughed softly.

"Don't think that any blade will wound me."

"Enkir." Milana's voice wobbled with relief, and then she stood straighter, and the darkness around them was illuminated by a silver light, blooming softly from Milana. "What are you doing here?"

"I asked where you were going," said Enkir harshly. Maerad peeked out from her mother's cloak; the light glimmered on the Bard, so she could see his face outlined in silver. His eyes were lost in darkness, and black shadows carved his face.

"What business is that of yours?" said Milana fiercely. "Are you blind? Are you deaf? Do you not know what has happened?"

"I thought you'd try to escape here. The secret ways of Pellinor are not unknown to me." Enkir stooped forward, staring into Milana's eyes. "I want your son. Now. Where is he?"

Maerad, close against her mother, felt her go very still. She didn't answer, but the light around her brightened. Dropping the sword, Milana lifted her hands, and Maerad's head buzzed with her power. She felt, almost like the clash of swords, Enkir's will answering her; the collision of the two forces shivered through her. Milana stepped back, her eyes wide with shock.

"So it was *you* who let them in!" she cried. "Treacherous

fool!" She stretched out her hands again, and a bolt of light hit Enkir. For a second it seemed that he would fall, but he collected himself and stepped slowly toward her, his face suddenly cold.

"No, Milana," said Enkir, with a cruel smile. "*You* are the fool. All your petty Bard powers are no use against me. I can crush you like an ant." He leaned forward and hissed savagely. "Your days are done, you Bards, prattling childishly of the Balance and jabbering your witless songs. I have seen the future; I know what it is. Only those with the wit will survive."

"You're mad!" Milana gasped. But then Enkir grabbed Maerad, pulling her out of Milana's grasp so suddenly that her nails raked Maerad's hand. Maerad screamed: his fingers pinioned her arm like steel. She felt something cold against her neck and screamed again. Enkir held a blade against her throat.

"Tell me where the boy is," said Enkir. "Or I will cut the girl's throat."

"I don't know," said Milana desperately. "I don't know where he is."

"I'm in a hurry! Don't play me for a dunce. You know where he is. I know he's not in Pellinor." Enkir pressed the blade closer to Maerad's throat, and she felt it cut her; a trickle of blood tickled down her neck. "Tell me, or the girl dies now."

Milana stood, white and still, the light within her fading.

"You'll kill both of us, anyway," she said coldly, after a long silence. "No. I won't tell you."

Maerad looked frantically at Milana. Was she just going to let her die?

Enkir paused, as if momentarily at a loss. Then he started to laugh softly. Maerad's skin crawled.

"No, Milana, I will not kill you," he said. "I do not wish to kill the boy either. I'll let the girl go too. Come, I can be a reasonable man."

Milana spat on the ground. "That's what the word of a traitor is worth!"

"Not to kill you would amuse me. That should reassure you. I could even make a few coins out of the deal." Enkir paused. "And you could have your daughter. Who otherwise will die, slowly, in terrible pain, in front of you."

"Don't!" screamed Maerad. "Don't let him hurt me!"

Milana's face contorted in an agony of indecision.

"Give her back!" she said suddenly.

"Tell me where the boy is!" He pressed the blade closer, and it cut Maerad again, and she started to weep. She stared desperately at her mother, terrified she wouldn't tell, that she would let this man kill her.

Milana's face suddenly crumpled. "He was taken to the Linar Caves. I don't know if he's there." For a second she lost all self-control, and hid her face in her hands.

There was an awful moment of stillness, and then Maerad felt Enkir's iron grip release, and he pushed her toward her mother. She stumbled over to Milana and clung to her legs, sobbing hysterically.

"See, Milana?" said Enkir quietly, a vicious triumph in his voice. "I keep my word. Now, I wish to see if you have kept yours."

He strode forward and grabbed Milana's chin, forcing her to look into his eyes. Maerad looked up in panic. What was he doing to her mother? Enkir's eyes stabbed red flames, and Milana didn't seem able to move, staring transfixed at his blazing eyes and shaking all over. Suddenly she collapsed, and all the light went out of her. Maerad stood trembling by Milana, staring dumbstruck at the tall man. He was standing over Milana's still body, his face shiny with sweat. He ignored Maerad completely, as if she weren't there.

"That's the end of you, Milana of Pellinor," he said, breathing hard. "There's a lesson in that. How easy it is to break your paltry kind!" He wiped his face with his hand and spat on the ground. "You'll make a slave, anyway. Not much of a slave." He kicked Milana's body, smiling with such malignancy that Maerad hid her face in terror, feeling the roaring in her ears, her world spinning, breaking, spinning . . .

Her cheek was pressed on cold marble, and somebody stroked her brow gently, saying her name. The roaring began to abate, and Maerad stirred.

"She moves," said the voice. She realized it was Cadvan. Maerad kept her eyes closed, battling to regain herself. She was in the Crystal Hall of Machelinor, she remembered now, at the Council, and at last she knew what had happened to her mother. . . .

Enkir, the First Bard of Norloch! Her whole being clenched in hatred. Treachery, treachery . . .

How could she have forgotten? The torment of the memory was its own answer. It had sunk to the darkest part of her mind. If she had let herself remember that—the merciless breaking of Milana, the malice of Enkir, her own childish terror—she would have gone mad. But now she knew, and she would not go mad. She let her head loll, feigning unconsciousness. How long since she fainted? What now?

"Perhaps she hit her head on the floor?" Saliman's voice was close by. She couldn't have been out for long, then. Perhaps a few seconds. She waited until her mind was a little clearer, and then moved, groaning.

Somebody slipped a hand under her head and lifted it. She fluttered her eyes open and saw Cadvan's face close to hers. He held a goblet filled with water. "Drink this," he said. She sipped obediently, and then sat up.

"I . . . I'm sorry," she said. "I don't know what happened." The sense of power that had so dizzied her before was still there, but now it no longer muddled her mind. She felt completely lucid, her mind clearer perhaps than it had ever been. Her first thought was that she could not let Enkir know that she recognized him. It would probably make no difference; he was no doubt signing her death warrant in his head right now. Her name was enough for that.

Slowly she got to her feet, and then turned to the table of Bards and bowed. She saw Nelac to her left, staring at her in concern.

"I ask the Bards of the First Circle and you, Enkir, First Bard, to forgive my weakness," she said. "I was overwhelmed by the honor of being here." Her voice was steady and certain, and Cadvan glanced at her with surprise.

"Then please sit down," snapped Enkir. She met his eyes, veiling her expression with polite humility; he stared at her coldly. She realized that he could do nothing to her here, in front of all the First Circle, without revealing his treachery. She took her place at the table, between Saliman and Cadvan, and the Council began.

Saliman spoke first, telling of increasing pressures in the Suderain: continual harassment from the forces of the Black Sorcerer Imank in Dén Raven, which was increasing in both frequency and power.

"We are now hard beset, and if we fall, then all Annar lies open to the Black Army," he said. "So the Circle of Turbansk sent me to ask for help. I have traveled north and east in Annar since this winter, and I think now that help cannot come. Your borders are already threatened. Yet still I ask." He nodded and sat down.

"We will consider this," said Enkir. "Thank you, Saliman of

Turbansk. And now, Cadvan of Lirigon. We hear that you come bearing news from the north." He glanced at Maerad as he said this, and despite her resolve, she shivered.

Cadvan spoke first of his capture and subsequent escape from the Landrost. "It is very clear to me now," he concluded. "From what I saw in the Landrost's throne room, I am certain that the Nameless One has indeed returned and that the recent troubles of Annar do, as some of us have feared, stem from his stratagems."

An audible stir went around the table.

"I remain to be convinced," said Enkir, staring at Cadvan with dislike. Maerad looked between the two Bards: surely they were somehow alike? A dreadful doubt began to stir within her; she struggled with some memory, something the Hulls had said. . . .

"But of course there are many of the lesser Dark who would like us to believe such a thing. You admit yourself you were weakened, and I question your judgment. How can you be so sure that you are not misled, Cadvan of Lirigon?"

"If I am indeed a Truthteller, then what I saw in the throne room was true," Cadvan answered. "But tell me, Enkir of Norloch,"—and here Maerad caught a flash of mockery in his eyes—"what makes you so certain that he will *not* return? Has not the Lore always spoken of that as a certainty?"

"The Lore is open to many interpretations, as well you know, Cadvan of Lirigon," answered Enkir. "I counsel caution on this subject."

"Hulls ride openly in Annar, the Schools are threatened or corrupted, we are beset from all sides: evil fears, long chained, are awoken in this land, and you counsel caution!" said Cadvan heatedly.

"What do you mean?" asked another Bard. "Saliman spoke of Hulls. . . ."

"I have not finished my tale, Tared," Cadvan replied. "I beg you, bear with me. Before I journeyed down the Empty Realm to the east of the Annova and was captured by the Landrost, I went, as I was instructed, north to Zmarkan. I traveled there from west to east, and I heard many rumors of unrest and travail. Many people, and not all of them fools, say that a black power has awoken there, an ancient power. I followed the rumors to their source, as far north as I could go. There, in the wastes, a shadow is spreading. I saw from afar the peaks of its fortress, and I felt its deadly breath. I can think only one thing: the renegade Elidhu, the Ice Witch, the Winterking himself, is now woken from his long sleep, and seeks to reestablish his sway over the north."

There was an astonished silence.

"Surely this cannot be!" said a short Bard on Cadvan's right. "The Winterking was banished beyond the circles of the world, long, long ago." He shook his head.

"It cannot be, Caragal, and yet it is so," said Cadvan, turning to face him. "Just as some say the Nameless cannot return, and yet he does."

Caragal nodded sadly. "The Flame ever darkens," he said. "I cannot argue that."

"Now," said Cadvan, "we come to the nub of this tale. For it seems to me certain, as I have said, that all the signs we have traced in the past years are, as we feared, the mark of the Nameless as he prepares his most deadly assault against the Light. And worse, that he has made alliance with the Winterking. I suspect that the Nameless himself brought him back."

"There are many kinds of shadow," said Enkir mockingly. "We must not leap in fear to the worst conclusions."

"I am convinced of his return," said Cadvan. "And I think if we do not move now, then we are lost."

"Move where?" Enkir smiled. Maerad thought it as cold as

the glimmer of winterlight over frost. "Always you were impulsive, Cadvan of Lirigon, and apt to leap where the more wise might pause and see an abyss."

"Do you claim that I lie?" said Cadvan. He seemed calm, almost serene, but Maerad sensed an overwhelming anger rising within him. There was a tense pause, and then Enkir smiled again.

"I would not have the temerity to say any such thing," he answered smoothly. "I say only that what you suggest is unlikely in the extreme. The Winterking, the Nameless: such figures are shadows from a child's tale of fear. I think, for all your well-meaning enthusiasm, that you are mistaken, Cadvan of Lirigon."

The insult was clear, and Maerad saw a faint flush in Cadvan's cheek. He took Enkir's eye and held it, and it seemed the two wrestled together, although neither moved. Maerad held her breath. They *were* alike. She could not say how. Her heart hammered painfully in her breast. At the last, it was the older Bard who desisted and looked down.

"Your arrogance will be your downfall, Cadvan of Lirigon," he said, and his voice was icy with rage. "It takes no Seer to prophesy that."

There was another uncomfortable silence. The Nine seemed all to be inspecting their fingernails, except for Nelac, whose face betrayed exasperation: whether with Cadvan or with Enkir, Maerad could not tell. At length, Caragal stirred. "I think, Enkir, we should give some credence to this. I myself am disturbed by the movements of Hulls."

"There is more," said Cadvan. "I have yet to tell the bulk of my tale, and the news of most importance."

Maerad looked at him with a silent plea, willing Cadvan to stop, to say nothing of his suspicions that she was the Foretold, not to betray her to Enkir. Mistaking it for nerves, he smiled at her reassuringly, and then plunged into the tale of their adventures. Maerad's heart shrank, colder and colder, as he spoke. She saw Enkir shooting glances at her, and each glance was deadly. How could Cadvan not know?

Suddenly, with a blinding shock at her own folly, she remembered what had been nagging her earlier. Cadvan had known one of the Hulls who attacked them in the Broken Teeth on the Edinur Downs. Likud. That was his name. What had he said? *Think we have forgotten, Cadvan, how eagerly you studied the secrets of the Dark?*

Maerad stopped listening and sank into a black reverie. Was Cadvan a traitor as well? Her soul felt as if it were dying within her, but she bleakly followed her thoughts. Treachery was what had killed her mother; if she wasn't careful, it could be the cause of her own death as well. Maybe Cadvan and Enkir were rivals in the service of the Dark; maybe that was the real source of the enmity between them. And if so, she was trapped, a trophy to be bartered between them, until such time as she was no longer useful.

She suddenly felt unutterably lonely, more lonely than even in the worst days at Gilman's Cot. She was on her own now. As she had always been, since her mother was murdered: murdered twice, she thought bitterly, once by Enkir, and once by Gilman. No, she had Hem, at least she had Hem. Now she had to find Hem and get out of Norloch, out of Enkir's clutches. Could she trust Cadvan? She always had; but perhaps the friendship he had shown her had all been sham, a pretense to lull her into his power. How well did she know him, really?

But now Enkir was speaking, his voice sharp with disbelief. Or was it rage? "And you are asking us to believe that this girl, who not three months ago was a mere slave, this girl, whom you admit freely can barely read, who has not the fortitude even to walk into the Crystal Hall without fainting, is the One who was Foretold?"

"I have told you the evidence," said Cadvan calmly. "It is compelling, and I think at least we have to say that it is likely. At the very least, we must instate her, so we can be sure whether it is so or not."

Saliman, who had been staring down at the table through all of Cadvan's narration, now looked up. "I think that perhaps the Dark is more apt to move than we are, and perhaps quicker to recognize its own danger," he said. "It would seem to me a serious misjudgment to forbid this. I too have heard the evidence, and I believe that Cadvan is correct. I urge you to consider his advice seriously."

"The Nameless returns, the Winterking stirs, and the Foretold appears in the guise of a wretched girl?" Enkir's eyes flashed with malice. "It is a pretty bundle of news you bring with you, and no mistake. You should be a troubador, Cadvan of Lirigon, and travel the hamlets, scaring the peasants. It will not do here."

There was an uncomfortable pause, and Enkir cast Maerad another look of dislike. "Do not think I have not had separate word of this . . . discovery of yours," he said. "You do not have a monopoly on information, Cadvan of Lirigon. If you think to surprise me, you are wrong. The only thing that surprises me is your temerity."

A clear vision of Helgar gazing at her spitefully during the Council in Innail rose in Maerad's mind. She felt suddenly certain that Helgar had sent word to Enkir of the Innail Meet. Perhaps Helgar, who was a Bard of Ettinor, was a Hull too? It was all so confusing. . . . And the force of the Light beating in that room seemed to be growing stronger again; it made thinking difficult. Her head began to pulse with an incipient headache.

Nelac spoke for the first time. "I am convinced of the truth of this argument," he said. The other Bards turned to look at him, listening gravely. "It would risk little to instate her, and I fear what may happen if we do not. I too strongly counsel this action. I recommend that we instate Maerad of Pellinor with the greatest urgency."

"The true treachery lies in those who seek to distract us with false fears, dispersing our proper vigilance," said Enkir dangerously. "I must ask why you seek to present us with such arguments, at such a time?"

There was an electric silence.

"My fealty to the Light is without question, and I wonder that you impugn it," said Nelac quietly. "I suggest you think again, Enkir."

"It is not your fealty I question, Nelac," said Enkir, unable to hide his spite. "I know you have a blind spot where Cadvan of Lirigon is concerned. Perhaps the soft partiality of a mentor for his former student might be excused, but we all know that Cadvan's history is a little . . . checkered."

At this, Maerad looked up. Had she been blind? Again and again people had hinted of something dubious in Cadvan's past. Why had she so blithely taken no notice of them?

"I do not doubt Nelac's good will," said a dark-haired Bard next to Nelac. "Nevertheless, I think, like Enkir, that Cadvan's tale beggars belief." Several others nodded. "There are so many other explanations for the ills that beset our realm. This is only the most fantastic."

Enkir glared at Nelac. "It is not so easy to become a Bard of the White Flame. It would be an insult even to consider instating a boy of this inexperience to such a height, let alone a girl. I forbid it. I will waste my time discussing this matter no more; my judgment has been given. We shall give thought to the other issues raised here, and make our doom known."

He looked around the table and met the gaze of each Bard of the First Circle. Only Nelac, Caragal, Tared, and another Bard, whom Maerad had not heard speak, shook their heads.

"Five against four. You are outvoted, Nelac. The First Circle has decided." Enkir looked to Nelac with a flash of triumph. "The petitioners are dismissed."

Maerad had listened to the debate indifferently. It no longer mattered to her whether she was instated or not. She felt a bile rising in her throat, a hatred of all these men, a hatred of Enkir most of all—Enkir, the most treacherous. He was, she thought, out of place at a round table; he should be in a high seat with his minions at the level of his knees.

All the Bards stood and bowed, and wordlessly Maerad, Cadvan, and Saliman left the Crystal Hall. Behind her, Maerad heard the Bards sit down again, their voices rising in argument.

She paced dully through the streets of the First Circle, blind to the beauty around her. Her thoughts made her feel nauseous. If Cadvan was a traitor, she felt that she couldn't bear it. But how could she trust him now?

XXIII

OLD SCARS

THAT was a total disaster," said Saliman disgustedly. He unbuckled his sword and leaned it against the wall. "Well, first things first. I sorely need a drink."

They had walked back to Nelac's house in oppressed silence. Maerad was wrapped deeply in her thoughts; she was scarcely aware of the other two Bards.

"A glass of good ale would be very welcome," Cadvan said to Saliman. "You'd probably get something in the kitchens, if you asked Brin."

"I'll see if I can find anything," said Saliman, and he left the room.

"I'm sorry," said Cadvan, smiling at Maerad crookedly. "I knew it would be a challenge to convince the First Circle; but I confess the depth of resistance to your instatement surprised me. I thought that there would have been room for some doubt there, given what we had to say."

Maerad glowered at him, and he looked taken aback.

"It's not the end of the world," he said. "There are other alternatives. When Nelac returns, we'll be able to discuss what to do. The best possible course would have been to have you instated in the sight of the Bards of Annar. That has now been strictly forbidden." Cadvan settled into a chair by the fire, taking off his own sword. "Sit down, Maerad," he said, waving his hand. "And look not so black; our failure is no reflection on you."

Maerad lifted her eyes to his and stared into him. For the

first time Cadvan realized the force of her fury, and for a second he looked staggered. He started out of the chair.

"By the Light, Maerad, what's wrong?" he said. "We just failed to convince a few Bards. That's a setback, I agree—"

"Where's Hem?" Maerad's voice was cold and hard.

"I don't know. Probably in the kitchens."

"I'll go find him." She turned to leave, but Cadvan took her arm and spun her around, earnestly examining her face. At last he spoke softly. "What's wrong, Maerad? What's happened to you?"

"Perhaps I have no need of you." Maerad looked at him with hatred. No, she wouldn't be taken in by his wiles this time.

"Have you gone mad?" Cadvan's face was pale, and the whiplashes stood out starkly against it. For a second Maerad faltered.

"No." She thought again of the Hull Likud at the Broken Teeth, and hardened herself. "Please let go of my arm."

"What's possessing you?" Cadvan said. "Where would you go by yourself? Do you think that you and Hem would have a chance, with Hulls all over Annar hunting you down?"

Maerad glared at him scornfully and shook herself free of his grasp. "I've managed before," she said. "I might do better if I'm not traveling with a Hull in the first place."

The blood drained out of Cadvan's face, and his hand fell nervelessly to his side. For a few seconds he was speechless. Then he gazed intently into her eyes, and spoke softly in the Speech. *Il ver umonor imenval kor, dhor Dhillarearë de niker kor.*

The words fell as gently as rain into Maerad's mind, but she winced as if they bruised her. "By all we have suffered together, by the sworn bond you owe me as your teacher, and by the deeper bond you owe me as your friend, I bid you tell me now: what has happened to you, Maerad of Pellinor?"

She stood mutely before him, her overwhelming suspicion and fear warring with other memories: her first sight of Cadvan in the cowbyre, and her instinctive trust of him; their many days together, riding side by side; shared jokes; Cadvan's face, innocent in the vulnerability of sleep, or stricken by the Hulls, or blazing with light, fearlessly standing against the Kulag and the wight. She turned her head away, feeling sick.

"You followed the Dark," she said thickly. "You betrayed the Light. I can't stay with you now." She looked into Cadvan's face, and he lowered his eyes. "Do you deny it?"

"No," he said. "No, I cannot deny it." Maerad had expected him to argue, and was momentarily at a loss. "I have never been a Hull, but I . . . did things I should not have done. I have paid for it, Maerad. And I have never betrayed you."

"Then why did you hide it from me?" She stared at him with a hostile intensity, and he looked away.

There was a long, painful silence.

"Maerad," said Cadvan at last. "I should by now have told you of this. I didn't ever seek to hide it from you. But it's painful for me to recall, and perhaps . . . perhaps I would like not to be always distrusted by those who don't know me well. I have been remiss. For that, I apologize."

"Then tell me now." Maerad's voice was as tense as a strung wire.

"Sit down," he said gently.

"No." She continued to stare at him, waiting for him to speak.

Cadvan shrugged his shoulders, glancing around the room as if he gathered his thoughts together, and then sat down. "It's a simple enough story to relate," he said, with an edge of bitterness. "I was a young Bard in Lirigon, newly fledged, arrogant in my powers, and despite my talent, ignorant of many things. There came another Bard there whose abilities almost matched mine, and we were rivals." He paused, and sighed. "Or, to be more precise, I felt he was my rival. He didn't think like that."

"What was his name?"

"His name was Dernhil of Gent." Maerad started, but Cadvan was not looking at her. "It happened that, in my pride, I brooked no rival, and I wondered how I could outdo him. In my spare time I had been studying the Black Arts, thinking as one does, when one is young and foolish, that I could take no harm from being merely interested. Warnings, I thought, were for those with punier abilities than mine. I had even been secretly in contact with a Bard who had been banned for practicing the Black Arts, although I didn't know then that he was a Hull."

"Likud," said Maerad.

Cadvan glanced up at her. "Yes, Likud. When Dernhil beat me in the duel, my vanity was badly hurt. I wanted to do something that would prove once and for all that my powers were greater than his. I decided the only way was to perform some magery that he would never dare because, as I thought, he had less nerve than I did. I called him to a place we both knew, a grove outside Lirigon, and there I meant to give him a demonstration of my powers." Cadvan stared at the floor, not speaking.

Unconsciously, Maerad had moved farther into the room, and she perched now on the edge of the chair farthest from Cadvan. "So, what did you do?"

"I summoned a creature from the Abyss."

"What, what creature?"

"A Revenant." Cadvan was now withdrawn, wrapped in an evil memory. "Like a wight, but not so powerful. I was not strong enough to hold it, and it broke my word of command."

He fell silent, and Maerad waited for him to start again. When he did, it seemed to be a struggle for him to speak at all.

"The Revenant nearly killed me. It wounded Dernhil badly. He has—had—a scar from his shoulder to his hip from that encounter. And it killed another Bard, a friend who was loyal, or foolish, enough to be there, even though she knew what I planned and had tried to persuade me not to do it." He stopped, his face drawn and haunted.

"And what happened afterward?"

"I had to send the Revenant back. I did so, eventually. It took a long time, because I was injured, and first had to heal, and then I had to find it. After that, I was almost exiled. I was, for a time, banished from all Schools. It was Nelac and Dernhil who saved me from that. They argued long for me." He fell silent again. "That is why . . ."

"Why what?" Maerad spoke more gently now.

Cadvan paused and then sat up, looking Maerad straight in the eye. "Maerad, these are black memories for me. I'll tell you more, if you wish, but I would rather not dwell on them. This is the sum of my dealings with the Dark. I have spent myself since in service of the Light and the Balance, more than any other Bard I know. I swear that to you, by everything I hold sacred."

Maerad nodded slowly. She turned from him and sat meditatively for some time, thinking over what he had told her. She now understood Cadvan's solitariness, she thought. She pitied the young Bard he had been.

"Who was . . . who was the Bard who died?"

For a while she thought Cadvan was not going to answer. When he did, his voice was muffled.

"Her name was Ceredin," he said. "She was very young, and very beautiful, and my love. She was a Bard of great quality. She might have been greater than me. She was certainly more wise." Beneath the bitterness in his voice, Maerad heard the anguish of an undimmed grief. For a second, as if she were a burning glass, Cadvan's emotion flashed through her, and she fleetingly saw Ceredin in her mind's eye: a dark-eyed, slender girl, with the same proud straightness she remembered of Milana. "I shall wear that death always," Cadvan said harshly, though Maerad heard a catch in his voice. "I cannot forgive it."

Maerad turned and gazed into Cadvan's eyes. For the first time, she used her Gift: she entered his consciousness, as she almost had that day, so long ago, when he had scried her. She felt Cadvan's flinch at her sudden intrusion and then his acceptance, how he let down the inner shields that protected his private self. For a brief, intense moment it was as if she *was* Cadvan, with Cadvan's memories and longings and regrets, and she felt his anguish as sharply as if it were her own. She looked as long as she needed to, no more; she could hardly bear such intimacy. Then she turned away and again stared out into the garden.

The black mood that had possessed her since the Council slowly lifted, as if the sun broke after a long, bitter night of the soul. At the same time, she felt an immense weariness sweep over her.

"I'm sorry, Cadvan," she said quietly, still looking into the garden. "I'm sorry I doubted you. I couldn't help it, when . . ." She trailed off. Cadvan's confession had driven the vision in the Crystal Hall out of Maerad's head. Now the memory returned, but instead of terror she felt a resolve hardening within her. Her collapse had been provoked by the darkness within the Flame; she was absolutely certain that it sensed her, that it sought to destroy her, to bewilder and obscure her mind. It had blighted her with a desolate hopelessness, and all around her had seemed foul and corrupt. She couldn't permit that to happen to her again.

"And now," said Cadvan, breaking her reverie, "you can tell me what caused all this." His voice was normal again, and she remembered what Nelac had said of him: *If he seeks to keep something hidden, it is near impossible to find it out.* Yet Cadvan had permitted her to see what he kept hidden, and his humility and trust in doing so had shaken her. She tried to order her thoughts.

She now told Cadvan why she had fainted and what she knew of Enkir. She could not keep the hatred out of her voice, her contempt and loathing for Enkir's treachery, and she felt the desire for revenge grow hot inside her as she spoke. Cadvan sat close by her, listening intently, and did not interrupt, though his face grew more and more grim. When she finished her tale, he stood up and walked to the window, gazing into the garden with his back turned to her.

"I thought you were betraying me to Enkir," Maerad said. "I didn't understand how you didn't *know*."

"I would swear on my life that Enkir is not a Hull," said Cadvan, turning to face her. He shook his head, as if he were trying to clear it. "Maerad, I can't tell you how difficult this is to believe. Enkir is ambitious and cold, I agree, and I do not love him, and I disagree deeply with much that he has done. But he has been a noble Bard, a man of great learning and great wisdom, and he is the First Bard of the Circle. He has done much in the service of the Light, great deeds of magery, and has spent himself without mercy. How could that be so? How has he concealed his designs and actions from so many Bards? For none of those who sat at that table are fools, or easy to deceive."

Maerad sat silently. It seemed perfectly obvious that Enkir was cruel and eaten up with malice. He did not seem noble to her.

"Perhaps the other Bards are like him," she said at last. Cadvan glanced at her swiftly, but did not demur.

They sat together in gloomy cogitation until the door unlatched, making Maerad jump. Saliman entered, and behind him a slim, handsome boy bearing a jug of ale. Maerad thought at first it was one of Nelac's students, then she realized it was Hem.

Saliman looked from Maerad to Cadvan, absorbing the atmosphere in the room. "What's been happening here?" he asked. Neither of them would answer him, and he raised his eyebrows. "Well, in any case, allow me to present Cai of Pellinor, who still insists on being called Hem."

"Hello, Hem." Despite herself, Maerad smiled; Hem bore himself with an awkward mixture of pride and shyness. His hair had been washed and cut short and, free of the dirt, was appreciably lighter than it had been. He was dressed smartly in the style of Norloch: blue breeches made of heavy silk, a long-sleeved crimson tunic of the same fine wool as Maerad's dress, and soft black leather boots. Self-consciously he crossed the room and put the jug of ale on the sideboard. "You look very nice," Maerad said. Hem nodded, on the verge of blushing, and sat down next to her.

"Saliman made me have a bath," he said. "I didn't mind *that* much."

"It's a complete transformation," said Cadvan, inspecting him. "Now indeed you look like a noble son of the House of Karn." Hem went scarlet.

Saliman poured four glasses. He looked at Maerad and Cadvan curiously as he handed them the ale, but did not inquire. "The least you can do is congratulate me on my magery," he said, sitting down.

"I congratulate you," said Cadvan ironically. He took a long drink of ale, and a silence fell on the company.

"Where's Nelac? He's late. We need him here," Cadvan burst out suddenly. He shook his head again, still disbelieving. "Saliman, it's much worse than we thought. Darkness fills the high seat of power, the White Flame itself. What will we do now?"

* * *

Maerad realized that it was late; the Council had taken more than three hours, and they had sat talking in Nelac's rooms while the dusk deepened. Cadvan had told Saliman of Maerad's vision, and although he had looked saddened, he did not seem surprised. "Cadvan, I have long told you that the Light is rotten in the north," he said.

"But at the very heart of the flame?" said Cadvan.

"Aye, it is bad," answered Saliman. "I had hoped it was not that bad. But it does not amaze me. Such are these times. Think of Maerad's dream."

Cadvan and Saliman were getting more and more uneasy at Nelac's absence, and Maerad was beginning to feel frightened. Something was happening, she could feel it. She watched the shadows lengthening outside with a growing sense of doom.

"Enkir will be forced to move quickly now," said Saliman decidedly. "And in that I think lies hope. What must have gone through his head when you announced her, Cadvan? *Here is Maerad of Pellinor!* She could pull down the whole castle. Do you think he has made plans for this? You saw, Maerad, how close he came to exposing himself in the Council. And Enkir is, I think, one who thinks through his plans carefully in advance, down to the last detail. He had dismissed Maerad. And *she* is the One! I think he is thrown. He'll do something imprudent."

"Perhaps," said Maerad. "But I think he has his own spies. He might not have been so wrong-footed as you think."

"You're thinking of Helgar?" said Cadvan. He was striding impatiently up and down the room. "Yes, I think it will not do to underestimate him. The Dark seems two steps ahead of us, always, though I think our argument that Maerad is the One took him totally by surprise. The Dark is blinded in many ways by its own nature; there are many things it doesn't understand. Enkir would not think a woman could have that power. And he doesn't know, or at least I don't think he knows, that we have found Hem. But I agree, Saliman. He will move quickly now. My guess is that he will try to get rid of us *now*, before we can do anything. We have to get out of Norloch. All of us."

"Where will we go?" Hem uncurled himself, and stared belligerently at Saliman and Cadvan.

Cadvan paused. "I think we should not flee together," he said. "We'll be pursued. We'll have to split up."

For a second Hem looked devastated, but he visibly collected himself with an effort of will, affecting a tough carelessness. He doesn't wish to seem like a child, Maerad thought, with a stab of compassion. But he is. She put her arm around him and pulled him close.

"I think Cadvan's right," she said softly. "But it's hard."

"The best thing," said Cadvan carefully, "would be for Saliman to take Hem south, and for me to go north with Maerad. For I think we must go north, and I think Maerad still needs my guidance. Yes, Maerad?" He looked across at her, a painful doubt in his eyes. Maerad met his gaze steadily. She hesitated for a long second, and then nodded slowly. She felt his surge of relief wash through her own body, and she was overwhelmed by a sudden emotion she couldn't name.

Next to her, Hem was struggling with his delight at the thought of going south with Saliman and his grief at having to part from Maerad. Maerad gradually became aware of him and looked hard into his face. Despite all Hem's willpower, a tear trickled down his cheek.

"Hey, be brave, little brother," she whispered. "We'll meet again. I know we will. And just think: you'll get to see the Falls of Lamar before I do!"

Hem didn't trust himself to speak, and swallowed hard, nodding.

Saliman looked at Hem with a deep empathy. "If Maerad says you will meet again, I think you will," he said. "And perhaps, yes, the Falls of Lamar will be some compensation, though no beauty can assuage the loss of those you love." Hem blinked and then sat up a little straighter. "Cadvan is right," Saliman added. "But first we have to get out of Norloch. I somehow think that will not be easy."

"We should pack, then," said Maerad suddenly. She looked down at her robes. "And I can't go like this."

"Yes," said Cadvan. "As quickly as we can."

It was a relief to have something to do, instead of just talking. In fifteen minutes they were all downstairs again, dressed in traveling clothes, Hem with a new pack like Maerad's, which Saliman had given him earlier that day. They threw their bags in the corner, and then sat down again to their tense vigil.

It was only ten minutes later, although it felt like an hour, when the door was flung open, and Nelac burst in.

"At last!" said Cadvan, turning quickly. "Nelac, we have news. . . ."

Nelac looked swiftly around the room. "Good, you're all here," he said. "I think I know your news, Cadvan. Do I guess right, Maerad? You saw the Darkness in the Flame, even as it perceived you."

Maerad stared at him in amazement. This was a Nelac she hadn't seen: all signs of age seemed to have dropped from him, and he spoke with a sure authority. "We have very little time," he said hurriedly. "The Circle is broken, and I do not know what will happen. I have spoken to Amdrith, the Captain of the City, and I think that not all will be loyal to Enkir, should he call out the Guard. That will buy us some time. But not much."

"What happened?" asked Cadvan, his face grim.

"Enkir has accused me of treachery," said Nelac. "And all

those who voted against him in the Council. He desired to imprison us all. The Circle would not agree to that. But he was only outvoted by one, and my heart misgives me, Cadvan; how deep does this darkness go? Enkir is in the tower in a black rage, and he drives the other Bards by fear and poisonous suspicion. You four must leave Norloch now, while there is still time." His eyes rested on the bags heaped in the corner and he nodded. "I see you already understand that."

"We were waiting for you," said Cadvan. "All is in readiness." He stopped his pacing. "You know that Enkir was at the sack of Pellinor?" Nelac glanced at Maerad in surprise.

"No," he said. "But I see already that Enkir is a monstrous traitor to all the Knowing of the Light. No, he's not a Hull," he said, putting up his hand as Maerad opened her mouth to question him. "He is too proud to enslave himself like that. Nor is he the Nameless himself, in the guise of Bard," he said, fending off another question. "He seeks rather to use the Dark to his own ends, and to make himself the seat of absolute power. He concealed himself in the very heart of the Light, following his recreant stratagems. I am sick that I did not see it." Nelac looked as if he were about to spit with contempt. "But in his arrogance he has forgotten the might of the Dark, and it has eaten him up, even as he thought he directed its ways. Cunning fool!"

Nelac glimmered with a light that threw shadows around the darkened room. But this was not the serene starlight Maerad had seen before: it flickered with rage.

"But come, we have no time to discuss treachery," said Nelac. "We must give thought of where you are to go."

"We have already," said Maerad. "Cadvan and I are going north, and Saliman will take Hem south. It seemed better so."

Nelac looked over her head into an unseen distance. "Yes, you are to go north, if we read the signs aright," he said at last. "That at least is clear. And you must find the Treesong. I do not know how. The Light will guide you. But your way is dark, and I cannot see far."

Nelac told them then that he had already arranged passage for Maerad and Cadvan on a fishing boat, which would leave as soon as they reached the quay. "It's owned by a fisherman, Owan, an old friend of mine from Thorold who petitioned me today," he said. "He was waiting in the hall when I came home. It's a lucky chance; I'd trust him with my life. I thought to send you all with him, but I see it is better that Hem and Maerad do not travel the same way. For I think Hem is as crucial to the Light as Maerad is, although what he must do is beyond my sight."

"What about Darsor and Imi?" asked Maerad.

"I have thought of that," said Cadvan. "Saliman and Hem must take them; they can send them on to Gent when they find other mounts. Darsor will bear my friend, if I ask him."

"But how are we to get out?" said Saliman. "Even on the best horse in all Annar, which I know Darsor is, it will be a challenge if the gates are held against us!"

"It is somewhat easier for you, my friend. Enkir is seeking Cadvan and Maerad, not Saliman, or not as far as I know," said Nelac. He took a ring off his finger and gave it to Saliman. It bore the seal of the White Flame. "The gates will not be held against this sign. And remember that Enkir doesn't know about Hem; it was lucky we thought not to discuss him at the Council. Tell them you bear urgent messages for the Suderain from the Circle. The Tall Gate in the Ninth Circle will be shut; it's already after dark. You'll have to leave by the messenger's portal."

"Shall we go, then?" said Saliman. Hem took a deep breath and stood up.

"Yes, you should leave now," said Nelac. "I don't know how long it will be before all the gates are sealed."

Saliman picked up his pack, signaling Hem to do the same,

and wordlessly the five went to the stables. Darsor snorted in greeting when he saw Cadvan, who stroked him and murmured in his ear as he hastily saddled him. Maerad kissed Imi on her nose and put on her tackle. Then she braced herself for parting.

She kissed Saliman on both cheeks. He looked gravely into her eyes. "The best of luck go with thee," he said. "You are a brave woman. May the Light shine on you, Maerad of Pellinor!"

She blushed at the unexpected compliment. She turned then to Hem and crushed him to her breast. When would she see him again?

"You'll find the Treesong," said Hem soberly. Maerad looked at him in surprise, and despite his distress, Hem smiled with a ghost of cheekiness. "I know you will, Maerad. I feel it in here." He thumped his chest. *Maybe, Maerad thought, but I don't even know what it is. . . .* She forced herself to smile back, and then boosted Hem onto Imi, who stood patiently while he scrabbled into the saddle. He settled and grinned down at her, suddenly delighted with himself.

Maerad wanted to say many things, but couldn't find the words. Cloaked and booted on a horse, Hem suddenly looked much more grown up. Besides, he had Saliman to look after him. He had as much chance as any of them. But she felt the parting as a wrench in her deepest being.

"Farewell, my friend," she said to the horse. "Guard my brother well."

Your brother? said Imi, pricking her ears forward in surprise.

"Yes," said Maerad.

I will, Imi said.

"I'll miss you!" said Maerad, feeling tears prickle her eyes again. She dashed them away impatiently. *Too many partings . . .*

And then, all too quickly, Darsor and Imi were clattering

over the cobbled courtyard. Nelac opened the broad outer
doors and looked out into the street. It was empty.

"Go now!" he said. "May the Light speed you!"

Then the horses surged out in a swift gallop. Within seconds
they had turned a corner and were out of sight. The three Bards
stood in the doorway for a little while after they had vanished,
Maerad with her head bowed low, struggling with her grief.

XXIV

FLIGHT

NELAC shut the outer door and locked it. Brin came out of the house with two burly students, and they began to barricade the doors with long, heavy bars of iron. "But what about us?" asked Maerad in surprise.

"We have to go another way," answered Cadvan. "Underneath the citadel."

Maerad didn't reply. Things were moving too fast. The Council, and then the terrible scene with Cadvan, and now losing Hem. . . . She was so tired, and the night was scarcely beginning. Subduedly they returned to Nelac's sitting room, which seemed suddenly very empty.

"Now, for the most important matter," said Nelac. "Maerad must be instated before you leave. There's only one way: the Way of the White Flame. Though now that I know what I know, I would not trust any other."

"The Way of the White Flame?" Maerad was caught off guard. She hadn't expected this.

"It is an ancient means," said Cadvan. "The way of Afinil. The very core of the rite. Not many these days know how to do it. Fortunately, Nelac is one of them." Suddenly he smiled at Maerad, his rare, brilliant smile, as if all shadows suddenly dropped from his soul and a great joy welled inside him. "And you shall come into your Gift at last, Maerad."

Maerad looked at Cadvan uncertainly, the dread returning like a black wind rising inside her. She feared the power within her, even as she felt it growing. And she felt a shift in her being, as if a heavy door shut irrevocably behind her and there was no way back.

Less than half an hour later, hidden from curious eyes in Nelac's private garden, Maerad of Pellinor became a Bard of the White Flame. Above blazed a field of stars where swung the waning moon, and the shadows of trees and flowers lay black and still on the silver grass. Maerad looked up and let the starlight fall on her face. She no longer felt afraid.

She stood alone beneath a flowering anarech tree, dressed in her traveling clothes. On her breast she wore the brooch of the Lily of Pellinor, and in her hand she held a switch of rowan. Cadvan stood about ten feet away, his hands clasped, as still as a tree.

Nelac came out of the house and he carried within his cupped hands a white flame. Maerad watched in wonder as he approached; the flame seemed to leap up from his palm and lit up his face from beneath, throwing the sockets of his eyes into deep shadow. When he reached her, he bowed his head.

"Maerad, Minor Bard of Pellinor, I welcome thee," he said, in the Speech.

Maerad bowed her head silently in return.

"Will you take the White Flame, in earnest of your vows to the Light?" Nelac asked.

"I will take the White Flame, in earnest of my vows to the Light," answered Maerad, and she held out the switch of rowan horizontally in front of her.

Nelac put the flame to the stick and it caught fire. Maerad resisted the impulse to drop the wood, holding it as the white flame spread along the rowan to her fists and then engulfed her hands. It didn't hurt; instead a strange, fierce tingling ran along her arms and through her body, as her entire body was sheathed in fire. Rather than heat, she felt coolness, but it was as if cold leaped and flickered as flame did. She felt more alive than she ever had in her life, as if her blood had suddenly woken from a long sleep; and she looked into Nelac's eyes with wonder. Then she heard, with a sense that was not hearing, a voice that was no human voice, but seemed rather the very tongue of starlight. *Elednor*, that was her Truename. Fire Lily. As the prophecy had said.

After a short time the flames flickered and went out, but the tingling continued, and the dim colors of the garden and the gentle starlight were almost more brilliant than she could bear.

"Thou hast passed through the White Flame, and have not burned," said Nelac. "Welcome, Maerad of Pellinor. Thou art in thy heart and in thy mind and in thy being a Bard of the White Flame." And then, into her mind, he said: *Samandalamë, Elednor Edil-Amarandh na, Eled Idhil na, Idhil Agalena na.* "Welcome, Elednor of Edil-Amarandh, Lily of the Briar, Briar of the Foam."

He stooped and kissed her brow, and then Cadvan welcomed her with the same words, and kissed her. Maerad looked at the rowan, which she still held in her hand; the switch was burned almost to ash, but her hands were white and unblistered.

Nelac took the switch from her and buried it under the anarech. Then, without speaking, they went back inside. The room that Maerad had left merely ten minutes before looked changed to her: the colors were richer and more profound, the objects pregnant with meaning. She almost flinched before the intensity of her perceptions. She looked around and blinked, and shook herself.

"I didn't know it would be like this," she said.

"One never knows how things will be," said Cadvan slightly dreamily, as if he remembered something in his own past.

A little of the radiance of the flame still clung to Maerad's skin, so as she sat in the room she shimmered slightly. Cadvan

looked at her in wonder; he thought he began to understand the
kinship Ardina had spoken of.

"Not all Bards pass through the White Flame," said Nelac.
"Not all Bards may. It was well done, Maerad." He stared at her
gravely. "A true Bard! And if I may say so, truly your mother's
daughter!"

There was no time for Maerad to absorb what had happened.
Into the sitting room came the sound of shouting in the street,
faint and far away, and the dim clash of weapons. Much closer,
there was a hubbub in the hall. Nelac looked up sharply. "It's
begun, my friends," he said.

Maerad sighed, and forced her mind to the present. They
had to escape Norloch. Saliman and Hem must already be out
of the citadel, heading south. She saw their figures in her
mind's eye, as if from a great height, galloping through the
night on the Meads of Carmallachen. Now she and Cadvan
must leave.

Brin ran into the room, looking agitated. "Master!" he said.
"Something is amiss. There's rioting in the streets! I saw soldiers from one of the high windows. . . ."

"I know, Brin," said Nelac calmly. "I am just sending off
these guests. Remember even the White Guard cannot force the
outer doors; they're barred with more than iron. And please, if
you could keep the students from panicking, we need to evacu-
ate them down to the lower Circles. I'll be back soon. If need
be, you know how to get to the Fifth Circle."

Brin nodded and left.

"Brin is my right hand," said Nelac, smiling wearily. He
leaned for a second against the wall. For the first time since his
return from the Council, he seemed old and tired. How old is
he? Maerad thought suddenly. Three times the span of a normal lifetime, Cadvan had said. . . . But Nelac interrupted her

musings. "Now it's time for you two to leave. I'll take you to the passage entrance—it goes straight from there, you can't get lost—and there I'll leave you. You two can defend yourselves. I have other urgent cares."

Cadvan and Maerad lifted their packs and followed Nelac. He led them along the great entrance hall, left into another wide corridor, and then through the huge kitchen, which was completely deserted. At the far end was a small, dark staircase, which they descended. Nelac made a light as they went down, and Maerad saw they entered a low-roofed vaulted cellar, which seemed to stretch endlessly around them. It was stacked to the roof with orderly rows of casks, glass bottles, barrels, and bulging sacks of grain. The walls were lined with shelves of fruit and vegetables: apples, turnips, carrots, and more. And from the roof hung strings of onions and garlic and long fragrant dried sausages. The air was cool and still, but dry. Maerad breathed in the pungent smells as they hurried through, reminded suddenly that they had not had time to eat.

Nelac led them to a low corridor on the other side, and here they went again downstairs and turned left into another passage, lined with a number of small, stout oaken doors. The walls here were more roughly hewn, and the air began to feel dank and stale, as if these passages were not often used. He stopped by the door at the far end, took a bunch of keys from his waist, and unlocked it. The Bard light wavered through the doorway, but all Maerad could see was a few gray stone steps, which vanished down into impenetrable darkness.

"Here it is," said Nelac. "This gives out on the cliff face far below, and from there it's a matter of picking your way over the rocks to the quayside. The tide is out for the next six hours, so you won't have to swim. I think Enkir does not know of this passage, but I certainly cannot be sure; there are others not so secret, leading out to the lower circles, which he may expect you to use. I don't believe the other opening will be locked; but I am not so sure of the quays. By now the citadel will be battened down, and I think Enkir will not have forgotten the sea. Be wary!"

He paused and wiped his hand over his brow. Cadvan looked at him intently. "Nelac, I wish you would come with us," he said. "I fear for you in this place."

"Nay, Cadvan," answered Nelac, and he smiled somberly. "I am too old for such ventures. I will not lie to you: my heart is full of foreboding. Now we are come to evil days. But I am needed here."

Cadvan did not argue, but the sadness in his face deepened.

"Now listen well," Nelac went on. "Owan's boat is called the *White Owl*. It has red sails, which bear the sign in white. You will know him; he is tall and dark after the manner of Thorold." As Nelac spoke, Maerad saw an image vividly in her mind: a dark, humorous face with eyes gray as the sea. "He said he would wait for you at the cliff end of the quay, and he knows your likenesses. Go there as quickly as you may. He is a man who may be trusted." He looked away from Cadvan and Maerad. "All my hope goes with you two. Do what you must. The Dark must not prevail."

Maerad brimmed suddenly with love for this old man, gentle and wise and human, yet stern and strong, she knew, as the very rock. She threw her arms around his neck and kissed his cheek. Nelac looked surprised, but smiled.

"Farewell, young Bard," he said.

"Goodbye, Nelac," whispered Maerad, still clinging to his neck. "Thank you." She released him and stepped back.

"What the Light wills, no frost can kill," Nelac said. "Remember that. The roots of the Treesong run very deep, and shoots emerge where you least expect them. Keep vigilant!" Maerad nodded. "Farewell, Cadvan." Cadvan embraced him without speaking. Then the two entered the passage and Nelac shut the door behind them. Maerad heard the key turn in the lock.

For a second it was completely dark. Slowly a pale silvery illumination blossomed in the blackness. The glimmer came from Cadvan, but he did not move. He was staring sightlessly ahead.

"I doubt I'll see Nelac again," he said flatly. "Though I would know—surely I would know—if he died. . . ." There was a strain in his voice, a pained doubt, and for a moment Maerad didn't answer.

"You don't know what will happen," she said at last, awkwardly. "And Nelac is strong."

"Yes." Cadvan sighed heavily, and thrust away his thoughts. "It would be easier if I had a staff to make the light," he said. "I don't use one much, but over long stretches of time it helps. Perhaps we can take turns; I don't wish to finish our journey too tired. I have no idea what we'll find at the other end."

Maerad looked ahead. The passage was roughly hewn in the rock, and before them the wall curved around, out of sight. The steps were steep and narrow, plunging down in a ceaseless spiral through the core of the cliff. There was a dampness in the air, and it was cold; she shivered and drew her cloak closer around her.

They began the long descent. There was no hand guide or banister in the wall, and Maerad felt a constant fear of toppling down the steps. As they went farther, it became damper, and trickles of water occasionally ran down the walls, making the stairs slippery and treacherous. After about half an hour, Maerad took a turn of making the light, and she began to see what Cadvan meant; it was tiring, in a deep part of her mind, to keep the illumination while concentrating also on making sure she didn't trip and fall.

They could hear distorted sounds vibrating through the rock, and once they passed what must have been a thin wall to a room or another passage, because they could hear the mumble of people speaking quite clearly on the other side.

"The pinnacle of Norloch is a maze of these tunnels," said Cadvan. "Many are used for storage, or for secret passage from one house or Circle to another. I don't think anyone knows all of them." Maerad wondered what was happening above their heads, in the citadel. Occasionally she could hear a faint boom, and when she sent out her hearing she could detect the echoes of men's shouts and the pound of feet on stone, but she could make no sense of what she heard.

The stairway seemed to go on forever, and Maerad's legs began to ache. The chill set in her bones, and she tired of the darkness and of the low roof of heavy stone, the oppressive sense it gave her of an increasing weight over her head. The constant circling of the corkscrew stairs induced a strange dizziness, always turning the same way inward; she thought that when they reached the bottom, her body would have a permanent bias and she'd never be able to walk straight again. She set her jaw and went on.

When at last the stairs stopped, her knees were trembling and her thighs burned with the unnatural strain of walking so many steps. She halted abruptly, looking at Cadvan.

"I've got to rest," she said. "Just for a little while . . ."

"I've no argument with that," said Cadvan. "I hate stairs." He put his pack on the ground and sat on it. Here the ground was damp, and a little rivulet of water ran down the edge of the tunnel, which plunged ahead of them through the rock into darkness. Maerad did the same, stretching her legs out in front of her and massaging the muscles. Now she could smell something new; a faint briny scent leavened the dead air.

"We're almost there," said Cadvan. "Soon we'll be out of here."

They didn't stop for long. After barely five minutes Cadvan stood up again and heaved his pack onto his back. Maerad followed him down the straight tunnel, which ran very slightly downhill. Now the going was much easier and they moved fast, possessed by a sharpening sense of urgency. They had walked for about fifteen minutes when the smell of brine grew stronger. Maerad saw a very faint glimmer of starlight in the distance, although she couldn't see the mouth of the tunnel; and then she could hear the crash of waves and, behind it, the ceaseless soughing of the sea. The tunnel became much less like a passage and more like a natural cave; their footsteps were dulled by sand, and the walls narrowed dramatically as they reached the end. They were forced to stoop lower and lower until they were nearly bent double. Then it suddenly ran steeply upward and they climbed the last few feet, scrambling out of a narrow opening onto a tumbled mass of boulders slimy with weed.

A dozen feet below waves scumbled the shoreline, a littoral of black rocks shining, dimly wet. The night was clear and bright, and Maerad breathed in the salt air, relieved to be at last out of the close, dead atmosphere of the passage. The black basalt cliffs of Norloch soared high above, and she saw over the water before them the narrow heads of the harbor, a gap of starlight between lightless walls of stone.

Now it was a matter of picking their way carefully over the rocks, trying not to stumble in the shadows or fall into the pools of saltwater that filled every crevice. It was tedious and time-consuming, but slowly they made their way around the base of the cliff, and soon Maerad could see the great stone quay looming before her. More ominously, she could hear shouts coming over the water, and sounds of armed struggle, and then suddenly she saw a leap of red light. Flames.

"Fighting in the Ninth Circle," Cadvan murmured in her ear. "I hope Owan still awaits us!"

"Nelac said he'd trust him with his life," said Maerad, wondering what they would do if Owan had already gone, driven off by whatever was happening in Norloch. They continued their scramble until they were at the base of the quay. Steps jutted out from the side, and silently they crept up. Just before the top Cadvan put his hand out to halt her, and cautiously poked his head over the edge. Then he beckoned her after him, and they crawled over the lip of the quay.

Farther up the wharf knots of people were fighting, grotesquely lit by flames. Three boats moored at the farther curve of the harborside were on fire, and their reflections glittered like blood on the surface of the waves.

"They're burning the ships!" Cadvan muttered. "Enkir is being thorough."

Maerad couldn't see clearly what was happening on the quay, but she could hear swords clashing and terrible shouts and screams. She shut her eyes; it was too like her memory of Pellinor. She couldn't afford to think of that. Not now.

They were hidden in the shadow of a large bollard, and, for the moment, unperceived. Nearby a number of boats clinked softly at their moorings. Crouching, Cadvan scanned them, his face anxious. Which one was theirs? They all looked deserted. Not far away, but too far for Maerad's comfort, was one with red sails, but they couldn't see its name from where they were.

"I think that must be the one." Cadvan nodded toward the boat. "Maerad, you can make a glimmerspell now, yes? Make yourself invisible. We don't want to be spotted. I can't see any Bards, though it's hard to tell in this chaos." Maerad concentrated her mind for a moment; she had never done this before, but it was easy. Cadvan lifted his eyebrow, and she nodded; and then they both stood up and ran.

They were almost at the boat, close enough to see a flying owl painted in white on its sails and the gangplank shifting on the stone, when there was a shout. A Bard had seen them.

"Halt!" A tall man bearing a mace and a fiery torch came running up to them. "Halt! Who goes there? None are allowed on these wharves, by order of the First Bard!"

They were still too far away from the boat to risk a dash. Maerad heard Cadvan curse under his breath. The glimmer-spell would not deceive a Bard, but perhaps there was still some hope of disguise. He turned to the man, his hand under his cloak on the hilt of his sword. "Mercy, sir!" he whined, in an accent Maerad didn't know. "Me and my boy are trying not to get ourselves killed." His hood shadowed his face, and Maerad shrugged hers farther over her head.

"You should have been off the quay an hour ago." Two other men were running up behind him.

"We didn't know," said Cadvan. "We were trapped. . . ."

"They're Bards," said a voice from behind the first. The man thrust the torch closer toward them, peering into Cadvan's face. Maerad moved behind him, trying to conceal herself in its flickering shadows.

"Bards, sir?" said Cadvan.

"Get Enkir," said the voice. "I think it's them." The third man ran off.

It was clearly too late for concealment. The two remaining Bards strode forward to grab them, shouting for help. Cadvan swept out his sword, Arnost, and they jumped back. The first man dropped his torch and took his mace in both hands.

In that split second Maerad looked around desperately. Dozens of soldiers seemed to be on the quay fighting, but she couldn't see who was fighting whom. More soldiers were running up to them. She saw the white blur of a face peep through the railings of the boat and instantly disappear. Owan.

He hadn't abandoned them. Without thinking, she drew her own sword and stood shoulder to shoulder with Cadvan, and they moved back to a bollard, standing against it. The water glimmered blackly behind them.

"You would kill me, Gast?" said Cadvan to the first man. The edge of Arnost gleamed dangerously. "I'd think again, if I were you."

"Silence, traitor!" Gast cried. "Death is your doom now." He lifted his mace and lunged toward them. Cadvan and Maerad leaped aside and the blow fell on the bollard, striking sparks. Another blade flashed and Gast fell to the ground, blood running darkly from his neck and mouth. He convulsed and then did not move. Maerad stared for a heartbeat, appalled at this swift death, but someone else swung at her with a sword. She parried the blow and leaped toward Cadvan, who pushed the soldier back brutally and then, with his left hand, flung up a sudden wall of white flame around them. The soldiers vanished behind it, and Maerad and Cadvan were enclosed in a blazing semicircle.

Cadvan turned to her, his face lit weirdly by the fire, the whiplashes livid on his white skin. "It's only thirty feet to the boat," he said. "Our only hope now is to fight our way there, and we can't do that with swords; there are too many of them. If we both hold a wall around us, we might make it."

Maerad nodded, breathing in gasps. Beyond the silver flames she could hear the shouting of many soldiers. She took Cadvan's hand, joining her mind to his, and the flames leaped up, brilliant and cold. Then, step by step, she and Cadvan began to move along the edge of the quay toward the boat. They had not gone three paces when she began to feel the pressure of a counterspell; the flames thinned and lowered, and she could see the dim shapes of soldiers beyond them. She pressed harder, and the flames leaped up again.

"There are more than two Bards out there," said Cadvan. Sweat was beginning to break out on his forehead. "I can sense five at least. I think we can make it, Maerad. Hold fast."

Slowly, agonizingly slowly, they moved toward the boat. Maerad felt her whole body burning with the strain. She dared a look over her shoulder, and the fishing boat still bobbed serenely in the water, apparently deserted. Twenty feet, ten feet: they were almost there. Her head throbbed with the pressure of keeping up the wall, but they would make it.

Then, with a dreadful suddenness, the flames vanished. Maerad reeled with the shock; it was as if they had been stamped out by a giant foot. Cadvan clutched her hand, dashing the sweat out of his eyes, and threw out another force of resistance to buy them a few precious seconds. Maerad blinked, trying to see. There were the red blurs of torches and a boiling mass of dark shapes, but in front of them was something else, a new power that had not been there before.

"Enkir," said Cadvan, gasping. "It's Enkir! He feels like a wight!"

Like a wight, thought Maerad with the rapidity of fear, but not like a wight: this power had not the horror of the grave, but the same living malice she had felt in the Crystal Hall. She could see Enkir's figure barely fifteen feet away, no bigger than any of the soldiers who milled around him; but a power gathered around him like an abominable shadow, so that he seemed to loom gigantically above them, hideous and terrifying. The soldiers were now scattering, cowering before him, but Maerad was barely aware of them.

Cadvan's resistance was fading and she felt, like a savage blow to her face, the force of Enkir's will, cruel and implacable. She crushed Cadvan's hand in hers and sent out a bolt of fire in panic, wishing fiercely that she knew how to harness the powers she undoubtedly possessed.

Enkir merely put up his hand, and the bolt shot up into the sky.

Maerad suddenly remembered what Indik had said to her in Innail, it seemed years ago now. "Intelligence is the key. You're not strong enough to be stupid. *Think!*" She gulped and steadied herself.

Enkir now stood still, and the black waves beating against them eased a little. He raised his arms, building a terrible force of darkness around him. Maerad perceived, with a sense that came from deep in her mind, that he was drawing on something outside himself. She felt her ears beginning to pop. He was going to crush them both with a single blow.

With a jolt to her stomach she realized the contemptuousness of the gesture; it was the same contempt with which he had destroyed her mother. She glanced swiftly at Cadvan, and he caught her thought. He nodded imperceptibly. They twisted their hands together, waiting grimly for endless seconds while the force built up to an almost unbearable pressure. The air vibrated with a sound like the screech of tormented metal.

Then Enkir released his blow. Together, Maerad and Cadvan flung up a shield at that precise moment, a shield like a blazing mirror. For the briefest instant it hung brilliantly in the air before them, and then Enkir's bolt hit it like a hammer. The shield exploded in fiery shards of dazzling colors and Cadvan and Maerad both staggered back, teetering on the very edge of the quay.

But the bolt didn't reach them; it rebounded back and hit Enkir. Gasping, Maerad recovered and sent a volley of lightning to follow it. The jagged flashes lit up the scene on the quay for a series of brief moments, as if they were unmoving images imprinted by fire on her sight. One man close by had dropped both his sword and his shield and had fallen to his knees, covering his eyes with his hands in a gesture of despair or horror.

Others were fighting with a kind of madness, as if they were possessed. There were at least four bodies lying outstretched on the ground, utterly still; but Maerad could see no sign of Enkir.

Then she and Cadvan turned and ran for their lives the last few feet to the gangplank and onto the boat.

Owan was laid out flat on the deck, his hands over his ears. He started up when they jumped in, but when he saw who they were he came forward to greet them. Cadvan was already pulling the gangplank in behind him.

"You took your time," Owan said.

"Quickly!" gasped Maerad. Owan went to the bows with seeming unhurriedness, although he was actually moving very fast, and unmoored the boat.

"A little help would be appreciated with the wind," he said laconically over his shoulder.

Cadvan stared at him for a second before he grasped what he meant. Then he lifted his arms and spoke. Maerad was still wondering what Owan had asked for when she heard a whisper of air, gathering in strength to a stiff breeze, and the sails flapped and bellied out. The boat began to draw steadily away from the quay.

Quicker, quicker, please be quicker, thought Maerad, but it seemed that Owan would not be hurried. After a short time they were clear of the other craft. Owan signaled to Cadvan, and the wind in the sails grew stronger, and they began to speed over the waves toward the headlands of the harbor.

Maerad looked back to the quay. She couldn't see what was happening, but she could feel now that Enkir was no longer there; that awful presence was gone. Had they killed him? She couldn't tell. The blast that Enkir had meant for them had thrown the whole scene into utter confusion. There was a loud hubbub, and still it seemed the soldiers were fighting each other. No one had yet noticed the tiny boat stealing out of the harbor.

Cadvan came up and stood beside her.

"Alas for Norloch!" he said.

"Yes," said Maerad. She clutched the rails to stay her trembling, the aftershock of the battle. Cadvan gazed back over the water.

"I'm glad we're going to Thorold," he said. "Maybe because it's an island, it has always been one of the most independent Kingdoms. If the First Circle issues a warrant on our heads, it will most likely be ignored there."

"A warrant?" Maerad turned to look at Cadvan with wide eyes. Cadvan shrugged.

"It is likely, Maerad. Blood has been spilled. And unless the First Circle is restored under Nelac, which seems a faint chance, we are outlawed now. We'll have made some powerful enemies tonight."

Maerad bowed her head, feeling oppressed. She wondered for a few seconds if she had the strength to flee both the Light and the Dark. It was too hard. . . . She had thought Norloch the end of her journey, but it seemed it was only the beginning of another flight, this time into the unknown, her fate more uncertain than it had ever been.

"I regret the death of Gast," Cadvan said, after a pause. "He was not an evil man, merely misled. He was doing what he believed right."

Maerad thought: He was going to kill you, but she didn't say it. "Did you know him well?" she asked, turning to face Cadvan.

His eyes were dark with sadness. "No, not well," he said. "He came from the School of Desor." He was silent for a time. "Civil war is an ugly thing, Maerad. It pits friend against friend, and makes enemies of those who by rights should be our allies. I had hoped never to see it. But such are these times."

They gazed over the water, listening to the ugly cries of battle, now beginning to fade with distance.

"Do you think Enkir is dead?" Maerad asked suddenly.

"I would like to think so," Cadvan said. "But I feel no certainty, which is perhaps a sign that he still lives. He draws his power from a source that is more than human, and that may have protected him. And if Enkir is alive, I fear for Norloch. He is still First Bard, the most powerful Bard in Annar, and if he is alive, he will use the chaos of tonight to his own ends."

"But maybe Nelac could stop him?"

"Perhaps," Cadvan answered. "But as he said, how deep does this darkness go? When people are afraid, they will give up almost anything for an illusion of safety. Only Nelac knows how deeply Enkir has betrayed the Light, and Enkir has already accused him of treachery. Nelac helped us escape, and I have killed one Bard, at least. You do not have to be evil to be mistaken." Cadvan's voice was bleak. "The weight of evidence may well seem to count against anything Nelac can say."

"But can't the Council tell what the truth is?" Maerad said with a sudden passion. "They're Bards, aren't they? Aren't Bards supposed to know?"

Cadvan gave her a tired smile. "Truth is not so simple, Maerad. You know that. It all depends from where you are looking, and it changes. . . . Do you think it is so easy to trace the workings of the Light? How do any of us really know that we choose rightly?"

Maerad thought of Norloch, high citadel of the Bards, now revealed as the center of Darkness, and then of Cadvan's confession earlier that night, and fell silent. She was filled with sudden disquiet. She had thought the Dark and the Light as easy to distinguish as night and day; but Cadvan seemed to be saying that was not the case at all, that certainty was but a comforting illusion.

"Do you think we are doing right?" she asked at last.

Cadvan did not answer her at first, and then he sighed. "Yes, I think we are," he said. "At least, we do the best we can, knowing what little we do. But sometimes there is no choice before you, except between bad and worse."

Then Owan called Cadvan over to him, wanting more help with the wind, and Maerad was left alone at the railings, brooding, staring back at the burning city.

As the boat crossed the harbor, driving a white furrow through the waves, the sounds of fighting died away completely beneath the soft creaking of the sails and the sough of the waves. Maerad gazed long at the citadel, feeling the trembling in her limbs gradually cease.

The ships were still burning along the quay, throwing a dreadful glare on the water, and with a stab of dismay she saw fire leaping in the higher Circles. The First Circle seemed to be all on fire. She thought of Nelac; he said he was taking his students down to a lower level. They would not be in the First Circle still, surely? She hoped bitterly that Enkir was dead. Perhaps then the Circle would be restored.

Despite everything that had happened in the past few hours, Maerad felt as if her blood were burning with life. She was weary, weary to the bone, but she wasn't at all sleepy. Slowly, looking across the widening water, she felt herself relax, and she thought, for the first time since it had happened, of her instatement: of the surge of fire that had passed through and transformed her. She was different now. She was the Fire Lily, Elednor of Edil-Amarandh.

She sat down on the deck and looked searchingly up at the stars. There, just as she had seen it in Gilman's Cot, blazed Ilion, solitary and bright. She thought of Hem: where was he now? Was he too staring up into the night sky, thinking of her? And maybe her mother, Milana, also had done just this; maybe she too had searched for the brilliant jewel of Ilion among the constellations, and thought of it as her star.

Here on the earth's surface, thought Maerad, people labor and suffer and die. Does any of that anguish touch Ilion? She wondered if the stars could sense the vibrations of human joy and wonder, of grief and despair. Did the stars know what was right and wrong? What were the Dark and the Light to them? She remembered what Ardina had said to Cadvan: *the Light blooms the brighter in the darkest places*. Perhaps, at this distance from human affairs, another pattern emerged from the chaos, another kind of necessity, and even evil became part of a larger music.

Maerad stared into the sky, feeling her heart pulsing in her body and her blood coursing through each tiny vein. She felt as if she keenly understood, for the first time in her life, the intricate relationships between all things, a web of infinite beauty and complexity. Between the small orb of her eye and the distant star, she felt the pull of a tiny glowing thread, one of the infinite gravities that wove together the living and the dead, the far and the near, the tiny and the immense, in one everchanging, everrenewing world.

As this understanding swelled inside her, the fears that haunted her gradually subsided and disappeared. For the first time since she could remember, she thought of her mother without sorrow. She saw her in her mind's eye, tall and unbroken and beautiful: Milana, First Bard of Pellinor. She would be proud of her daughter now.

Maerad breathed in the sweet night air with a fierce exultance. This night, she thought, she did not care what the future held, what perilous journeys and dimly guessed terrors awaited her. For tonight, the present was enough.

HERE ENDS
THE FIRST BOOK
OF PELLINOR

APPENDICES

A BRIEF HISTORY OF
EDIL-AMARANDH

THE difficulties of dating the extraordinary civilization of Edil-Amarandh, or even of pinpointing its exact geographic location, are well known. Estimates vary wildly, dating its mysterious disappearance from 10,000 to 150,000 years before the beginning of the last Ice Age. Initial theories, which saw the Annar Scripts as confirmation of the persistent accounts in Plato, the *Mabinogion*, and elsewhere of an Atlantean nation overwhelmed by flood, have generally been discredited, since Edil-Amarandh appears to be far older than these texts suggest and has sharply divergent cultural differences. Some people, however, have suggested that the continent of Edil-Amarandh may be sunk beneath the Atlantic, west of the African and European coasts, as was theorized of Atlantis.[1] However, despite these arguments, the voluminous records available make it possible to elucidate a detailed history of Annar and the Seven Kingdoms.[2]

The Bards used two principal calendars: the reckoning of Afinil (indicated with A) and the Annaren or Norloch Calendar (indicated with N). These calendars were in general use throughout Edil-Amarandh. The events recounted in *The Naming* took place in the Year N945, which is to say 945 years after the Restoration of the Light under Maninaë.

The history of Annar and the Seven Kingdoms is divided into three Ages (the Great Silence is not regarded as an Age), according to the *Chronicles* of Istar of Norloch (N398), from which this account is mainly taken.[3]

The Age of the Elementals

The Age of the Elementals ended approximately a thousand years before the founding of Afinil, that is, about 5,000 years before the time of this story. Thus by the Restoration, much of its history was lost, and the little that remained was partial and fragmentary. However, after the founding of Afinil, the Elementals who remained recounted many of the events of that Age,[4] and so many stories and songs were preserved through the Bardic tradition, although again only scraps of that lore were preserved after Afinil was razed by the Nameless.

Elementals (or the Elidhu) were immortals and were so called because they bore affinities with natural forces such as fire, water, earth, air, the sun, the moon, and the tides. They were often associated with particular places or regions, such as rivers or mountains. After the Elemental Wars, many of the Elidhu retreated into their pure forms and were not seen again as sentient beings, although some still remained as visible spirits. They could take different forms at will, and in the days of Afinil often visited that city in the guise of humans and learned from the Dhyllin the arts of speech, song, and music, in which they especially delighted. The Lady Ardina was the most celebrated of those Elidhu who became part of the human world. After the dominion of humans and the estrangement between the two races, for which the Nameless was in large part responsible, most withdrew into their elemental forms and were rarely seen. Their number was not known.

The Age of the Elementals was marked by the dominion of the Ice Witch, Arkan, who came from the north and covered Edil-Amarandh with a perpetual winter. At this time the Elementals threw up some of the mountain ranges of Edil-Amarandh, the Osidh Elanor (the Mountains of the Dawn) and the Osidh Annova, in an attempt to bar Arkan's approach. All living things at this time suffered greatly, and it was said that humans at this point almost disappeared from the face of the earth. The Ice Witch was resisted and finally overthrown by an alliance between some of the Elementals and the peoples of

Edil-Amarandh, led by the Elidhu Ardina and the King Ardhor. The final war against Arkan convulsed the entire continent: "The sea poured in over what had been land, and lands rose where had before been sea."[5] When the war ended the coastline was entirely different, and became the shape presently mapped.

Human history and songs are recorded from that time—the legend of Mercan, for example, which was preserved in the Scrolls of Lir at the Library of Lirigon—but the years were not logged. Small communities of men and women lived in settlements east of the Osidh Annova, and there was a strong and proud people who lived near what is now the Lir River, the descendants of whom later became the Dhyllin.

The Dawn Age

After the wars, the Dhyllin settled the areas to the north later called Lirion and Imbral, and it is said in this time the *Dhillarearën* first appeared in Edil-Amarandh, but little is recorded until Afinil was first founded. This time is called the pre-Dawn, or Inela.

The Dawn Age dates from the Founding of Afinil, about a thousand years after the end of the Elemental Wars. Afinil was the first city founded and settled by the *Dhillarearën*, although they were by no means the only peoples who lived there. The city was founded by the great Bard Nelsor, who among other things invented letters, and was the first to write down and formalize the Speech. The script he invented was still the one most commonly used by Bards more than four thousand years later.[6]

Afinil was never a city of Kings, but of Bards, and it was built between Lirimal and Inchan, the major cities of the realms of Lirion and Imbral. Its site is long lost, but it was on the shores of a lake that was said to be so deep the stars were reflected there even in the daytime: the Ilimican, or Mirrormere. Afinil was reputed to be the most beautiful city ever to have been built in Edil-Amarandh and it became a center of high learning and culture. There were established great

singing halls and libraries, and it was famous for its gardens and terraces, which were said to perfume the air for miles around.

This was the first great flowering of the Light. Afinil prospered for
many years, and as it prospered, so did its surrounding lands. Bards
began to travel widely, and found their kin in many places: most
notably in Turbansk to the south, an ancient city founded before the
end of the Age of Elementals, and also in the lands to the west, along
the coast of Edil-Amarandh. People moved east as well over the
Osidh Annova and established the Kingdom of Indurain in the fertile
lands they found there.

The first sign of trouble occurred in A1567, when Sharma, the King
of Dén Raven, a small mountainous realm to the south, traveled to
Afinil and demanded tuition, offering gifts of gold and jewels. The
Bards, who valued such things only for what beauty they found in
them, laughed and gave him tuition for nothing. "What is the cold
light of a gem next to the living Light?" asked Gel-Idhor, First Bard of
Afinil, when Sharma approached him. "Nay, keep thy jewels."
Sharma, who was proud and quick-tempered, was deeply offended
by the Bards' gentle mockery; but he concealed his anger and bent his
mind to study.[7]

Very soon it was apparent that Sharma was the most precociously
talented Bard seen in Afinil since the days of Nelsor. He studied in
particular the making of things of power, and also the mysteries of
binding, and he was very curious about Arkan, the Ice Witch, and
spent much time speaking with the Elidhu who came to Afinil of the
history of those wars; but he concealed his intent. It only became clear
later that Sharma was interested in making himself immortal and as
powerful as the Elidhu, who could not be killed. There were those in
Afinil, including the Lady Ardina, who were disturbed by Sharma's
questioning and did not trust his ambition, and who counseled
against his education; but the Bards did not see why their Lore should
be kept from such an apt pupil, and such disquiet was brushed aside.

When Sharma had made himself the most powerful Bard in Edil-

Amarandh, he returned to his own kingdom; and it was then that he made the Spell of Binding that cast aside his Secret Name and ensured that he would never pass through the Gates to the Uncircled Open of Death.[8] This was a great blasphemy; for a Bard to so challenge the Laws of Balance was unprecedented. The casting away of his Name and his abjuration of Death signaled the beginning of the grievous wars that ended, five hundred years later, in the overthrow of Afinil and the utter defeat and destruction of Lirion and Imbral and all the Lore and beauty that had existed there.

After he cast off his Secret Name, Sharma was called the Nameless One. He attracted followers, to whom he promised unending life and absolute power, and many Bards went to his side, betraying the Light; and these became Black Sorcerers, and were known as Hulls, for they were but the shells of Bards. The Nameless also made alliances with the remnants of the Elidhu who hated and feared the Light, most notably the Elidhu Karak, who held dominion over the realm of Indurain, east of the Osidh Annova, after the armies of the Nameless had destroyed it and slaughtered or enslaved those of the Dhyllin who had lived there.

The campaign of the Nameless One to overthrow the Light in Annar succeeded in A2041, when his forces overwhelmed the last desperate alliance of Lirion and Imbral on the Firman Plains near the Findol River. That defeat was the end of the Dawn Age, and the beginning of the Great Silence.

The Great Silence

The Great Silence lasted from A2041 to A3234. At this time the Light retreated in hiding to the areas that later became known as the Seven Kingdoms: along the coast of Edil-Amarandh, and to the south. The Bards did not build cities or towns, and lived in great hardship, working always against the Dark; but they did not succeed in overthrowing the Nameless until the coming of Maninaë, heir of Laurelin, in A3157. Maninaë, a Bard, united resistance in the Seven Kingdoms and after many years—a story too complex to even begin to relate here—he succeeded in casting the Nameless off his throne and restoring the Light to Annar. He then became the first King in Norloch, and the first to rule over all Annar.

A new year-count, the Annaren Calendar, was then introduced. It was also called the Norloch Reckoning.

The Restoration

When peace was restored, Maninaë founded the citadel of Norloch and the system of the Schools. Twenty-five Schools were founded across Annar and the Seven Kingdoms, and roads were built across the country to allow free movement between all of them. At this time more areas of Annar were settled, although there were large regions of wilderness in the center of the land, and Edil-Amarandh was always a continent more thickly populated near its coast than at its center.

Once again there was a great flowering of Bardic culture, and the tenets of Afinil were restored. But Maninaë also gave thought to martial strategies, and the culture of Norloch was warlike, unlike that of Afinil. For Afinil had never been a city of Kings, and although all Bards were routinely trained in the arts of the sword, they never gave them especially high honor.

The Restoration lasted for 300 years. After that came a period of consolidation, called the Middle Years, in which all the Arts flourished in peace and harmony. At about the year N720 came the first promptings of disquiet, and also the last King; for the heirs to the throne made war on each other in an argument about succession, and in the strife the ruling line of Norloch was destroyed. The Seven Kingdoms at this time revised their alliances with Norloch and restated their autonomies.

After this, the Bards ruled alone in Norloch, incorporating into the authority of the White Flame the triple scepter of the Kings of Norloch; and after the destruction caused by the rivalries of Kings, it seemed to some this was better, and that the Bards, constrained by their vows to the Light and the Balance, would rule more wisely. But there were others who said this was a distortion of the Balance; and they also pointed out that women were no longer placed in authority in Norloch, as they continued to be in most other Schools, and saw this as another symptom of imbalance.

Gradually, over the next two hundred years, it became clear that things were amiss in Annar. The fortresses in Dén Raven were rebuilt, and the sorcerer Imank made war on the Suderain, although he was fiercely resisted. There were other signs of imbalance: the White Sickness, never seen before, began to ravage parts of Annar, and some Schools began to be estranged from their people, demanding high tithes and begrudging their services, which caused an enormous loss of the Bards' prestige in many parts of Annar, and sometimes outright and violent resentment. There were more frequent sightings of wers and other servants of the Dark, and for the first time since the Restoration, Hulls were seen in Annar. More disturbingly, some Bards began to report a disturbance in the Speech itself, which they found impossible to express, but which troubled them deeply; they said that it seemed to them the Speech was losing its ancient virtue. However, it was not until the School of Pellinor was sacked and burned to the ground in N935, followed by Baladh and Jerr-Niken in the south within the next four years, that a few Bards began to suggest that the Nameless One had at last returned.

OF ANNAR AND
THE SEVEN KINGDOMS

ANNAR, sometimes called the Inner Kingdom, was the greater part of the continent of Edil-Amarandh, and was generally held to be that land south of the Lir River, west of the Osidh Annova (the Mountains of the Earth) and north of the Southern Deserts.

The Seven Kingdoms were smaller, situated in a loose ring around Annar along the western coast: from the north, they were Lirhan, Culain, Ileadh, the Isle of Thorold, Lanorial, Amdridh, and the Suderain. The Suderain was close to the realm of Dén Raven—sometimes called the Lost Kingdom—a poisoned country that was the stronghold of the Nameless One, and that continued to be the biding place of Hulls and his surviving servants even after his defeat by Maninaë the Great and the Restoration of the Light in Annar.[9]

Maninaë united all of the Seven Kingdoms under one rule for the first time after the Nameless One was thrown down, ushering in a long peace. Maninaë was unusual in that he was both a King and a Bard, although in him the Barding was not strong and he forswore Barding when he became King. With one other exception, the Kings and Queens of Norloch had never been Bards; and this was considered a crucial element of the Balance.

The Monarch's authority over the Seven Kingdoms was extremely limited, and was freely given rather than asserted by force; the situation parallels more closely an alliance of city-states and the loose autonomous regions surrounding them. It is telling that the only name for the whole continent was the extremely archaic Edil-Amarandh, which dated from before the Dawn Age, and that this name was seldom used. The unity of Edil-Amarandh was a result of the influence of Barding, rather than any enforcement under Kings. The Bards were also a source of the relatively loose hierarchies in Edil-Amarandh; since a Bard might come from anywhere, even the poorest of communities, it was entirely conceivable—and commonly happened, especially in the first centuries after the Restoration—that the lowest might hold sway over the Wise.[10]

The regions were called kingdoms, but they were not strictly kingdoms or principalities in the generally accepted sense. This was because of the dual authorities of Barding and ruling authorities, both of which shared governance of their various peoples, and which by their complex nature mitigated against absolute rule. Over many years this evolved into a complex political and social system, differing in each region, of mutually interdependent autonomous structures. It appears that in many Fesses—the regions around the Schools—and other regions there operated a variation of democracy: stewards were elected by popular vote, and all adults over twenty-five, no matter what their social status, had the right to vote. Only the monarchy operated on a system of hereditary rule, and many Bards saw this as a primitive system, tracing from this "original sin" the subsequent demise of the monarchy.[11] However, it has to be admitted that the monarchy, within its limited powers, governed over a peaceful kingdom for several centuries before it degenerated into civil war.

The dual system—which only roughly parallels the medieval division of secular and religious power between church and state, although it is a tempting syllogism—was considered to be at its most ideal in the community of the Dhyllin, where Bards and the community lived and worked closely together, to their mutual benefit and pleasure. It was not in practice always ideal, and at times disagreements or rivalries led to bickerings and even war, sometimes between Bards and monarchs, sometimes between rival regions. All such occurrences were regarded by the Wise as a corruption of the Light.[12]

THE SPEECH:
SOME GENERAL NOTES

T HE Speech, the defining attribute of a Bard and the central mystery of the Knowing, is a topic that exercised many Bardic thinkers over many centuries.[13] Much therefore might be written about it, of which only the barest sketch can be given here.

The Speech behaved like a language, with certain crucial differences, and could in fact be learned; it was, for example, spoken by the Dhyllin people as their first tongue. But in the mouths of those who learned it, rather than in those with the Gift, it had no Bardic virtue.

Bards used it when speaking of matters of gravity and importance, because it was considered impossible to lie in the Speech. This was, in fact, not accurate: Hulls used the Speech and were able to lie, although this usage was not considered to be the Speech proper, and was sometimes called Dark or Black Speech. There was also the question of those who attained the Speech but were never taught the Knowing of the Light and, more crucially, never came into their Bardic or Secret Name (also known as their Truename). This was a circumstance that usually had tragic consequences, since such people were unable to properly understand or channel their powers, and were never able to enter their full Gift. This, generally, was rare, if more common as the Schools fell into disrepute after the demise of the Monarchs of Annar. There were also the cases of those who had only a slight Gift. Such people might have been village witches (hence the expression "witchspeak"), and they generally spoke a truncated and bastardized version of the Speech, with no more than a few words of potency, although sometimes they could attain considerable, if limited, power; but they were not considered to be Bards, since they did not attain the whole of the Speech, nor did they know their Names. Consequently, they were sometimes referred to as the Unnamed, which is to be distinguished from the Nameless, who had rejected his Name.

This clearly makes possession of the Speech less straightforward than it might at first appear. The fact that the Speech could be learned by those without the Gift suggests that the virtue of the Speech was not inherent in the words themselves, as was argued by many Bards in the Middle Years, but that it expressed the mysteries of the cosmos itself within its syntactic relationships and the vibrations of its utterance, from which were drawn its unique powers.[14] The chief reason given for the argument that potency was inherent in the words themselves was the priority and importance given to Names in the Speech, and to Bardic Names. The truth quite possibly resides in an amalgamation of both arguments, as was pointed out by other Bards.

Bards were the only people who bore Secret Names, and a Bard's Name was and remains a central mystery that can only be partially discerned and puzzled over. The only complete written record of an instatement and Naming ceremony occurs in *The Riddle of the Treesong*,[15] which confirms rather than negates the ritual's crucial importance. Other writings indicate that the most important mysteries were not written down but kept in the "rings of living memory." In the *Treesong* text the authors felt compelled to defend their choice to record it, remarking that since entire forests of knowledge had been hewn down by the Dark, "it is necessary to preserve, even in such a crude way, such Secrets as are known to us, in case the Knowing vanishes from the earth."[16]

It appears that a Bard's Name was much more than a mere appellation or signifier of status or origin: it *was* a Bard's being, and its achievement was a sign of a Bard's maturation into full power. One who knew a Bard's Secret or Truename had power over him or her, and thus Names were guarded closely and given only to intimates as a sign of ultimate trust. Rejecting one's Name was unheard of until Sharma's Spell of Binding, and was regarded as the ultimate blasphemy. Sharma of Dén Raven, however, remained the only Bard to successfully do so. Hulls did not use their Names, but were unable to reject them completely, and those who possessed the Names of Hulls could still destroy them.

Because the Speech was not learned in the normal way, and so was not subject to the same forces of change or cultural variety, it remained more constant than other human languages. Bards from vastly differing regions had no difficulty understanding each other if they used the Speech, despite the gulfs in tradition and culture that separated them. Nevertheless, the fact remains that there were variations in the Speech; although it sprouted, as it were, always from the same stem, different environments encouraged its growth in differing ways. There was, for example, a noticeable, if slight, difference between the Speech of Afinil and the Speech of Maerad's day; and, to Maerad's ear, Saliman's Speech, being from far south of her region, would have had the equivalent of an accent.

Those with the Gift used the Speech for all the Arts of the Knowing. The use of the Speech was central to healing, to song— which was held high as an art of wisdom—and to all spells, as well as to investigations—such as astronomy or natural science—we would be accustomed to thinking of as scientific. The Bards made no distinctions, as we do, between art and science, considering them parts of a single Knowing. The Speech also enabled those with the Gift to converse with animals and, less frequently, plants. The Speech did not need to be physically spoken to be potent; Bards could use it effectively merely as a mode of thought. This raises the most important and difficult differences between the Speech and other languages, which are the subtleties of its registrations as a mode of mental communication. These, crucial as they are, cannot be explained, and here must be glanced over by reference to the Bardic paradox that the "center of the Speech is Silence." It is also why, despite the fact that Bards had a very sophisticated written culture, orality, and the mnemonic arts that go with it, still held precedence.

OF THE BARDS:
HISTORY, SOCIETY,
AND CULTURE

History

It was generally considered that those with the Gift, known as the Starpeople—the *Dhillarearën*—or the Singers, first appeared in the Inner Kingdom at the end of the Age of Elementals, some five thousand years before the events recorded in *The Naming*.[17] Records or even a count of years were not kept until the founding of Afinil during the Dawn Age, more than a thousand years after the end of the Age of Elementals. There was a tradition that claimed that as the Elementals withdrew into their natural forms, "somewhat of their power dispersed from them and was taken up in human form; and so there appeared, in all places where the Elementals had dwelt, the Starpeople. And they were so named because their eyes held a distant fire, as if they had themselves come from the stars, and they delighted in the fire of the stars and so, unlike other peoples who feared and cursed the Darkness, they loved the Night, and called it sacred."[18]

There were, of course, other traditions, including a durable theory that Bards arrived from the west shortly after the disastrous Wars of the Elementals reshaped the lands of Edil-Amarandh. Another account held it that the Bards appeared first in the north, being forced there from the lands now inhabited by the nomad peoples of Zmarkan. The truth behind these competing theories, which became popular after the Restoration, might well be that many Bards of Annar found their linking with the Elementals, however far back, to be disreputable, for the Elementals had been held in distrust by Annarens since the alliance of the Ice Witch with the Nameless One. It was this alliance that led to the defeat of Recabarra, Queen of Lirion, and

Laurelin, last King of Imbral, and the evils that followed: the slaughter of the Dhyllin, the razing of Lirion and Imbral, and the tyranny over the Inner Kingdom that came to be known as the Great Silence.

The Restoration of the Monarchy and the Bards was chronicled many times. "The story of the downfall of the Nameless One is long and hard and desperate, and many parts of that tale never returned from darkness," wrote Ghoran of Desor. "I have often thought of those who fought him, lonely and afraid and hopeless, knowing no whisper of their courage would meet any new dawn. For many generations the land was in thrall, and the Keepers of the Light fled and hid in far places, keeping secret the Knowing, the Lore, the Singing, the Speech. And in time a King appeared from the west, where the bloodline of Laurelin, last King of Imbral, had been kept alive in hiding. Maninaë, helmed with Light out of the deeps of time, took up his fell inheritance, and through great suffering the powers of the Nameless were turned against him, and at last the realm of Annar was released from slavery and the Balance restored. That was a time of great joy."[19]

Maninaë is credited with the establishment of the Schools (the Libridha) around Annar, and decentralizing the influence of the Bards: "And at that time Maninaë determined to make his seat in Norloch, southward in Annar at the mouth of the Aleph River, and he built a great and fair city, and appointed the Circle of the High Bards, and there he and the Queen Marva dwelt in peace. But neither did he wish that the Lore and the Singing should become hidden and secret, the knowledge only of a select priesthood. He decided the Lore would be more safely kept in many centers, and so across Annar he established the Schools."[20]

Twenty-five Schools were established in every region of Edil-Amarandh and became centers of learning and culture. To an extent this was merely a formalization of a situation that had already occurred: communities of Bards existed in all the Seven Kingdoms, where they had been driven during the Great Silence, and had been instrumental in the defeat of the Nameless One.

Norloch flourished as the center of the Light in Annar, being both the seat of government and the highest School of the Light—two authorities that were at this stage formally separated by Maninaë's relinquishment of his Bard status.

Society

It is not only the origin of the Bards that remains shrouded in mystery, but the reason for the appearance of the Gift in any individual. Bloodlines were no guarantee of a Gift, which could die out in a family in which it was previously strong and appear in a family in which it was previously unknown. This characteristic had a profound effect on the social and political organizations of Annar and the Seven Kingdoms.[21]

Bardic communities, partly for this reason and also by reason of Bards' longevity, sometimes more than three times the lifespan of an ordinary human being, were remarkably tolerant. Bigotries of sex or race were unknown in Afinil, as prejudice of any kind was thought to cloud judgment and was abjured as a sign of corruption of the Mystery of Barding. The Bards also venerated what they called "The Way of the Heart," which was considered a major component of understanding the Silence of the White Flame; there were mystics who wrote long poems on this subject, the most famous being "The Birds of Anakatin" by Lorica of Turbansk. The Bards had a sophisticated culture of erotic art, although the western idea of the libertine was unknown, and romantic love was considered a central mystery. Homosexual love was not considered aberrant, and was never persecuted as it was in some less-civilized regions of Edil-Amarandh. It was celebrated in many popular lays, such as *The Lay of Lamark and Colun*, just as the lays of Andomian and Beruldh or Ardina and Ardhor celebrated the love between man and woman, or man and Elidhu.

Bearing children and child-rearing were also honored, and were interestingly related to eroticism in a way that again is unknown in the west, though some vestige of that might be discerned in the

Archaic Greek child-god Eros. The long life of Bards—which meant that child-rearing occupied a relatively small proportion of their lives—meant that women were never considered merely procreators of children, as they are in some traditional dogmas; and it appears that child-care was considered a responsibility not only of both parents but of all adults socially connected to a child. The family was a much broader concept than the contemporary nuclear family, or even the older extended family.

This ethos of tolerance lasted better in the Seven Kingdoms than it did in Annar, where the machinations of the First Circle during the Middle Years began certain imbalances, including the appointment of fewer and fewer women to the Circle.[22] By N945, no women had been appointed as Bards of the First or Second Circle within living memory, and this in itself became the justification for appointing no more. This tendency was strongly resisted in the Schools of the Seven Kingdoms, and was often condemned as a distortion of the Balance.[23] Nevertheless, from circa N500 on, a patristic ideology was aggressively argued by successive Bards. Studies of Bard lists in the various Schools revealed some fascinating figures. They show that by N700, every member of Norloch's First and Second Circle was male, and there were only three female Bards in the entire School. This contrasts sharply with Schools such as Baladh, Pellinor, and Innail, where the instatement of Minor Bards and appointment of Bards to the Circle largely reflected the demographics of the surrounding population: the proportion of women instated and appointed to positions of authority was generally about 52 percent, and Bards came from all social classes.[24]

Moreover, in Norloch the lists reveal that the Bards instated were for the most part from more powerful and wealthy families, and there is evidence that minor Bards from low-status families, such as Pilanel, and women, were sent to try their luck at other Schools—actions that were explicitly against the Charter of Schools set down by Maninaë.[25] This shift—which progressed slowly but inexorably over the centuries—began with the incorporation of the Triple

Scepter of the Monarchy into the authority of the White Flame until under Enkir of Norloch at the time of the events of *The Naming*, the writings of women began to be actively suppressed, and women were at first forbidden to be taught the arts of self-defense or warfare, and, finally, any of the Arts at all.[26]

Culture

The Bards created an extraordinarily sophisticated culture. It is still almost impossible to comprehend the extent of the Annaren Scripts, which are believed to consist of almost the entire Library of Norloch, itself a repository of many scripts from other Schools. Translation of the scripts has so far barely scraped the surface of what is available and here I can give only the most basic outline of Bardic achievement. While some scholars have wished to compare the Bardic culture with Medieval Europe, citing its relative technological backwardness, its culture was much closer to the humanistic Renaissance in its scientific curiosity and complexity. The truth is that neither comparison applies: both obscure the essential strangeness of the Bards.

They did not distinguish, as we do, between art and science; the alienation of these branches of knowledge in contemporary society would have baffled a Bard, who was accustomed to thinking of all knowledge as part of a single Knowing. A major reason for this was that their system of representation was not based, as Western knowledge is, on Aristotelian notions of categorization, but on systems of relationship.[27] This profound difference accounts, perhaps, for the very sophisticated understanding the Bards had of what are now known as sciences of complexity (the biological sciences, for example). A science that depended on laboratory experimentation, for example, simply didn't exist, although it is known that the Schools of the Suderain included extremely advanced mathematicians and that the Bards of Baladh formulated and used physical laws in their astronomical observations. They were aware of atoms and subatomic particles, and theorized matter and energy as musical vibratory forces, anticipating

quantum physics and string theory, and the Bard Thorkon of
Turbansk proposed something that looks very like the theory
of relativity.[28]

More astonishing discoveries include the fact that the Bards had a
working theory of evolution and natural selection, which becomes
very clear in the many texts written about the game of gis, which was
very popular in Bardic culture. Many Bards wrote about the game, but
it was Intathen of Gent who first theorized gis as a model of competing populations of species, and even of evolutionary tendencies
within a single psyche.[29] Malikil of Jerr-Niken theorized genetic inheritance in N755 in *The Loom of Light*, which recorded her meticulous
observations of breeding and cross-pollinating ikil plants. It is even
possible, given the prevalence of the symbol of the double helix in
Bardic writing, that the Bards knew about DNA.

Unsurprisingly, their medical skills were highly advanced,
although many practices also depended on the powers that were associated with the Speech, and so remain mysterious. The Speech, which
the Bards considered to be the basis of their magical powers, is something of which we still understand very little. Most experts believe
that Bards knew about bacteria and viruses, and some argue it is
likely they observed them; there is evidence from astronomical observations that the science and practice of optics was highly developed,
and it is possible they may have invented microscopes, although there
is as yet no proof of that. It is known that medical practice stressed the
importance of hygiene to prevent infection and that Bards practiced
inoculation against disease. There even exist instructions for produc-
ing antibiotic potions to "extinguish the invading disease-spores."[30]

Bardic literature and arts are astonishing in their variety and profu-
sion, and include great masterpieces of music, poetry, and painting.
Bards had developed a complex system of notating music, which they
venerated as the art closest to the Light, and much of the music so far
deciphered sounds very "modern" to the listening ear. They delighted
in metrical and linguistic inventiveness and employed a wide range

of forms in their poetic literature; their aesthetic abhorred dogmatism of any kind as a "dimming of the Light." Only the beautiful illuminations of the scripts now remain as reminders of their visual art, although the writings tell of extraordinary architecture and signal the widespread prevalence of murals and sculpture in all Bardic communities. The most complete picture of Bardic culture yet discovered is in the *Riddle of the Treesong*,[31] and it is widely speculated that this book was written to combat misinformation about Bards then widespread in Annar.

Unfortunately the central spiritual tenets of Barding—what was meant by the Light, for example, or much beyond general and extremely ambiguous notes about their idea of the afterlife—remain beyond our understanding at present. In part this was because of the Bardic practice of communicating the most important mysteries orally: it is crucial to remember that in Bardic culture orality and literacy ran side by side, as occurred in Classical Greece during the few centuries of its greatest achievements.

It is also critical to understand that pivotal concepts like the Light and the Balance did not imply an anthropomorphic notion of God. Without disputing the spiritual significance given to the Light and the strong moral imperatives contained in the Balance, it seems fair to say that they were much closer to forces of nature than to monotheistic notions of a punishing and rewarding Creator.[32] It is tempting, if perhaps anachronistic, to speculate that, despite their magery, the Bards may have created one of the most genuinely secular societies ever known.

NOTES FOR THE APPENDICES

1. See *Possible Geographies,* by Jacinta Crowe (Melbourne: Gondwana Press, 1991), and *History of Atlantis,* by Lewis Spence (London: Ryder and Co., 1926).

2. For much of the information on the history of Edil-Amarandh, I am indebted to Jacqueline Allison's wide-ranging study *The Annaren Scripts: History Rewritten* (Mexico: Querétaro University Press, 1998).

3. Other major sources are the *History of Edil-Amarandh and Its Peoples,* by Lanorgil of Pellinor (N307), and *The Riddle of the Treesong,* by Maerad of Pellinor and Cadvan of Lirigon, Library of Busk (N1012).

4. *Lays of the Elidhu,* by the Bard Jikarren, Afinil (A237).

5. *History of Edil-Amarandh and Its Peoples,* by Lanorgil of Pellinor (N307).

6. A fascinating and authoritative study of Bardic scripts can be found in *Die Urschrift von Annaren,* by Anschelm Juster (Northeim: Bundes Studienverlag, 1999).

7. *Sharma, King of Nothing,* by the Bard Nindar, Library of Busk (A2153).

8. For discussion on what is known of Bardic ideas of the afterlife, see chapters IV–VI of *Knowing the Light: Comparative Studies in Annaren Spiritual Practice,* ed. Charles A. James (Oxford: Cipher Press, 2001).

9. For a history of Dén Raven, see *A Chronicle of the Black Kingdom,* by Callachan of Gent, translated by Jessica Callaghan (Albany: Coromandel Press, 1996).

10. A full discussion of the complex societies of Edil-Amarandh can be found in *Genealogies of Light: Power in Edil-Amarandh,* ed. Alannah Casagrande (Chicago: Sorensen Academic Publishers, 2000).

11. See Cantos 54–58 of Saliman of Turbansk's poem cycle *The Circle of Living* (N915).

12. *The Balance,* by Lilidh of Turbansk (N419), was considered the most comprehensive articulation of this idea.

13. See Jérôme Casson's pioneering study of the Speech, *La Parole d'Edil-Amarandh* (Paris: La Deuxième Université, 1996).

14. Arguments raged between Bards on the origin and power of the Speech for centuries; however, the principal disagreements were best summarized by Hulmir of Norloch (N367) in *The Light of Words: A Discourse on Sacred Names* and in a series of dialogues called *The Skins of Speech,* by Salmira of Jerr-Niken (N456), reportedly destroyed in the sack of Jerr-Niken. Subsequent commentaries and partial copies that survived indicate she was the first to authoritatively theorize the syntactical nature of the Speech.

15. Book 2: *The Riddle of the Treesong,* by Maerad of Pellinor and Cadvan of Lirigon, Library of Busk (N1012).

16. Ibid.

17. See *The Annaren Scripts: History Rewritten,* by Jacqueline Allison (Mexico: Querétaro University Press, 1998).

18. *The History of the Starspeech,* by the Bard Menellin (A1464).

19. *Out of Silence,* by Ghoran of Desor, Library of Desor (N134).

20. Ibid.

21. See *Genealogies of Light: Power in Edil-Amarandh,* ed. Alannah Casagrande (Chicago: Sorensen Academic Publishers, 2000).

22. *Women of the Stars,* by Anna C. Jones (Toronto: Pimon and Huster, 1997).

23. See *Of Women,* by Selimor of Norloch (N808), for an example of the anti-female argument; and for its condemnations:

The Circle of Living, by Saliman of Turbansk (N915), and *In the Name of the Balance*, by Oron of Innail (N960).

24. *Women of the Stars*, by Anna C. Jones (Toronto: Pimon and Huster, 1997).

25. *Paur Libridha*, by Maninaë, King of Annar (N23), was the most authoritative and influential text on the constitution of the Schools. Its importance might be compared to that of the *Magna Carta*.

26. Book 3: *The Riddle of the Treesong*, by Maerad of Pellinor and Cadvan of Lirigon, Library of Busk (N1012).

27. For a full discussion of this issue, see *Uncategorical Knowledge: The Three Arts of the Starpeople*, by Claudia J. Armstrong (Baltimore: Grayden University Press, 1999).

28. *Of the Substance of Light*, by Thorkon of Turbansk (N615).

29. *The Breathing Waves of Gis*, by Intathen of Gent (N560).

30. *The Healing Arts*, by Malbul of Lirigon (N238).

31. The most comprehensive analysis of the *Naraudh Lar-Chanë* is Christiane Armongath's *L'Histoire de l'Arbre-chant d'Annar* (Nice: L'Institut d'Etudes Supérieures, 1995).

32. *Knowing the Light: Comparative Studies in Annaren Spiritual Practice*, ed. Charles A. James (Oxford: Cipher Press, 2001).

ALISON CROGGON is an award-winning Australian poet, playwright, editor, and critic. She is also the author of *Black Spring*, a tribute to *Wuthering Heights*, and *The Bone Queen*, a prequel to this quartet. Alison Croggon started to write the books of Pellinor when her oldest son, Joshua, began to read fantasy. "I had forgotten how much I loved this stuff when I was a kid," she says. "My first real ambition as a child was to write a fantasy novel, and Josh's reading reminded me. So one day I sat down and started writing a story. I had no idea what would happen, but one character appeared, and then another, and before long I had to finish the story to see how it turned out."

That story was *The Naming*. She says she was surprised by how the series seemed to unfold, already formed, before her. "Perhaps it's been waiting to be written for thirty years."